BORROWED WINGS

RUTHIE MORGAN

LUCKY ARBUCKLE PUBLISHING

Cover illustration by Kate Louise Powell

First published in 2016 by Lucky Arbuckle Publishing.

ISBN 978-0-473-36410-6

Book layout and cover design by ebooklaunch.com

For my family –

far and near.

"We are all broken.

That's how the light gets in."

Ernest Hemingway

PROLOGUE

I was drawn to him.

That morning I felt the call and flew close where I waited, circling and swooping in the early light, watching the house in the pale dawn. The air was still; it too was waiting. Soon he would come and we would guide him.

Dawn breaks gently, the gradual lifting of dark making way for light. Contours of land and form rise through the slow dawn. The waking world of day emerging from the blackness of night.

Rising, rising, higher and higher in the breathless air I swoop then plummet, diving recklessly, dropping like a stone, waiting for the moment when instinct pulls me skyward to safety. My performance perfect for an audience of none.

Light glints on glass as he steps out, rakish eyes fixed on the sky. He knows as I do, flight is imminent. He runs through the long grass below, shedding layers till naked and new he calls to me. His footsteps cut a slick path through the dewy grass and he raises a hand to the sky as I guide him to the edge. Flight lies beyond his mortal grasp, but as I swoop and plummet watching from above, delicate buds sprout and push through pale skin. Unfurling slowly as he runs; downy, feathery, white.

In the thick of the bush he is no longer visible, swallowed by the weight of trees and vines, the scene is still and the light grows. Fingers of sunlight pushing through the horizons boundary, stretching to the waiting land. Rippling water painted orange, red and gold.

He appears close to the cliff through the edge of the bush, the canopy of leaves opening to hopeful morning sky. Searching wildly his eyes meet mine. Joy and hope glitter in those eyes that see more than the sunrise, the jagged cliff and the ocean far below.

He reaches out a hand, believing I might carry him away, but his body succumbs to the pull of gravity. Twisting and turning in yearned for flight he is welcomed by the waves. No trace, no resistance, no second chances.

The lights' assault persists; rays bright and glaring strike waves and coast in angry protest to life taken too soon. Waves beat against the rocks sounding out the passage of time and the sun rises from the edge of the world. The call is gone, the ocean still, and I swoop and fly in careful arcs above that place where he is. I wait, watching the waves ready him for flight with borrowed wings - from this life to the next.

Evan F. Skylark: March 13th 1981 - November 9th 2007.

Son of Mary (nee O'Shay) and Frank Skylark of Belfast, Ireland, husband to Billie and father to Evie and Sunny.

Painter, sculptor and local architect Evan Skylark's premature death has shocked the community of St. Cloud. Death by drowning has been ruled accidental by the coroner and a memorial will be held for friends and family at St. Anne lookout point at 3pm on November 19th. Evan Skylark will be remembered for his contribution to St. Cloud's architecture and city design. St. Cloud International Airport, due to open next year is the product of his talent and passion for St. Cloud and its community.

Family request that those wishing to send flowers should instead make a donation to: www.whitewings.com, *a charitable trust supporting mental health.*

(Extract from St. Cloud Herald, Obituaries, November 12th 2007)

Billie

When I was small I'd play *happy families* as little girls do. Tea parties with dolls and stuffed toys; teddies my boy babies and plastic dolls with pink cheeks and blinking eyelids my little girls.

I'd play house where I was Mom, and the toys my brood of adorable children. But my version of house always involved two Dads. Two different and equally wonderful Dads; which is funny seeing as at that particular time I didn't have one.

The Dad's in my games would go to work, come back for dinner, fix things then help me put the toys to bed. All very traditional aside from the fact there were two.

I wonder now if I was making up for the missing place at our dinner table; the Daddy I didn't have. I wonder if seeing Mom alone made me overcompensate in those childish games. In real life my Mom mightn't have a husband but in my world of make believe I'd found her two; just in case.

My Mom would have two husbands who loved her, and were kind, and funny, and handsome and strong. They'd have to be strong because my Mom deserved that. Mommies weren't meant to be alone. That was how it worked and this was how I played. And strangely, or maybe sadly this was how it was to play out. Not for my precious Mom but for me. A real life parallel quite different yet so aligned in theme these arbitrary childhood memories return crystal clear.

This is how my path was moulded, a fate contrived for the child who believed two loves were better than one.

Although later Mom would meet and marry a wonderful man who would become the perfect father, somewhere deep an idea had taken root. A belief so layered in conformity I no longer recognised or cared to acknowledge its existence.

Looking back, in light of how things turned out, I wonder if I'd created a space within myself that could only ever be filled by two great loves.

Loved for the things that separated them and the way they so seamlessly fit into the puzzle of my world. My two missing pieces.

Evan and Jack. Two loves, one life, one taken, one lost.

Chapter One

February 19th 2008

Billie

> *It's good to write your name.*
>
> *I want to say it aloud, see if it sounds the same now that you're gone, but I don't. I know the sound will be strange and you'll feel further away than before. How long has it been since that other part of our lives, the part before all this?*
>
> *I try to see you again, laughing, the sun on your face, smiling for me. I fool myself, believing that smile was only for me. But I know you smiled for him. Now that he's gone I wonder if I'll ever see you smile again.*
>
> *I'm sorry for everything, not that it matters. Not that we can change anything or sorrow can bring him back. I wish it were different, all of this. That he was still here and you were happy, even if none of that happiness could ever be mine. And although I know it's wrong I relive that night in Seacrest over and over. I reach for you, wanting that again, the perfection of you in my arms.*
>
> *I love you, though I can never have you, but there it is.*

Jack

⁊

Dropping the pen roughly on the scarred, wooden work desk he stares at the words, the letters in ink; another layer of permanence in a new and strange reality. He closes his eyes and exhales long and slow, then in a flash of motion slams a fist on the table and crumples the letter into a tight ball.

He writes to her, he has to, but she'll never see the words.

∽

Jack

The house has never been so quiet. He'd always thought quiet was what he needed, what he wanted, but that was before. This quiet is not still, but unsettling and empty, a quiet that echoes the barren landscape of his life. A blanket of uncomfortable silence that settles after the sounds of life are gone.

Picking up the sandpaper from the bench he crouches to reach the underside of the boat and rubs methodically, smoothing the roughness of unfinished wood. The movement feels good. He's been sanding the hull for weeks now, a job that should have taken him half the time, but he's in no hurry. There's an odd comfort in the repetitiveness of the task, the predictability of movement and certainty of outcome. His mind can wander freely while his hands do the work.

He ought to hurry this boat along. He's already behind the deadline he set himself but the thought of starting anew is too much. So many changes lately. He'll stick with this boat a bit longer; its solid form a physical link to the time before.

He'd started it the day he met Evan on the wharf, when they'd talked awkwardly and he'd tried to speak to him about the drugs. One of the last times he saw Evan alive.

He's replayed those last few weeks so many times, wondering if he could have done anything to change what happened in the end. He's consoled himself with the reassurance that it wouldn't have mattered. Evan would never have listened to him.

The truth is the guilt won't go because he knows Evan could feel Billie slipping from him. A gradual movement toward Jack and he can't deny it, that's what he wanted. He'd wanted her for years and for every mess Evan made, Jack was there to clean up and comfort her. He's not stupid enough to think that didn't contribute toward the events that last night.

He's been sanding the same spot for too long. The wood is smooth and the gritty paper has lost its rough edge. This is the way it's been since; his head can't seem to stay in one place without retreating back to that night. A night where everything he'd guiltily wished for was within reach for a few short hours before the fall that tore life in two.

The phone rings from underneath a pile of rags, wood shavings and tools and he takes his time reaching it, digging around till he finds it; neglected and dusty.

"Hello" his voice cracks, rusty from days of quiet. He clears his throat and tries again, "Hello?"

"Jack?"

"Mama," the familiar voice makes him smile.

"You don't call like you used to Jack."

"I'm just working Mama. How are you?"

Ignoring his question, she continues. "Always working, you work too much. Come home, come see your Papa."

Jack catches the inevitable *no* he is ready to deliver to the familiar question. "Maybe soon. After I finish my boat." He hears her sigh on the other end of the line.

"Always another boat."

It's been too long, he should have gone months ago, but home is the last place he's wanted to be lately. He's never been able to hide at home and he doesn't want to have to explain his inertia, this stalemate he's come to.

How can he tell them he screwed up again? Made another mistake. One with consequences that ripple and spread; it's a story he can't reconcile. He hadn't meant for it, had tried to avoid it. The more he'd pushed it all away the more certain it seemed. Despite knowing there could be no happy ending, he'd quietly loved her, never expecting the ending that was to come.

So to go home and see his parents now would be too hard; Jack the great disappointment. He can't face his father's judgement and bitterness. His well-contained temper feels dangerously close to the surface and it makes him wary. Since that night, a lifetime of carefully stored emotion threatens to break the surface and create a wave he's not ready to deal with. When he's with his parents it's too hard to escape the past, and right now the present is hard enough to deal with.

❦

They've been meeting at Santos again every Thursday night for a month. Trying to get some sort of routine back. Meet up like they all used to, have a few beers, spend a few hours together and talk, about anything really, anything but the fact that someone's missing.

Santos never changes and he likes that. Rough hard wood floors, a few well used booths lining the back wall, cracked red leather seats either side of the bare wooden tables. The walls adorned with island memorabilia; beach shots, yellow edged photos of local's mid party, posters advertising bands, fiestas and street parades. Faded over time, partly covered over with newer versions; Friday night's band, next month's reggae festival. It's all comfortingly familiar.

A long wooden bar runs the length of the far wall, a line of sturdy stools prop up the front. Behind the bar the back wall is an array of bottles; shelf upon shelf of glassware, every colour and variety of liquor available. The impressive collection of bottles is framed by the owner Bastian's collection of international notes and coins. Over the years he has fastidiously pinned and stuck each one to the wall.

Santos has been around as long as Jack can remember and Bastian has always been there. He hasn't changed much either, less hair perhaps and a little heavier around the middle but like everything in the little bar, Bastian is comfortingly predictable.

For Jack, Bastian is like family; one of the familiar St. Cloud local's he's grown up with. Originally from Germany, Bastian arrived in St. Cloud in the seventies. Long haired and flared he was ready to surf and party before returning home to begin a career as an accountant in Leipzig. Somehow, that planned future never quite worked out and Bastian, having had enough of the limited choices in island beer, decided to take action. In the late seventies he opened *Santos* - version one - a small bar, better described as a portable beer cart. Licensing laws on the island were loose so he custom-fashioned a travelling bar which moved from beach to beach selling European beer in long necked bottles. Having secured a shady *no questions asked* shipping deal, Bastian managed to supply real beer to the people of St. Cloud, a populace who had only ever tasted watery lager from the island's only brewery.

Bastian and his beer were soon so popular he was able to set up permanent residence in the city, securing Santos's current site and building the small bar from scratch with the help of a few friends. Around this time, he met his Mexican wife Josefina, who christened the bar *Santos*: little saint. Although some would argue it mightn't be saintly to sell liquor for a living, Josefina and Bastian have saint-like status with the island's beer drinkers and lonely souls.

Santos has always been a place to go where the welcome is warm. And on an island where home may be far away, a warm welcome, cold beer and friends on tap comes close to heaven.

This bar has seen Jack in many different phases of his life, some prettier than others. Bastian has been there through it all, Josefina at his side.

Jack at sixteen with the surf crowd, feeling like the big shot, drinking beer at the bar. No-one cared about ID in St. Cloud back then, he had the beginnings of a beard so they served him. Later, stupid and reckless, with his brother Raife and their friends, drinking too much and causing trouble, getting kicked out by Bastian who never made much of a fuss. He'd take them firmly by the elbow and guide them out the door using a few German expletives. He'd tell them to come back when they could handle their beer like men.

Later when things got bad, and Jack had nowhere else to go, he'd drink alone in Santos. He'd drink to try and forget that he'd fucked up and life was a mess. Bastian didn't ask questions. Josefina would feed him, give him a bed for the night and a place to be when he didn't seem to fit anywhere else.

Here he is so many years later, still heading to Santos, not to get drunk or to forget, but to remember. To try and figure things out in a place that never changes despite life's turmoil.

The bar is quiet, familiar faces at tables or tucked in booths, country music plays low, muted conversation interspersed by the mournful sounds of Garth Brooks.

"Jackie boy! Good to see you brother, where you been hiding? You don't like my beer anymore?" Bastian greets Jack with a smile, barely looking up from the glass he is polishing.

"What's with the music?"

Bastian shakes his head, reaching for a bottle of beer. "Josefina, she's just discovered country," he shrugs passing the beer to Jack. "Could be worse, last month it was Lady Gaga. I blame the internet." Jack smiles raising the bottle to his lips as Bastian continues. "How's life? That boat coming along well?"

Jack shrugs setting the bottle back on the bar. "It's good." He's about to say more but another customer approaches the bar and he's saved the unappealing prospect of having to talk about himself. He'd rather not, there's nothing to say; he'd rather sit here and watch life go by for a while, although Garth Brooks is seriously depressing him.

"Jack." A hard slap on his back announces the arrival of Felix. He's beaming, looking relieved he's made it, his bulk and mop of spiky blond hair cast a shadow across the bar.

"Easy there, almost knocked me off my stool." Jack grins.

"Don't know my own strength." Felix sits down beside Jack and gives Bastian a wave.

"Does Zoe know you're out?"

Felix is married to Zoe and together they have two boys, Matty and Nate. Felix is usually the last to arrive anytime they get together and usually sports the look of the frazzled, sleep deprived father. His wife Zoe is a whirlwind and they all marvel at how Felix manages to keep up.

"She does." He smiles warmly, shrugging, used to the jibes from his friends about being henpecked by his over-achiever wife.

"Felix!" Bastian approaches with a glass of dark beer. Apparently real Germans prefer not to drink from bottles. The men greet each other with a firm handshake before Bastian passes the glass to Felix.

Felix has lived with his American wife Zoe in St. Cloud for six years. Originally from Munich, Felix's accent still forms words and phrases with clipped, guttural, Germanic sounds. There's no mistaking where he's from. Bastian however, has been away for so long his accent has formed a strange Germanic/island hybrid, soft drawn out vowels that transition to clipped consonants. It's an intriguing sound and often tourists will try and guess where he is from; few get it right.

"Danke," Felix takes the beer, gaze fixed on the amber glow and frothy top before drinking deeply.

"Nichts zu danken," Bastian's smile reflects Felix's. A small taste and sound from home. They chat in German for a time, Bastian's accent changing immediately back to the way it sounded in the seventies.

Dan enters the bar with Jed ten minutes later, and after greeting Bastian the four men take their beers to the pool table where they can find comfort in each other's company and conversation has a focus. It's only been a few months since Evans death and they need each other, but no-one has the emotional energy to talk about it anymore.

Dr Dan or DJ Dan, depending on which hour you meet him is always immaculately groomed. Direct from the pages of *GQ* or maybe if you know him a little better *Out Magazine*, his chiselled features an alluring advertisement for other gay men. Dan is a doctor on the island who moonlights as a DJ by night. Jack has grown up with Dan and their friendship is an anchor.

Dark haired with olive skin suggesting Italian or South American heritage, Jed, like Jack and Dan has also grown up on St. Cloud. Jed's youthful appearance and unwillingness to settle down had given him a bit of a playboy reputation on the island. A reputation now in tatters as a result of meeting Sadie, a pretty dreadlocked Canadian who came to St. Cloud for a month, two years ago. Another traveller who didn't get around to leaving. Jed's other reputation however, the one that really matters, is thankfully pristine; Jed is St. Cloud's number one barista.

Without Jed island life would be a few shades more stressful for the entire population. As owner and manager of Beaujangles, St. Clouds best coffee shop, Jed is a popular guy. Along with Santos, Beaujangles forms the heart of the St. Cloud community; another home from home in a city full of immigrants on an island far from everywhere.

The evening is pleasant, comfortable and undemanding. For a short time, Jacks' head feels grounded. He remembers: this is home, the only one he knows.

"Hey Bastian can you please change that music? You're about to see four grown men cry." Dan calls across the bar to Bastian who shrugs and calls to Josefina in the kitchen. She's busy making Chili

Rellenos. There's laughing and swearing in Spanish before Garth Brooks stops dramatically and is replaced by Lady Gaga.

A chorus of men's voices holler in protest from around the pool table as the smell of fried Poblano Chilies and melted cheese wafts through the bar. The music changes again to Peter Tosh and everyone breathes a sigh of relief (in St. Cloud no-one complains about reggae). The game carries on amicably and soon a chuckling Josefina arrives, bearing a tray of hot chili rellenos.

Since they've been coming back, coming back without Evan, Josefina always cooks for them. Every Thursday night she arrives with a smile and a tray of comfort food. It's the unspoken language of grief; offerings and tributes when words won't do.

Josefina is small in stature, and standing next to Jacks 6ft 3inches she resembles a child. But there's nothing childlike in her determined manner as she pushes the tray of food under his nose.

"Eat," she watches him steadily as he reaches for a relleno and bites down through the crisp fried coating to the hot green chili and its molten cheese filling.

"Josefina," Jack breathes between bites. "You're wasted here with this old German, come live with me."

She slaps him affectionately. "You know I'd never leave that crazy old German. He'd be lost without me."

"You boys leave my girl alone!" Bastian shouts from the bar, his hearing always perfectly attuned to conversation, gossip or trouble in Santos. Josefina rolls her eyes and leaves the tray on the table, returning to the kitchen and her home-made corn tortilla.

"It's a good thing I can't cook these myself, I'd lose my figure and these hips won't look this good forever." Dan licks a greasy finger then reaches for a paper napkin.

Jack isn't really listening. He leans on his pool cue, eyes focused on the table, attention elsewhere.

Dan turns to him, "What's up lover boy? You look like shit."

Jack can't help but smile. "Go easy with the compliments."

"Don't get used to it. Go take a shot and show Jed how it's done. He's a cocky little ass. Always thinks he can win. I've got the next round resting on our victory." Dan gestures toward the table where

Jed and Felix stand smugly, arms folded, sure of certain victory after Jed's last play.

Dust scatters as Jack chalks the top of his cue.

"Come on baby, show them what we're made of." Dan is confident as Jack leans over the table and steadies himself to take aim. The cue rests between thumb and first finger and his aim is perfect, it always is. But his head is crowded and the cue seems to know. As the tip of the cue makes impact with the white ball it quivers and jumps sending the ball off target to collide with the green cushioned edge of the table, potting one of Jed and Felix's balls in the process.

The others laugh as Jack swears and Dan shakes his head. "Man, you're in worse shape than I thought."

March 13th 2008
Isle of Arrasaigh,
Scotland

Dear Jack

I keep waiting to wake up. Waiting for that moment when reality starts to bend and I realise that this isn't the real world at all.

I am here, Evan is gone and that chapter of life is over. I lie awake and think of the many ways I might have stopped it, might have seen it before it happened. I lie awake and wonder if I helped push him to that place where he ended his life alone.

How do we keep going? I can't see beyond each minute and I'm terrified for the twins. Will I always feel this way? They carry on, unaware the sky has fallen. They laugh and play and they ask for him. They ask for you, for Louie and Bets and the beach. I need a story to tell them to make sense of it all but my words are gone.

Did he know Jack? I can't help but wonder. Did he know?

I will stay here in Arrasaigh until I'm strong enough to come back, until I can survive these equal measures of grief and guilt. I can't stop thinking that my love for you contributed to catastrophe, yet here I am holding you like a lifeline.

Billie

There's a box under the bed that holds all the words I want to say, I open it at night when the house is dark and quiet, and place another letter inside. Letters to Evan, to Jack, to the twins, to Cam, to Mom. Conversations I must have, questions I must ask and apologies I need to make. I write letters I will never send like my life depends on it. Maybe it does.

I hear them at the foot of the stairs, the hushed tones stop me in my tracks. Pressing myself against the wall I listen to another concerned conversation about me.

"It's time Cam, you have to talk to her son. She'll listen to you." I picture Cam rubbing his eyes or running a hand through his hair, thinking carefully about what he's supposed to say. I am not the only one who is suffering, but the thought isn't enough to shake me from my grieving stupor.

"I'll talk to her Nell, she's not strong enough. I don't want to rush her." I hear the fear in Cam's voice and slide down the wall to sit on the hard wood floor of the upstairs landing, head on my knees. "The doctor said to give her time." Cam's voice sounds unsure and I imagine Nell taking his arm and squeezing it in reassurance, but when she speaks I know I'm mistaken because she's firm and authoritative.

"The girl needs to be out of bed. She needs to be with those wee ones, she needs to taste a wee bit of life if she's to carry on. Of course she needs to grieve, and she'll keep grieving, but she needs to live."

There's a pause and I imagine an embrace. I imagine Nell pulling Cam, weathered and worried into a mothering embrace. In that moments silence Nell's last four words crowd me, pressing on closed eyelids, unwilling to pass by and let me hide away in my own selfish grief. *She needs to live.*

This is my new reality; Evan, my husband, is dead and I am here, hiding away at the home of my stepfather Cam, and Nell, housekeeper and surrogate grandmother. I ran here to Arrasaigh, another island, this time in Scotland. An island as far away from St. Cloud as I could manage. I hide here, far away from the real world that waits.

Downstairs my children wait. Their understanding of the present simple, perfectly so; they live. I hear Nell's words again, in a quiet voice that sounds like mine, a whisper repeating. I *need* to live. As the simple message sinks through my grey mist, the very reason I *need* to live screams in chorus down the corridor; two small voices in harmony.

"What are you two up to? Now what's that you've got in your hand Ms Evie?" Nell's voice changes tack, full of indulgence. Giggling follows as a small child is tickled or cuddled.

"Nell's told you about that before. Don't put it in your mouth, it's Samson's toy." A tussle ensues, Nell must be wrestling the dog's toy from Evie and despite my curled position on the floor, and the tears that lie wet on my cheeks I can't help but smile.

"Ganda, Ganda…" little hands are being clapped together; Sunny must be holding out his arms to be lifted. The chant turns to laughter and I picture Sunny in Cams arms being nuzzled by his stubbly chin.

"Let's get some dinner fixed, then we'll get you in a bath." Nell bustles away, I imagine the twins in tow as Sunny yells, "Bye bye Ganda. Bye bye."

The words summon a dusty memory; my own grandfather, Mom's Dad, a farmer back in Kansas. I remember his plaid shirt and leather work hat, the smell of tractor gasoline and the way his hands were hard and calloused but his smile soft and warm.

There's a moment where I'm looking down at my sorry self from above. I see the pale, curled form below through the eyes of another. I see myself feeling the weight of the world, wallowing in helplessness. Maybe it's through the eyes of Grandad, long gone, looking down, shaking his head. Or, maybe it's through the eyes of Mom, her arms folded across her chest telling me; *Enough now Billie. Get up off the floor and start walking. It's time to start walking.*

There's a sensation of ice cold water, a bucket thrown unexpectedly over my head. My eyes spring open as I gulp in a sharp breath. It's time.

Pressing my palms against the floor I feel the wood below me, comfortingly solid. Easing myself up to stand I take a moment to breathe evenly. Breath by breath, in and out. I listen to the laughter downstairs, the twins and Nell and the creak and groan of farm gates outside as Cam retreats to his predictable animals. Life all around and I must step back in. I need to live. Awkwardly I place a cold foot on to the floor and move forward. One step at a time. I walk slowly, but with intention, to reach the shower where I will wash away some self-indulgent grief to make room for my babies who need me.

"I used to come here as a wee boy and swim in the rock pool." Cam's stride is long and I struggle to keep up with him as we walk along the track that forms a rough path through the valley.

"On your own?" I have this image of Cam as a little boy, alone, maybe with a dog in tow, a bit like now.

"Sometimes," Cam smiles down at me, my walk breaking into a jog to keep pace.

"Shall we slow down?" he asks kindly. Months in bed with a box of hankies for company have left me thin and unfit. I'm ashamed of my weakness and nod, stopping to tie a shoelace which hasn't really come undone. I catch my breath as Cam stands waiting, hands on hips, admiring the scenery he never tires of.

Glen Rannach is breath-taking any time of year, but today it is warm and the sun bright. Arrasaigh is not known for its warm sunny climes and the day is a gift. Stones crunch beneath our feet as we follow the well-tended track that leads from the edge of the village up over the brow of the hill to the lush valley below. A brown, peaty river runs alongside the path, widening here and there. Water bubbles over rocks and mossy banks into deep pools where the flow appears still for a time.

We follow the path side by side in companionable silence. Cam carries Sunny on his shoulders and Evie sleeps on my back, snuggled into a backpack whose weight makes my shoulders ache. I steal a glance at Cam; he is lost in thought, the sight comical. His face is set and serious but Sunny's head lies atop Cams; a sleeping hat, mouth open and drooling despite the bumpy ride, chubby arms encircling Cams neck. That anyone could sleep so peacefully in such a position makes me laugh aloud and Cams head jerks toward me. My laughter is an unfamiliar sound these days.

I gesture to Sunny, and Cam smiles. We walk on in the afternoon sun, only the sounds of the river and the odd call of a bird overhead to interrupt the quiet. As the path changes from gravel to grass even our footsteps are silent and we walk, step by step, side by side, till we reach the rock pool from Cam's childhood memories.

Evie and Sunny wake as the motion of our footsteps stop. We unload a small picnic and let them paddle by the edge of the cool water. The surrounding hills are vibrant in the sun. Deep greens mixed with the lemon yellow of gorse flowers in bloom.

Cam unwraps a sandwich and takes a bite, eyes fixed on the twins, careful they don't venture too deep. "What will you do Billie?"

The question takes me by surprise, but his manner is nonchalant, his mouth half full as he speaks. "Have you thought about it yet?"

I suppose I've been waiting for this question since I arrived, but my answer is only really half-formed and I'm afraid it's not the answer he's hoping for.

"We'll go back." I bite down on my sandwich, wishing I could say more, could feel more definite in my plan for our next chapter. Life without Evan.

Cam nods and chews thoughtfully. "Evie lass, come back a wee bit," he calls gesturing Evie to come to him and away from the water. Mischievous as usual she takes a step back but slips on a mossy stone and ends up sitting in the pool, cold water up to her tummy. She cries balefully at the shock and Cam hops up to scoop her into his arms. "Come and sit with Granda and we'll get you dried off." She looks up at him, then at me and smiles, wet bottom forgotten she cuddles Cam and Sunny follows. Wherever Evie goes Sunny is inevitably close behind.

"Have you decided when?" Cam asks, ruffling Sunny's hair.

"In a few more months." I nod as I speak, hoping to convince him and myself, that by then I'll be ready.

"Are you sure?"

I keep nodding, afraid to trust my words.

"What will you do love?" Cam eyes are kind. I know he will support whatever decision I make. It's what he's always done, but I see the sadness and the worry and I wish I could take it away.

"I don't know."

Tears are never far away and I don't try to hide them. Cam pulls an old cotton hankie from his pocket and I dab my eyes and start again. "I don't know. But I do know I've got to go back. I've got to try and start again." I stop and take a breath. "St. Cloud is our home. I'll figure things out when I get there, but I know I'll never be able to start again if I don't go back." I nod, the words said aloud making sense of months of quiet thought. I must go back to move forward. I need to be back in St. Cloud, in our home, with our friends. I need to make peace with my memories to carry on.

Cam nods, his eyes on the pool and the bubbling river flowing merrily into its depths.

"You won't stay then?"

"You knew I wouldn't."

"I know, but you know you can. You could move in here and I'd have these two milking cows for their keep." He smiles gesturing to the twins who are squabbling over a cookie. Evie wallops Sunny in the face sending him toppling backward. He sits, eyes wide as cold water pools around his tummy. Evie is quiet for a split second, secretly impressed with her own strength until Sunny starts to giggle and splash and she barrels in after him determined to be where the fun's at.

Cam and I laugh together and he rummages around in his backpack emerging triumphant moments later with a tarnished silver hip flask. He winks as he unscrews the silver stopper and takes a long slow sip.

"Cameron McMahon, tell me that's not whisky!" I pretend to be shocked.

"Not just whisky Billie…Laphroaig. Here!" He throws the flask into my lap and I roll my eyes, undoing the stopper and inhaling deeply. "No, not just whisky," he shakes his head with a look of reverence on his unshaven face. "Single malt. Try it, you can taste the peat."

I wrinkle my nose, "And that's a good thing?"

He smiles. "You'll see what I mean," he nods again toward the silver flask.

"Bloody hell! What's become of me?" I smile, raising the flask to my lips. "Hard liquor and it's not even a weekend."

"A weekend? Christ." Cam laugh. "It's been daily for me since dealing with these two urchins." He gestures to the twins.

I laugh feeling the hard tang of whisky evaporate on my tongue. The depth of flavour takes my breath away, and just like Cam says I can taste the peaty riverbank where the water flowed as it made its way to the whisky barrel.

When I open my eyes Cam is staring at me. "Are you okay lass?" I nod. Warmth emanates from my chest as my heart reaches out in love.

"I'm fine." Something quiet and sleepy is wakening and I remember how it feels to have hope. And although it's probably just the whisky and the Highland air, I breathe in that taste of happiness and know in time I will be.

Later, on the return journey with Evie and Sunny snuggled on our backs and shoulders, the sun is low in the sky, and the gentle sound of birdsong echoes from the hills as dusk approaches. Evan appears, unbidden in my memory, a clear vision, and for a moment I can hear his voice.

"What I'd give to fly Billie…to feel the flow…just to fly."

In the world we lived in, together, not so long ago I'd answered: "But you'll never know."

In this world, my new world, where Evan flew with his birds, I wonder if he did know. If he always knew this is how it would end. That death was the flow he'd have to surrender to. Maybe he tried to prepare me, maybe he never knew himself.

The image vanishes and the birds sing and Cam squeezes my hand. "Be brave Billie, be brave."

He returns to a light flashing on the answer machine.

The room is dark and shadow less, the moon hidden under low cloud. The red flash breaks the dark intermittently, throwing the room briefly into the seedy tones of city nightlife.

Disinterested, Jack ignores the machine and flips on the light as he crosses the room to open wide wooden doors to the deck. The night is heavy and the complete darkness comforting. Kicking off his shoes, he walks barefoot to the edge of the deck and leans heavily on the rail. His eyes strain for a glimpse of the ocean. From here the view is best, he built the deck to face the sea, and with tea trees framing either side his view is private and almost always clear. But tonight there isn't a glimmer of moonlight on waves. The sky is black and the ocean follows suit. He hears the water only barely, the low hum of insects in the bush masks the gentle lap of waves below.

He should feel differently about the ocean, especially here, at this very point on the island; the point where Evan fell to his death. It should feel tarnished, ruined somehow. A place of beauty and peace now one of heartbreak and anger. But it remains the same, Evan hasn't taken that away, although in his darker moments Jack wonders if he maybe he wanted to.

He never wanted to be angry, to feel this rage against fate and circumstance…against Evan. But the anger is there nonetheless and it shames him. He stands leaning on the rail, eyes focused on the darkness beyond for a time until the red flicker interrupting the solitude of blackness annoys him enough to head inside.

Sinking on to the sofa he hits the play button, instantly the red light is replaced by a once familiar voice.

"Jack, you there? Pick up, it's me Raife. Hey…I know it's been a while but I need a…" There's a noise in the background that's hard to define, a low beat, voices, a distant siren. "Look, don't sweat it, it's all good. Forget it for now. I'm in…" The message abruptly ends as the caller is cut off or hangs up deliberately.

Alert, Jack hits the play button again, listening to the voice that used to be as familiar as his own. A voice now so strange and unexpected it takes his breath away. Raife…what the hell? Where was he and why would he call now? Bets sidles over on the sofa and rests her head on his lap, sensing tension and wanting to relieve it. Jack exhales slowly, rubbing the dog's ears distractedly. The message has unnerved him.

By three am he is asleep on the sofa with Bets by his side and Louie curled by his feet. The doors to the deck open to the still, black night, the phone thrown to the floor,

His dreams are exhausted and black, dark imaginings, faces from his past and present, boats and babies, Billie and his brothers and the sound repeated in an emotionless tone, *It's me Raife…pick up Jack.*

The smell of coffee wafts down the driveway that leads to Felix and Zoe's house. Jack breathes in the welcome fragrance as he climbs the back steps leading to the open kitchen door.

"Smells like I'm just in time." He enters without knocking as is expected of him.

"It's mine, I told you not to touch it, I said, like three million times, the blue light sabre is only for Luke Skywalker." Six-year-old Nate is wrestling a plastic light sabre from his younger brother Mattie who is not about to give up without a fight.

"You did not, you said I could have it! You said I could, cause you wanted to be Darth Vader and he only uses the red one!" Mattie looks around for support, someone to confirm that indeed the blue light sabre is his and Nate really should be Darth Vader. Jack steps into the kitchen just as Nate pulls the light sabre so hard it flies from Mattie's hand knocking over a plant, spilling damp soil over the rug.

"Shit." Nate breathes in a serious voice as his mother rounds the corner with a murderous look on her face.

"Who taught you that word Nathaniel?"

She ignores the plant that lies crumpled on the rug. Her hands are on her hips and Nate looks around the room for help or an escape route. He knows he's in big trouble; she's just used his Sunday name.

"Dad says it all the time." Mattie pipes up suddenly ready to stick up for the brother who was about to flatten him for a light sabre only moments ago.

"Does he really?" Zoe answers, nostrils flaring.

"Yeah," Nate has found his voice, sensing Mattie's on to something. "He says other stuff too Mom," his expression is all serious, "like…"

"Okay you can stop there. Get this mess tidied up, then get outside." Zoe is blushing as she notices Jack leaning against kitchen counter. She rolls her eyes and heads toward him, "Coffee?"

"Wonder what else Dad says?" he grins opening the milk carton and pouring some into the steaming mug.

"I'll kill him."

"Kill who?" Felix enters the kitchen holding the remains of the sorry plant.

"You!" Zoe grabs the plant and punches his arm as she passes with a brush and shovel to help Nate and Mattie clean up.

"What did I miss?" Bemused, Felix shrugs and heads to the coffee pot.

"Zoe was just getting a few tips from the boys on your parenting style." Jack smiles, sipping his coffee, surveying the cluttered kitchen with its mismatched paint colours, pots hanging from the ceiling and kid's art stuck to the fridge.

"Shit, they didn't tell her about the x…"

Zoe breezes back into the kitchen, her timing perfect. "The x-box? Oh I've known about that for a while. I've just been waiting for the right moment to bust your ass."

Felix opens his palms in a gesture of supplication. "They're boys Zoe, it's just games, they love it."

"You didn't buy it for the boys, it's for you…and you know I don't want them on video games. Did you think I wouldn't see your little set up out there in the garage?"

Felix looks sheepish. "You never go in the garage."

Zoe turns to Jack, eyebrows raised. He laughs, raising his palms. "Leave me out of it."

"I give up." She sighs. "Pour me a coffee will you?" Jack passes her a steaming mug and Felix, sensing a window of opportunity, pulls her in from behind and kisses the top of her head. He places a hand on the small of her belly.

"How is she today?" He touches her tummy which swells below her loose shirt.

"Will you stop with the she? It's probably a he and you'll give him gender issues *in utero*."

"It's got to be she! What the hell will we do with another one of those?" He gestures toward the backyard and all three turn to see Mattie and Nate in the middle of a mud pie fight.

"Oh man. I'm getting the hose." She makes for the door, "Jack, there's fresh bread on the counter, eat something will you? You look awful." She breezes into the garden and the two men hear the splash of the hose and ensuing screams of delight as the little boys race around muddy and wet.

He'd promised to help Felix take down some walls and the job takes longer than expected. By 4.00pm they stop for a cold beer outside. The air is warm and damp. Zoe has taken Mattie and Nate to the beach and the house is unusually quiet.

Felix exits the kitchen carrying two beers, his blond hair now white with dust from the wreckage. "Zoe's going to flip over the mess." For a minute he looks concerned then his face breaks into a smile.

"Can't believe she knew about the x-box all this time," he shakes his head. "I was sure she'd have a fit, must be the pregnancy, most women get grouchy but it's the only time Zoe goes easy on me."

Although the baby wasn't *planned* according to Felix, Jack suspects differently, he's pretty sure Zoe had plans for another baby all along.

"I know I shouldn't say it, but God I hope it's a girl." He looks to Jack with mild concern, "Not that another boy wouldn't be great, but I think if it's not a girl she'll want to keep going." He blows out a long breath of air in a slow whistle. "I'm not sure I'm up to it."

Jack smiles and claps him on the back. Felix, his strong, reliable friend looking genuinely terrified at the thought of his wife's hormones and a football team of kids.

"Come on then, let's get finished before they get back." They head inside, a trail of dust in their wake, the mission to clear the way for the new baby's bedroom still a few hours from completion.

With each swing of the sledgehammer the once solid wall chips, cracks and crumbles. Jack swings harder than necessary, the rough physical action a relief. Every bang releases another layer of frustration, but by the time each loose brick is cleared the feeling returns.

At seven, Jed arrives to find Felix and Jack ghostly white, leaning on their sledgehammers, surveying the day's work. The once three room corner of the sprawling house has been opened into a wide airy room which when the sun rises and the dust clears will begin its transformation into a baby's room and play space.

"Holy shit, what happened here?" Jed stands open-mouthed, eyes creasing into a smile as Jack and Felix turn to face him. "Does Zoe know you're demolishing her house? Jed claps his hand on Felix's shoulder surveying the mess.

"Are your here to help or be a pain in the ass?" Felix asks.

"Both. Zoe sent me down to tell you guys to call it quits, she says the banging is driving her crazy and… hang on let me get this straight…she said to tell you, to shower and go play on your x-box."

Jack laughs and claps his hands together in a bid to rid himself of some dust as Felix stands hands on hips, open-mouthed. "She said that?" his smile dazzles through the dust.

"Just kidding, she said to get your ass up there and help her get the kids to bed." Jed punches Felix on the arm. "Had you going there."

"Fuck off."

"Easy, I'm the good guy. Anyway I was looking for Jack, been calling your place all day, figured you were either in the boat shed or here."

Jack dusts his shoulders with his shirt. "What's up?"

Discomfort flashes over Jed's usually cool demeanour, but by the time he answers his tone is casual. "Raife called the shop yesterday, said he was trying to track you down, didn't know if he had your number right. One of the girls answered and gave him your number and address." His expression is careful. "Hope that's okay. I know you guys haven't been in touch for a while."

Jack closes his eyes, rubs a hand over his mouth and waits for Jed to continue, but Felix pipes up first. "Who's Raife then?"

No-one answers, Jed continues. "Sorry man. He must know where you live anyhow, right?"

"Don't worry, it's okay." Jack's voice is stiff. "Listen, I'd better head, got to do some work on the boat." He smiles at Felix. "You want me back tomorrow to finish this?"

"Sure." Felix nods as Jack heads toward the door. "Who's Raife?" He mouths the question to Jed.

"His brother." Jed stage whispers to Felix while Jack's back is turned.

When Jack turns both Jed and Felix are watching him. "See you first thing." He nods to Felix and pulls a dusty t-shirt over his head as he exits the room.

"Stop in for coffee. Not too early though!" Jed shouts through the open doors, but Jack is already reversing quickly down the drive.

Speeding around the dark bends toward Frontiere Point Jack's head is elsewhere. It's back in an era he doesn't like remembering. But if Raife is set on seeing him, he'll have to face it again. But he doesn't know if he can, not right now, with Evans death still fresh and the loss of Billie still raw.

The truth is, she was never his to lose, so why is it so damn hard?

The dark bends in the road suddenly feel threatening. The heavy line of trees cloyingly close. He's back, just for a moment to that time, another night when everything changed. Another slice across time; a before and after that has clouded the years since.

Breathing unsteadily Jack pulls the truck carefully to the side of the road. Eyes closed, he grips the steering wheel, hands slick with sweat. He concentrates on his breath and heart rate, willing calm to return. It does, slowly, with the hesitance of a disloyal friend. Frustrated and ashamed at his loss of control he starts the car shakily and begins the slow drive home. Maybe it's finally time to deal with Raife, time to try and heal old wounds?

As the trucks' high beams alight on his house the dogs bark and race to meet him, certainty descends. It is time. He needs to face Raife and try to heal old wounds. But this time he'll face him as a man, not a boy.

Chapter Two

Billie

The music is loud, and the club dark and crowded, it's hot and the smell of beer and sweat hangs like a mist. It should be repulsive, but somehow here the smell fits. Combined with a beat that runs below the floor and reverberates from the walls; the picture is complete.

A thousand conversations: mouths moving, words that flow then disappear unheard in the crowded haze of smoke and music. I watch from behind the bar, a voyeur, tasting the nights flavour through the senses of others. Unheard, my words are understood amidst all voices and music. They give me money and I give them drinks. I pour and mix, pass bottles and pints, a willing observer of the primal connection of man to music.

The colourful microcosm of the basement nightclub is captivating. Uninhibited displays of the human condition, exposed and on show. Inhibitions lulled by beer and spirits, darkness, strobes of coloured light, and loud music that pulls at desires normally bound tightly in a world of social etiquette.

I work here four nights a week, a London nightclub where the music is wild and the characters wilder. I love and hate this job from minute to minute. It's a thrill to watch and experience the heady buzz of London nightlife, but the hours are long and I often finish feeling hung over, although I haven't drunk a drop.

Tonight is busier than usual, its midsummer, and the city's population swells. There are six of us behind the long bar that runs the back wall of the club. For every bottle or glass passed over in exchange for a bill there is another line of hands waiting outstretched, money at the ready. It's hot and I'm damp with sweat as the music gets louder and the crowd thickens.

I see him at the corner of bar watching me and don't know how long he's been there. The DJ plays the Arctic Monkeys and the dance floor heaves. He leans against the wall mouthing the words, his head moving to the beat. '*Bet you look good on the dance floor.*' I know this track; he'd play it in his studio on repeat. Catching my eye, he smiles and I work my way down the line of waiting drinkers toward him.

"I love your work," he says, half smiling as I pass him a beer. He reaches a hand across the bar and tucks a damp lock of stray hair behind my ear then slants his head toward the exit sign. We play the game, I know what the sign means; it's not a request but an order and I slip away from the crowded bar to follow him.

The Arctic Monkeys play on as I weave my way through the sweaty bodies, taken by the night, the booze and the beat. A hand finds mine and guides me to a corridor lit with dim red bulbs, leading to the stairwell up on to street level. He pushes me back against the wall, hands either side of my shoulders, forehead close to mine.

"Who are you anyway?" he asks tipping my chin up to kiss me and I feel the smile in the kiss as he brings his hands to my waist and pulls me higher to reach him. The music, the darkness, the smell and taste of him and the illicit forbidden feeling of knowing we shouldn't, works every time. Reaching my hand to his trousers I feel the swell and am taken by a force dizzyingly powerful and erotically addictive.

I pull away and walk through the crowds knowing he will follow. This is the game.

The *Staff Only* sign hangs above a curtain leading back to a storeroom and bathroom. I walk quickly now; he is on my heels. The liquor storeroom is small and once inside I close the door and turn to him. A neon strip bathes the scene in cheap white light.

Evan hums the song and his head still nods to the beat whose base we can only feel now. There are times I look at him and wonder if I really know him at all, but it doesn't matter. In these moments there is a need more powerful than knowledge. His hand circles the back of my neck pulling me in, the kiss; rough and urgent. There's no time for anything else. Hands under my top, he murmurs as he touches skin before yanking my shirt to expose breasts to his mouth.

Flailing hands and deft fingers undo belts and jeans and he lifts me to him, legs circling his waist, back pushed up against the storeroom wall. The sex is urgent, fast and hard, and when it's done we slide slowly to the cool concrete floor and begin to laugh. The aftermath of mania and the relief from such physical desire leaves us giddy.

Evan tidies me up, smoothes my hair, kisses each breast and sends me back to the bar. "See you at home Cinderella."

A phone rings downstairs and I jump, sitting bolt upright in bed, disoriented and shaky. I hear a hushed voice pass by my door. "No dear, her light's off, she must be asleep. Aye, I'll have her call you in the morning."

Shaking I reach for the glass of water beside the bed. The cool sensation helps return me to the present. I wasn't asleep, it wasn't a dream, just a clear memory. One of those hazy memories that descend before sleep comes. Memories that let themselves in when my guard is down.

Unsettled, I rise and listen for any sound from the twins next door. Usually when I wake they do and we sleep the remainder of the night together here in the big bed with its patchwork quilt and old wooden frame. The bed they were made in. The thought drops me to my knees and grief rolls in again.

Nell didn't remember that this was the room Evan and I stayed in a lifetime ago, and I didn't want to tell her. Part of me wants to lie here again, in this bed and remember him, maybe that's why these memories come to me at night, crystal clear in detail.

I walk across the cool floorboards to the bathroom where the harsh light assures me I am indeed awake. The nightclub scene, the heady, illicit sex with Evan was just another memory. I turn the heavy taps in the old claw foot bathtub and strip, knowing that hot water and bubbles are a comfort to the saddest of souls. A long, free standing mirror in the corner reflects my naked image and I turn fully to face myself; pale and stripped bare. My hair falls drab and unkempt, its sheen lost. My legs and arms hang limp, barely supporting a frame that has lost something vital. Breasts once shapely droop, baggy and apologetic.

I raise a hand to my mouth in shock. My wasted frame symbolises all I have lost.

The girl in the store room, in the nightclub with Evan, full of lust, fearless and ready to run at life, she's gone. She isn't coming back. I stare, startled by my reflection; who is this that looks back at me? I don't know her. So busy looking back and mourning at what's been lost I've let her be, let her suffer and struggle alone.

I straighten up and take a step toward the mirror, running a hand along a thin arm, tracing the line from shoulder blade to clavicle. Pulling the limp hair from my face I examine my eyes and see that although the rest of me has changed, they remain the same. I am not the Billie of before but I carry her with me in an older, wiser body. I am a mother and a daughter, a friend but not a lover. That chapter has closed and I must focus on the chapters that remain open and hold me together.

Sliding into the hot bath I let my head submerge fully under the fragrant bubbles and hot water. As steam clouds the room and the water eventually cools, my head is clearer and my heart stronger. I realise that I am beginning to manage my grief, these snapshots of Evan are part of my journey to letting him go. That with all the good memories will come bad ones and those too might be relived then tucked away to rest, so that in time I might move on and begin again.

Jack

Gravel crunches under tires as the truck backs out of the drive. He reverses slowly, like he used to when Evie and Sunny were next door, when the thought of a stray toddler had him creeping along the driveway, checking his mirrors constantly.

Passing the Skylark house, silent and empty he feels the familiar rush of sadness. The house once full of life now barren and deathly quiet. He hits the accelerator and takes the corner too quickly, the trucks tyres skid, the road damp from a night of rain.

St. Cloud is at its most beautiful this time of day. He loves the quiet waking of the world, the first moments after the sun's rays break over the horizon and daylight skims the ocean. Mornings after heavy rain are best, when tails of steam rise from leaves and branches. When grass sparkles and glints in the early light and the warm, damp tarmac smells like boys and bikes and summertime.

He thinks of his brothers now; Raife and Saul. You could tell they were brothers by their physical similarities, but there the resemblance stopped. Their personalities and how they had chosen to live were poles apart. Raife just a year older than Jack, and Saul five years older again. Although youngest in years Jack has always felt himself wedged in the middle of his brothers; the missing link that brought all three together. A little like Raife, a lot like Saul. He'd like to think that's the way it is, but he wonders if the truth is that he's a lot more like Raife than he cares to admit.

Louie and Bets sit up in the flatbed of the truck, mouths open, tongues lolling in the small breeze the truck cuts through the still air. A duffel bag lies wedged between them, and as the St. Cloud city outline becomes clear, Jack remembers the promise he made to Felix.

"Shit." Shaking his head, he cuts across the city to Beaujangles; home to St. Cloud's best coffee. The streets are quiet and he pulls up out front as Jed sets chairs and tables on to the wide sidewalk.

"Morning sunshine." Jed slides the last few chairs beside the street-side tables and heads inside beckoning Jack to follow. "Haven't even got the coffee on. No-one gets here this early!"

"I won't make it to Felix's. Can you let him know?" Jack shrugs and fingers the day's newspaper on the counter.

"Where you heading?" Jed pours dark, fragrant coffee beans into the grinder and flips it on. Jacks words are drowned by the noise. Distracted by the act of making coffee, Jed's expression is far away. He smells the ground beans before distributing a few scoops into the heavy handle that locks firmly into *Monica*, his red, shiny, chrome espresso machine. The fact that Jed named his espresso machine and engraved the name on the side is a source of conversation and humour in the cafe. No-one has managed to get the real story of why the beloved machine is called Monica, but most can guess.

"So where did you say you were going?" he asks raising an eyebrow before turning the nozzle on the milk frother, which makes more noise than the grinder and Monica put together. Jack sighs and checks the paper again. He'll wait.

Moments later Jed places a perfect coffee on the counter. Just as Jack likes it. Triple shot with a single spoon of creamy milk on top. "Taking a road trip, heading out to see my folks in St. Eloise. I'll drive to Bastille Bay then take a boat. Might drive the long way, take a few days." Jack reaches for his coffee and mixes the dark and light shades of espresso and milk slowly with a spoon.

"Sounds good, must be a long time since they've seen you."

"Too long really. I should check on them, spend a little time."

Jed looks carefully at his friend. "You okay?"

Jack glances up quickly from his coffee. "Just need a change."

Jed nods. "Sure."

"The old man will drive me crazy within a half hour, but it'll be good to see them."

Jed smiles, stacking cups to warm on top of Monica. His next question is lost as the door opens and Dan breezes in, perfectly groomed and smelling of expensive cologne.

"You guys knew I'd be up early eh? Fixed me a welcoming party?" He doesn't wait for an answer but addresses the espresso machine. "Monica you are the light of my life, don't disappoint me today." He turns his clear blue eyes to Jed. "One to go pretty boy."

"What's up with the crowd this morning? Usually I get this half hour to myself. It's sacred." Jed shakes his head. "You're killing me." He gets to work on Monica, smiling despite his complaints.

"What's this I hear about Raife being in touch?" Dan turns to Jack who almost chokes on his coffee.

"What is it with this place?"

Jed raises his palms to Jack in awkward apology. "Sorry man, I just mentioned it to Dr Big Mouth here."

Jack shrugs. "I don't know, he left some garbled message on my answer phone and called here. He probably needs money."

"He always does." Dan answers. Both men sit, coffees to hand, facing Jed who's busy setting up for opening.

"I don't think going to see him is a good idea." Dan shakes his head. "He's never easy to deal with, and you always come out worst."

"I'm going to see my folks and Saul, nothing more, a little time out." Jed and Dan watch him expectantly. "I need to get away. I can't build boats, and I can't stay in that house and be reminded every fucking minute of everything that went wrong."

"We all miss them man," Jed answers quietly.

Jack breathes deeply, he said more than he meant to. "I know."

Dan claps a hand firmly on Jacks shoulder. "Go, do your drive, hug your mama, help Saul with the farm and come back with a fucking smile, or I'll be slipping some happy pills into your morning java."

"Right." Jack stands, downs the last of his coffee and leaves with a wave. "Hey don't forget to tell Felix."

"Sure thing, drive safe." Jed replies to his retreating back as Dan lets out a long slow breath.

They watch Jack hop into the truck and take off with Louie and Bets in tow. Dan's eyes remain fixed on the road long after the truck disappears. "Raife Kelly," his words are barely audible, the image conjured by the name leaves him unsettled.

There's something about driving and music that clears thoughts of the present. Scenery, smells, and well-chosen tracks can easily turn a road trip into a journey of nostalgia or a pathway to an imagined future.

The road to Bastille Bay is a long winding journey. Easy routes and highways don't exist in St. Cloud. The small port town is a ten-hour drive from the city on a good day. The winding route traverses the islands most beautiful points. He'll take his time, maybe stop for a night along the way. He has his tent; he'll get there when he's ready. He'll need to be ready to deal with his father.

The cab of the truck is lonely and he pulls over to let Louie and Bets hop into the passenger seat as the coastline flies by. His mind wanders, childhood memories of these beaches as a boy.

He remembers fishing with Saul, catching his first tuna, and the pride of fighting the pull on the line till finally the fish came whipping from the water, all silvery skin and flapping body. His pride turned to fear as Saul unhooked the slippery, writhing body and thrust his pen knife into the neck of the fish. The fighting and flapping on the deck slowed gradually and he'd watched horrified as that life dimmed to nothing; still, motionless and bloody. His doing; dead on the deck.

At seven he'd cried and Raife had laughed, the scene would be ammunition for boyish teasing for years. Saul had knelt down and lifted the fish to him, made him hold it and feel it. He'd told him that this was what men did, it was the law of the land and fish were made to feed men. Jack had believed him, and together they gut and cooked the tuna on an outside fire. Later when he heard Saul and Raife laughing about the incident he'd decided not to be the baby anymore.

As boys Raife and Jack were alike in height and build, from a distance easy to mistake one for the other. Closer, their differences distinct. Where Jack has his mother's dark hair and olive skin, Raife is fair and sandy, his features finer. Raife was an attractive boy, and Jack often felt those looks gave permission to a host of normally unacceptable behaviours. Jack became the fall guy, copping the blame when things got broken, the boys were late and chores went unfinished. He never made a fuss; he too basked in Raife's golden glow. The only one seemingly immune to Raife's charms was Saul; solid and grounded. He favoured neither of his brothers, treated them equally, bashed them equally and made sure they were both on the right track when he could.

He remembers his mother; Amandine, young and beautiful, possessive of her boys and unsuited to conflict; an inevitable presence in three teenage siblings. Saul rarely got involved; the age gap enough to rule him out of their petty disputes over chores, food and later girls. His mother hated it. She'd yell, lash out with a wooden spoon, then resort to tears. That would always get them. They'd stop and go to her, and soon forget what had been such a big deal before. That was when they were younger. Much later, when things really became a big deal, they'd break her heart and no-one would ever really get over it.

It's late when he pulls into the quiet cove on the far eastern side of the island; a small sheltered beach just off the beaten track. Maybe he's delaying his arrival home - maybe not - but the extra forty minutes to get here has been worth it. He admires the surf and enjoys the feeling of being completely alone. Just Louie and Bets, and they're easy company.

Jack sets up the small tent a short distance from the truck and wanders down to the water's edge. Here the ocean beats against the shore, and the tide pulls strongly on retreat, the force urging him in. Cool salt water; a perfect antidote to the day's hot drive in a truck cab with two heavy breathing dogs. It's dusk, and the beach his alone. He strips and runs into the waves diving deep below the cool white foam, where the water is calm and the rush of surf frames the quiet undertow.

The rip tugs and pulls as he swims toward shore and he remembers Evan on the beach. A lifeless body so close to death he'd feared it was too late; but that time had simply been a practice run for the real thing. He should have seen the signs. But could he have stopped it if he'd known? Worse still, did he sense it and choose to look away? He can't answer the last question, and again Evans death is all around, tainting the water, the beach, his memories.

He staggers back toward the tent tired but refreshed by the struggle against the rip and the swim to shore. The dogs bark and race along the sand and he lies, naked on the beach, the last rays of sun beating on his chest as he breathes, remembering the last time he lay like this, sundown on sand. The memory is jagged but absorbing. He wants to tuck it away, but uninvited it finds its way to him as the sun lowers and the dogs settle on the still warm sand.

I love you Jack. Her words are clear, heavy with emotion but he knows she's been drinking, they all have. *I love you Jack.* He's heard the words from lovers before, but never like this. Then the endless wait for the reply that never comes, the words he didn't say.

He never told her, she never knew, never will. She'll go on thinking that she betrayed Evan, and amidst the pain of dealing with his death she'll never know he'd always loved her. And that one night on the beach would always have to be enough.

There was never going to be a happy ending, how could there have been? He hadn't meant for it, he'd pushed it away, but it wouldn't go, and there she was every day. The whole thing from start to finish was his worst nightmare. He grew up with Raife; he understands drama and abhors it. Yet all he's done is attract it.

He'd built the boatshed and house to get away. After the mad years, after his doomed relationship with Claudia, after the haze of drink and marijuana lifted, he'd needed to be alone. Back then it wasn't a choice, it was the only way he thought he'd get through. A simple life; he couldn't survive anymore chaos.

It was less than a year before they arrived and the quiet simplicity he thought he wanted was gone. The Skylarks and their baggage, and their noisy, chaotic lives were everywhere. He remembered what it was to want a family, joy and pain in equal measures. He'd watched her, and loved her and their children too. He'd watched Evan like a train wreck in slow motion, knowing it could never end well, but watching - like the rest of them.

Back against the warm sand, eyes to the slowly setting sun he brings a hand over his face. *What a fucking mess.* Despite the regret and the sadness, the remembrance of Evan and the man he was; despite it all the facts remain the same: Jack is in love with Evan's wife.

That's what won't go away, that's what keeps him awake, and that why he can't move on. He loves her in a way he knows won't happen again this lifetime. And life's kick-in-the-ass is that they have no future together. Evan is immortalised in every fucking wave that beats the sand. She'll never be able to let go. He couldn't have planned his departure more perfectly.

The bitter thought makes him nauseous. Maybe he needs to move away, start again. Pulling on his jeans he makes his way back to the tent waiting forlornly on the far shore. He will stop thinking about her and what can't be. Avoiding thoughts of the past is how he's managed up till now. He'll avoid thoughts of her; he has to. Turning slowly back to the receding ocean he watches the glow of crimson light disappear below the horizon. As the last light leaves the day Jack wonders where to leave these thoughts of her.

⸎

We watch the boat approach in the distance, a tiny speck of black and white on the horizon, gradually finding form.

"Mommy, Mommy, the boat, it's the boat!" Sunny is thrilled; the arrival of the ferry into Arrasaigh is a daily treat. We come to watch it dock most days, hear the horn blast as it approaches and see the passengers disembark. They walk down the gangplank to excited friends or relatives, or just head home after errands on the mainland. We count cars as they drive up the ramp from the underbelly of the ferry; the twins amazed at how many cars, trucks and people the Arrasaigh ferry carries.

Evie and Sunny are three and a half. They run around, get up to mischief, talk lots, giggle lots and whinge a lot. Their conversations are cute and funny and I love to hear them chat to one another. Most of it makes little sense but they always seem to understand each other perfectly.

Evie is the boss, she calls the shots and usually, Sunny follows. It's not that he's afraid of her little temper; he always gives as good as he gets, it's just that he adores her. He happily follows her lead and together they are a team.

I gather the buckets and spades, then pull on brightly coloured rain jackets over small squirmy bodies. A familiar drizzle descends on the island as we head up from the sand to reach the terminal where the ferry will dock.

The Arrasaigh terminal comprises of one small building, home to a ticket office and a kiosk serving hot tea and sausage rolls. There are two rows of plastic benches and a table with the day's newspapers. As the rain falls steadily we shelter inside and watch from the window. The boat now so large it dwarves the port, and as it docks it sounds the arrival horn three times.

I see her edge out of the open doors and sniff the air before heading warily down the ramp. Iris, in a yellow sundress, red sandals and a fifties hair do. Her high heels wobble under the weight of her bags and she scans the dock looking for me.

"Iris, over here!" I yell to her as she stands scanning the small crowd. Her face lights and she drops the bags and runs to envelop me in an expensively perfumed hug. We stand hugging in the rain, Iris, spectacular and colourful, me a little grey and washed out. The twins are quiet now, both holding on to my trousers, unsure of who this wild woman is that's squeezing their mother.

Later back at the farm house with Iris unpacked and settled we sit around the kitchen table with hot mugs of tea and a plate of scones courtesy of Nell. Cam is out on the farm and the twins play on the floor with toy cars and Lego.

Iris looks around smiling; her eyes are wet but she's not one to cry. "It's a lovely place to stay for a while." I nod, outside the rain falls heavily but a small fire glows in the kitchen hearth.

"I'm not sure what I'd have done if I hadn't come here."

She reaches out a hand and rests it on my arm; waiting for me to say more. This is the first time we've seen each other since Evans death, since I arrived back in Arrasaigh. I hadn't wanted any visitors and until now I hadn't felt ready.

"It's okay." I clasp her other hand across the table. This is what I knew I'd have to be ready for; to comfort others who arrive to comfort me.

"Sorry Billie."

"Don't be, it's okay."

"Ah, but it's not really is it?"

"No," I shake my head feeling a rogue tear slide down my cheek. "But it will be."

Iris nods and we hold hands, and I ask her about her fiancé Marcus, her life in Dublin, and her family. We chat for a while, sipping hot tea, eating Nell's home baking, and for a short time I can almost forget why we're here. That Iris has come to visit me, not to tell me about her life, and her exciting future and upcoming wedding. But that she's here to try and comfort me because my husband killed himself a few months ago and I have two small children and an uncertain future.

We don't talk about any of that the first day, or the second. We enjoy each other's company, enjoy the twins, walk, bake, sit by the beach and reminisce. But even that has its dangers; our shared memories of university involve Evan.

Iris stays for four days before she has to head back to work, her visit has lifted me. Her vivacious presence and infectious source of energy are a tonic. The twins adore her and I feel some of her colour seeping into me.

On our last evening we stay up late after everyone has gone to bed and the farmhouse is quiet. We drink wine and finally we talk - we talk about Evan.

I tell her everything; how I miss him, how I loved him and hate him. How I'm so angry with him and myself. I tell her how afraid I am, and how there's a hateful part of me that amidst the grief feels relief. Relief that maybe now he's finally happy, and that I am not responsible for his happiness any more.

I tell her how I screwed up, and I'm afraid the weight of that will never leave. That he was too much for me in the end and I wasn't coping, but hadn't told anyone and didn't know what to do.

I tell her of all the events leading up to Evans death; of the depression and darkness, the drinking and the night he almost drowned. I talk till it's all out, and finally I tell her about Jack.

When eventually I stop talking the wine is finished and Iris sits holding my hands, still listening intently. She lifts her glass to her lips, drains the last mouthful and sits the empty glass carefully down on the table.

"I'm going to say a few things now Billie, and you might not like them, but you're going to listen." Her voice is firm. "You are to blame for nothing, do you hear me? Evan's life was not yours to watch over, and no matter how much you loved that man, it wouldn't have mattered. Evan's path was his and you didn't push him there."

She takes a breath and squeezes my hands. "He made choices, he was sick, and if you carry on taking the rap for how things turned out you'll get sick yourself. And I mean sick! Those kids rely on you, you can't fall apart, and you will if you never find a way to move on."

I can't look up. She squeezes my hands again. "Do you hear me Billie? You have to find a way to move on." I know that I'm crying but need to hear her out. I blink away the tears and urge her to go on.

"Evan loved you, anyone could see that, but love wasn't enough to stop any of what happened and Evan wants you to pick your ass up and live!" I nod as she speaks, her hands so tight over mine I lose sensation in my fingertips.

"Take those babies, his babies, and find a way to parcel up that grief. Remember what's real Billie. Evan was no angel, don't give him wings. He screwed up more than once, and you were there to pick up the pieces each time. I know it hurts, but he screwed up again, and you can't fix this one. But you can forgive him and move on. That's what he'd want, just that you'd love him, despite it all." Black droplets course down her cheeks as mascara marks trails of tears.

"So love him Billie, for what he was, but know he's gone and it's time for you to go on too. Start again. Go back and do what you have to do to make a new life. Take your time - maybe it's Jack, maybe not. Go slow, but go. I don't think you can wallow here anymore."

She stops abruptly and raises her empty glass to her lips, parched from the long soliloquy. She sniffs and dabs her stained cheek with the back of her hand. "Jesus, pour me another drink will you?"

My head is spinning with her words and I'm dizzy with wine and the relief of talking it over. How heavy all those unsaid words had become. I open another bottle and refill our glasses. When Iris sips, the red wine leaves a rim around the top of her mouth that looks like a smile. I gesture to her face and she shrugs taking another sip.

Suddenly I feel the need to laugh rather than cry, to laugh like I might never stop. Iris stares at me warily, anticipating a flood of tears, her lipstick smudged, her face striped with black and her fifties hairdo collapsed on one side. I feel my mouth twitch and her eyes open wide in surprise. Then it starts. The belly laugh that is as cleansing as six months of tears. We laugh until we ache, then later, after the wine and the talking and the laughing we hug and head to bed, grateful for each other and the power of friendship.

Jack

Jack sits on the deck with Louie and Bets at his feet. St. Cloud fades into the distance as the passenger ferry makes its slow and steady journey to St. Eloise. It's a six-hour boat trip but not unpleasant, he'll stay on the deck and watch the ocean, maybe sleep a while. He hadn't settled well last night after the ocean and the thoughts of his family then Billie. He woke early after a night of broken dreams and dark imaginings.

The quiet of St Eloise will be welcome, it's a small island; too small for most, the community tight knit but prosperous. You either fish or live somehow from tourism. It's an island of contrasts: the older side is full of fisherman, markets, small community and farmland; the newer more recently developed side a small but exclusive tourist haven. Only the wealthiest tourists go there, mostly for privacy and guaranteed sunshine.

Jack grew up on St. Cloud, but his parents moved to St. Eloise fourteen years ago after the shit hit the fan. By then Saul was already there; his wife Jess had grown up in St. Eloise and together they took over Jess's family farm. It's a small holding with only a few animals but they make their money on island fruit and fish. It's more of an orchard, with a profitable side-line in fresh fish. His parents, Amandine and Joseph, moved over and Saul built them a cottage on the far side of his land. That way he had privacy but could watch over them. St. Eloise was what they needed; a quiet life.

Tall palms and golden sand frame the island, and as the ferry approaches, it rises up picture perfect from sparkling aquamarine water. Imaginings of the tropics, crystal water, tall palms and white beaches end here; this small island is paradise. So far only touched by tourism and too small for business or industry, St Eloise makes St. Cloud feel like a thriving metropolis.

He sees Saul's van from a distance away. He knew he'd be here waiting; always dependable. The image of his brother, tall and unkempt leaning against the old beat up van makes him smile. Jack raises a hand in acknowledgement and Saul salutes. Once the boat docks Jack jogs along the dock, the men embrace and Saul steps back to look at him, cupping a hand to the side of his face. "Good to see you."

"Room for three of us?" Louie and Bets jump and bark excitedly at Saul's heels as he opens the van doors. "Jesus Saul, do you ever wash this thing out?

Empty fish crates are stacked against the back wall and the odour is overpowering. "You get used to the smell." Saul grins throwing Jack's bag in the back with the fish crates, beckoning the dogs to follow. Even Louie and Bets recoil slightly but Saul claps his hands and they're up and in, tails wagging.

Jack enjoys the easy silence that rests between them. They drive along the narrow roads, busy at first as tourists embark on to coaches that will take them to the other side of the island. Saul turns on to a coastal road and beach after beach speed by until the road turns to gravel and the ride becomes bumpier.

"How long you here for?" Saul asks, eyes on the dusty road.

"Don't know, probably just a few days. Thought I'd check in, Mama called giving me a hard time." Jack glances over at his older brother, similar in build and colouring, but with distinctly different features. Saul's eyes are pale green and his features soft, his face has a permanently gentle expression although his manner is not always so. Jack can testify to that.

"Listen before we get home I need to talk to you about Raife." Saul steals a quick glance across the van cab at Jack.

"What about him?"

"Damn." Saul bangs the heel of his hand on the steering wheel. "I don't like the way you say that: *what about him?*" He imitates the tone and Jack bristles, feeling like he's fifteen. "The '*what about him*' is that I think he's in trouble again and we need to find him."

"There's no *we* in this Saul. You want to find him? You go find him. I'll stay here and take care of things for you but I'm not going looking for him - not this time."

"Shit Jack, I knew you'd react this way."

"Then why are we having this fucking conversation? If Raife wants to talk, he knows where to find me. I'm not the one who ran away." Jack turns to Saul. "As far as Raife's concerned I screwed up his life, so when you ask me to go look for him you can sure as hell bet my answer will be no." He turns to the ocean trying to get a breath of air amidst the smell of fish and confrontation. Louise and Bets bark as the van hits a bump.

"I get it. I do. But he's our brother." Saul hits the gas and the old van complains. "Raife's been stewing on the past for too long, behaving like an asshole; feeling like the world owes him something. He needs a kick up the ass!" He sighs running a hand through his tangle of dark hair. "He needs another chance Jack."

Jack shakes head. "He'd never take one, he made his decision years ago. If he needs us, he'll come to us."

"And you'll give him another chance then?" Saul's voice is even. Jack leans back in his seat, trying to breathe evenly. How can he say no? All Saul's ever wanted was harmony between them all. But Raife is another story. Raife won't ever ask for help, especially not from him. He feels secure when he answers "I will," knowing he won't ever have to.

The rattle and bump of the van's tired suspension punctuates the silence as they turn on to a dirt road and the farm comes into view. Saul glances at Jack. "Listen, I meant to talk to you about Mama…" He's interrupted by Ziggy Marley singing from his mobile phone, his ring tone of choice. He sighs and answers, quickly distracted by details of a new fish order from a local hotel, present conversation forgotten.

"Hey, hey, my baby's home!" Amandine rushes to Jack holding him tightly and he's transported in time; boyhood in her touch and smell.

"Mama." He bends to plant a kiss on her forehead as she smiles dabbing her eyes with a cotton hankie before she drags him through the small house to the back porch where his father, Joseph, sits smoking and reading. The greeting is awkward and formal. His father stands extending his arm for a firm handshake.

"Good to see you son."

"You too." Jack clasps both hands around the one his father offers, hoping this small gesture will somehow convey the words he can't say. "You look well."

"You don't. You need a haircut and some new clothes," he gestures to Jack's ripped jeans and work shirt, shaking his head at his unkempt hair. "You're as bad Saul." His father sighs, sinks back into his chair and reaches for his pipe.

"I heard that?" Saul emerges on to the porch with a large slice of watermelon. Amandine fusses, taking Jack by the hand to a small tidy bedroom with a single bed, washstand and fresh towels. No-one mentions the fact that Jack hasn't been home in four years. No one acts like it's been that long and for that, he's grateful. Saul heads home to work promising to return with Jess at eight for dinner.

Amandine pats the bed spread and fluffs the pillow, glancing out of the window distractedly. She seems smaller and it makes his heart ache. She has grown thin since he's been away, her diminished frame chides the neglectful son he knows he's become. As a boy his mother was his world, her willowy frame and long auburn hair, beauty personified. Amandine was the gentle contrast to Joseph's hard edges and in her presence Joseph had been softer. But it's been a long time since Jack's seen the softer side of his father. A bitterness descended after Raife left, sadness turned black. A smouldering seed of anger that burns brightly in Jacks presence.

Amandine sits on the bed, forehead furrowed in a frown, hands knotted on her lap.

"Okay Mama?" Jack sits, placing an arm around her shoulders, her frail frame a shock to his hands.

She starts as though from a daydream and smiles pulling his free hand into hers to rest in her lap. "So good to have you home." She kisses his rough fingertips and stands smoothing her skirt, gaze fixed on the view from the window then clicks her tongue in annoyance. "He's here again, what does he want this time?"

Jack follows her gaze to the yard. "Who?"

"I don't like that man. I wish he'd stop bothering us." She shakes her head, walking briskly to the door. "I'll tell your father, he'll get rid of him."

Moving to the window Jack sees Saul alone in the yard throwing a ball for Louie and Bets. When he turns she's at the door, and he catches the words he's about to say. He's confused, uncertain if he missed something or simply misheard her. But as he stands by the window, watching Saul and the dogs in the late evening sun, confusion is eclipsed by denial, and Jack Kelly does denial pretty well.

❧

Jess breezes through the door at eight, dwarfed by the casserole she carries. "Jack!" She squeals happily, pushing the large dish into Saul's arms she throws her arms around him. "Where the hell have you been, and why do we have to wait this long to be graced with your company?" She throws her hands on her hips and for a second he thinks she might really yell at him, but the frown is quickly transformed to a smile brimming with affection.

Jess really is Saul's perfect match; together since their teens, it's hard to imagine one without the other. They are one of those unique couples who seem to complement each other in every way.

It's only as she envelops him in a bear hug that he feels something different, and as he pulls away holding her at arm's length he shakes his head turning from her expectant smile to Saul's.

"And you guys were going to tell me when exactly?" He gestures to the compact bump Jess had cleverly concealed behind the casserole dish. He pulls her into another hug, gentler this time then claps Saul hard on the back. "Congratulations, I can't believe you managed to keep this from me all the way home in that stinking van! And you…Mama, not a word? What's with that?" He hugs Jess again.

"She made us promise," Saul gestures toward Jess who smiles brightly. "Wanted to tell you herself…good thing you didn't wait another year to come home." Saul grins and cracks open a beer and Jess pulls Jack by the hand to the sofa.

Much later at the dinner table the atmosphere is one of togetherness and Jack feels happier than he has done in months. It's been wrong to stay away so long, he has missed this. Perhaps the tension and implied blame were never that bad. Maybe time has added weight to his dread of home and family expectations. No-one has brought the conversation round to Raife - not yet.

The thought seems to pass via the wine bottle from him to his father. Joseph has been in good spirits but has drunk too much, and as he pours himself another glass, Jack catches the brief exchange that passes between Saul and Jess.

"So, you built me a boat yet Jack?" Joseph asks, tone laced with an edge of frustration.

Jack shakes his head smiling. "Not yet Papa, but I will, one of these days, and when I do you…"

"I'll what, son?" The loaded reply is a blow.

Jack lowers his head, knowing what happens now. Joseph pauses dramatically as if waiting for Jack to answer, knowing he won't. His eyes are clear, ignited with bitterness, in anger he is alive, vital and resolute.

"I'll be happy? I'll forgive you? Is that what this little visit's about? Grace us with your presence, clear your conscience? Your Mama…" he gestures toward Amandine who examines her hands clasped tightly in her lap. "Your Mama, she waits for you." He takes a deep breath then turns the corners of his mouth down slowly, deliberately, in disgust. "I say, Amandine, why wait for him to come home? Jack will do what he's always done, take care of himself." Joseph stands, hands gripping hard edges of the table, leaning heavily as the bitterness finds voice.

Saul reaches a hand toward his father. "Papa, sit down." Joseph's balance wavers a little as he swats Saul's hand away and continues undeterred.

"Build me a boat eh? That will be the day." He points a shaking finger but Jack isn't watching. His eyes are pressed tightly closed, head still lowered, fighting to retain control.

"Joseph stop." Amandine stands and moves toward Joseph, reaching for him, but he dismisses her with a toss of his head.

"Stop what? Stop trying to tell him to sort his life out, stop wasting it away like a hermit?" Fingers twirl the stem of his half empty wine glass, mouth twitching as he listens to the internal conversation directing his conduct. He looks up, glazed eyes on Jack. "Of all the things you could have done…look at you?" He points a shaking finger as Saul stands abruptly and puts a hand on his father's shoulder.

"That's enough to drink Pa, you're out of line."

"Get your hands off me Saul, I'll be the judge of when I've had enough. I'm still the man in this house." He glares at Saul who takes a deep breath and sits down slowly. Joseph's flabby expression is transformed; rigid with anger. They sit quietly, the scene too familiar, childhood memories cripple adult reactions. It's always been this way, this undercurrent of volatility. He used to keep it under control, know when to stop, but since Raife left he doesn't bother trying.

Air is sucked from the room, all eyes on Joseph, each carefully anticipating what comes next. Joseph shakes his head then looks back to Jack his gaze barely focused. "I'm making a point Saul. I'm making a point to Jack and he's going to listen."

Jack doesn't look up, he's trying to breathe and not react. It's all coming back, this is why he's stayed away.

"Where's that wife of yours anyway? What sort of a marriage was that? What the hell were you thinking? That's always been the problem with you Jack, never made a smart decision in your life." The words are teasing jabs, the beginning of the inevitable boxing match. "Look what your decision did to your brother," he pauses, "and that poor girl."

Jack looks up. Anger turned to sadness he sits like a remorseful teenager waiting for the punishment, taking the blows.

"Stop it!" Amandine is crying and Jess looks afraid. Joseph hears no one, taken by anger and thrilled by the audience and opportunity to unleash it on the son he knows won't fight back.

"Are you so ready to forget Raife? If it weren't for you he'd be here, he'd have a family, he'd have a life. Look at him now, stupid son of a bitch is going down the tubes and anytime you care to remember him, remember this…it's your fault."

"Stop it Pa! Jesus Christ, stop it." Saul stands to face his father and Joseph turns to him squaring his shoulders. Jack is on his feet. He won't see them fight over him.

"Go home Saul." Jack's voice is low, he gestures to Jess who sobs openly. Saul's hands, balled into fists are white at the knuckles. He nods warily, guiding Jess to her feet and out through the kitchen door.

Suddenly Amandine starts to sing, not a soft hum that might distract and diffuse the atmosphere, but a jolly TV jingle. Jack stops in his tracks turning from Joseph to stare slack-jawed at his mother, whose eyes are closed, fingers drumming on the cotton tablecloth, singing the Luxaflake laundry detergent commercial loudly.

The sight knocks the wind from his sails, anger fading to confusion as he watches, trying to find an explanation more palatable than the one he suspects to be true.

Joseph holds his ground, seemingly unfazed by Amandine. Either ignoring, or so used to the strange scene he pays it no mind. He wants to carry on where he left off.

"What are you going to do son, hit me? For telling you how it is? Go on, give me your best." The old man sticks his chin toward Jack, eager for the blow. Jack turns slowly, running his hands over his head as though to erase the evening and start again. Joseph juts his chin out again, awaiting the sharp thrill of the blow.

"Mama, I'm sorry" he bends to his mother who smiles happily, she has stopped singing. "I'm going to go."

"I know." And she really seems to, she shrugs her shoulders like she's got it all figured out, then stands to begin clearing the table. He turns to leave with a last glance back at his parents, heart heavy and mind racing.

His father has slumped back into his chair scowling silently as Jack leaves the room to reach the small bedroom. He grabs his bag, whistles to the dogs and leaves. Amandine is by the door.

"I love you Mama." She nods and silently mouths her love in reply as he descends the steps and walks out into the dark night.

Saul is waiting at the gate, and without a word joins step, guiding Jack across the farm to his place where Jess has a bed ready.

"Fuck Saul, what am I doing here? It's always the same."

"I don't know why you came home, but I'm glad you did."

"Why didn't you tell me about Mama?"

Saul shrugs looking awkward. "I meant to, then we didn't have the chance. It's just sometimes. She's okay but when she's tired she gets confused."

"How long has she been like this?"

"A while. It's been worse lately, but hell, she's seventy-four. I lose track of things all the time, at her age she's entitled to forget. It's par for the course right?"

"Is it?" Jack rubs a rough hand over his face. "What does Papa say?"

"Won't talk about it."

Jack shakes his head, hands pushed deep in his pockets, reeling from the evenings turnaround. Here is a new layer to an already weighty reality. They walk in silence the rest of the way, knowing there's too much to say.

At the gate to Saul's drive they stop and Jack lets his bag fall to the ground where he bends to rub Louie and Bets behind their ears and feel the unconditional love they offer. "I'll go. I'm making everything worse. I need to think. I can't be around Papa, it's bad for both of us."

Saul's stands arms folded, blocking the path. "Don't leave feeling like this. Screw the old man, his resentments are so big he doesn't know what he's angry about anymore. Come home with me, spend some time at our place. I could sure do with the help and Jess would kill me if I let you head home. She wants you to stay a while."

"I can't Saul, you saw what me being here does to him."

"I don't give a shit about him. We've all pussied around him for years. I'm not giving you a choice, besides he never leaves the porch, you won't even see him."

"I'll stay the night and we'll talk tomorrow."

"You make a plan with Jess. She's a got a few weeks work in mind for you and you can't say no to a pregnant woman right?"

Jack shakes his head; story of his life.

Chapter Three

Virginia and Sadie walk side by side, stride for stride, in silence. Bark and leaves on the forest floor carpet the sounds of determined footsteps. The trail winds and climbs through the bush emerging finally on to the sand at *La Misere*, St. Clouds most beautiful beach. They walk together, a friendship formed through tragedy. There's intimacy here, deep in the heart of the bush where filtered green light gives little hint of time, and the quiet hum of insects are the only sounds of life.

"Look, there it is again…" Virginia points toward the yellow-flowered tree on which a small bird alights, tail spread in a soft arc against the bark. Aware of their gaze, it performs a small show of acrobatic flight landing softly on the path near their tired feet before flying on to rest then repeat the performance.

Sadie is transfixed, native birds and bush still unfamiliar, "It wants to come with us." Her face glows in the pale golden, green light as she watches the bird fly to and from the path to the tree over and over, following their steps then guiding them forward.

"It's a fantail," Virginia smiles, her gaze following the little bird who swoops and sings in their wake.

Sadie's reply is disturbed by a cough she's been trying to suppress. The spluttering sound makes the fantail flee, disappearing into the bush as the cough rushes forward in a spluttering explosion. Virginia frowns as Sadie holds a hand out, palm up, shaking her head. "I'm okay, just something stuck…in my…throat." Virginia proceeds to clap Sadie vigorously on the back, despite her complaints.

"I think you're just unfit," Virginia says a little smugly. "I need to get you out hiking more often."

Sadie smiles, composure returning as her chest clears and her breath relaxes. "Maybe I'm allergic to something in here." She gestures around at the dense green forest on either side of the trail. "Damn, I've frightened the fantail away."

"Oh, he'll be back. You watch and see." Both women survey the forest. "He won't be far away. He'll be keeping close because he knows our footsteps will rustle up the undergrowth and unearth some breakfast." Sure enough, as they watch the Fantail swoops behind them, and pecks at the leaves they have disturbed with their footsteps. Mission accomplished, it disappears back into the trees.

They walk on in companionable silence until the dense growth finally breaks out on to a sandy beach, the contrast startling after the protective cover of forest and fern. Virginia claps her hands together, drops her backpack and sinks into the warm sand. Sadie walks on to the water's edge where she stops and lets her gaze take in the breaking waves and ripple of cool blue water.

She dumps her pack on the sand and pulls off her hiking boots, letting the cool water run between her toes and up around her sore muscles. Wading into the waves she beckons to Virginia who is already on her way.

"Heavenly." Virginia closes her eyes as the exquisite coolness of water soothes away aches from the hot hike. "I sometimes wonder how I survived in London for so long."

Since moving to St. Cloud ten years ago, Virginia and her husband Mike haven't managed to return to London, even to visit. Absorbed in their careers at St. Cloud's city hospital and content in a new life in the tropics, London's fast paced hustle becomes less attractive year by year. Virginia, St. Clouds' top gynaecologist, is immersed in the island community. She has a job that challenges her and a community of friends to stave off the lonely hours; her husband Mike, a cardiac surgeon, is a workaholic.

"I thought you loved London?" Sadie's hands rub her chest gently, massaging residual tightness, gaze still fixed on the edge of the ocean, water lapping around her knees.

"I did. I do. I just mean, how does one manage to be happy so far from the sea?"

"You are the only person I've ever met who actually uses the word *one* to describe herself," Sadie teases. "Apart from Colin Firth and Mr Darcy I didn't think people really talked like that."

Virginia extends an arm theatrically toward the ocean, "One can't help being of fine stock." She sighs lowering her arms into the water, letting her hands cool before placing palms on either side of her flushed cheeks. "Colin Firth would be nice though."

"Not my type!" Sadie laughs.

"What about you? Don't you miss home?" Virginia asks.

Sadie closes her eyes as though trying to conjure a memory. She nods and wrinkles her nose. "A little."

"Just a little?"

"Believe me Saskatchewan gets a little old when you've lived there for twenty years. I needed to get away." Her arms swing like a child's. "I'm happy here. Besides, I have Jed."

"Yes you do." Virginia smiles at Sadie whose gaze rests on a spot far out to sea, wistful youth seems long ago. "Damn, look at the time, we better start heading back, I've have to be in clinic at one."

Sadie cups some water in her hands, splashes her face and hair. "Well, we should hurry, those island vaginas won't wait."

"It's true. I'm a woman of purpose." Sadie laughs as Virginia continues. "Being a gynaecologist is a lesson in life, you wouldn't believe the things I hear and see." They sink on to the sand to struggle with wet feet and hiking boots.

"Don't go on, I can imagine." Sadie's smile is followed by a frown. "Ginny, when you met Mike, were you ever…well…"

"Was I ever well what?"

"Were you afraid? You know, scared about marriage and all."

"No, I can't say I was. I was sure. But then I was almost thirty, we'd been together for a long time and I was ready to start a family."

"Has Jed asked you to marry him?" Virginia is careful with her tone, conscious not to sound shocked.

Sadie laughs heartily. "Only every day since the day after we met. I keep saying no of course, I mean, he's not really serious even though he thinks he is."

"Is that why you keep saying no? Because you think he's not serious?"

"Even if he was, I'd still say no. He has no idea what he'd be getting into. I mean, he hardly even knows me. It's ridiculous." Sadie's fingers fidget with the dangling straps of her pack as she strides step for step in front of Virginia.

"You've been together a while now, I'd think he probably knows all he needs to."

"He doesn't."

"Is there something you want to tell me?" Virginia frowns at Sadie's back.

Sadie stops suddenly and Virginia ploughs into her back.

"Sorry." Non-plussed that her abrupt halt has sent Virginia toppling into the bush, she offers a hand. "Yes, I want to tell you I'm pooped." Taking a deep breath, she wipes her forehead and reaches for her water bottle drinking deeply. She splutters, choking back another chesty cough. "I think you're right, I am so out of shape."

Virginia brushes her shorts off. "You're changing the subject. You were about to tell me if everything was okay with you and Jed."

"No I wasn't."

"You are now."

Sadie laughs, recovers then sighs. "Things are fine. Better than fine - they're great. Jed's great. It's just..." she blows a stray hair from her face. "It wasn't the plan."

Virginia shrugs. "Sometimes letting things go unplanned is for the best."

Sadie squeezes Virginia's arm, tightens her pack straps and they begin their steady pace once more along the trail, where the bright sunlight diffuses to a pale green glow. Sadie's pace is slow but sure. "You know Ginny, I almost bought that line. But you're the most well-planned person I know. How can you be sure of that?"

Virginia smiles at Sadie's back feeling a rush of regret. "I planned my life so beautifully I didn't leave enough time for children. Then when I decided the big plan could fit them in, it was too late."

Sadie doesn't turn around, doesn't respond with an insubstantial answer. She nods, keeping their pace steady, the rest of the walk passing in easy silence.

Jed

At 12.30pm Sadie, sun-kissed and smiling, breezes through the door of Beaujangles. The cafe is crowded, lunchtime rush in full swing, the fast pace of food prep and coffee creation accompanied by the frenzied banjo playing of Mumford and Sons through the speakers. The intoxicating scent of grilled goats cheese and roast peppers mixes with aromatic freshly ground coffee beans and just baked cookies. A sensory overload of smells, sights and sounds.

Sadie stops for a moment by the door to take in the scene; she closes her eyes and smells the air, listening to the buzz of conversation and laughter that bounce from the brightly coloured walls.

A familiar voice yells above the hum of cafe chaos.

"Hey! Quit dreaming over there and get your ass behind this counter - I'm dying here!" Jed raises his palms to the ceiling in exasperation. "I keep telling you I need you, but I don't think you get it!"

Rolling her eyes, she walks leisurely through the maze of customers and tables. Sadie doesn't do rushing. "Oh I get it." She smiles lazily, eyes fixed on Jed's boyish grin. "You need me for my plate scraping and dish washing capabilities. It's flattering." She slips in behind the counter, passing Jed on the way to the cafe kitchen. "Breathe a sigh of relief, I'm here to save you."

Jed shakes his head at her retreating behind and turns back to the next customer, "She is you know."

By 8.30pm the light outside is low. People stroll along the sidewalk heading to bars or restaurants, pace slow and relaxed. Jed stacks chairs and pulls heavy tables under the street side awning outside Beau

Jangles. He loves this time of night, the gentle wind down of day and the warm smell of sunshine that coats the streets as the cool breath of evening descends. Warmth radiates underfoot, concrete storing the day's heat and passing it on as night falls.

He's always come home, wherever he'd ended up; travelling and surfing, trying on different lives. He'd wondered for a while if growing up in St. Cloud would limit his understanding of the world. He'd felt he had to travel, take some time to figure out where he wanted to be, what he wanted to do. Funny that after three years of wandering, surfing and working cafes for a living he'd come home, realising that St. Cloud was where he wanted to be. He'd loved it all; Europe, Asia, North America, Australia. But after a while, when the novelty of each place wore off, he'd pine for home and the familiar smells, sights and people of St. Cloud.

He picks up the Beaujangles sign that sits on the sidewalk and carries it into the brightly lit cafe. Sadie smiles, armed with a mop and bucket, the last of the evenings clean up tasks complete. "Hope I'm getting a pay rise!" She snaps off her gloves and wipes her forehead.

Jed grins, motioning toward the door, flicking off the cafe lights. "Come on, let's go."

"I'm beat." Sadie slides a hand into Jed's as they reach the sidewalk. "The hike with Ginny this morning, then eight hours' hard slog with you. I hope there's something in it for me." She smiles and squeezes his hand.

Jed tugs her in the direction of the beach. "Let's swim." He leans in to kiss her on the forehead then leads her in comfortable silence in the direction of the ocean.

It's been like this since they met. Easy, like he'd always known her. There are conversations he doesn't have to have with Sadie. She gets it, she gets him and he's never had that before. He never knew that being with someone could be so easy and feel so right. Sadie walked into his life, actually his cafe, and after that everything changed.

He hadn't wanted a girlfriend, not then. He'd had enough trouble before, never seemed to meet the right girl. Beaujangles took all of his time and energy; it had been a few years since he'd been in a proper relationship. The guys teased him about it, and he took it good humouredly. He was happy with the odd fling here and there, no strings, no complications. Beaujangles was his baby girl and with her, he knew what he was doing. Women were different.

It's dark by the time they reach the beach. The transition from day to night is almost complete and the stretch of beach is deserted. They walk barefoot, the water lapping at their feet until the lights of the city twinkle and the sounds of cars and street life fade. Sadie drops her bag and shoes under a tree before stripping off and heading confidently for the water.

Jed watches her retreating behind, wondering how he got this lucky. He's never met anyone like her. In fact, he hadn't realised women like Sadie existed. Calm and self-possessed, comfortable with her body in a way he's never known another woman to be. She is beautiful but he doesn't have to tell her, although he does. Her quiet, self-confidence drew him in from the beginning.

She'd walked in to Beaujangles and asked him for a job. He'd been busy and was short with her, barely looking past the dreadlocks. An hour later she was still sitting at the window seat, slowly sipping her coffee. He'd told her if she didn't move on soon he'd have to charge her rent. It was then that she smiled and he'd been struck by that smile. She'd asked if she could work for food and somehow persuaded him to give her a trial for a day to see if he wanted to keep her.

Of course he did, and here they are almost two years later. Her hair is piled high on her head and she walks carefully into the waves before diving and disappearing under the black water.

She'd disappeared once before, decided she needed to travel some more, be without him and figure things out. He'd been stunned. He'd believed that they were together and there were no questions. The memory makes him shudder despite the warmth in the air. There had been no warning; she'd turned up at the cafe halfway through a busy Friday, back pack on. She told him she was taking off and asked if he wanted to go with her. What was he supposed to do? He couldn't drop everything, and anyway he'd said before; he was done travelling. She'd told him she wasn't big on goodbyes and she was leaving but she'd be back sometime. Sometime? He was floored by the unexpected departure and angry for a while. Angry with her and angry with himself, wondering why he didn't tell her how he really felt. He'd just assumed she got it, understood without words - they were so good together.

She did come back and he'd been so happy. He knew then he'd have to figure out a way to keep her. Then Evan had died and life turned on its head. She'd been a rock and he'd fallen into that feeling of inevitability that came with their relationship; they were meant to be together. But lately he's become nervous. He keeps coming back to the hurt. The scars of her unexpected departure haven't quite healed over and it bothers him.

"Are you coming in?" She interrupts his train of thought. "You're staring over there like a creepy old guy, get your clothes off and get in here!"

"Easy with the old guy." Jed peels off his clothes and jogs into the water, diving toward her. She screams and tries to swim away but he catches her ankle and pulls her in.

There's the pretence of combat, struggling and splashing but they know how this plays out. Jed lifts her hips as she wraps her legs around his waist, reaching to pull his face close to hers. When she finds his lips he's smiling. He can't help it. She's smiling too but he hardly notices as the kiss that follows is deep and urgent. He'll save the smiling for later; when his heart rate is back to normal.

The first time he'd told her he loved her she'd smiled and said "I know." The self-assurance was disarming. She'd waited for her own moment, much later that night, when he'd been about to fall asleep, to tell him she loved him too. He hadn't replied "I know", because truthfully up until that moment he hadn't.

When she tells him now it's like a drug. There's a high that accompanies those three simple words and he can't get enough of it. Tonight, as the dark water beats against them she tells him again. Hands in his hair, legs wrapped around his waist she whispers the words in his ear. Jed closes his eyes and breathes her. He breathes her and the night; the salty ocean air and fragrant humidity. Tilting her hips to meet him he pulls her in, she gasps and bites down on his shoulder, breasts tight against his chest. There's no holding back with

Sadie - sex holds the drama of a grand finale each and every time. For a brief second, Jed considers the possibility; what if it were? The thought is gone before it takes root; all thoughts evaporate as sensory pleasures take over. Sadie takes control, guiding him deeper before slowly releasing, her rhythm matching the gentle pull of the tide.

Jed loses himself in the exquisite sensation of making love in the ocean; the contrast of body heat and cool water in the buoyancy and tow of the waves.

"Stay with me Sadie."

"I will."

He sucks in his breath pulling her deeper. "I mean it."

Her eyes are open, fixed on his face as he comes. A small gasp escapes his lips, parted in pleasure. She whispers in his ear. "I know."

Dan

It's almost 7.00 pm when Virginia pulls her car into the driveway.

Turning off the ignition, she sits quietly for a moment watching the neglected façade of the house. It could be a place she's never been before, so changed. All the life sucked out, a shell of its former vibrant self where life was everywhere.

It's been six months since she's been here. Six months for the weeds to wander, the grass to grow and wild flowers to bloom in the most unexpected places. The house looks neglected, unloved but not without a past. Overspill of emotion oozes from cracked weatherboard walls and chipped window panes. Regret and despair seep from salty windows, ocean air leaves traces of briny neglect. Windows reflect no sunlight and inside is blurry and disfigured behind the haze of time passed and tragedy.

She shivers and squeezes the steering wheel tightly, eyes straight ahead. Virginia, always practical, always level-headed, is having a moment. Her eyes squeeze tight shut, knuckles white from her determined grip on the wheel. One tear pushes forward and rolls uncertainly down her cheek; the next, less wary follows, trickling down the bridge of her nose where she intercepts it quickly with the back of her sleeve. She blows a slow breath outward, her fringe lifts and settles and still the hot tears flow.

"Damn it." Releasing her fingers from their stranglehold on the wheel she delves into her handbag for a handkerchief.

"All right in there?" The voice makes her jump in her seat.

"Don't you knock?" Virginia answers, dabbing her red eyes quickly before leaning over to open the passenger door.

Dan smiles, easing himself into the adjacent seat as gracefully as a cat. "Sorry, didn't realise you were indisposed. Shall I hop out and start again?"

"No you moron. I was having a moment. Stay here will you, but don't look at me." She continues to sniff and dab her eyes. Dan reclines the passenger seat and leans back letting the expensive sunglasses that rest on his head fall forward to hide his own eyes. After five more minutes of sniffing and a loud nose blow, Virginia is ready and turns to him.

"Ok, that's it. I'm good. Thank you."

Dan nods gently and gestures toward the house. "Shall we go in?"

Virginia looks straight ahead, composure regained. "Let's do this."

Both car doors open simultaneously, creaking a welcome to the still autumn night. The sun lies low in the sky and the air is sweet and fragrant with late summer blooms.

Standing outside Billie and Evans house, Dan and Virginia are sombre. They have to go in, they've promised they would. They must check things over, clear a few things out and get the house ready for Billie's arrival home.

Dan pushes the key in the lock and fiddles for a moment, twisting it left and right, till reluctantly it clicks and the door opens in a yawn. It is a house in hibernation. As light slices through the shadows a frantic rush of wings and feathers burst through the opening gap. Dan drops to his knees and Virginia screams.

A trapped bird. Its unexpected exit triggers overreactions borne from wary anticipation. Billie and Evan's home has been locked up for six months.

"There must be an open window." Dan's voice is shaken, his cool exterior ruffled.

Virginia stands behind him, a smile slowly transforming her anxious expression. "You okay down there?" Dan is still on his knees in front of the gaping door.

Dan doesn't miss a beat. "It's an ancient tradition, I'm honouring past ancestors." He looks up encouragingly to Virginia before lowering his forehead to touch the dusty doormat. "There." He winks, rising awkwardly, dusting down his designer jeans. "Should be fine, think I've cleared the way." Rolling her eyes Virginia follows him inside.

Fingers of late afternoon light weep through cracks in closed blinds, deep golden rays, peppered with dust motes, alight across floors and walls. The morbid still is a crushing contrast to the fleeing bird's fight for freedom.

A light linen drape flutters in a far corner, a small, open upper window evidence of the birds' recent entrance. They stand silently in the doorway, motionless, embodying the aura that settles all around. They wait, the house waits; a home without a family, quietly anticipating life's return.

The house had been cleaned and cleared after Billie and the twins' departure for Scotland; a job left mostly to Virginia and Zoe. Billie had been in no state to manage practicalities. Surfaces lie free of clutter, toys are packed away, windows closed and blinds drawn. The task of clearing Evan's studio had been left for a time. No-one could face the scene of devastation. Art mimics life. Life mimics art.

Finally, Dan had faced the job with the help of Felix and Jed. Together they had cleared the chaos of broken wings and bodies, perfectly sculpted creatures of flight. Even the most mechanical, those with the hardest lines, the most rigid bodies had seemed to breathe life. That was Evan's gift; the things he created with his hands sparkled with life. His creative world was blindingly bright and it stole the light from his days.

Virginia snaps out of reverie and moves with purpose opening curtains and blinds, prising open windows, letting air flood the stale space. Dan follows, still a little shaken by the unexpected flight of the escaping bird.

As air and light fill the house the solemn mood lifts gradually. Hope accompanies the light. As the room colours with late afternoon sun, the seed of a new beginning seems possible.

"How does she sound?" Dan unlocks and slides open the doors to the deck.

"Hard to say. Better I think, said she was ready to come home." Virginia dusts off the countertops and shakes cushions purposefully. "Right, let's get some sheets on beds." She directs Dan to the bedrooms and he salutes in response, happy for once to have her boss him around.

The bedroom is heavy with Billie and Evan's presence despite the passage of time. Virginia stops by the foot of the bed to gather herself before continuing on in her usual no nonsense fashion.

Sheets billow in the air then settle, crisp cotton layers of practicality on the barren double bed. "That's better." She bustles around, room to room, cleaning, airing, and readying the house for Billie and the twins' return. Dan, redundant amidst Virginia's whirlwind of domestic capability, sinks in to the swing seat on the back deck.

The ocean sparkles in the changing light, just visible through the tree break. A distant formation of sea birds fly together, forming a shape like the tip of an arrow. Their sleek bodies glint in the sun and its reflection on the ocean below. For a moment they disappear, the light creating a magical illusion. Turning and twisting, bathed in colour and sparkling sunlight then gone.

Virginia emerges half an hour later, sleeves rolled up, cheeks flushed. "Don't tell me, this is another ancient tradition. By relaxing out here while I do all the work you're somehow honouring St. Cloud ancestors." Her expression is only half serious. The readying of the house has done her good, a practical step away from the past toward the future.

"Virginia, have I told you before you are both brains and beauty?" Dan opens his hands out toward the garden and view. "You'll be happy to know our ancestors are pacified." He smiles apologetically toward her. "Sorry."

She shakes her head and pushes the awkward apology away with a flick of a hand. "It's fine."

Dan nods and turns back to face the glimpse of ocean at the end of the sprawling yard.

It isn't fine. It hasn't been fine for a while now. It's something else, something forced, a game of make believe. They move on using routine as a crutch, it helps pass time and only time can truly help. Since Evan's death they've carried on, each of them trying to live in a tragically altered reality. Nothing is fine. It can't be.

He thinks back to the night he'd packed up the last of Evan's clothes and belongings. Jed and Felix had helped but it had been a hell of a task. Virginia had insisted that by doing this one thing for Billie they'd be helping her manage her grief in stages, when she was ready. Coming home would be hard enough.

They'd sorted through and packaged everything up. Working in silence they'd removed most traces of Evan, and despite knowing the task was necessary it had all felt wrong. The process was too intimate, a forbidden glance into the private world of another. A life laid out in art supplies, broken sculptures and rumpled clothing.

They knew that sorting through his studio would be hard; they'd been ready for that. Clearing the carnage left behind after his last night in life, the splintered wood and crushed wings, years of painstaking work and passionate construction crushed and broken.

Strangely the chaos in the studio was not the hardest to deal with. It was the simple possessions and everyday objects, small symbols of Evan's life that left them hollowed out.

Inside the untidy closet it was the worn sneakers and crumpled shirts, the balled socks and his faint but still present scent. Linseed oil and charcoal, oil paint and citrus.

When the sorting was over, they'd hugged. None of the usual back clapping, high fiving guy embraces. But a hug where they had given and received comfort, no words or apologies for the intimacy of holding each other in grief.

It took a few weeks for him to move on from the wrenching experience of packing Evan's life in boxes. His dry, sarcastic wit was gone. He faked a flu and stayed home wallowing in *the blues*, listening to opera on his retro Dansette record player. He moved cocktail hour to 2pm and spent the mornings in bed reading Orson Welles until the hour approached and he could listen to Maria Callas and drink dry martinis. Dr Dan was out of commission and his evening persona, DJ Dan, was incommunicado.

After a week Virginia came banging on his front door armed with a brown paper bag containing organic produce and some herbal iron tonic. For backup, she was flanked by Jed and Sadie armed with takeaway coffee and blueberry muffins.

After his solitary week of the blues he was ready to be coaxed back into the land of the living. And although he protested half-heartedly, he was happy to shed the layer of self-prescribed sorrow. The knowledge he was loved more replenishing than any tonic.

"It's ready." Virginia rubs her hands together. "Ready as it will ever be."

Dan nods and stands slowly, gaze shifting toward Jack's house, another shadow of its former self. Shuttered and quiet, another casualty of the fallout from Evan's death.

Jack's place was always alive with the sound of a radio, power tools, dogs barking, a guitar strumming. Jack has been gone for three months and no-one knows when he might come home. A visit to see family, although they all know his departure is more than that - much more.

Dan brings his gaze back to Virginia, blinking as though to clear his head. "What now Mary Poppins?"

Virginia smiles, a layer of tension sliding from her composed features. "Beer. Let's go to Santos. I could murder a Corona."

Dan smiles warmly linking arms and leading her back through the sliding doors. Through the dust free, sparkling room and out through the door that will remain closed until Billie's arrival. "You're a terrible influence Ginny." He opens Virginia's car door and she slides in with a sigh.

"And you, Dan Wilder are a terrible tease." She reaches to find her seatbelt and clips it firmly in place. "Now, I know I've mentioned it before but really, you should think about donating. You have such wonderful genes darling." Her expression is wistful, then exasperated. "And let's face it, the female race will never see your swimmers. Truly, think it's your duty to donate that sperm."

Dan opens his mouth, about to respond to their usual tête-à-tête, but she's too quick.

"Just think about it." She raises a palm to shield herself from his predicted negative response to the tired topic before backing out of the drive. "Come on then, I'll buy you a Corona." Accelerating quickly, a hand waving from the window, Virginia is gone.

Dan smiles wearily, shaking his head as he steps into his Chevy, easing carefully on to Frontiere Point Road. He'll follow her into the city, to friends, a quiet beer and later, a few hours on air. Tonight's show is worrying him a little, there's no knowing how things might turn out. But he's made a promise and he'll keep it.

Chapter Four

God the truck smells bad. Saul's fish van had been the only option for escape. He'd lain for a while on the bed Jess had hastily made but sleep was far away.

With every pot hole the truck hits, another pungent wave wafts through the thick muggy air. Jack feels nauseous but maybe that's just a result of the evening. With a free hand he rifles through the scattered CD collection on the passenger seat. Turning onto the smooth main road, a base guitar and steady drumbeat reverberate as the sound of the Foo Fighters thrum from the stereo.

He should have known. It's always the same, although usually he might have had at least twenty-four hours to settle in before Joseph's tirade. This is why he doesn't come home.

Every visit since, every conversation, each moment of eye contact with Joseph: loaded. Maybe the blame is his? The expectation of inevitable confrontation willing the moment's transformation from guilt to action. This conflict now their default position: Jacks presence highlighting Raife's absence and everything that spiralled from there.

The night is heavy with regret. No starlight in the bleak darkness. As the van nears the coastal road a pale, insubstantial moon grazes the quiet ocean with tired light.

This wasn't the plan. He breathes deeply trying to stop his thoughts from spiralling in regressive circles. "Damn it!" He bangs the steering wheel with the heel of his hand and pumps the gas. Actions interpreted as threatening were he not driving a strong smelling fish van with a maximum speed of 60 kilometres per hour.

Twenty minutes later the van pulls into the parking lot of a busy ocean-side bar. A snap decision, the music and dark mood have made him thirsty. Not a thirst he's comfortable with, but recklessness is brewing along with his need for a beer.

There is comfort in the company of strangers and the bar is the small escape he needs. The beach bars' closer to the touristy side of St. Eloise are busy and anonymous. No need for polite conversation. He wants to have a beer alone, let the dark anger brewing dangerously settle and subside.

An overwhelming lack of control jostles him through the crowd to the bar where he finds a seat and orders a beer. The woman behind the bar nods and passes him a dewy green bottle, no words needed. In this business she is only too familiar with the smell of despair.

There's a cover band in the corner: three men in their fifties and a heavily made up woman whose cleavage attracts more attention than her voice. They start up another tired number that no-one pays much attention to.

Jack nurses his beer, trying to still his thoughts and find some calm. But stillness is elusive and the bottle which usually hits the spot, misses the mark completely. He needs another.

"You don't look like you're on holiday." She smiles pushing the second beer before him. A name badge pinned to the breast pocket of her shirt reads *Aubrey*.

Jack smiles reluctantly, he doesn't feel like conversation. He shakes his head before taking a long slow drink from the bottle, hoping this small action will satisfy.

"You here with the construction lot? I wish they'd stop with the condos over in La Moliets. Soon there will be more condos than beach. Man, I hate that shit."

Her bad pronunciation of La Moliets suggests she's another run-away. Another post college traveller in limbo, still tending bar ten years later. Career dreams forgotten; white picket fence, 2 kids and prematurely balding husband traded for eternal hippiedom in the tropics.

She's staring at him, arms folded. "It's rude not to answer. I'm just being polite."

Jack blushes, caught up in his own thoughts he hasn't said a word. Doesn't really care to. "Sorry. No, I'm not with the construction guys."

She smiles. "You have got a voice!" She stops drying beer glasses and thrusts a sticky hand toward him. "Good to meet you. You can call me Aubrey."

Jack takes her hand, slightly amused by her persistence. "Jack."

"Well Jack, what the hell are you doing here, looking like you just got done at a funeral?" She pauses, frowning. "Shit, you didn't just get done at a funeral, did you?"

He smiles and shakes his head again. "No."

"Aha." She winks then claps her hands together. "I get it, the one-word answer. I'm desperate for conversation, I guess it'll have to do." A man hollers an order from the other end of the bar and she gives him the finger without looking around. "In a minute, I'm busy." She cracks open a bottle of beer, leans in and clinks the bottleneck with Jacks. He can smell her; shampoo and cigarette smoke. The top of her cleavage is visible from the open neck of her shirt and she lingers a moment before moving back, smiling and heading over to the waiting order.

"So Jack, I'm right. You're not from around here." She shouts over the music from the other side of the bar, hands deftly mixing a cocktail. He shakes his head, a little more interested in the amusing distraction she is becoming. "That's not even a word." She bangs the cash drawer closed and heads back toward him. "Silent type. I like that - less complicated."

"Do you ever let up?" He's enjoying her now. She's attractive and sassy and he's just finished the second beer. Things are feeling better.

Aubrey claps her hands and laughs deeply. "Five words! I did it."

The band plays on and slowly the night loses its hard edges, even the cover songs sound better. By beer number five he's progressed to full sentences. This is the place he'd sworn not to go again. The crossing point where is doesn't matter. Where everything is good and consequences happen to other people. Coated in the protective armour of the invincible drunk, Jack forgets he's no good at this; that he's still cleaning up the mess he made last time he lost control.

For now, everything is possible and his hazy head entertains the thought that he should be spending more time in bars; it feels good. All the stress he's put himself though, all the work and avoidance to hold it together. Right now he believes he's come home, and as he catches Aubrey's eye, he knows exactly how the night will go.

At 2.00 am the bar is empty. Aubrey grabs a set of keys and a leather bag. Jack is in the same seat at the bar. He's lost track of beers and time. There's a dull throb in his temple; an omen of sorts. Rubbing his hands over his head he pushes the pain away till later. He'll have this now.

She walks to the far end of the bar and takes a brush from her handbag. He watches as she pulls off her bandana emblazoned with the bar logo, and brushes. Long, wavy, bottle blonde hair. Pulling a tube from her bag she applies gloss to her lips, dabbing the corners then smacking them together. She admires her reflection, oblivious to Jacks stare.

"Going somewhere nice?" Jack asks as she walks toward him flicking lights off as she goes.

"Come on sunshine, I'll give you a ride."

"You will?"

She smiles pulling him to his feet. "You're not driving anyplace tonight."

"So you'll take me home?" He lets her pull him toward the doors. Why the hell should he resist? Why stay faithful to someone he'll never have? He needs this.

"Hell no." Aubrey guides him out of the bar. The air feels good on his face. She turns to double lock the door and flip the switch to the outdoor lighting. He stands behind her, hands on her waist as they're plunged into darkness. His need is suddenly insatiable, it's been so long and now he can't wait. Aubrey grabs his hands and places them on her breasts. He pulls her round to face him, hands moving beneath her shirt, pushing his body into hers.

"Easy," she murmurs, pulling away gently and leading him by the hand across the deserted parking lot.

"Tell me we're not doing this in the bushes." Jack groans, his erection almost painful.

"Here." She drags him around the side of the bar where a small camper van is parked. She fiddles with another key and throws open the back door. Inside is a mattress and the faint smell of incense, her home on the run. Life in a few basic possessions; clothes and a duffle bag, books and some blankets.

He pushes her backwards on to the mattress, tugging at her shirt and bra, pulling off his shirt roughly. She's on her back naked from the top up. Jack straddles her, taking his fill of her breasts before moving to her belt. He peels off her shorts and underwear; he can't stop or he'll sober up enough to change his mind. His body shudders in anticipation; this is what he needs. This one physical act will cleanse him. That after this everything will be fine. This is all that matters. Right now he believes it.

She thrusts him a condom and in seconds he's inside her. He starts slow but she urges him on and the sensation clears all thoughts from his mind. As their pace intensifies she begins to buck and moan loudly, too loudly, and it stalls his rhythm.

She pushes him on to his back and sits astride him, pulling his hands to her breasts as she moves and cries out. He opens his eyes, the air suddenly thick in the hot dark van. Pale, grey moonlight illuminates her face and form. But now her breasts seem to sag and droop as they sway close to his face and the flesh around her middle gathers in his hands. Slowly, slowly the haze in his head is clearing, and as their sweat mingles he feels a physical wrench, a vice in his chest that tightens as he longs for another body; another face; another woman.

Eyes closed, she holds her arms high above her head, moaning, hands twisting and turning, hips rising and falling gracelessly. The illusion dissolves with each awkward thrust. In one urgent movement, he flips her on to her front pushing in from behind; sickened with the sobering knowledge that he can't finish while seeing her face.

Jack doesn't sleep, he waits until she wakes. "I'm sorry."

Aubrey takes a moment, eyes clouded with sleep, she sighs heavily before answering. "Don't spoil my fun Jack. Don't say another word. I get it and it's okay."

"I don't normally drink... I didn't mean..." she holds a palm up to his mouth, sealing in the words that will follow. Moving her hand into his she turns on her side, back to him, pulling his arm around her, forcing the hold that must end soon.

"Just stay a while." She draws him closer, and as they lie she strokes his hand. "Don't say anything else. I know I'm not her, whoever the hell she is, but it's okay. I had a good time." She squeezes his hand and falls quickly back to sleep.

Dawn brings sadness. Steadily brightening light and darkening despair. He lies behind her, not quite touching aside for the hand she clings to. He's another one of *those guys* - the bastard who takes what he needs and leaves. Bitter daylight reveals truths carefully hidden in the night's black cloak of acceptance. When it's late, and the world is quiet and dark and you believe for a time that comfort and release, however it's found, is yours to take as need beckons. He'll never see her again. She won't remember him, it doesn't matter…but somehow it does.

It does. And as the light brightens through the grimy camper windows, it matters more that he's here. That it's come to this. That he used her to fill a space. The fleeting satisfaction a poor reward for the heaviness that lies in his heart.

What the fuck was he thinking?

Prising his arm from her, he pulls the clothes he can find from the mess around them. He needs to be outside and away from this unsettling chaos. She rustles as he leaves but doesn't wake. Cool morning dew embraces his shaking arms as he gently closes the door. He won't say goodbye, she'll expect him to be gone when she wakes.

He stands in the low light for a moment - maybe more - eyes closed, face raised to the cool air and gentle light of dawn. He tries to breathe steadily but his head pounds and his body aches from guilt and alcohol. With quick urgency he runs, heading for the bush that leads away from the bar down to the sandy undisturbed beach. At the tree line he doubles over, hands on bent knees and vomits.

When it's done he walks till Aubrey and the bar and the booze are far away. Jack keeps walking, till the incoming tide laps around his body and the waves try to wash away the night before.

Santos is crowded when they arrive. Virginia gets there first, Dan's vintage Chevy no match for her sports car. Making her way to the bar, she smiles and greets the local faces she recognises. It's hard to be anonymous in her profession and Virginia likes it that way.

Virginia waves across the bar where Josefina is leaning on her elbows chatting. When she catches her eye, Virginia blows her a kiss, gestures to the beer fridge and holds up two fingers. Josefina winks and heads toward her collecting two bottles of cold Corona on route. Beers in hand, Virginia weaves her way through the crowded bar to find her friends. She's relieved to see them huddled around their usual table. She sighs, "Shifty up then, I've had a hell of a day."

Sadie nudges Jed who shuffles along the cracked leather bench. "How was it?" She asks laying a hand on Virginia's arm as she sinks into the soft seat with another loud sigh.

"Okay. I think it's all ready." She tips the bottle to her mouth taking a long, slow sip.

"Those both for you?" Jed gestures toward the beers lined up in front of her.

"Dan's on his way."

Jed frowns. "Doesn't he have the show tonight?" He looks at Sadie, then back to Virginia. "He never comes in on a Thursday!"

Sadie laughs and nudges him, "What do you care?"

"I don't, I just…"

Dan emerges from the crowd looking tired. Seeing them, he grins and makes his toward their booth. He leans over and kisses Sadie on both cheeks before sinking into the leather seat opposite.

"What about me?" asks Virginia, proffering her cheek forward in anticipation of a kiss.

"Twice in one night? Ginny, you're wearing me out." He smiles, reaching for the beer she pushes toward him. "Where's Felix?"

"On his way with Zoe," Sadie answers scanning the crowd. "Her Mom's in town so they're making the most of the free babysitting."

As if on cue the couple enter the bar, Felix's blond head clearly visible over the crowd. He waves and shouts something in German to Bastian, then cuts a path toward them, Zoe and her protruding tummy tucked safely behind. Seeing them, Zoe rushes forward to kiss everyone before squeezing herself in beside Virginia. Felix grins and pulls a stool over to the edge of the crowded booth.

Bastian arrives with a pint of dark brown beer of German origin and an iced tea with mint and lemon. "Bastian, you shouldn't have. Table service isn't necessary." Zoe smiles grabbing the pint glass.

"Hey you, pass that here!" Felix calls across the table.

"Just a tiny taste?" Zoe lets the beer touch her lips and sighs. "God I miss beer." Felix reaches over and commandeers his pint, pushing the iced tea in front of her. "Bleh!" She smiles up at him, foam from the beer coating her top lip.

Felix shakes his head reaching over to wipe her lip with his thumb. "Hey Bastian, pull up a chair."

Bastian is already heading back to the bar. "Too busy, maybe later."

"Hope you're tuning in to the show tonight." Dan calls after him, "I got a great line up of music." Dan turns slowly and winks at Jed who looks mildly alarmed.

"We'll have you on full volume." Bastian glances briefly over at Josefina. "Just promise me no country music. She's been playing Garth Brooks and Shania Twain for weeks. It's driving me crazy."

"You bet, no country music. I have my standards." Dan pretends to look offended. Bastian gives him a thumbs up and returns to Josefina's side behind the bar.

Half an hour later Dan rises to leave, blowing a kiss to the table as he departs. "Full volume, don't forget."

"Yeah, yeah. We hear you!" Zoe says. "Don't worry - the world will stop and we'll all hail when the show starts."

"Easy fatty." He quips retreating before she can throw something at him. He turns briefly raising his eyebrows at Jed who nods quickly, his face pale and distracted.

Zoe turns to Virginia. "So the house looks okay?" Virginia nods and smiles. Zoe continues, "They're on their way right now, this time tomorrow she'll be home. It'll be so good to see her." She hesitates, "Will it be okay to talk about it?"

"Of course." Virginia is reassuring. "Billie has had time and she's strong. We can't avoid it. She'll want to talk and we have to be here for her. We have to do our best to support her, help her to move on."

"I wish Jack were here." Zoe pauses. "But maybe it's good he's not... oh, I don't know." She looks at her hands and twists her wedding band. Virginia is about to reply when Jed stands abruptly and pushes past them, knocking over a beer as he goes.

"Jed!" Sadie calls after him. "Where are you going?"

"Forgot something at the cafe, be back in a minute." As he jogs from the bar, Sadie shrugs and carries on her conversation.

Out in the street Jed grabs his skateboard, overcome by a rash of nervous energy, he takes off on the wrong side of the road at full speed. Luckily there's hardly any traffic and he's a skilled boarder. He lets out a crazy guy wolf call and boards like a mad man, weaving around the scattered traffic toward Dan's studio where the nights broadcast is about to begin.

Back in Santos the crowd has thinned considerably and they can actually hear each other speak without shouting. Bastian arrives with a pitcher of dark brown beer, some glasses and a basket of unshelled peanuts. He pulls up a stool and pours himself a glass, launching into conversation as Josefina turns the volume up on Dan's show. Dan's voice is smooth as he introduces the show before playing the first track of the night.

"Where's Jed?" asks Felix.

Sadie starts, deep in conversation with Zoe. "He should have been back by now, said he had to pop over to the cafe." Josefina interrupts arriving with another round of drinks. Jed is momentarily forgotten and conversation continues until Dan's voice becomes annoyingly loud through the speakers.

"Calling Santos! Are you guys listening? Bastian? I told you to turn the volume up. Don't let me down man."

Bastian looks around sheepishly as though somehow Dan must be able to see him. "I turned it up!" He opens his palms to the speakers as though to placate the demanding Dan.

"Okay then, tonight I'm going to dedicate a track to our dear friend Billie and her kids who are on the way over the oceans as we speak, heading back home. Billie we can't wait to see you. This track is also for Evan our dearly departed friend. Hope you got some aerodynamic wings up there buddy. We miss you. Bastian, don't turn me down, you hear?"

Bastian keeps looking around like Dan must be sitting in the bar somewhere watching him. "My hands are on my beer!" They all laugh, the track begins, and people nod and smile, recognising the music and understanding its significance. When it finishes Felix calls out a toast to Billie and Evan and they raise their glasses.

Dan chats on, entertaining with snippets of local news, gossip and some well-chosen music. He introduces a new local reggae band, plays a few of their tracks and takes some local calls. As the show comes to its conclusion there's an awkward pause, silence as the last track concludes. They imagine Dan taking a long slow breath. When finally he speaks his voice is tight, the pitch a little tense. His unusual tone has everyone's attention.

"Okay guys, this is it. It's a first and I want you to move to the edge of your seats while you're listening. If you're driving, pull over and cross your fingers, because my friend here is doing something crazy. Something brave and something you probably won't hear again on my show."

Zoe raises an eyebrow and motions everyone to be quiet. Conversations stop and ears are trained on Dan's voice, wondering what he's about to do. Who is his friend and what's going on?

"I'd like to welcome my buddy Jed here to the show, a guy we all know and love, artisan of the finest coffee in the South Pacific, owner of Beaujangles cafe downtown. If you haven't been there, you shouldn't be listening to my show; so turn off your radio and don't come back till you've tasted Jed's coffee."

At Santos, everything has gone quiet. Those drinking in booths or at the bar all know Jed, and now everyone is wondering what's about to go down.

Felix nudges Zoe, "You know what this is about?" She shrugs looking bewildered and reaches out a hand out to silence Felix as Dan continues.

"Well, I'm going to put Jed on then pour myself a stiff drink, and thank God I don't have to ever go through this. I'm hurting here Jed, the floors' yours."

There's a sound of someone clearing their throat, then the familiar tone of Jed. His voice a little strained, not the usual relaxed guy they're used to.

"Hey out there." There's a pause like he expects an answer, then a short nervous laugh. "Santos bar, I'm hoping you're all listening. In fact, I'm hoping one person in particular is listening. Her name's Sadie." There's a pause as Jed takes a breath.

In Santos everyone is listening; Virginia casts a quick glance at Sadie who is completely white aside from two red blotches on her cheeks. Felix starts to laugh and Zoe nudges him again.

"Sadie… this is crazy I know. But I'm here on Dan's show tonight to ask…"

There's an awful pause like he's about to chicken out of asking the question they suspect is coming. Sadie's eyes are wide and she stares at her hands.

"…to ask if you'll marry me."

The bar is silent, all eyes on Sadie who doesn't move or look up.

"I know I won't hear your answer till I see you. I'm going to skateboard over right now. So get ready baby. I love you."

Dan's voice returns and is quickly replaced by another well-selected track. All eyes in Santos are on Sadie. When she finally raises her head, she has the look of a deer in headlights and no-one knows what to say. It's beyond awkward because she's not smiling and they know Jed is on his way to hear her answer.

"Oh fuck…" Felix mutters under his breath and receives another nudge from Zoe. Josefina hurries over with a tray of drinks trying to break the tension around the table but Sadie stands quickly, apologising, climbing over legs to get out of the booth and exit the bar before Jed arrives.

As she reaches the swing doors Jed bursts through, meeting her face to face. He's all smiles, positive expectations beam from his flushed face. But her dark expression stops him in his tracks. She pushes past him as he stands frozen in the doorway. "Damn." Jed sucks his breath slowly through his teeth then turns on his heel to follow her.

She is running down the street and when he catches her she's crying. "Shit Sadie, what is it? I'm sorry, I thought…"

"What the hell did you think Jed?" She stands with her back to him, shoulders slumped.

Jed pauses, reaching a hand to her shoulder, turning her around to face him. "I thought you'd say 'yes'."

She bangs a closed fist on his chest. "Christ Jed, you dumb ass! That was the single most embarrassing moment of my life."

"Is that a 'no'?"

She grabs the skateboard he holds under his arm, turns on her heel and sprints down the street, throwing the board to the ground and jumping on, full pace, heading away from Santos, from Beaujangles and Jed.

"Shit." Jed brings his hands to his mouth. "That went well."

He stands for a moment, watching her speed off on his board. "Fucking Sadie." He says it aloud, then repeats the words again, louder the second time. Sinking his hands into his pockets, he retreats back to Santos where he receives a standing ovation, some conciliatory back slaps and a few complimentary beers.

"One never reaches home. But where paths that have an affinity for each other intersect, there the whole world looks like home, for a time."

Hermann Hesse

Billie

The low drone of the plane has finally lulled Evie and Sunny to sleep; now it's my turn, but I can't settle. We are heading back to St. Cloud. Arrasaigh, Cam and Nell are far away and presently I am somewhere between homes; somewhere above another vast ocean, somewhere between two lives, anchored by my children.

This time tomorrow we will be back in Frontiere Point, back in our *home*, starting again. Moving back was never a question. My heart is in St Cloud, it's where our children were born, where Evan died and where my life needs to begin again. I need our friends and the familiarity of our house, the view, the beach and the sights and smells of St. Cloud. Despite the knowing, despite my certainty about this next step, our new beginning; I am afraid.

I'm afraid of how I'll feel when I walk in the door.

Will I be overwhelmed with crippling grief? Will it be like I never left, the weight of tragedy leaving me helpless again? These past few months I've begun to see things differently, to understand a little more clearly. I'm not angry anymore. I'm not angry with Evan or myself. All that anger passed to wracking grief, then more gently to sadness. The sadness never leaves and I don't want it to. It reminds me of him, of us, of what we had and what we lost. I can live with the sadness, I can function for Evie and Sunny without fear of crumpling under the weight of guilt and despair. Sadness colours my world but allows the light to filter through. I know now I'll make it.

I think of Jack and am torn still with longing and guilt. I know now that nothing I could have done drove Evan to his death. I understand he was ill and fate led him to the cliff, and that circumstance conspired to end his life early.

What would he have told me now? I have imaginary conversations with him. I ask him what I should do, where I should go, how I should start again. And I have to trust that the intuitive feeling I experience regarding what to do and how to be are a guide from him. Because despite it all, Evan loved me, and I know he wants the best for us now.

For now, here in the dimly lit plane I'm not sure what that *best* will mean. I still don't know how I'll feel back in St. Cloud, but I know I have to go home. Home is the start point for everything.

I signal the airhostess and politely ask for some wine. I need to sleep. I chug the glass faster than considered proper and close my eyes, one arm round each child. Letting my mind drift to thoughts of St. Cloud. I ache for home.

The airport looks different but I can't figure out why, I'm too busy rounding up bags and children, feeling flustered and suddenly unsure. Everything is bright and shiny and anxiety rises in my chest as I look around, hoping to see something that feels like home.

A crowd await arrivals and every face is unfamiliar, I feel panicky and unclear on why we're here. Then, I see him. He stands, hands in pockets, a head taller than everyone. His eyes are on us and his careful smile fills me with relief. It will be okay. I've done the right thing - this is home. I walk warily pushing my luggage and the twins through the concourse. The crowd seems to move for me. All my uncertainty over the future is gone, there's no grief or anger and no guilt. Each steady step toward him feels right, an inevitable path to my new future. A future that was always mine to take.

Jack waits for me, his dark eyes intense.

The twins are so quiet; the calm certainty of the moment seems to have affected them too. I stop the trolley and walk round to stand in front of Jack who looks just like he did the day I met him. He opens his arms and I move toward him, suddenly desperate to hold him. Pulling his face down to mine I kiss him. The kiss is needy. I pull him to me and kiss him till I'm out of breath. This time he doesn't stop me and there are no words. All sounds have dimmed to nothing, only the noise of blood rushing in my ears.

A loud *Bing Bong* sounds all around the terminal and I pull away from Jack to see things moving in slow motion. The crowds have cleared and the pilot approaches, cap on, head down, flanked by gorgeous air hostesses. They walk in a line, a procession of perfection, suited and suntanned, pulling along wheelie cases. Entwined in Jacks arms I turn to watch, disoriented. As the pilot passes he tips his cap and winks; Evan.

I drop to my knees as he keeps walking, an airhostess gently stroking his back. Pressing my eyes closed I try to reboot the scene. But when I open them the airport tannoy is playing *YMCA* at full volume. Evan spins on his heel, throws his airline cap in the air and starts singing "Young man…", pointing to Jack who is now wearing a hard hat and builders vest, his arms in the air joining in with the actions.

"Mommy, Mommy, Mommy…"

Oh God what now, where am I?

"Mommy, Mommy?" I jump sending the empty wine glass resting on the tray table into the air.

"Shit…" Evie is pulling on my sleeve pointing to the window, the shade half up, sunlight streaming in through the gap. The *fasten seatbelts* sign flashes on overhead and I take a deep breath, not sure whether to laugh out loud at my dream or worry over its interpretation. I kiss Evie on the forehead. I can tell she is trying to work her mouth around the cuss word I've just uttered. Sunny sleeps on, relaxed and unaware of the next big change on the horizon.

Jack

St Eloise is hellishly hot. Hotter than St. Cloud, but maybe it's just his mood. He's been angry and frustrated for days.

Jess has him working around the farm and the physical labour has been good. In one month he's built her most of the furniture for the nursery. He's happy to do this. It makes him feel good; one light amidst a dark few months.

Most of his days he's been outside with Saul in the orchard or on the boat. The time with his brother is exactly what he needs. Saul is grounded and Jack hopes some of that steadiness might rub off. Not so far. It's been a long time since he's felt this way, dark and restless, stuck with a head full of regret and a future he can't see.

"How's it coming along in here?" Jess breezes into the nursery, a tray with coffee and cookies balanced above her small bump.

Jack's smile is warm. "You tell me boss, what do you think?" He stands back, dusting off the small dresser, opening out the top surface on brass hinges. The dresser now a sturdy baby change table.

Jess breathes out slowly, lowering the tray to the floor. "Jack."

"Is that '*Jack it's pretty good*' or '*Jack I hate it*?'"

Jess's hands cover her mouth and her eyes fill as she takes in the lovingly carved dresser. Pressing her lips together she fans her eyes for a moment. "It's perfect."

"Then what's with the tears?" He pulls her into a hug as she stifles a small sob.

"God, I'm a wreck." She pulls away and sniffs. "Sorry, you'll get used to it, I just cried over a batch of burnt cookies before. I'm hoping this phase stops pretty soon." Bending down she passes him a mug and offers the plate toward him. He raises an eyebrow. "Don't worry, these are the good ones."

They sit down on a few upturned crates and look around the nursery. "It's hard to believe." Jess sips from her mug, eyes fixed on the cream coloured walls and crib. "We've been trying for a long time... I just never thought it'd happen." Jack smiles. "I thought maybe there was something wrong with me. God, or worse still, wrong with Saul. Can you imagine him in a fertility clinic?" She rubs her belly and carries on. "He's so happy Jack, I'm just..."

"Just what?"

"I'm afraid it won't be okay? There's still a ways to go and... well Saul's pretty sure it's a done deal. He's sure it's a boy. He's bought a little fishing rod and has a name fixed and..."

"Hey." Jack lays a hand on her arm. "It'll be fine, you'll be fine. You've come this far, that baby will be a stubborn little guy like his Dad, he won't be going anywhere."

"It might be a 'she'."

"Most likely." Jack grins again. "Saul will teach her to fish any-way."

Jess nods. "Thanks Jack."

"For what? My great advice?" He stands up and moves to the dresser, running a rough hand over its smoothly sanded surface. "I'm the last person to listen to around here. I'm an expert on screwing up, but not much else." She raises a hand to silence him but he carries on. "That baby is a blessing and you guys will be great parents."

Jess sits quietly, looking around the nursery while Jack sips his coffee, gaze fixed on his brother at work at the edge of the orchard. Despite the open window and glimpse of cool ocean, there is no breeze. Heat radiates from the ground, and the air is heavy and still.

"I want you to do something for me." Jess speaks carefully. He doesn't turn around, he knows the tone, and he knows the topic. He doesn't feel like talking about this. "I feel like we've given up on him." She speaks tentatively, as though she's rehearsed the line many times before.

His jaw tightens but he doesn't look around.

"When he called, a few months back, he sounded different. I think he's asking for help Jack."

Jack lets out a breath, eyes moving from the sun drenched orchard to the dusty floorboards. "Of course he's asking for help Jess, nothing's changed. The only time we hear from him is when he's in trouble, when he needs money or a place a stay." He puts his mug down on the windowsill and turns to her. "Don't worry about Raife. He'll be fine."

"But he's not." Her words bristle. "He isn't fine. Don't pretend you believe that because I know you don't. You know the truth: Raife's still running." She pauses and takes a slow, calming breath. "This is what families do. We support each other…" She stops, breathless, cheeks flushed, "…through everything."

The close scrutiny makes him uncomfortable but he doesn't respond. He won't give an inch, not yet.

"Will you look at me?"

He raises his eyes, he'd like to make a joke to clear the tension but her eyes flash in warning.

"We support each other…through everything."

He nods needing to pacify her, calm her down. And she's right, that's what families are supposed to do. It's what he wants to do and he's ashamed that he can't.

"I just think you'd feel so good if you went to him, to see if you could help. Saul and Raife were never close, and I think you're the only person he'll listen to. You need to give him a kick up the ass Jack. God knows he needs it. It's time to move on. It isn't healthy. And we could do with the help around here, Saul is pretty much on his own right now." She gestures toward her belly. "You need to go tell him we need him, that his family want him to come home."

She stands wearily holding her hand out for his empty coffee mug, "I don't think we can wait on this." The anger is gone, replaced with sadness. "Raife needs to know about Amandine." She holds his gaze and he nods quickly before looking away. Her certainty adds weight to his worry. His mother is slipping, and Jess is right, his brother needs to know.

Jack closes his eyes and sighs heavily. "Jess, if I thought for a moment he'd listen, I'd go tonight. But you know him, you know what he's like now. It'd be a waste of time."

"Maybe, but don't you think he deserves one last chance? He's been through a lot. Yes, he's a mess, but maybe, if you could stop moping around, you'd see he's asking us to help him." She barrels on before he can interrupt. "You might get there and find you can't help, he won't let you, whatever. But you'll know you tried. You did your bit. Then, you can head back to St. Cloud and feel sorry for yourself…or whatever."

He listens, arms folded. "Are you done?"

She mirrors his pose. "Yes."

"Are you sure?"

"Yes…I need to go pee." She gives him a quick smile and hurries from the room.

"Damn it." Jack begins sanding again, knowing there's truth in her words, knowing that right now he probably is the only one who can help Raife. Hearing Amandine in the garden he looks up, she's crouched over on the deck speaking in hushed tones. He makes his way out to the garden to see her. "Mama…"

"Jack!" She turns, her smile bright. "Darling, so good to see you." She reaches up to kiss both of his cheeks. "I was just feeding Saul's cat."

"Come in, Jess has just fixed some coffee." He leads her by the arm toward the house, glancing back he sees one of Saul's running shoes stuffed with scraps of food.

"Give me ten minutes." Saul nods as Jack hops from the van and jogs toward the house. Ten minutes to say a quick good bye. He heads to the back porch where he knows Joseph will be sitting, puffing on a pipe, ensconced on the swing seat.

"Finally." The voice calls out to him before he's even up the stairs. Joseph has been expecting him. Jess must have told them about his plan. "What took you so long?"

"Papa I'm leaving." Jack doesn't want a lecture or any harsh words between them. "I'm going to visit Raife and spend a little time with him." He stands facing Joseph, hands pushed deep in his pockets.

Joseph doesn't look up from his newspaper. "I heard. It's a good idea." Jack nods, Joseph's support unexpected. "Have you spoken to him?"

"No, but I know where he is."

Joseph looks up, softness in his tired eyes. "You talk to him Jack, bring him home." Wearily he extends a hand but doesn't stand.

"'I'll try Papa."

"Don't tell him about your mother."

"I…"

"I don't want that to be the reason he comes home." Jack extends his hand and Joseph grips hard, bringing his free hand to rest on Jacks' forearm, squeezing in uncharacteristic tenderness. "She's asleep, don't wake her. I'll tell her you're gone. It'll be easier that way."

Joseph's hand feels small and unsteady and Jack holds it firm, thrown by the unfamiliar intimacy with his father. He leaves moments later in the van with Saul, heading for the boat, then the airport; unhinged by the ties of family and bonds that bind them.

He'll find Raife, he knows that much; the man leaves a trail of chaos in his wake. It's not the finding that keeps him awake through the long flight to Los Angeles. Raife wants to be found, but what else does he want and why now?

From a notebook he pulls out a page covered in pencil drawings, beginnings of ideas for his new project; a boat gathering dust in his workshop back in St. Cloud. He turns the page over and begins to write. He writes to Billie; another letter he won't send. He tells her of his mother and father, Saul, Jess, the baby, St. Eloise and Raife. That he's going to find his brother and doesn't know when he'll be back. And that he's sorry - sorry for everything.

Touching the page, he imagines the reply. The letter she won't write him, because there is no hope for them. There never was.

Exiting the plane, he crumples the paper into a tight ball, stuffs it into a garbage can and turns to face the chaos of Los Angeles International Airport. Weaving gracefully through the mass of travellers and tourists he emerges, determined but unsettled out into a dark red smoggy sunset.

Chapter Five

Jed

It's midnight when Jed skateboards home through town, a little buzzed from all the free beer and more than a little apprehensive.

He's not sure how he feels about Sadie's reaction to his proposal. He was sure she would bust out laughing, shocked but happy. He had visions of her yelling '*Yes!*' out to the listening crowd at Santos and he'd skateboard in to applause. Then there'd be one of those movie moments where she run into his arms, he'd lift her up and twirl her around. She'd say *yes* again, and they'd kiss while people cheered then yelled at them to *get a room*.

Man, it didn't work out like he'd hoped. Right now he's not even sure she'll be home, but where else would she go? God, she was mad. It's almost funny, what a cock up. He isn't looking forward to seeing her, and he's delayed the confrontation by staying at Santos, where he could drink a few beers and make light of the whole thing.

The cool night air is sobering and as the beer makes way for awkward emotion, he's overwhelmed. He thought it was pretty funny at first, then he was mad at her over reaction, now he's not really sure how to feel.

There is no traffic at this time of night and the quiet roads allow him to weave smoothly on his board, past dark shop windows and cafe's, businesses and offices. The few bars still open have pulled in their signs and are ushering out straggling drinkers. He had to stop by Beaujangles for his spare board after Sadie stormed off with his other one.

Jed doesn't like to think too far ahead, hates to have to think about more than his moment, which for the most part works pretty well; until he met Sadie. As he glides smoothly down the moonlit street he wonders what all this means, and if she really doesn't love him enough to stick around. The thought knocks the air from his lungs and he jumps from the board leaving it skittering on aimlessly before crashing into a street-side bench.

What if he's wrong and this isn't the real thing for her? What if he's been reading her wrong all along? Maybe she doesn't love him at all - maybe she's just waiting until it's time to move on again, find another guy on another fucking island. Shaking his head, he catches his breath, suddenly unsure of everything. He stands in the middle of the road, fingers laced together, hands on the top of his head pressing down the negative thoughts rushing in from all sides.

"I'll be damned!" Breathing out slowly he lowers his hands to his waist and stands shaking his head wondering how the hell he believed she might really love him.

A car horn beeps loudly and he jumps but doesn't move. Stopping behind him the driver rolls down his window. "What's up bro? You need a ride?"

Jed turns to the bright lights, raising his palms. "Do I look like I need a ride? I'm thinking here man, give me a break." He turns away but remains fixed in the middle of the road, hands on hips, thoughts on Sadie.

"Move your ass off the road then!" The driver honks his horn and Jed sighs and strolls back to the waiting car.

"What's your name brother?" He leans toward the open window.

"Stanley. Now will you get off the fucking road and let me go home."

Jed nods and thrusts out an open hand. "Good to meet you Stanley. Yu know much about women?"

Stanley takes his hand, mouth forming a wide grin, "Shit. I saw you standing there and knew it had to be women trouble."

"You got it." Jed leans in on the driver's side window. "I just asked a girl to marry me and she damn well turned me down."

Stanley chortles and hits the steering wheel with the heel of his hand. "Is that all? Oh boy, you got to get used to that kid. That's the game. You've just got to try again."

"Really?"

"Trust me, I've got three ex-wives and a fiancé, I know what I'm talking about."

Jed smiles widely and slaps Stanley on the shoulder. "Stan, you're the man!" He claps his hands together and points to Stanley. "Get on home now, to that fiancé." Jed bangs on the car door and Stanley accelerates.

"You got to do it right is all. You even have a ring?" Stanley's voice fades as the car lurches forward.

Jed stares at the back of Stanley's shiny car. "No, I don't." He looks around for support but the streets are empty.

"I didn't even have a ring."

The apartment is dark when he gets home but he knows she's there, the door isn't locked. The simple gesture of the unlocked door gives him hope.

He creeps into the bedroom and peels off his clothes, before sliding under the sheet beside her curled form.

"You smell like shit." Her voice makes him jump backward from the edges of sleep.

"Honey, I'm home." He groans, shielding his eyes as she snaps on the light.

"What were you thinking?"

Jed takes a breath, wills his headache away and sits up sheepishly, eyes adjusting gradually to the glare. "Holy shit! You cut your hair."

Sadie sits up, pulling the sheet around her. "And?"

He's shocked. It's not that he loved the dreads, in fact he didn't really care much for them, but she'd always had them…until now. "Baby… you look so…" He reaches a hand out to stroke the soft blond hair rising in tufts, the length barely past her ears.

"So what…what do I look like?" The question bristles with anger but she's betrayed by her eyes, wide and brimming with tears.

"Beautiful." He says the word quietly, carefully. "You look beautiful."

Sadie starts to sob. He's never seen her cry and for a moment he doesn't know what to do. The sudden vulnerability makes him love her more. If there was ever a question that she was his girl, that eventually he'd convince her to marry him, it's gone with the dreadlocks.

"I love you. Nothing else matters."

She shakes her head and tries to push him away but he catches her hand and holds her steady. Moving closer he trails his fingers over her soft downy scalp then down, slowly tracing the steady flow of tears.

"I'm not ready for anything else Jed. What we have now, it's all I can do, and if it's not enough…" Her last words are muffled by another sob.

"It's enough."

"When I'm ready I'll tell you but you can't do that… it's too much."

He shushes her with a finger. "I'm sorry. I didn't mean to rush you. I just…"

"I love you Jed, but the forever stuff I can't do. I won't ever be able to give you what you need."

"Okay, I get it. I understand, I'm an idiot." She shakes her head in reply. "I understand you're not ready, but I'm not afraid to say it Sadie." He pauses, gathering his words carefully. "I need you. I want you here with me, but I won't pressure you. I'm here, and if you go, I'll still be here, waiting for you to come back to me."

She rests her eyes on his face, so serious in his heartfelt declaration of love. The tension between them disperses as she smiles, letting the sheet that protects her slide slowly to the floor.

"I don't want to go anywhere."

"God, I hope you mean that."

He catches his breath at the sight of her pale body, smooth and still in the low light. He wonders at her still serenity when his own body thrums in anticipation. Pushing her gently back on to the bed he runs a hand over the soft cap of short golden hair, down over her shoulders to her breasts where he lingers, trying to control his breathing.

"I can't get used to your hair."

She laughs as he kisses her. Slowly at first, each touch a request for forgiveness, permission, and understanding. This Sadie seems somehow smaller, softer in her vulnerability. It's a way in, past the fortifications she's built against him, it's a chink in her armour and he loves her more for it. He loves her more and he doesn't want to rush the makeup sex, he wants to drag it out, be with her like this forever. His face pressed into her neck her hands tracing lines on his back, her lips on his ear.

But it's too much. His restraint takes off at a run for the bedside drawer where he keeps the condoms. He needs her, and his body can't help but want her. She reaches for him, hand stroking and guiding and he follows her lead. She holds his shoulders as he sinks slowly into her. He catches his breath as she takes control, moving slowly, gradually, easing his rhythm to her pace.

When he comes he cries out her name, it's the best sex of his life, he'd tell her but it might kill the moment. As ripples of exquisite release slowly fade to quiet calm, he opens his eyes to find her smiling up at him, face flushed but wet with tears.

Billie

I wasn't sure what I expected. I wasn't sure how I'd feel. And here I am, in the dark in my bedroom, our bedroom, with the twins asleep next door; and so far I'm okay.

I'm waiting for the crescendo of wailing and thrashing, the disbelief and denial, yet I'm calm. Calm but wary that this might pass at any moment.

The house has been cleaned and cleared. It still looks and feels like our house, but traces of Evan are gone aside from a few photos in frames. A happy young couple outside a church in Belfast, another, taken on the back deck of this house - Evan with his arms around a very pregnant me, and a family shot - both of us with a swaddled baby in our arms.

I'm not sure how I feel about this cleansing, this removal of Evan, but my stronger self tells me this is another step forward. He is gone, that cannot change and I must live here without him.

Zoe brought us home from the airport. The twins have slept since our arrival, exhausted and overwhelmed from the journey. They didn't register where we were or who was missing, but let themselves be tucked into little beds with fresh sheets. They must somehow recognise home, despite the long time away they are calm and comfortable and for that I am grateful.

Zoe was quiet and considerate. We probably said more in the hug we exchanged than in words. I know she expects little of me for now. Anxious of how it would feel to be here, afraid the twins would immediately ask for Evan once home, tired and wrung out, I was quiet. She squeezed my hand and brought me home.

Zoe is glowing, radiant in these last few months of pregnancy and I am so happy for her. I keep saying that to myself…I am so happy for her, so happy. So why do I feel sad? Why do I feel jealous? I don't want another baby; I am genuinely happy for Zoe. It's just that part of me can't help but be jealous that her *happy ever after* is working out so beautifully, so to plan, where mine is beyond hope. Abandoned, lost - but not forgotten.

I jump from the bed feeling the imminent slide into despair approaching. I can't slip, not this early. I'm doing so well.

Walking through the house from room to room I see that everything is almost as it was, everything aside from Evans studio. The chaos has been cleared. A couple of boxes line the walls and the shelves are bare. Two scented candles sit on the window sill happy in fulfilment of their mission to remove his smell; linseed oil and charcoal, wood glue and whisky.

I can't stay here, not tonight, so I move back toward the den and the long glass sliders that lead to the deck and the garden beyond. From here I can see the glimmer of moonlight on water and it soothes me. Despite it all, the moon shines on dark waves as before. All is as it was.

Glancing over to Jacks' house there is only darkness. No signs of life. I wonder where he is and how he feels. I wonder if he has moved on with his life, forgotten us, forgotten me. All the letters I wrote to him travelled back in my suitcase. Letters he'll never see. I screwed things up for everyone, but none of it matters now. Despite it all, I miss him. His empty house fills me with sadness and I don't know what to do.

Creeping back to check on Evie and Sunny, I reassure myself they are asleep and return to the garden, wandering out to the deck and following the path down to that place. The place where it all ended. I know I shouldn't, I know it will be too much, but I need to go. I need to feel him and talk to him tonight. I need to imagine him listening.

I am careful and the moon is bright, I follow the path through the bush, listening to the noises of the night, just a little afraid. Too soon I reach the opening, the space where the trees clear and the ocean yawns below. Now I am afraid. I knew I would be but I force myself forward; as close to the edge as I dare. I watch the ocean below lap the rocks and gradually feel my fear ebb away. The scene is calm and quiet, and I feel the moment is meant as an opening.

"Evan?"

My voice cracks in the quiet. A brief sound then nothing; an uninvited noise swallowed by the night.

I take a breath and try again, "Evan…"

I don't know if I'm waiting for something, a reply from the heavens or a celestial thumbs up to carry on.

"I miss you. I'm sorry for everything. I didn't know, I didn't realise things were…so bad." I catch my breath again and stifle a sob. "I want you to know that we're here again because I love you and I want to hold on to my memories of you, of us and Evie and Sunny here, in our home."

I stop for a minute but the silence around me continues like an ellipse awaiting its conclusion. "I need to carry on Evan." I pause, unsure of what I'm going to say exactly, until the words push forth, pouring out.

"I need to carry on living without you. I want you be happy for me, no matter how things turn out. Do you know what I'm trying to say Evan? Goddamn you! I don't know how to do this without you, but I have try."

I'm sobbing but it doesn't matter and there are no celestial cuddles of comfort delivered from on high.

"You really fucked things up…do you know that? Yeah? What's that? You think I did too? Well you'd be right! But I stuck around, I'm still here, living with it. And you want to know what else? I never stopped loving you, ever. But you pushed me away and I fell in love with Jack. Is that so wrong? What's so wrong in loving two people for different reasons? I never thought it would come to this."

Now I'm really sobbing, all that cool calm stuff is gone with the wind, but it feels good to yell and shout at him like this. Like a normal argument, the fight we should have had but never had the chance to. And now that he's gone all the unsaid words become hard and painful to carry.

I'm the one to blame, poor Evan was sick, I never noticed, I was too busy ogling the guy next door. Evan worked hard, while I frolicked around with my other fella. He never wanted to bother me with his worries and look what happened.

You see? This is how it can play out in my head. I need to yell and shout, just for a while and I want him to yell back. I want him to tell me I was a self-absorbed cow, that I couldn't see his problems because I was so wrapped up in myself and my woes of being a mother. I want him to tell me he knew I was in love with Jack and wondered how long it would take before I messed up.

I want to scream at the unfairness of fate that we can't ever have that fight, that I can't take the rap or give it back. Or that together we can't share it out, and later work it out and maybe be stronger together in the end.

I hate it all and I cry for it.

I cry until I'm done and I'm calm and the ocean remains, gentle and quiet.

I walk slowly back up through the bush and into our house where I crawl into bed and find deep, dreamless sleep.

❧

Here, the water feels different. Despite the heat of the day the ocean is cold and the waves small and insubstantial. The tide's roll on to the sand leaves dirty lines on the beach, no seaweed or shells, just a film of the city absorbed by the sea to be washed back on the shore.

A swim seemed like a good idea. After the plane and the city traffic, he'd made his way to the beach. He'd left his pack on the sand and walked to the water to try and wash away the travel and let the beat and rip of the ocean fill him with the spirit he needs to deal with Raife. Now, treading water looking back at the beach littered with bodies, he wonders why he came. Santa Monica Beach couldn't be further from what he's used to and he doesn't like it.

Instead of a spiritual boost from nature, he feels weighed down by people. Toned and tanned, beautiful people litter the sand, oiled and postured for maximum sun. Bikini-clad bodies jump and dive for volleyballs; tight asses and breasts that don't move. There are no kids, no dogs, none of the usual associations of the beach and home. Here the beach is a grooming ground, everyone behaving as though someone is watching, as though someone else cares.

Jack exits the water and dresses on the sand, aware of the eyes of others. He doesn't fit and he's glad. Its 4pm and he knows if he walks inland toward the bars and clubs of Santa Monica he'll eventually find a trail that will lead him to Raife. Raife's been playing gigs in this part of Los Angeles for years. It could take a while, part of him hopes it does. He's not sure he's ready.

Bikes, power-walkers, joggers with headphones and rollerblading women crowd the beach path. He waits - bemused - unable to traverse the concrete ribbon that wraps around the edge of the beach, separating it from the palm trees and busy road beyond. The smell of the ocean is gone, replaced by gusts of sweaty armpits and expensive perfume.

Jack is alone, a fact felt more keenly by the crowds. He'd always been fine with the uncomplicated position of solitude, but since Billie something has shifted, the feeling is no longer peaceful. Sadness has settled where there used to be relief. Here in LA the sadness is weighty, amongst the sheen of effervescent smiles and surface-deep perfection.

He walks for a while before heading inland toward Santa Monica Boulevard. He needs the movement, meditative steps through unfamiliar streets to steady his head and settle his body after the flight.

Gradually the light softens as he veers inland. There is no peace to be had in this beach community. Noise is everywhere; car horns and voices, the thrum of traffic and loud blare of stereos. Pale evening's fall into night ignites sounds less familiar in St. Cloud's sleepy city; raised voices, deep bass, tinny speakers and breaking glass. During his walk from beach to boulevard, Jack has decided one thing: he needs to bring Raife home.

By 11pm he's been in almost every bar on the Boulevard and he's beginning to wonder if maybe he got it wrong. Tired and hungry he buys a slice of cheap pizza from a street side vendor and sinks to a bench on the sidewalk. A reflection catches his eye from across the street. A bright shop window, gleaming glass and clean white lights illuminate the man, bearded and unkempt, elbows resting on knees, a picture of dejection. A guy who's had it hard, needs a good scrub and a sleep. Of course it's him, and the realisation makes him blink in surprise. Shaking his head, eyes still on the unfamiliar reflection he smiles wryly; he really does look like shit.

The pizza's gone but he doesn't move from the bench, not immediately. It's easier to sit a while and imagine that maybe this past year has been a bad dream. But then he'd have to give up the memory of the night with Billie, and despite everything he's not ready to do that.

"You looking for spare change man? This is my area! You best move on."

A teenage kid with a nose ring and a sleeveless shirt scuffs a worn sneaker on the sidewalk as he stops in front of the bench and eyes Jack suspiciously.

"Don't worry kid, I'm not staying" Jack stands and the boy grins loosely, several missing teeth pock mark an attempted smile.

"Wise move dude, I'm bad ass. Got a reputation around here. Don't wanna have to rough you up for getting on my area."

The confidence of the skinny teen makes Jack return the smile, the kid's no threat. He pulls a crumpled note from his pocket and thrusts it in the boy's hand which is already open in anticipation. "Here, rent for using your bench."

The boy sniffs and nods, pocketing the note quickly, staring at Jack suspiciously. "I don't do no favours, you don't get nothing for this."

"I get that." Jack turns to walk away.

"You one of them undercover's trying to catch me out?" The scrawny teen's voice follows him. "I'm too smart for that shit."

Jack waves a hand and keeps walking, pace steady, determined to leave LA as soon as he's done. Smog from the city has settled on his skin. He feels unclean. He's sick of checking bars, ordering beers he doesn't drink and sitting like a voyeur, watching the crowds for Raife.

Three girls pass; arms linked, drunk and giggling, barely twenty. God, he feels old. One turns back, smiles and blows him a kiss. Eyes drawn to retreating behinds; short skirts and tanned legs, his response is physical, breath catching he stops abruptly and closes his eyes. He sees Billie, more clearly than in a long time and the chaos of pleasure and pain is everywhere.

When he opens his eyes the girls are gone but Los Angeles still looms before him, and somewhere out there Raife, his brother, waits for him.

He hears the music before he sees the club.

The steady drumbeat pulses under the rhythm of a bass guitar, sounds merge seamlessly. A lead guitar rises and there's melody amongst the stirring depths of the heavy beat. They're good, and he's ready to stop cruising the streets. The music guides Jack off Santa Monica Boulevard and under the neon sign, into the bar where the music is loud but the crowd sparse.

It isn't what he expected. The band plays in a corner behind a small dance floor where a few people are dancing or just watching the musicians up close. A long liquor bar lines one wall, brightly lit serving hatches line the other revealing a busy kitchen within. Waiters move around taking orders and delivering food to tables, people eat, drink and listen to music. Instead of the stale liquor smell of most bars the smells here are incredible; chipotle chicken, peppered steak and fried calamari. The atmosphere is a chaotic blend of restaurant, beach bar and live session; and it works.

Above the small stage where the band plays is a neon sign in scripted writing: *The Virgil.*

Jack wanders through the small crowd, past tables of couples and groups of friends sharing food, toward the bar where he finds a stool and orders a beer. He might stay a while, screw Raife; maybe he'll actually finish this beer and enjoy the music. He'll find someplace to stay and start again in the morning. The urgency he felt only an hour before has faded. He'll find him, just maybe not tonight.

The lead guitarist strums a few final chords before moving to the mike to thank the audience. There's a chorus of applause and a few hollers for more. Jack claps warmly, feeling himself finally relax.

"Thank you so much." The guitarist nods modestly. "We thought we'd give you guys a treat tonight." Much clapping and whistling ensues. "We've got someone joining us for a few numbers. He hasn't played around here for a while, but I know if you've heard him before, you'll remember him."

More whistling, the barman is nodding and smiling and the crowd keep clapping.

"We bumped into this guy a few nights ago and persuaded him to come join us. We're hoping he might stick around."

Jack sips his beer, more interested in the crowd than the next act. More clapping as the hotly anticipated musician heads on to stage but Jack isn't watching, distracted by the barman who is juggling three liquor bottles.

A sudden quiet in the room unsettles him; maybe he's not quite as relaxed as he thought. His eyes move over the crowd of people and tables till his gaze comes to rest on the darkened stage area where the band have been joined by another figure sitting on a stool with an acoustic guitar resting on his lap.

The bassist hits a chord and the band follow, in a flash they are bathed in light and for a moment Jack is back on the bench in the street, shocked at his reflection in the shop window. But this time it's not a reflection, this image is Raife. A worn, hollowed out Raife, bedraggled and unshaven but smiling, blinking in the bright spotlight before moving his gaze to his guitar, he taps his foot and begins to play.

Shock is quickly followed by relief as Jack watches his brother do what he does best. Raife plays and sings and his low melodic voice fills the room. Sounds of the crowd, the kitchen and the busy bar are silenced by the ragged beauty of his voice. And in this moment everyone in the room is feeling something unexpected but equally powerful.

The simple melody and sound of Raife's voice captivate the crowd and a magic rests around the bar. Each response to the sound can be read in expression; wistful, dreamy, emotional, entranced. Faces glow as his sound captures memories or inspires dreams for projected futures. Raife owns the room. His guitar's even sound smoothes the rough edges of his voice as he leads the audience chord by chord.

The song finishes and the room erupts in applause. Raife bows his head gracefully before raising his eyes to the crowd. His smile is dazzling; his smile has always been dazzling.

Caught by the scene Jack can't look away although he wants to leave, wait outside and talk to him when it's over. But he stays, transfixed by Raife's glow. As Raife's eyes pass the spot where Jack sits he stops, gaze directly on his younger brother. He sees him, there's no doubt, but his expression remains the same. Lowering his head, he strums one long slow chord then begins finger picking the guitar till it sings. When he joins in, the effect is breath-taking.

Later, when the crowd have made him play *just one more* for another hour, Raife finally exits the stage to huge applause. The remainder of the band are forgotten and Jack has lost sight of why he's here.

Raife looks like shit that's for sure, but he seems to be managing just fine, still able to turn on the magic. Just like when they were kids. Raife always had a following; kids that wanted to be his buddy, just to bask in his glow and maybe try to score a few of the girls left in his wake. Socially Jack didn't even have to try, as Raife Kelly's kid brother everyone wanted to be his friend. He was admittedly one degree removed from the main attraction, but those kids were happy to settle for second best.

Jack shadowed Raife for the first seventeen years of his life. Sometimes because he wanted to, and others because there was no place else he fit. He was Raife's brother and this gave him status. He admired Raife, loved him, but Raife was reckless, he'd do anything to get what he wanted and more than anything he wanted to cut loose, be free of small town St. Cloud, party and play music.

The energy in the room has changed. Things relax and bluesy jazz floats through the sound system. The stage area has been cleared and filled with tables and chairs already occupied by cocktail drinking LA residents. The barman is busy but beelines toward Jack with an already open bottle, smiling in admiration. The beer bypasses Jack and slides to a stop to his left where Raife eases into a stool beside him. A quiet moment passes as mentally they circle each other - like dogs before a fight.

"What you doing here Jack?"

Jack surveys his brother for a moment before answering. "I thought you'd tell me."

Raife shrugs. "Nothing to tell, same old shit." He sips from his beer, eyes still straight ahead.

Jack swallows his frustration. "So what's with the calls? Are you in trouble?"

Raife turns to face Jack igniting his million-dollar smile, "Just wanted to see if you'd come." He slaps Jack on the shoulder then pulls him into a half hug. "…and here you are."

Jack rubs a hand over his eyes and exhales slowly. "Where are you living?"

Raife ignores the question and takes another swig of beer. "How's Mama?

"You should come home and see her."

"Hey Jonas!" Raife calls out to the barman. "Get my brother here another beer." Jonas is quick to respond but Jack raises a hand.

"I'm good, thanks."

Raife laughs. "Are you?

"I don't drink much."

Raife nods slowly eyeing Jack carefully, expression steely and clear despite his haggard demeanour. "Of course you don't."

Jack is suddenly bone tired. "Raife, I don't know what the hell is up with you, but for some fucking reason I'm here. Don't tell me you don't need me because I know you do. I'm tired and I need to get some rest."

Raife's eyes narrow and a smile twitches around the edge of his lips. "Poor Jack, he's come a long way to rescue the black sheep."

Jack stands wearily, this is going nowhere. He needs to get out of this bar before he hits Raife or drowns his sorrows.

Raife grabs his shoulder. "Where you going? I'm messing with you. Take it easy." He stands, pushing his empty bottle across the bar to Jonas who watches them with interest. "Wait here while I get my stuff." He squeezes Jack's shoulder and heads to the back of the club where he disappears back stage.

Half an hour later he hasn't returned.

"You okay man, can I get you anything?" Jonas is hovering, anticipating drama.

"I'm good." Jack rubs a hand over his eyes. "Can you check if Raife is still back there?" Jonas shrugs and heads backstage whilst Jack stands surveying the thinning crowd. Not a great start to the fraternal reunion.

Jonas is back moments later, palms raised "He's gone man. No-one back there now, just the manager and he said Raife left half an hour ago."

Jack nods slowly in response. "Thanks." Face set, he hoists his pack on to back and strides out into the night. Jonas is calling something after him, but he doesn't care to listen. He wants to go home, to be anywhere but here. But here he is, bound to the brother destined to despise him.

Anger rises slowly with each step, anger reserved for Raife, red and fiery hot but always tinged with the cooling haze of guilt. No matter how much of a dickhead Raife can be, how self-indulgent and bitter, Jack will always wear it. He'll restrain his first impulse because Raife deserved better and Jack is at the heart of it.

Outside the cooler air does nothing to diffuse his mood. Despite the ocean's proximity the air smells heavy with city life; garbage and hot tarmac, exhaust fumes and frying food. It's 2am and Jack's angry and beat. Tomorrow he might feel ready to deal with Raife again but tonight he's had enough. Let Raife play his games, he won't run after him, not this time.

He doesn't know where he's headed but knows if he walks long enough the anger will eventually seep from his soles. He needs to move and let the tangle of emotions teased out by his brother unravel. It's always the same; Raife creates an internal maelstrom Jack is unequipped to deal with. All tied to one cruel flash of fate. The past can't be undone and around Raife he can't hide, because Raife hasn't moved on. Jack is mired beside him and together they are toxic.

Eyes gritty with weariness and city air he shuts them tight and in the dark behind his eyelids he sees her, just a flash of dark hair and pale skin. A face divided by an angry red line. A contrast of beauty and tragedy, eyes mocking and lips pale. The image is gone as quickly as it appears but it takes his breath away. The proximity to Raife brings her back and the walls he's erected around himself shake with the pressure of memories grown tired from neglect. He doesn't want to remember, but the truth is, he can't ever forget.

Following the lead of night traffic that flows steadily despite the hour, Jack begins a slow walk uptown. He needs to find a place to stay, he's too tired to deal with it now. The streets are littered with people out at night for all the wrong reasons and he doesn't want trouble. Making a snap decision he changes route, veering off the main drag, taking the quieter route that leads behind the bars and clubs.

He's only a few blocks away when a familiar voice raised in anger stops him in his tracks. Again, the voice answered by others, one, two, now three different voices shouting, cussing, a loud bang against metal and the singular thud of fist against bone. Instinctively, he throws his pack to the ground and runs toward the sounds; an alleyway between the back entrance of two bars. Yellow security lights illuminate the dark, throwing the sprawling figures into a jaundiced glow. Three flailing bodies dance awkwardly in and out of the shadows. He doesn't have to see their faces to know Raife is amongst them.

Here lies a pause in time, a moment he will think about after the event has passed. Jack pauses by the entrance to the alleyway, seeing Raife amidst the chaos, watching fists reign down on him. Time stops, and maybe the passing is a mere second, maybe simply the pause between thought and action, but Jack does stop. He stops in the shadows and witnesses the blows to Raife with a brief trace of satisfaction.

Something bigger than resentment takes over. In seconds Jack is in the midst of the ugly brawl, it becomes his fight, in that moment the fight is the reason he's here. It's his chance to make up, to make amends and to release the anger that's been simmering for months.

Raife recoils, huddling against a dumpster, bruised and bloody. There's a second, maybe two when Jack believes he can change everything by fighting for Raife. The men come at him on both sides and with every punch he feels something wretched leave his body; an ugly exit given freedom through violence.

It doesn't take long, in minutes they're gone, running, and afraid, this wasn't what they'd bargained for. The alleyway glows yellow and Raife cowers against the dumpster. Adrenalin coursing, Jack scoops him up under the arms and drags him from the harsh light onto the side street. "We need to get out of here, where do you live Raife?"

Raife's head lolls, blood oozing from his bottom lip. "What you doing here Jack?"

"Where do you live? We need to move before they come back." Jack drags Raife toward his abandoned backpack.

Raife's face breaks into a garish smile, teeth coated red with blood. "You've still got it." He grabs Jack's forearm hard, face suddenly serious. "Now get the hell out of here, you think I can't handle myself?" He slumps down on the sidewalk. "Always the tough guy." He raises his face. "Come on then, give me what you got, I'm ready for you champ."

Jack slaps Raife hard across the face with the back of his hand. "Wise up! Tell me where we're going or they're coming back, with their friends to kick our asses." The slap sobers Raife enough to slur an address Jack can barely understand. A street name, not much, but enough. He manages to hail a taxi, hoping Raife will remember where he lives on route.

Cool air from open windows and the cabs dark interior shifts the energy. Rap plays on the radio and the cab driver's head nods to the beat, he doesn't turn to look at the brothers or talk. He drives. Jack slumps, exhausted and bruised against the vinyl seat and Raife lets his head fall into his hands as downtown LA flashes past; a blur of street lights and neon signs serenaded by car horns and the angry rap beat.

The cab takes West Olympic Boulevard heading to the Pico suburb. West 11th was the only information Raife offered and as they reach West 11th Street he signals the driver to pull over outside a liquor mart. Raife exits, his movements slow and wary, unsure of who might be waiting to greet them. Jack pays then follows down the side of the liquor mart where Raife fumbles in a darkened doorway. A buzzer panel is lit by a narrow strip of light, names and apartment numbers form a line below; Raife's name isn't there.

The door opens on to a flight of stairs, lit by a single low bulb. Four flights up they follow the dimly lit corridor to another door which Raife unlocks on to a single bedsit room. He flicks on an overhead light and locks the door behind them. He's quiet now, his movements seem sober and assured.

Jack drops his pack on the floor, eyes alert, still wary, but the small room reveals no surprises. A bed against the wall under a curtain-less window and little else. A few possessions lie scattered, and a small counter with a sink holds the remnants of last night's takeaways. The bottom half of the window is covered by the square grate of an air conditioning unit but the room is hot and stuffy.

"It doesn't work." Raife gestures to the air con unit and Jack nods, wondering why he's explaining the shitty air con when so many other questions need answering.

"Is this your place?"

Raife shrugs sinking on to the edge of the bed. "A guy I know let me have it for a few weeks, I played in his bar. I'm between apartments."

"Right." The air is thick with unsaid words but it's late and they're bone-tired and bleeding.

"You have any ice?" Jack asks, the light revealing the swelling around Raife's eye and jaw.

"Are you kidding? I don't even have a refrigerator, the place is a dump."

"You'd better get cleaned up." Jack gestures to Raife's face then heads to the sink to run water over his own swollen knuckles. Raife nods, cocky backchat gone, he bends down, removes his boots and sinks back on to the unmade bed. Jack throws a cold cloth on to his chest. "Here, clean the blood off."

Raife grimaces as he dabs the cloth around the cut by his right eye. "I had it under control."

Jack doesn't look at him, scooping water on to his face and hair he rubs his eyes. "Right, next time I'll leave you to it."

"You should have. I'm really screwed now."

"Looks like you were screwed already. Hey, and by the way, you're welcome." Jack dries his face and sits on the opposite side of the bed, kicking off his boots. "Who were they anyway?"

"I owe them money."

"Of course." Jack sinks back, feeling like he hasn't slept in years. "Why'd you take off? Do you know how much that pissed me off?"

Raife lies back carefully; estranged brothers side by side, unexpected intimacy in siblings relegated to strangers. "There's your answer."

"You're an asshole." Hands behind his head, Jack closes his eyes and city street sounds recede as he drifts reluctantly toward sleep.

"You knew that already, so why did you come?" Raife's swollen eyes are closed too, both supine bodies still and finally relaxed, feet dangling off the end of the short mattress.

Jack breathes in slowly, "Because it's time."

"For what?"

There's a long pause, as Jack pulls the words from the middle ground between wakefulness and sleep. "For you to come home."

The sound of the word *home* drifts into quiet surrender as Jack falls deeply asleep. Raife opens his eyes, focusing on the cracked ceiling and bare light bulb. He breathes out; long and low, his exhale disturbing stale air in the dark room.

"Home." He echoes, trying the word for size, there's comfort in the soft vowels. He watches the cracked ceiling until his gritty eyes become heavy. "Home." Night pulls him closer to sleep and he speaks quietly as he drifts.

"Thanks."

Unheard, the word floats around the grey room alighting on Jack's sleeping form. But Raife's moment of sentiment has passed. His legs twitch with the beginnings of guiltless slumber and gratitude falls flat on sleeping ears.

Chapter Six

Billie

I hate wallpaper.

I do, I really, really hate it.

At this moment the patchy, sticky strips that cling to the living room walls and shred between my fingers are the reason my life has turned on its head. Every time I pull and ease that paper from the wall, it remains stuck in obstinate patches of resistance. I cuss under my breath before attacking again; this time with more fervour, driven by the need to cleanse and change my outlook.

Strip by strip I pull and tear and sometimes - only sometimes - one beautiful whole strip will peel gracefully from top to bottom. An intact paper record of years of bad decor, layer stuck to layer of florals, stripes and textured prints, leaving a naked section of plain but beautiful wall. Mostly, I sponge and scrape and peel shred by shred and it sticks under my fingernails and peels only when inclined. After several hours the living room wall resembles a patchy, pitted canvas. It looks awful, worse than before I began, but I can see those perfect plain white walls gleaming underneath the mess and know that the potential for a new beginning is waiting.

There is work be done. Today is about fresh starts and a stronger, brighter outlook on the world and my place in it. I will strip the house back, room by room and remove layers of the past. Underneath those flaking layers, my walls are plain, but strong and quite lovely.

It's barely 6am and the sky is pale, no sun yet but a change in the dark; a lift. I feel it too. As the wallpaper peels and I take my anger out on every gaudy layer and sticky clump, I feel that same lift.

Stripped of Evans love, a calmness and certainty descends, a side of me overshadowed by desire and my need to be loved. Without him I feel plain, bare and revealed. As the darkness lifts, it takes with it something heavy. Standing barefoot in the chaos of torn wallpaper, something fragile gets a royal kick up the wahoo as a wary realisation rises slowly with the sun.

I have been a victim for too long.

Victim to lust, to love, to betrayal, fate and the rest; my life spinning like an old movie reel. Events rushing past the screen frame by frame. There I am in each frame; the damsel in distress, hair pinned in twenties style curls, face pale, lips red, hands clasped to chest, mouth open in an expression of despair: *Help me!*

Help me! My mother died. *Help me!* I'm alone. *Help me!* I'm in love with an obsessive madman. *Help me!* He cheated. *Help me!* I'm pregnant. *Help me!* I'm alone again. *Help me!* He's gone.

Each sad, pathetic image of Billie 'the victim' flashes by, frame-by-frame. Whilst in the background two small children move in and out of view, trying desperately to get stricken Billie's attention.

On cue, I hear a thud, followed by little feet running down the corridor, one set followed closely by another. The door is pushed so hard it bangs against the supporting wall. Two small bodies run on solid little legs calling my name: not *Billie the victim*, but *Billie the Mommy* - the stronger me I am growing into.

The capable, self-assured, *victim-be-damned* Billie steps confidently into a ray of sunshine beaming through the glass slider. Knee deep in discarded wallpaper, I stand with my arms out, basking in the light of my new beginning as my babies run toward me, squabbling as to who gets the first hug. The Mommy I want to be answers with a start: *I'm done.*

No more backseat role for me. No more waiting for the world to deliver me my happy ending. No more wondering what I did wrong and blaming myself for loving two men at the same time.

I'm done.

I hold the words in my hands like virgin snow, precious and new. Perfection in simplicity. Quickly before they melt away, I compress them into a tight, icy ball. As Evie and Sunny barrel toward me, their smiles as bright as the rising light, I throw that icy ball out into the waiting day yelling goodbye in a loud, overly cheery voice.

I'm done.

The twins stop in their tracks as I throw the imaginary bundle of inner baggage to the non-existent breeze. They watch me warily. Unsure if they're in trouble they wait until I beam my *this-is-our-new-beginning* smile at them. They relax instantly and sprint as fast as two chubby-legged toddlers can, into my open arms and we cuddle till we can't anymore.

Later amidst the mess, as I sip my coffee and watch Evie and Sunny race around in the debris of discarded paper that litters the room, I know I can do it. I know that I will love Evan forever. And though part of me will forever grieve for him, and the life he should have had, I know that life is waiting, like a gift. A new life for a stronger, more resilient Billie. A Billie that needs no man to bring out her colour. A Billie that can make it through anything.

It's another cheesy Oprah moment…but I don't give a shit. Oprah would be booking me in for a feature interview right now but I'd tell her I'm too busy. I have my kids to look after and a new life to build.

By midday the entire open plan living room/kitchen/dining/hallway has been stripped of wallpaper. Badly I should say, there are stubborn sticky clumps dotted liberally on every wall surface, but I don't care. The floor is an autumnal display of crunchy paper leaves in a variety of colours and patterns. With pure joy in chaos, the twins, roll, tumble and chase one another in the mess, forgetting to ask about who isn't here.

"Good God! What's happened here?" I hear the familiar voice before I see the face. I hadn't heard the doorbell, absorbed in my cathartic task of disrobing the house.

"Dan!" I barrel toward the slowly opening door as Dan and Virginia's puzzled expressions come into view. I run at Dan like an All Black in for the tackle, so happy to see him. Forgetting that at this moment neither he, nor Virginia know about my newly found, fabulous self.

His shocked expression is evidence. He expected a more pathetic, crushed and broken version of me. A little like the one that arrived last night, unable to speak too much for fear of an endless flood of tears.

I want to tell him and the darling, reliable Virginia about my breakthrough, about the wallpaper and my decision to lose *Billie the victim*. But it wouldn't come out right and it's the first time I've seen them in over six months, so instead I just hug Dan like I might never see him again. After a long enough period for him to readjust his *I-love-you-I'm-here-for-you-face* he smiles, a little warily and holds me close.

I pull away, lean in, kiss him on both cheeks then move to wide-eyed Virginia, and do the same. She embraces me warmly and holds me tight for a long time. I don't want her to break my tranquil new found *strong-self* mantra. I'm praying she doesn't say: "How are you? We're just so sorry," because, although I'm the *new* Billie, I'm not that strong yet and can deal with wallpaper but not people.

Virginia releases me from the hug then holds me at arms length. "Darling girl, you look fabulous." I press my fingers to my mouth in a bid not to cry. I know she's full of shit; I look ten years older. I breathe in deeply before releasing those fingers and hold them to either side of her face then hug her again. I am just so happy to be here, to be home.

After more hugging and catching up I'm forced to explain the chaos. "So, I thought I'd get started on some re-decorating." I'm holding Dan's hand and walking him through the mess of shredded wallpaper. He holds Evie and Virginia follows, a little wild-eyed, carrying Sunny. "I think we all need a fresh start so why wait?"

Dan who is looking a little concerned, turns on a supportive smile. "Absolutely, why wait? I say it every day when I'm shaving! Why wait wrinkles? Harbours of forty-something-ness! Bring it on, I'm ready!" His hand is raised to the heavens and I laugh, imagining his conversation with the mirror.

Dan hasn't a wrinkle of course but I love that he's pretending for me. I punch him playfully in the arm. "Seriously Dan, I'm going to start painting tomorrow. The whole house." I throw my arm around theatrically.

"Good girl…and you're planning to farm these two out for child labour for a few weeks while you paint yourself away to serenity?"

I stop, reflecting on my excited plans and their lack of practicality. "Of course not. I'll paint while they sleep."

"Whilst they sleep?" Dan is frowning.

"Yes."

"And, when do you sleep?"

"Oh, I try not to. Dreams aren't my friend so I stay awake at all costs."

Virginia frowns too and tilts her head to the side as she rests her eyes on Dan. Sunny is wriggling so he sets him down to race around.

"I hate to say it darling but I have alarm bells illuminating my solar plexus. How about a few quiet weeks to get settled back in. Ginny's managed to organise the twins into kindergarten. You can relax and have a few hours to yourself and…" he pauses and I take a deep breath knowing what will come next. "Get over things."

The minute the words are out Dan blushes, looking awkward. So far we haven't mentioned the elephant in the room.

"Dan." I take his hands and look up at his handsome face with as much patience as I can muster. "I love that you care about me and how I'm doing, but I'm okay…" I pause, unable to lie. "No, that's not true, of course I'm not."

I feel Virginia's arm drape around my shoulder. "Of course not."

I have a slight lip wobble but reign it in quickly. "A part of me will never be fine." I take a breath, asking that stronger, *new beginnings* Billie to step forward…and she does. "But, there's another part of me that's okay. She's good, and she knows what to do and I'm trying my best to listen to her and follow her lead."

Dan nods like he gets it and Virginia's grip tightens on my shoulder.

"And, you just have to understand and not molly coddle me. I'm okay and I'm getting better every day. So if I want to rip the wallpaper off, dye my hair purple and change my name to Buffy, you're going to say. *Hey, good girl, do what you need to.* Because, right now, I have to listen to the other Billie… I just have to." I stop for breath and pull my hands from Dan's, placing them on my hips for effect.

"I like your hair blonde," says Virginia.

"Me too" nods Dan. "I can't help it. I know it's shallow. I have a thing for blondes."

I start to laugh. I can tell they're not sure at first, but soon they can't help it. They join in and we're all laughing and it feels so God damned good. It's the first time I've laughed since Iris's visit when I got a little hysterical and that memory makes me laugh even more. I laugh till my cheeks hurt and Dan pulls me into his chest and holds me tight, and I know all the laughing has somehow turned to crying, but it doesn't matter. We hold each other and again, again and again I know, I am home.

❧

Three weeks later, I'm still painting. Admittedly, I was a little optimistic, my plan for rejuvenating the house took about three days in my head, but the reality has been weeks.

Evie and Sunny have settled into kindergarten and I was that cliché mother who cried at first drop off despite fantasising about solo time for ages.

The thing is, in my situation you get away with stray tears anytime. I'm coming to realise that people expect it of me. I feel bad smiling publically; it's not in the etiquette of *recently widowed woman.* This is a little challenging considering my newly found strong woman approach to life. I want to smile in the face of adversity, and everyone keeps looking at me like I should be wearing black, have my hair in a bun and pray to my rosary on the hour. I don't know how to be a widow; I don't want to be one. *Widow* sounds like a spidery old Sicilian granny. It's not me. So, I have decided to flounce convention and do my very best to smile at all costs. To be bright and breezy even when I feel like crying. Soon people will move on and maybe eventually forget that my husband jumped off a cliff.

The flippantly worded thought drops me to my knees and paint spatters on the drop sheet below me. "Shit."

"You okay?" Jed looks down from his position at the top of a ladder. Sadie and Jed have spent a few nights this week here with me, painting, listening to the radio and drinking beer. The company has been nice.

"Fine."

Sadie appears from the corridor. "So cute." She presses a hand to her chest and points back toward the twins' bedroom smiling. "Still fast asleep, I was sure they'd wake up with the radio."

"I can't believe how much they've grown." Jed shakes his head as his paint brush follows a careful line between ceiling and wall.

I smile. "That's what they do Jed. You should try getting yourself a few, bet you could train them to make great coffee." As I glance up at his easy smile, I feel Sadie's glare from across the room.

"Don't get any ideas in his head Billie, next thing you know he'll be advertising for the mother of his kids on the radio."

I wrinkle my nose in confusion as Jed blushes. "Is there something I've missed?" I ask, watching the colour from Jed's face pass to Sadie's as he nods in her direction and resumes painting. Sadie, forced to spill the beans, tells me how Jed proposed to her on Dan's radio show. Before she has a chance to finish the story, there's a knock on the back window. Dan, is outside armed with what looks like take-away pizza and his best smile. I wipe my hands and open the door.

"Pizza boy's here. Take a break kids." The smell of expensive cologne mingles with the odour of wet paint as Dan makes his entrance. He sidesteps the mess making his way to the kitchen where he sets the boxes on the counter and helps himself to a beer from the fridge.

"How is it possible that warm, greasy bread in cardboard can smell so good?" I follow him to the kitchen, stomach grumbling. I have missed too many meals lately, my new identity as DIY diva has been a little absorbed. I dive for the box, extracting the biggest, cheesiest slice possible.

The inequality of fate is displayed carelessly in pizza dimensions. Even in the predictable world of pizza somehow one slice gets the 'bum share'; the least topping and the smallest measurements. The oily pepperoni and stringy cheese pack a punch, and as I close my eyes and chew slowly, savouring the taste and texture, I deliberately pull myself from another slide into self-pity. I was about to compare my lot in life to the smallest slice in the pizza box for heaven's sake! When does the pity party stop?

Each bite of cheesy heaven brings me back to my moment. The simple pleasure of tastes and textures, good friends, home, sleeping children, freshly painted walls and the mixing pot of smells that drift around the room: pizza, cologne and paint. It works. It's a good moment, and it's the only one I need right now.

"So Dan," I speak between mouthfuls. "I hear you've diversified your role in the community." Dan looks confused. "Matchmaker, proposal deliverer, that sort of thing? You could become a Justice of the Peace then you could even do the odd wedding on the show." I smile and lick my lips. "God, that's good pizza."

"You'd be St. Cloud's one stop shop," smiles Sadie, leaning forward to select a slice. "Just think, locals could pop in for some antibiotics, listen to a debate on local politics, relax to a few good tunes, then, what the hell? Get married! All on the same block downtown."

Dan grins, tapping a finger on his temple, nodding. "I like it." He bites carefully into his slice then frowns. "But all that extra responsibility might get in the way of my yoga schedule."

"Don't mess with the yoga," chimes in Jed, happy to steer the conversation away from marriage and radio proposals.

"Anyway," Dan grabs Jed and knuckle rubs the top of his messy hair. "The pup's suffered enough, let him be. Love does crazy things to a man."

We all laugh as Jed nods in agreement, winking at Sadie as though the unexpected proposal was only to be expected. Because, as the town's wise man Dan says: *Love does crazy things to a man.*

We're chatting and eating, sipping beer, faces splattered in paint blemishes, all turned to face the setting sun. Through the sliding doors, out past the deck and down past the rolling lawn and tangled bush, the ocean glints. The sky is burnt orange and colour-washed crimson. Buttery golden light casts low shadows over the garden, past the trees and up to the room where we stand. Gradually we become quiet, taken by the scene and the light that changes as we watch.

Beyond the window four soundless reflections gaze back, seeing through us and beyond. And I look past them, past the comfort of friendship and familiarity of form to the quiet darkness of Jack's house.

"Where's Jack?" It's the first time I've said his name aloud in many months. The silence from before lingers, but changes, edged now with apprehension.

Dan breaks the moment. "He went home."

"Isn't that home?" I gesture to the dark house realising with regret there are so many conversations I never had with Jack. Might never have with Jack.

"His parents moved out to St Eloise a while back. He went to spend some time with them."

"Oh." I'm about to ask a whole bunch of questions; *why didn't he ever tell me about his family? How long will he be away? Is he okay?* One question crowds the others out, sounding panicky and scared, but I won't say it out loud: *Will he come back?*

Sadie interrupts before I can speak further. "Dan, don't you dare sneak that last pizza slice. I see what you're up to." She slaps Dan's hand as it hovers over the last lonely slice. "Hand it over." She taps the kitchen counter with one hand and extends the other toward Dan. "Come on."

Dan, about to raise the aforementioned slice to his open mouth pauses, giving Jed a *Is she always like this?* look before handing the pizza over to a grinning Sadie.

"Good boy, I need it more than you. I've been painting for hours."

"Yeah, and I've been downward dogging for at least that."

"All the more reason you've just done the right thing." She beams as she bites down, "Pizza is a big no-no in the world of hot yoga. You should know that. Try sweating those calories out! Stick to carrot sticks."

Dan tosses his hair theatrically. "I will. Enjoy those cheesy calories when they come to rest on your ass." He pats Sadie affectionately on the bottom as he passes, heading down the three small steps that lead from the kitchen to the living/dining/everything room.

"Billie, I love your work." He folds his arms looking carefully around the room, stripped bare and half painted. "I had no idea you had it in you." He looks around, inspecting my corners and edging, noticing the patches where the wallpaper refused to budge and I painted right over top. He turns critically to meet my gaze, head inclined toward the lumpy wall. I shrug and we both smile. He takes my hand and gives it a squeeze. "One day at a time, right?"

Much later when everyone has gone home and I've cleaned up the day's mess and checked the twins, I head outside to the recycling bin, armed with the empty pizza boxes and beer bottles. The night is clear and cooler than normal, the stars bright, and the sounds of crickets and tree frogs buzz and drone lazily. My legs ache and I sit on the edge of the deck for a moment, letting my feet swing and my eyes wander the dark.

St. Cloud is as before. All is as it was - except it's not.

A momentary flash of light surprises me and my eyes are drawn to Jack's house. But the light is gone and I wonder if maybe I imagined it. Sitting quietly, eyes trained on his house I see it a minute later, a small flash of light from within. I know the light is probably nothing of concern but decide I should be a good neighbour and check.

My feet are silent on the cool damp grass as I walk the path I have walked a thousand times before. But my footsteps are unsure despite my certainty of direction. I'm not sure why I feel the need to go inside, to see Jacks house and feel the hard wood floors under my feet. But I do, and I decide to trust the instinct that moves me forward in this darkest part of the night.

Standing outside the locked ground floor workroom, a cloak of familiarity wraps my shoulders and I'm comforted, although not sure why. The heavy scent of Agapanthus is all around, unkempt flowers lining the edges of the garden connecting our homes and lives. I stand for a moment at the foot of the steps that lead to the deck, eyes closed, lost in images and scenes from before.

"Where are you?"

I've spoken aloud although I didn't mean to, and as I carefully climb the steps, the question repeats over in my head. Reaching the deck, I walk to the edge and hold firmly on the rail that looks out to sea. I see the view of life from Jack's eyes and grip the rail, pressing my fingernails into wood till they make indentations that remain.

Through the old French doors, I can see the light is only a flashing answer machine but now that I'm close, holding the cold metal of the door handle, I have to go in. I need to go in.

The spare key, in predictable fashion is under a plant pot on the deck. I slide it into the lock and turn the handle. The door clicks submissively and opens to allow me entry to the man-cave Jack calls home.

In the dark only the outlines of basic furnishing are clear: the futon sofa, woodstove and bookshelf, a guitar in a corner and the radio on the long wooden bench that forms the kitchen. Nothing has changed, and I breathe in the smell of the room till I'm dizzy, then lower myself back onto the sofa. So desperate to know the comfort in his scent, my heavy breathing has made my head spin. I pull a rough woollen blanket around myself and smell him again. Of course this is where the crying starts. How could it not?

I sniffle and sob into the blanket, wondering why the hell I can't just make things easy and forget. My days are spent trying not to see and smell traces of Evan in my own house and here I am next door, in the dead of night deep breathing for signs of Jack. These feelings I have for him seem so wrong, cruel and disrespectful to Evans memory? Yet they remain, and being here in St Cloud, they gather force day by day.

My new strong woman persona stands at the foot of the sofa, staring me down. Her arms are folded across her chest and she's shaking her head saying; *Really? Is this what you want? Another man to distract you from yourself? Another relationship to lose yourself in? Another man to wait for?*

I shrug in response: *Maybe.*

She's mad and turns on her heel heading for the door. I have her attention. "Didn't you tell me to take care of myself and my needs for a change? Maybe Jack might be just what I need. Do you want me to grieve till I have saggy boobs and a face like an old lacy bag?"

This stops her in her tracks, she's near the door, about to make a dramatic exit. When she turns around she's morphed from a *Straight*

Sally version of me, to a red-lipsticked, head-scarfed, buxom-bosomed, World War Two gal recruit. Her shirt sleeves are rolled up and she flexes a tattooed bicep at me. She's got arms like Popeye and in a stage-whisper says; *You're right girl, a good shag is just what you need.* Winking saucily, she turns to go. I'm yelling after her and the sound of my voice wakes me from my brief doze on the sofa.

Good God. I rub my eyes and smile. If only feeling better were that easy. The thought makes my cheeks flush; shame and desire in equal measures.

With this in mind I make my way to Jack's bedroom where sheets of moonlight lie on the unmade bed. I unpack my heart and leave it scattered on crumpled linen, bathed in silver light.

At home I sleep with the rough blanket from his sofa around me. Lying on the floor in the narrow space between the twins beds I drift, lulled by whispered words I think are mine.

He'll come back, he has to.

Dan

A warm glow emanates from the windows of Beaujangles café. Outside darkness rests, the heavy blanket of night uniformly broken by pale streetlight. The slow surrender to dawn is close, the long moment of deepest darkness that exists before the light.

Dan watches Jed inside the café, moving around with rhythm, in time to music he can't hear. He flips switches, sets down chairs, snapping his fingers with the carefree air of a man without a worry. It's nice. Dan smiles as he watches his friend, thinking how good it would feel to approach life like just another day on the beach.

Jed's been living his *life's a beach* philosophy as long as Dan's known him. 'Some days the surf's good, and some days it's not, and there isn't a damn thing you can do about it.' He says that line every day like he's only just come up with it.

Dan likes it, even though he's heard it too many times. It's that rolling-with-the-wave's thing, knowing you can't control any of it.

That's it, if he could just quit trying to fix the surf, he'd be a happier guy.

Jed is unshaven, his scruffy hair covered by a bandana. He jumps as Dan raps at the window. Rolling his eyes Jed taps his watch before heading to the locked door to let Dan in. It's a routine, their set piece. Every day of the week Dan arrives at 6am, thirty minutes before opening time. Jed pretends he's too early, reluctantly lets him in, then begrudgingly makes him a coffee and they chat while the cafe is quiet. It's the only quiet time either of them will have all day.

"Morning sunshine." Jed doesn't wait for Dan to reply, he's already back behind the counter firing up *Monica*. "What's up?"

Dan shrugs, pulling a stool out from the counter. "Do you know you say the same thing every morning?"

"I do?" Jed slides a hot coffee along the sleek wooden countertop to where Dan's hand waits perfectly positioned to receive it.

"Every morning." Dan raises the cup and breathes in deeply, savouring the aroma.

"Well?" Jed places a stainless steel jug of hot frothy milk on the counter and grabs another warm cup from the rack on top of Monica.

"Well what?" Dan's eyes glaze over, the coffee's good.

"Well…what's up?" He frowns at Dan who looks like he's contemplating the meaning of life.

"Apparently, Bette Midler crossed with a bit of Johnny Depp." He gestures to Jed's bandana and just-woke-up stubble.

"Thought you loved Bette Midler." Jed disappears into the kitchen.

"Yeah, well, right now I'd rather have Johnny."

The oven door bangs and Jed emerges carrying a tray of warm croissants. "Billie seems good." He doesn't look up, carefully transferring the warm pastries on to a rack.

"Yeah, she does." Dan nods watching the croissants warily.

"You want one?" Jed offers, pushing a buttery golden croissant toward him.

"When did I ever eat a croissant for breakfast?"

"Never." Jed grabs the croissant, takes a huge bite and grins.

"Then why do you ask me every single morning?"

Laughing, Jed stuffs the remainder of the pastry into his mouth. "One day you'll come over to the dark side." He wipes his mouth with the back of a hand. "A man shouldn't have to start the day on juiced spinach." He disappears back into the kitchen humming some familiar tune.

"I never juice spinach."

"You've got something green in your teeth."

Dan rolls his eyes, runs his tongue over his teeth and checks his watch. "Where's Sadie anyway? I could do with some proper conversation."

Jed bustles through, tea towel draped over his shoulder, cheeks red from the warmth of the oven. "She'll be in later, got something on this morning." The phone rings and he answers, receiver cradled between shoulder and ear, he shines latte glasses with a free hand whilst placing an order with a supplier on the line.

By the time the call is finished Dan's coffee is gone. "I'm off, catch you later."

"Okay bro, take it easy. I'll tell Johnny you said hi."

"Do that." At the door Dan stops. "Meant to tell you, Jack left a message. He'll be back in town next week."

"Did you tell him Billie's home?"

"Nope. Sounds like he's got enough going on right now." Dan shrugs. "He's bringing Raife home."

Jed looks up from the list he's writing. "Shit." he pauses, taking in the news. "I really thought Raife was done with St. Cloud."

"Yeah well, he's a hard guy to read."

At 9.15 am Sadie breezes through the doors of the doctor's office, smelling of tiger balm and patchouli. "Good morning, I have an appointment."

"I'm sure you do," answers Muriel, Dan's ancient receptionist who doesn't look up from her computer screen when she answers (she's on the Crafts-R-Us website and doesn't want to be distracted).

"I'm here to see Dan," Sadie offers.

Muriel waves a hand, shooing her to a plastic seat in the waiting room. "So is everyone darling." She turns from the screen briefly to take a look at Sadie. "You know much about decoupage?" She sighs at Sadie's blank expression. "He'll be right out."

Sadie nods and sits in a seat beside a gnarled pot plant, a yucca that's been indoors too long. Its foliage leans heavily against the window where a few lucky stems rest sweatily against the glass. On the table are copies of GQ, Homes & Gardens and Men's Health, a magazine collection so *Dan* it makes her smile.

"Okay Muriel. Hit me up, what's it to be?" Dan breezes in from the corridor at the far side of the waiting room. He wears an open necked linen shirt and crisp khakis.

Muriel jumps, turning to face Dan, a free hand subtly closing the webpage, revealing an illuminated screen of appointments, names and ailments. Painting on a smile she gestures to Sadie, sitting in the corner, framed by the sweaty Yucca plant.

Dan frowns, recovers and steps forward, a palm extended toward her, the other to the corridor where his quiet consultation room waits.

"Sadie." He inclines his head and smiles as she rises, following him down the corridor. "What a pleasant surprise."

Dan's office is bright, white and airy, a calming contrast from the stuffy confines of the waiting room. Out of range of Muriel's interested gaze, Sadie sags and sinks heavily into the chair across from Dan's desk.

Professional hat on, Dan doesn't ask why she didn't mention she was coming to see him. The Sadie before him barely resembles the pizza-hogging girl from last night at Billie's. She slouches in the chair across from him, picking a fingernail and chewing her bottom lip. His smile is warm as he settles into his chair behind the long beech wood desk, watching as Sadie does her best not to make eye contact.

"Okay darling, what's up?"

She jumps to her feet and moves quickly across the room, suddenly interested in Dan's collection of local art. "This is beautiful." Standing with her back to him she gazes at a framed photograph; a close up of a leaf bathed with morning dew. The glistening light that emanates from the pale green leaf shimmers and reflects what seems like a thousand smaller images, thousands of tiny leafs shimmering in their own dewy light.

"It's one of my favourites." Another long silence. "So, you're here to plan a heist of my art collection? It'll be an easy job - most night's Muriel forgets to lock up anyway."

Sadie turns to face him, her cheeks flushed. "Sorry, this is awkward."

"It doesn't have to be. It's my job. I'm good at it. Now sit down…" He's out of his doctor's swivel chair and across the room in one elegant move. "Here." He guides Sadie by the shoulders and gently but firmly sits her back down on the chair. Flipping a switch on the electric kettle in the corner he plops a teabag in a pretty china cup, which when brewed, he places gently on the desk in front of her.

"Green tea, take a sip and spit it out." Sadie frowns, "I mean what's up…spit out what's up, not the tea. Good grief it's going to be one of those days."

She smiles, visibly relaxing and does as commanded. "Nice tea." She turns her head quickly to the window. "It's hot out there."

"Darling, I see through you. Don't change the subject. Tell dear old Dr. Dan before he calls for Muriel."

"Oh my God." Sadie plops down the green tea and raises her palms in mock horror. "Anything but Muriel!"

His expression is gentle. "Sadie, I'm a professional, I've seen it all before."

She flushes red. "No, it's not that Dan! Oh God…" she covers her hot cheeks with her hands. "I just need a confidential chat. I need some advice and I didn't know where else to go."

"I'm all ears." He leans back in his chair, plops his feet up on the desk and closes his eyes. "Chat away."

Sadie smiles. "Oh Dan."

"Say it again, my favourite two words," his eyes are still closed.

"Stop teasing."

"I'm not."

"I'm trying to be serious."

"Me too. Go ahead, I told you, I'm a pro."

She breathes in slowly, closing her eyes, hands held carefully in her lap. "So… I can't marry Jed."

Dan's expression remains unchanged, eyes closed, trying to channel little zen. He needs a smooth start to his day, not a counselling session with Jed's girlfriend on her commitment issues. "Uh huh, I got that part."

"See the trouble is…" she pauses, hands twisting in her lap. "It's not the timing, or the mad proposal, and it's not that I don't love him either." She pauses for breath. "I do."

Dan likes Sadie, she's a little bossy, but he likes her. She's honest and warm-hearted and his buddy Jed loves her. But right now he's getting a little narky. This is not his area. Write to the *Problems Page* in the Island Times, go talk to a girlfriend, I'm a doctor not an agony aunt. He doesn't say any of this but tries instead to find his most sympathetic self.

Bringing his feet carefully down from the desk he opens his eyes and turns to face her. He's about to say; *Sadie, I wish I could help but I can't. I'm Jed's friend, and he's a great guy, and you could do much worse, and finding love is pretty damn lucky, and maybe you need to address your hang ups before you lose Jed.* But when he looks up she's crying. Fat, silent tears that spill down her face on to her pale grey Beaujangles t-shirt.

"Hey, talk to me?" His mood has quickly changed from impatient to concerned. The sadness is something bigger than boyfriend issues.

"You see I didn't want to have to be *that girl* here. When I came to St. Cloud, I thought I'd just stop a while and move on before it might become an issue. I thought with travelling, people not knowing me from before, I could stop being that other Sadie." She jabs at a stray tear with the heel of her hand. "Don't you see Dan? Jed's screwed it all up for me, and I don't know what to do without hurting him."

"Sweetie I'm sorry, but I'm lost, you've got to tell me a little more before I…"

Sadie brings a hand up to silence him. "God, it's a real mess now. Now that he's got this *together forever, you're my girl, let's get married* thing, he won't drop it. I thought it might work out at first." She sniffs heavily, eyes fixed on Dan should he try to interrupt her flow. "If we'd just carried on like before, you know…summer fling, then I could have headed away for a while, come back, it'd be all good. No expectations or big commitments, no one gets hurt."

Sadie puts her hands over her eyes while Dan watches helplessly, wondering what the hell to do. "I thought you loved him, you two seem so good for each other."

"I do dumb ass!" The angry outburst causes another flow of hot tears. Dan holds his hands to his heart looking wounded. "I do. I just can't marry him, I can't stay with him, because I'm sick." Dan's hands drop from the wounded pose. "God, stop with the deer in headlights look would you. I'm not dying, not for a while…at least that's what the research says."

"That's what it says about us all," Dan replies calmly.

She flashes a small smile then wipes her eyes again. "Yeah, that's right." She's quiet for a moment. "I have CF." She pauses, watching him. "Cystic Fibrosis."

"I know what it is."

"I manage it. I'm okay, but you know the stats - I'm no material for long term anything."

Dan takes his time before answering, letting this news sink in, following its ripple, quickly assessing the facts, and choosing carefully how to react. "Treatments get more advanced every year, things are changing."

"I know. I have a specialist back home. I have a stack of meds I eat like candy. I take care of myself, eat well, do my exercises, all the things they tell me too. I do all the right things but still, my life expectancy is thirty-one. Thirty-one years old, you do the math, less than ten years to go."

"You're reading the wrong research." He's unsure of how much to say, he knows the odds, he understands the condition and now it all makes sense; the tough exterior, the elusiveness, the aversion to commitment.

"Maybe. I hope so, but really, thirty-one, forty-one - whatever - the facts are the same. It's not fair to commit to Jed."

"Have you asked him what he thinks?"

"No."

"Don't you think he should know?"

"No. Like I was trying to tell you before, that's not the Sadie I want to be here. I grew up with it Dan. All my life I've had people treat me differently and feel bad for me. That's why I decided to travel, to pack up my life and move away. I wanted to start again and if I got to the point I had to explain and be *that* Sadie again I'd pick up, leave and start over."

Dan listens, leaning back in his chair, watching as she releases her worries into the confines of his office. As she talks a gradual change becomes apparent; a subtle softening. The barriers she's built to contain her secret have formed a wall around her and its crumbling as she speaks. The borrowed defensiveness bleeds out with her words. With the secret set free she looks tired but softer, surrounded by a quiet peace.

"I made a plan with my specialist; they'd fax my notes to the nearest hospital of any place I stayed for more than a few months. I go away every six months to get all checked out, my prescriptions are faxed and I get my stash of drugs from the hospital pharmacy." She shrugs. "That's what I've done for the past few years."

Dan clasps his hands together, bringing his index fingers together in a point. He rests his chin on his fingers while Sadie watches him. He's about to speak when she jumps in. "And that's not the worst part. In fact, that part's okay, it's what I know. The worst is the way people react, the having to tell, the being different. And the sympathy, God, don't get me started on the sympathy - it kills me." She frowns. "Bad choice of words. It's just, this part is all new and I don't know what the hell to do." She looks up at Dan, her expression desperate. "I've never done the being in love part." Another fat tear slides down her cheek.

Dan reaches across the table, hoping she won't thwack him. He takes her hand and holds it, she lets him. "Sorry, I'm being such a bitch about it."

"No, no." Dan grins, squeezing her hand. "I like the bitch, I'm comfortable with her. The crying thing I wasn't quite ready for, but the bitch? She's fine."

She smiles mid-sob, "It's just, I'm so mad. Before, it was just about me and I could handle that. But now I've really messed up. It's about Jed too. You know him Dan, he won't cope with this."

"You might be surprised."

"He's a marshmallow."

"A brainless marshmallow." Dan shakes his head. "I don't get how you've managed to keep this from him."

"Oh he's easy," she laughs affectionately. "I nap a lot when he's not around. When I've overdone things and I'm coughing I tell him I smoked a lot of pot in my teens." Dan shakes his head incredulously. "I know." Sadie blushes. "I'll never get to heaven." She shrugs. "At the beginning I didn't want to hand him all that baggage, then I just couldn't and now…"

"And now?"

"Well, now I have to, or…"

"Or what?"

"Or, I just leave. Let him think I'm a heartless bitch who just didn't love him."

"Didn't you try that before?"

"I know, but this time I'm not doing it for me, I need to do it for him." She looks up at Dan like he should understand. "So he can get on and find his 'forever-girl.'

"That stinks of really bad idea."

"What do you suggest? Last night he asked me again when I was going to back down and say 'yes'. I know he thinks it's funny but I know it's what he really wants. He wants a family, and all of the forever stuff, and the truth is, I can never give him any of that."

"You don't know that."

The office is quiet, the first silence in the flow of emotion and words. Outside the sun shines, the view of the distant ocean sparkles brightly, and a baby cries down the hall in the waiting room. "There are no hard facts, everyone is different, you could have a family, plenty of women with CF do."

Sadie eyes are on the view outside. "My specialist at home was pretty clear on the facts." She deepens her voice and her face forms a scowl: "Carrying a baby will significantly reduce your lung capacity

Sadie, think very carefully about your future." Her voice sags at the last few words.

"Do you know for sure if Jed even wants kids?" Dan is still holding her hand.

"No, but I'm pretty sure."

"Okay, here's what we're going to do." He sits up straight taking her other hand. "For now, you're going to keep on being a bitch; all this emotion is too hard for me. I'm going to talk to a few friends and get some real facts before you make any decisions. And…" he stops for breath.

"And?"

"And you're going to promise, that after we know the facts, the most recently researched, up to date, real facts…you're going to talk to Jed and let him be part of whatever decision you're going to make." She turns away, eyes lowering, mouth drooping at the edges. "It's only fair Sadie."

"Is it?"

"Don't do anything till you speak to me. I'll call you tomorrow, I promise." She opens her mouth but its Dan's turn to interject. "And no, of course I won't! I'm a professional darling, we already discussed that. This is Dr Dan's *Dome of Silence*." He gestures grandly around the walls of the gleaming office.

"Shit!" Sadie's gaze has stopped on the wall clock which displays the time: 10.50am.

"Shit!" Dan echoes.

Sadie grabs her bag and envelops Dan in a hug. "Thank you." He winks in reply and she's off, racing for the door. "Jed's going to kill me, I'm an hour late for my shift!" She's gone in a flash of patchouli.

The buzzer on his desk rings loudly, he presses the intercom button reluctantly. "Muriel, I thought you'd forgotten me."

Muriel's tone drips with sarcasm. "How could I dear? Someone comes through the door asking for you every three minutes."

"Oh, you know how to make a guy feel popular."

"Only too glad to help. The waiting room is at capacity and you're running…let me see now… fifty-five minutes late."

"Right. Well, I just hate to crowd your waiting room Muriel. Send my first happy customer this way."

Dan rolls his eyes and sinks into his chair with a heavy heart.

Chapter Seven

Jack

Sunlight frames her standing pose, hands resting playfully on tilted hips. Golden rays trace her silhouette and throw dazzling pinpoints of light on her shoulders.

All that light but he can't see her face, she's dark and in shadow. Her voice playful, teasing. "Come on Jack." He's on the ground looking up at her. Again: "Come on Jack." He's shaking his head and she's laughing.

Another voice, strong and familiar. A voice used to getting its own way. "Come on Jack." He won't shake his head now. He'll come - he always does. The light is eclipsed as Raife stands behind her. His height blocks the light and dwarfs her smaller body. His arms encircle from behind and he leans into her neck whispering in her ear. Still the light is gone; it hides behind him. They're laughing at Jack but she holds out a delicate arm. She likes him; she likes all the guys. He reaches for her hand but Raife pulls her away.

All is dark and he can smell the rain. He's driving and they're beside him. She whispers in his ear smelling of sweet liquor and weed. Raife pulls her close, they're fooling around. It's so dark. He's dizzy.

"Come on Jack." Now, the words are angry and ugly. He turns to her in the dark. Raife's gone and her words become loud and hysterical. He's afraid. He reaches for her, pulling at the hands that cover her face. And there's light everywhere, a thousand spotlights shine down on the scene. Illuminated and still, she is ghostly pale and expressionless. Eyes open but empty, an angry scar divides her perfect face, forehead to chin. Billie.

Jack's eyes flash open in the dark. His face is damp. He breathes heavily, running a hand over his face, wiping his eyes. Reality returns slowly, breath by breath. This is home, this is his bed, this is his house and this dream is old.

He sits up and Bets rouses from her basket on the floor. "It's okay girl." He whispers as her eyes rise to meet him. Sensing all is well she flicks her tail, tucks it back under her curled body and settles back to sleep.

He won't sleep for a while now. It's the first time he's had the dream in years.

Taking a long slow breath, he runs both hands through his damp hair before rising. Billie was never in the dream before. God, it's having Raife around. He knew it would happen. With Raife here in St. Cloud, in this new part of his life, the past is too damn close. This is how he knew it would be. This is why Raife's been running and he's been hiding. It's why Joseph hates him and why Amandine's years of quiet sadness have turned in on her.

He thinks of his mother in the garden and absently rubs his chest where his heart hurts. Amandine, the family sentinel, her mind creeping toward a place where no-one can hurt her.

Outside the night is black. There are no stars to break the thick blanket of dark. Billie's house is barely visible, a dark outline against the night on the other side of the yard. He wonders if she's home, if she's asleep there, or if maybe she decided to stay away, start again. Another escapee running from the past.

They'd arrived back in St. Cloud late last night. He'd brought Raife home in darkness and somehow it felt fitting. In the light of the coming morning he'll decide what to do. He doesn't have a plan, he never did, but he owes it to Raife to help. He sees that now. He'll try to help his one last time and maybe then, he can let go.

In the kitchen he splashes his face with cold water and fills a glass. He hears Raife stir on the sofa. He mumbles, words too hard to define, his mind freed by sleep. He speaks again. The sounds are angry but the words jumbled. Jack watches his brother's face as he dreams. In sleep Raife looks younger, free of anger and regret. He looks like he did in the dream: holding the girl, teasing his little brother.

Jack had wanted to stop in St. Eloise on the way back. Raife needs to see their parents. Jack had hoped a visit from their favourite son would bring Amandine some joy and Joseph some peace. But Raife said he didn't feel good, he wanted to wait, get himself together.

He watches Raife turn restlessly on the sofa. It was a good idea coming here first. Raife needs some time. Jack needs time to talk to him about Amandine, prepare him for when he sees her, but he's not sure how. He'll let him settle a while, give him the time he's asked for, then they'll go together.

Refilling his glass, he hears a long sigh. Raife's hands are behind his head, eyes open staring at the ceiling. "God this place is hot."

"Did I wake you?"

"I don't know if I was even asleep. There's no air in here." Raife sits up slowly and pulls his t-shirt over his shoulders, eases out of his trousers and throws them on the floor. "Was it always this hot?"

"Always." Jack passes him the glass of cool water.

Raife drinks greedily, setting the glass down and sinking back. His long legs hang over the edge of the sofa, arms raised above his head in a cat-like stretch. "I don't know if I can live here again."

Jack walks to the window, looking out into the blackness. "You don't have to."

Raife sighs again, closing his eyes. "That's right Jack, you've got all the answers." There's a long silence. Jack hopes Raife's fallen back to sleep, he doesn't feel like talking. But Raife isn't done, he's only thinking. "What do you do out here anyway? There's nothing here, doesn't it drive you crazy?"

Jack's gaze rests on the outline of Billie's house. "Sometimes."

"Then why'd you stay? You've got nothing here, nothing real. No-one would notice if you stopped building boats. Can't be much business for you." He yawns and sighs again.

"I like it here. I don't need any more." Jack works on keeping the edge from his voice.

"You got a girl?" Jack doesn't answer and Raife laughs, "You're not still screwing around with…what was her name?" Jack remains quiet. "Jesus." Raife laughs again. "You should remember! You married her. God that's funny." He shakes his head, enjoying the joke. "You and her married, what was that about anyway?"

"Shut the fuck up will you?"

Raife knows just how to push his buttons. Claudia, the girl he'd married young after she'd told him she was pregnant. What had started as a drunken fling ended in a shit load of despair. A miserable year, there had never been a baby. When he left she took everything, and he didn't care, he just wanted her gone. Back then Claudia was another bad decision he'd had to live with.

"Take it easy. I'm playing with you."

Jack rubs a hand over his eyes. "Do you know what a pain in the ass it is having you here?"

Raife smiles, eyes closed again. "I can guess."

"Well, how about we make a deal. While you're here, sorting your shit out - stay out of my shit."

"I get it. Relax, you never used to be so uptight. Don't worry, I'll stay out of your business. Nothing much to stay out of by the looks of it." Raife pulls the sheet up over his chest. "Soon you'll be begging me not to leave."

Jack shakes his head and walks back to the bedroom. "Good night…oh, and when you wake up tomorrow, try not be an asshole."

"Will do Jackie-boy."

Ten minutes later Jack can hear the quiet snores of his brother. It's another hour before he falls into a fitful sleep. Rising early, before dawn, he's happy to hear the gentle calling of a native bird in the trees singing the morning in. It's a joyous sound and he's missed it, the gentle melody ringing out in the dark. As the light lifts the others will join, and the air will be full of chatter and birdsong. Jack is sure of one thing; he is where he belongs, and despite everything - it is home.

Billie

There's a scene in *The Grapes of Wrath* where Steinbeck writes about Tom Joad meeting the old preacher, Jim Casy, under the shade of a willow tree. Casy is unkempt and weathered, changed since they last met. He tells Joad he's lost his faith in Jesus.

They face each other, sharing a single line of shade cast from the gnarled trunk of the willow. Casy tells Joad of his new understanding of faith; one he can't preach. That the human spirit is the Holy Spirit. That thoughts and actions aren't of heaven or hell, but of man, all men, connected; all the same.

I read that scene again last night. The words shared between those men; the ex con and the old preacher, the Oklahoma accents you can hear, and their simple honesty. I went to sleep with that scene. Drowsy clarity accompanied the veil of sleep and I saw that the preachers' conflict over feelings and actions, right and wrong is eternal and everywhere. That our struggles and demons, addictions and obsessions are based on that same struggle. How we feel, what we do, and how we reconcile it all in a world where what's expected is written in bold in the subtext of every conversation. Where the lines between right and wrong, *shoulds* and *shouldn'ts*, blur our vision whilst we struggle through the swampy grey areas on either side.

Casy threw his faith away because when he felt closest to God he wanted to make love. He couldn't reconcile his feelings and actions with the way of Jesus. And I like him - despite his indiscretions, he's a good man, but he's just a man. Just like the rest.

And here I am, weighed down with my own matching luggage set of conflicting feelings. Knowing what's expected, what's deemed right and wrong, struggling with love, grief, hope and despair. When I woke, I was thinking about Casy and Joad again, and their words brought me quiet comfort. There is no right or wrong in a feeling, and there are no rules to loving, grieving and living on. We are all of the same, and love is what makes us tick. I wish I'd been there under that willow tree. I'd have given Casy a hug and told him he didn't need to give up on faith because he loved women.

It's early and the house is silent as I sit up in bed scribbling my thoughts on a notepad. Catching my reflection in the mirror, I can't help but smile. I could be Patsy from Ab fab; hair askew and face crumpled from sleep. A glass of champers wobbling in my right hand would just about complete the look. Coffee will have to do - definitely the better option - although I don't rule out anything in my slippery slope of self-pitying decline.

I've done a lot of crazy in the past few months. I speak out loud regularly to Evan, have become a compulsive DIY diva, eat more cookie dough ice cream than *Fat Albert* and reflect daily on my current status in recovery. I suppose creating a cameo role in John Steinbeck's *Grapes of Wrath* is progress from comparing oneself to the 'most-meagrely-topped-pizza slice-in-the-box'.

Poking my head into the twins' room to check they're still alive, I breathe easy seeing their peaceful sleeping forms. Closing the door silently, I tiptoe to the kitchen for coffee, my reliable, available friend.

Always this light; the softness of dawn in St. Cloud lifts me. That, and a little help from my morning java and Patsy might soon be replaced by Elle McPherson. This thought is a nice one, impossible of course, but nice, and I try a sexy swagger across the living room to the deck to sit down for the remainder of the dawn lightshow.

I'm sexily swaggering when out of the corner of a still sleepy eye I see him.

Although I've imagined seeing him like this for months, the sight and surprise makes me dizzy. The sexy swagger stops abruptly and I spill coffee down the front of my night-shirt. My belly is burning but I don't take my eyes from him. He hasn't seen me, he's out on the deck, elbows leaning on the rail, right about where I left my nail marks, staring out to sea.

I'm hyperventilating and might need a paper bag. Just the sight him - the solid square of his shoulders and slant to his waist, those arms and hands - leaning on the rail, cradling a coffee cup.

Before I can think any further, I'm out of the sliding doors and walking down the damp grass toward the fence. I watch him from behind as he watches the sun slowly rising. A bird swoops and dives from the gum tree beside his deck and he follows it with his eyes till it lands on the rail. For just a moment, I see him in profile and as he turns, his eye catches my movement.

The world stops here. Jack stops, dead still, eyes fixed on me in my coffee stained nightdress. Me, stuck to the spot, unable to walk on, unable to move, or blink, or breathe, praying that it's not another dream, and that Jack has come back here, where he belongs.

I raise a hand about to wave then stop mid-way, realising how insignificant the action would be. My hand travels instead to my mouth where it stays, fingers resting shakily on my lips, willing myself not to cry or make a scene. I don't know how long I've been standing motionless, hand to mouth, but Jack breaks the moment. He walks toward me; along the deck, down the steps and slowly toward the fence that separates our gardens. I'm walking too, but I'm not sure how, a magnetic pull that matches my stride for his. Slow and controlled. One foot at a time.

We reach the fence at the same time.

I take a breath, long and slow, trying to control my overflowing emotions. I face him, eyes locked on his. It's that same feeling of comfort and safety since I first met him, right here, just a few feet away in this garden. But now the comfort and safety is obscured by another stronger feeling, one that was always there, a feeling that remained hidden amidst the confusion of a tangled heart.

Longing. The need to touch him and hold him. I long for him, but I take that breath and will my stronger self to the fore. I must not be needy and weak. He smiles and that weakness I'm shooing away, rushes straight for my knees and I focus to keep from wobbling.

"You're here."

He nods. "I am."

"I wasn't sure if…" I pause and try to breathe evenly. "Sorry, it's just…"

He reaches out and runs one finger down the side of my face and I close my eyes as a fat tear slides down my blotchy cheek. He wipes it with a course thumb and if it weren't for the fence that divides us I'd throw myself into those arms and have him hold me. I'd soak up that warmth and make it mine and I'd let him feel all the trapped longing that waits for him.

Instead, with the fence between us, I hold out my hands and he takes them and we stand there smiling gently at each other in the dawn light.

"You grew a beard."

"You spilt your coffee."

I'm laughing, having forgotten the wet coffee stain, the hair and the nightdress. It doesn't matter, Jack looks at me like I am Elle McPherson. I squeeze his hands and shake my head at the hairy face, teasing him gently, telling myself to tread carefully.

Jack hops the fence and we walk warily side by side to the edge of my deck where we sit and watch the sunrise together. Our conversation is gentle, we could be strangers, but the intimacy of tone gives us away.

After a while Jack tells me a little about where he's been. That he's brought his brother home, that his Mom isn't well and he's soon to be an uncle. I tell him about Sunny and Evie, how they've grown. I tell him about Scotland and Cam and Nell and the farm, about my best friend Iris and her fiancé. We talk together about St Cloud, about the local news, about Zoe and Felix, Jed and Sadie, Dan and Ginny. We talk like we did before; before everything.

We try, in the way that people do, to act *as if*. *As if* it's all okay, *as if* we know how to live in this new reality, *as if* we understand the strange and complicated relationship we circle around. *As if* we can cope. *As if* we're getting there - to that place; that place where we really are all of those things. As though by acting *as if*, we might make the transition easier.

"And so Evie and Sunny have started kindergarten. God, you should see them with their little backpacks and lunchboxes." Jack looks incredulous at this piece of news, and I can tell this mostly because he raises his eyebrows, the beard is seriously getting in my way.

"Are they still sleeping?" He glances behind us to the house.

"Yep, believe me, we'd know if they were awake. I'd say we're probably on the countdown as we speak." I can't wait for him to see them and equally for them to see him. So much has changed and I cling to things that are familiar for them. They will be so happy to see Jack.

There's another moment of silence between us. We've run out of all the safe topics. Jack turns to me, reaches over and places a hand over mine. "Billie…"

We haven't spoken, not properly since *the night*. We never spoke of the kiss, of Evan, of who is to blame or not, of how to move on, and even now I don't think I can.

I shake my head quickly. "It's okay Jack." Three useless words.

I should tell him how hard it's been, how I blamed myself, how I hate Evan and love him at the same time, how I hated myself, and how I thought of Jack throughout it all. But I don't. I say "It's okay," and nod feeling the warmth of his hand over mine, knowing that at this moment it really is okay.

The light is layered pink and orange when we hear two thumps followed by the distinct sound of little feet running heavily on wooden floors. We both jump and turn in time to see two small faces squished against the sliding doors, lips flat and noses turned up as they press against the glass. I clap my hands and jump to my feet, pulling the doors open and kneeling down to hug Evie and Sunny who peer questioningly over my shoulder at Jack.

"Look who's here! It's Jack! Our buddy from next door, remember?"

They hide behind me for a moment, feigning shyness. Evie pokes her head out first, her nose wrinkled, scrutinising Jack, who stands with his arms folded, staring back.

"You can't be Evie Skylark. She's much smaller than you." Jack says shaking his head.

"Am too."

"Are you sure?"

"Mama, tell him."

I turn around hands on hips. "This really is Evie Skylark."

Before Jack can respond, Evie pipes up. "Jack has dogs." Her little brow is furrowed, as she looks him up and down.

I shrug apologetically and Sunny, who is hugging my legs pokes his head around. "What's on his face?"

"That's a beard, honey." Sunny looks up at me for clarification, "It's like hair on your head, but on your face." This sounds so funny I giggle and so do the twins. Jack's arms are still folded and I can tell he's smiling under all that facial hair. He rolls his eyes, sticks his thumb and first finger into his mouth and whistles loudly. In seconds Louie and Bets hurdle the fence and barrel toward us, jumping and wagging their whole bodies in happiness.

"Doggies! Doggies!" shouts Evie, clapping her hands together, while Sunny jumps up and down.

"You remember Louie and Bets?" We crouch, letting the dogs lick and paw and love us like we've never been away. Sunny has thrown his arms around Louie's neck and Evie is off to find a stick for Bets.

Jack looks wounded. "What about Jack? Do I get a hug? Sunny turns to look at him again, giggles and runs off.

"You might have to lose the beard first." Without thinking, I raise a hand to touch it. He freezes but I let my hand remain. The roughness on my palm feels good, warmth radiates from his face sparking happiness in my heart. And I could stand here all day, because I feel seeds of joy bud and bloom in my heart. Like an echo distorted over time and distance, past happiness is tinged grey with regret and grief. This innocent feeling of joy is pure and untouched, unaffected by time or tragedy.

If I stand still here in the morning sun, my hand on his face, my heart alive, I can almost forget the sad yesterdays and unknown tomorrows.

But the world doesn't stand still, it spins and all we can do is hang on. We must hang on, must stand firm taking little steps on tired feet, because wings and flying are only for birds.

Raife

Raife stands by the kitchen window, just far back enough that he won't be noticed if they look his way. He watches as the woman in the nightdress reaches up to touch Jack's face.

"I'll be damned," he shakes his head. "I'll be damned."

He watches as Jack looks down at her, her hand on his face. The look exchanged between them needs no interpretation. Raife's smile twists to a grimace as he turns away, bringing his hands to rest on his head. He breathes slowly, each controlled breath an effort that drains colour from his cheeks. Lowering his hands to rest on his temples he closes his eyes then in one quick motion, pushes his palms hard into the sockets till colours flash and sting behind his eyelids.

"Fuck, fuck, fuck."

When he opens his eyes they're still there, in the garden. He turns away and starts toward Jack's bedroom where he stands, naked from the heat, surveying the space with calculating eyes. In a few minutes he has gone through the drawers and wardrobe, filtered through Jacks meagre belongings - so little to see.

He finds a photo of her: the girl next door. She's pregnant, in a sundress, saluting the photographer, smile wide, cheeks flushed. Underneath the photograph, folded carefully is a newspaper clipping, an obituary: *Evan Skylark, husband and father...* he doesn't read on. Carefully, he re-folds the newspaper and replaces the photo.

Returning to the sofa, he finds his jeans and wanders to the kitchen for coffee. He pours and stirs, letting the coffee change gradually from black to pale brown. Milk slops on the counter and floor as the spoon clatters on the side of the mug. Coffee overflows, mixing with spilt milk and sticky sugar remnants. He is watching Jack through the window.

Jack takes the steps two at a time. He's happy, it's clear.

Raife nods his head slowly, glancing up as his brother enters the room. "Morning sweetheart, made you some coffee..."

Billie

Evie and Sunny are never quiet, never, unless of course they're asleep. Even then, there are no guarantees. They chatter and laugh, cry and scrap, whinge and make *broom broom* noises always. It's funny how quickly you become used to this new level of volume in the world.

Gone are the days when I'd turn the radio on for company in the evenings, when the twins were asleep and the house felt too quiet. In those days, there were no words, just crying and at night, I needed the sound of adult voices to bring back some sense of reality to my isolated world. These days, the quiet of night is like medicine. I take a shot of that peace and stillness. It's a beautiful thing. I don't want the radio or television, I crave that quiet space, where there is no noise and no demands.

As they figure their way around words and their meanings the air is full of chatter. I love the nonsense talk, the reasoning out and brutal honesty that comes when words precede social sensibilities. "Mommy that man has no hair." (Sunny pointing, voice raised in the supermarket). Or, "Mommy why's that lady got big boobies?" (Evie discussing Muriel, Dan's receptionist, very loudly in the doctor's waiting room).

Kids don't need a quiet audience; they don't care if someone is already talking, singing or shouting loudly before they join in. Two voices are better than one right? Little conversations, observations, questions, songs or just random words they like the sound of. All in synch. It's like my own little radio frequency tuned in to babble station with no volume control.

Today we are on the way to kindergarten, a routine I'm still getting used to. My goodness, who said breast feeding was the hard part? Getting two pre-schoolers dressed, fed, toileted and out of the door by 8am takes a whole new level of organisation and discipline. By the time we three are dressed, ready and belted into the car, there's the feeling that a great miracle has occurred. I turn the ignition and wait for a round of applause. Instead what usually happens is I realise I've forgotten one, maybe two crucial items and spend the next five minutes racing back in and out of the house, locking and unlocking the door. When finally, I feel secure that everything is packed and ready, Evie or Sunny, or maybe both, decide they need to go 'wees' again. Worse still, they might not have realised the wee in question was coming. Then we have the clean-up-and-start-again scenario which can add another fifteen minutes to our E.T.A. So, like I say, the getting to kindy by 8.15am part is really quite something to be proud of.

So far this morning has gone particularly well. We're driving, dressed, packed and singing to the radio. No-one is crying or whingeing and its 8.10am. Five minutes to spare.

Paradise Park Kindergarten feels like a little slice of kiddie-heaven. The colours are warm and bright. Kid's art and photo displays of smiling children hang from the walls. Egg box creations painted in primary colours, stuck with silver foil and felt shapes line display shelves. It always smells like scones and sounds like humpty dumpty. I wonder how the teachers ever have a bad day here.

What happens when you come to work with PMT? When you're crabby and blue? You can't be a kindergarten teacher on a day like that. You just can't - it goes against the laws of teaching pre-schoolers. Kindy teachers must always be smiling, wear bright colours, be good at giving hugs and wear silly earrings.

Evie and Sunny were welcomed into Paradise Park Kindergarten like they were family. The experience of arriving there and being welcomed so warmly was so unexpectedly beautiful, I had to be led to the teachers' room and given a box of hankies and a maternal cuddle myself. All that kindness and love, all those little people starting out, full of life and joy and hope. (Okay, there were a few tantrums and squabbles and wails for mommies to come back, but for the most part it was a beautiful thing.)

The twins arrived at Paradise Park like they'd been there every day of their short lives. They breezed right on in and went straight to the craft tables and new toys, climbing bars and new friends. That's when the tears started, you see I'd expected the clinging to Mom's leg, crying not to be left, me feeling terribly needed and having to be shooed out by the kindly teachers, who'd tell me 'they'll be fine when you're gone'.

Except it wasn't like that at all. They were off with barely a backward glance, even Sunny, my little softie. Gone.

Of course I was proud. "Gosh haven't you done a good job." said Miss Mandy, the fifty-something portly teacher with a kind smile and dangly cowbell earrings. "Wonderful to see little ones so confident and ready to get involved."

I kept smiling proudly, only aware I'd started to sniffle when Miss Mandy led me kindly by the elbow to the teacher's room. You see, all I could think was that my poor babies were relieved to finally have a break from Mommy. I wondered how much I'd carried my grief for them to see, wondered how much they'd felt it too. Maybe kindergarten felt like a place they could start again, where they didn't have to hold my sadness.

I'd blurted this all out to Miss Mandy. She held my hand then made me a cup of tea and nodded reassuringly, telling me again how well I'd done. Of course she doesn't know how well, or not well I've done at all, but the kindness was humbling. I stayed there in the teacher's room for a while, watching Evie and Sunny from a distance, playing with their new best friends, climbing and running and exploring, not looking for me. And when I felt ready, I slipped away, knowing they were happy and that I was doing everything the best way I could.

I had taken to going to the library after kindergarten drop off. The quiet calm and musty smell of books felt like exactly what I needed. I thought of London and Paris and the libraries there that inspired me, back in my other life. I thought of my book, the only one I'd finished and the joy I'd found when writing. So I started again: notes at first, ideas and plans, quotes and scenes. I started writing and it felt so good I cried again, my tear ducts barely holding up.

Like saying 'hello' to an old friend, the simple act of beginning a story that wasn't mine felt like freedom. My writing since Evans death has been self-absorbed, focused on thoughts and feelings, exploring my grief and recovery. This was a step forward - a right royal leap. I was writing outside of self-pity, beginning the makings of someone else's story.

Today I spend an hour in the library, a good hour planning and writing, then head to Beaujangles to meet Zoe and Virginia. It's a ten-minute stroll and I walk slowly, savouring the perfumed smell in the air. It rained heavily last night and as the warmth of the sun dries the pavements and palms a sultry smell that is specific to St. Cloud lingers.

The main street leading to Beaujangles is lined with palms interspersed with benches on the sidewalks. Town is busy but never crowded, and I can see the outside tables and chairs of Beaujangles spilling on to the pavement near the end of the street. The hum of chatter and the soft low beat of reggae drifts towards me as I approach.

"Billie girl, there you are! My morning is complete." Jed is behind Monica, smiling as he multitasks, frothing milk with one hand, setting down cups with the other.

Sadie drifts around the corner from the kitchen carrying an order of eggs and toast. "Hey Billie, the girls already ordered for you."

"Thanks." I smile and weave through the busy tables to a booth in the corner where Virginia and Zoe sit. The table groans with cups and plates. "Did I miss the crowd?" I gesture toward the stack of pancakes, milkshake, round of buttered toast, croissant and savoury muffin.

Zoe dabs her mouth with a napkin. "It's all for me sister, can't stop! I'm growing as we speak." She pats her large bump lovingly. "I know you must be wondering how I can fit anything else in here. It's amazing. I keep waiting to pop but so far I'm just hungry." She pauses for effect. "All the time." She bites into a slice of toast and smiles up at me. "Sit down, I might even share."

"Holy cow, you've grown since last week." I touch her tummy. It is as hard as a bowling ball.

"I know, she's unstoppable. I keep thinking maybe I should go easy on the food. I mean how big will she be by pushing time? But then, I start thinking about macaroni cheese and it's all over."

Virginia laughs. "You'll be fine. It's number three. You'll sneeze and that baby will be out."

"Don't say that!" Zoe looks horrified.

"I'm kidding, but seriously…" Virginia sips her coffee delicately. "It's almost always the way with the third baby - two pushes and they're out. Easy labour, quick recovery. It's Mother Nature's way. She knows you've got be back on the front line quickly."

Zoe frowns. "It's true. I'll be back making the macaroni cheese myself the next day." She gives her head a small shake then turns to me. "You look great Billie, what's different?"

I'm not sure this is a compliment. "Washed my hair?"

"That'll do it, good girl, about time." I elbow her and she laughs. "I'm kidding, you do look good though, and it's more than the hair."

"I'm writing. Not much really, but a start, I need to get going again."

"That's great Billie." Virginia is overly enthusiastic. She's about to carry on but Zoe interrupts.

"Holy crap, who is that?"

We all look around to the front of the café, and our triple head swivel is so obvious the man in question looks straight at us. He's over six feet tall with sandy blonde hair and chiselled cheekbones. For a second, I see Jack but realise quickly it can't possibly be, this is a blonde, less hairy, finer version. It must be.

"Jacks' brother."

Virginia and Zoe turn open mouthed to stare at me. He's at the counter now, shaking hands with Jed, and I know I must be right.

"Jack's brother?" Zoe looks puzzled. "Hang on, back up, but Jack's not here, is he?

"Why didn't we know he had a brother?" says Virginia, eyes still on the man at the counter, tongue practically lolling.

"Virginia." Zoe nudges her. "Pull yourself together."

"Jack is home. I saw him yesterday."

"Oh?" Zoe still looks puzzled; she hates not to be first on the scoop. I can tell she's unsure how to follow with her next question. "Did you speak to him?"

"Of course."

"Oh. And the brother, what's the story?" Virginia and Zoe's eyes are trained on me but I'm studying the brother, who can't see me staring from here.

"I don't really know. He's been away in the States for a while and decided to come back, I guess." I know there's more to the story. Jack hinted their relationship was difficult but it's not my story to tell.

"Funny, we haven't heard about this brother before." Virginia's gaze is back at the counter where Jed and Jack's brother are still in conversation.

Zoe wrinkles her nose, and returns to her muffin. "Actually, now that I come to think of it, I'm pretty sure I remember something about Jack having a couple of brothers. All used to live here, parents moved away a while ago, not sure about the rest."

Virginia sucks in her breath, sitting up straight. "Okay, I'm calling him over."

Jack's brother turns when beckoned by Virginia and smiles a smile which manages to look both shy and quietly confident at the same time. He walks toward our table carrying a large cup of coffee.

"Ladies." He towers over our food covered table, eyes lingering on each of us in turn.

Virginia leans forward, hand extended toward him, cheeks flushed. "You must be Jack's brother."

"Actually, Jack's *my* brother." He extends the smile further and offers his hand. "I'm Raife."

Virginia is holding his hand, and the rose in her cheeks deepens by the second, "Nice to meet you Raife. We're Jack's friends. I'm Virginia, you can call me Ginny." Zoe kicks me under the table and I yelp. His eyes turn and fix on me. "And that's Billie and this is Zoe."

Raife reaches out to shake our hands one by one, holding on just a little longer than necessary, maintaining eye contact for an excruciatingly long time. Virginia has turned to putty, and is blabbing on, asking questions. Raife manages to answer without giving too much away.

I study his face as he talks, so very like Jack yet so different, and I wonder what it was that came between them. What could be so bad that you wouldn't see or speak to family for years? Life is too short.

I think of Cam and how very far away he is, and feel an ache in my chest. I take a fortifying gulp of coffee and turn to Zoe who continues her eating marathon, oblivious to *Ginny*, Raife, and to me. She spreads a thick layer of butter on some toast.

"So you're Billie."

I nod, "We live next door to Jack. It's really nice to meet you."

I'm not sure why I feel unsure of him. Maybe it's the 'I'm-too-sexy-for-my pants' look, or just knowing there's been difficulties between him and Jack in the past. But every family has its share of drama, and I shouldn't judge. Besides, he's quite nice to look at.

Virginia's not the only one swooning. As I glance around Beaujangles there's a trail of wide eyed, open mouthed, ladyfolk in his wake. He's straight from a Calvin Klein add, drop-dead gorgeous but without the designer clothes.

"Jack told me about you."

I wonder what Jack might have told him. "But we haven't met yet right?" I worry I've had a momentary memory lapse, but realise that of course I would remember meeting him. He's quite unforgettable.

"I saw you in the garden."

He staring and it's a little uncomfortable. Zoe kicks me again under the table and I'm tempted to kick her right back but she stands up and starts waving madly across the café. Dan has just walked in the door.

We follow Zoe's wave, all eyes turned to the door where Dan breezes in, slick and suntanned. The google-eyed pathway of women Raife only just swept through, turn now to the vision of male perfection that is Dan. The effect is almost exactly the same. Where with Raife, the reactions were open mouthed and wide-eyed; who was this gorgeous stranger? With Dan the look is all open admiration. They all know who Dan is; they just wish he was straight.

"Dan, over here! Got time for a cuppa with us?" Zoe's is a fog horn. She stands to greet Dan and as she turns her bump is pushed into the side of my face. "You okay down there?" Giggling, she eases herself back in to a sitting position. "That was hard work. Pass me my milkshake."

Dan is heading our way, smiling and signalling to Jed as he weaves his way through the crowded café. My newly resurrected novelist's head must be playing games with me. First my suspicious uneasiness around Raife, and now, as I watch Dan approach and see Raife, I notice an odd change in Dan's expression. An emotion visible for a brief moment before his face forms a smile. But it's the same smile he uses in the doctors waiting room, for greeting patients he's never met before, or ones he already knows and maybe wishes he didn't. It's a shiny, wide smile, but it doesn't reach his eyes.

Raife sits on my left and I can tell that his attention is now fully on Dan. He seems to have a way with that - *'Hi, I'm Raife, I'm looking in your eyes and you're the only person in the room'*, thing. But as Dan approaches he doesn't do the *'Hi I'm Raife'* line, he breathes out slowly and rises to meet Dan. There's an unspoken history. I see it in Dan too.

Before he says a word, Dan nods at Raife, acting as though the arrival of this new and dazzling secret brother of Jack's was a prior arrangement.

"Raife." Dan doesn't hold out his hand to shake or hug, his hands push deeply into his trouser pockets and he nods. It's a little awkward and an embarrassed silence slips over the table.

"Good to see you Dan." Raife thrusts his hand out anyway, palm open, ready to do the manly handshake.

I feel an anxious creep of uncertainty flow over the table as we watch. What's up with Dan? Here follows a long, excruciating moment where we're all sure he's not going to shake Raife's hand.

I'm just about to jump up myself, grab Raife's extended hand and on behalf of Dan say; *'Good to see you too! You two obviously know each other, but in your absence Raife, Dan has acquired a hearing impediment. You might think he's being rude but actually he can't hear you.'*

Virginia clears her throat unsubtly. Zoe chews her bottom lip.

"Been a long time Raife." Dan finally extends his arm and there's a collective sigh of relief around the table. The sigh is quickly preceded by lively chatter as we all begin to talk at the same time, trying to cover the social awkwardness.

Sadie arrives with Dan's coffee and sandwich and Virginia introduces her to Raife. Again, the full attention and long eye contact. Sadie looks unphased; nothing seems to rock her boat. She clears the table, squeezing Dan's shoulder affectionately before leaving laden with debris from Zoe's food fest.

Sitting at the opposite side of the booth, Dan isn't forced into further conversation with Raife. He bears down on his sandwich, eating like someone might steal it if he stops for breath.

"So Raife, are you planning on staying in St. Cloud for a while?" I ask politely.

Raife shrugs, and sips his mug of coffee, eyeing me carefully. "I might, I haven't decided."

"What do you do?"

As soon as I ask, I realise the question is horrible. It's one of those 'open ended, interpret how you want, make you feel awkward if currently you don't *do* much' sort-of-a-question.

He smiles wryly. "I do a lot of things, which one do you want to know about?"

I'm blushing. "Were you working in Los Angeles?"

Raife sets his coffee cup down and stretches his arms out in front of him, lacing his fingers together and extending his palms. "I'm a musician."

Zoe perks up beside me. "What sort? Are you in a band?"

"Not any more. I play gigs, mostly solo."

"So you sing?" I ask surprised. I'm not sure why this seems so unlikely.

He smiles, "I do."

"Were you playing in LA?" Zoe is suddenly awestruck, appetite satiated she looks properly at Raife. "Wow, like, paid gigs? Would we have heard of you?"

Raife smiles. "I doubt it. Not here in the boonies."

Dan looks up. "Yeah Raife, why would you ever come back to *the boonies*? Can't be much for you here, not after living in LA."

Raife shrugs again. "This is where I grew up remember?" Dan raises his eyebrows a little, and again there's that tension. "I might hang around a while, catch up with some old friends, take it from there."

He stands to leave, glancing around, smiling at us all before tipping an imaginary cowboy hat. "It's going to be nice, getting to know you all." He turns to Dan. "It's real good to see you again."

Dan shrugs, looking like he's privy to an entirely different commentary on the scene than the rest of us. Raife leaves, waving to Jed on the way out, the ripple of appraising female eyes following his slow stroll.

Dan

It's a fabulous record player.

If only he had a bigger collection of records to play. It's either Maria Callas or Nat King Cole. Maria's too emotional for tonight and Nat makes him feel like he should be wrapping Christmas presents.

Dan pulls off his glasses and rubs his eyes, the glare of the computer screen illuminates the dark red wine that waits untouched in a large glass beside the keyboard. Pushing the chair back from his seat at the table, he strolls barefoot across the cool tile floor to the old 'Dansette'. The turntable clicks as the record spins and slows to a halt, the arm returning smoothly back to its resting point.

He was given the player by a patient, an elderly lady he'd visited at home until her death. She'd known he'd loved her old retro player, a blue and cream striped wooden box on four legs. She'd left it to him in her Will along with a few records, and the scratchy sounds of those smooth melodies are part of his downtime routine. Late at night, when the day's tasks are done, he clips open the box lid, stacks a few records and lowers the needle carefully on to the spinning ebony discs. Those grooves create a magical sound you just can't recreate with anything else. It sounds like the past.

He would have fitted in so well there, back in that era. He'd drive a shiny new red Chevy with white leather seats and wear a cardigan with his name on the back. The past is so easy to think about, reference to and enjoy. It's the future that causes all the problems.

He doesn't want to listen anymore. He's restless and edgy. Returning to the computer he settles back into his seat and stares at the screen, reading and re-reading the text.

'*…incurable genetic disease… clogging of lungs… suppressed immune function…*'

Dan reaches for the wine glass without taking his eyes from the words. He takes a long slow sip, skimming over the paragraph he's read too many times.

'*…damaged lungs, scarred from infection cannot effectively supply sufficient oxygen to the body making the sufferer susceptible to suffocation.*'

Setting the wine glass down he closes his eyes, nodding slowly in thought. When he opens them his expression is focused. He clicks on the email icon and begins to type. Message composed he presses 'send'. The message on its way to his friend; Dr Jan Roitner, Head of Clinical Research at the James Lewis Cystic Fibrosis Centre in Baltimore.

Dan knows the prognosis, understands the facts, but before he talks to Sadie he wants to be sure he's aware of any new research which might give her future hope; hope that the current statistics clearly don't. The whole thing has thrown him off kilter.

Pushing back the chair, he raises his bare feet and crosses them on the corner of the table. Lifting the glass, he swirls the wine around, watching as it clings to the inside of the glass leaving a thin film of translucent red. Another sip, the taste full, the slow hum of alcohol seeps gracefully into his bloodstream flowing smoothly to his brain. The world slows down and so does he.

There are days when the usual philosophies and mantras just don't cut it. Even with the Dansette playing, the wine and the night; spectacular with smell and sound - there remains an edge he can't smooth. Dan likes things in their place: people, emotions and possessions. He likes the comfort of clean lines and smooth edges.

Right now, things don't fit. Something in the fabric of life all around is unsettled, and he's unsure how to fix it.

But hey, it's been a long day. He's feeling drowsy after his 5 am yoga start. Wine glass in hand, feet crossed on the table, Dan's head lolls forward as his eyes droop. He wakes only when the red wine soaks through his shirt and the glass smashes on the ground. The accompanying shock sends him tumbling from the chair on to all fours on the floor.

A loud knock at the door startles him from his incredulous position on the floor. It's like a scene from 'Freddy's Revenge': Dan's white shirt is red with wine and his palms and knees bleed from the broken wine glass he un-ceremonially landed on.

"What the fuck?" Another knock. "Hold up! I'm just bleeding out in here. Let me seal up a few arteries and I'll be right with you."

"Dan, its Jack. You okay in there?"

Dan hobbles to the door.

"Jesus, what happened here?" Jack is wide-eyed.

Dan's pretty wide-eyed himself, from drowsy slumber to awake on the floor; drenched in wine and shredded by his own glass.

"Oh, this?" He glances down at himself. "Just a suicide pact with the cat gone wrong."

"Good to see you - I think."

"Well come in quick before I lose any more blood. My floors will never recover." He looks down. "Goddamn, look at my shirt. This is Armani. The wine will never come out."

Dan limps back through the house, heading for the bathroom. Jack follows. "Was it a party for one?"

"Something like that."

Jack looks around at the glass and wine on the floor and heads to the kitchen for cleaning supplies. "I've only been away for a few months. I didn't expect to find you in such a state." He bends to brush up the glass.

"Well, you never called, what's a guy to do? Jesus… that hurt." Dan's voice is raised from the bathroom.

"Okay in there?"

"Just removing a few glass shards."

Minutes later Dan hobbles through, wearing some loose trousers and a clean shirt, a few sterile strips on his hands. Jack has mopped up the wine and is looking in the fridge for beer.

"Heard you were back today. Wondered when I'd get to witness the hairy face myself."

Jack grins. "News travels fast."

"You bet. Billie sent me a text this morning - three words: *Jack's gotta beard!*"

"Big news then."

"Big news…for Billie." Dan watches him carefully.

Jack turns away, his eyes skimming over the slick appliances and stainless steel surfaces in Dan's kitchen. "How've you been?"

"My God, finally someone asks about Dr Dan! I'm thrilled you're here. I knew someone would care. How long do you have?"

Jack turns back to face him, eyes narrowed in concern.

"Relax, I'm kidding. Same old, same old here. Every day's another day in paradise, right?"

"Right." Jacks smiles gently. "Severing that artery has made you cynical."

"Yeah well, I've been a doctor around this place for a long time. A guy can know too much." He pauses, turning to look out the window at the settling darkness. "Sometimes I think I'd like to start again, a new place where I didn't know anyone or their business. I wouldn't know who's got boils and bunions, who's divorcing who, having a breakdown, or on Prozac."

He turns back, lifting an injured hand to the light, examining it for further glass remnants. "Just for today I'd like not to know. Then I'd be able to imagine that everyone's life was '*happy, fucking, joy, joy*'." He shakes his head slowly, sighing wearily. "That's the trouble Jack. It never is."

"Bad day?"

Dan looks up and shrugs. "I'm just tired. Some days there's more bad news than good, and usually I'm the guy who has to deliver it."

Jack nods slowly. "I wish I could help you man, but I agree. Feels like nothing's been easy for a long time." He sinks heavily into a chair. Dan follows and they sip their beer in silence for a moment before Jack continues. "Amandine's not herself, I'm not sure what to do."

"What wrong with her?"

"She's getting confused, forgetting things, then gets real upset."

"How long has she been like this?"

"I'm not sure. Saul won't talk much about it. Jess said it's been a while and it's getting worse." Jack leans forward, elbows resting on his knees. "She can't remember things, gets all mixed up. Sometimes she starts talking like its twenty years ago, then starts crying about her Mama's death like it just happened."

There's a long pause as the information settles. Dan nods slowly. When Jack looks up his expression is expectant. The look of hope crushes the word waiting on Dan's lips: *Dementia.* He won't say it out loud, Jack already knows. But still, his eyes are fixed on Dan as though he might have the magic answer and will prescribe a nice tonic to bring her back to herself.

"Has she been to a doctor yet?"

"Joseph won't take her and won't let anyone else. Denies there's anything wrong. Whenever anyone tries to talk to him about it, he says she's tired. Even said me being around is the problem, brings all that sadness back."

"He's an old bastard."

Jack nods ruefully. "What can I do?"

"Do Jess and Saul keep a close eye on her?"

"They're there every day."

Dan surveys his friend closely taking a moment before answering. "I guess for now they need to be watching her closely, make sure she's not getting worse or endangering herself. Get the old bastard drunk and get her to a doctor. She's going to need some help if she deteriorates."

Jack sits up and rubs a hand over his beard, his eyes troubled. "So, there's not much chance it's something that will get better."

Dan shakes his head slowly, heart heavy. "I'm sorry Jack but I don't think that's likely. I could be wrong. But from what you're saying, I think it's more likely she'll get worse."

"God damn!" Jack makes a fist, nursing it in his palm. "God damn." Quieter this time, tone resigned, fingers running over the knuckles of his balled fist.

"I'm sorry man."

Jack gathers himself, shaking his head, waving a hand briefly in protest. "I asked you."

"Want me to talk to Saul?"

"No." He shakes his head decisively. "No, its fine."

Silence rests in the room as the hard facts of a new reality build another wall that must be scaled. Jack's eyes are on the window, lost in darkness and pinpricks of hopeful starlight. Dan examines his hands, deft fingers and smooth skin; healing hands. The thought brings frustration to the contemplative quiet - *healing hands* - what a fucking joke.

Jack turns from the window and smiles wryly at Dan's expression. "Well, you'll be feeling better now that I dropped by to cheer you up. All that cynical *'life's a bitch'* talk, you'll be glad I came to join the party."

Dan is glad for the return of humour. "How did I get by while you were gone? My own little ray of sunshine." He folds his arms sighing heavily. "Oh, and by the way, welcome home."

Jack grins, sips the last of his beer, and pushes his chair back to stand. "Well, it's been a real fun time but this ray of sunshine's got to go."

"Hey, I'm kidding…sort of, stay a while. I'm on an unlucky roll, if you go that wine glass might come back for me."

"Can't, just swung in on the way past. I've got to pick up Raife. He's at Santos, trying to sweet-talk Bastian into a gig."

Dan keeps nodding. "And you guys are okay?"

Jack shrugs noncommittally. "I'm going to help him get on his feet."

"Think I've heard that before."

"Yeah well, this is the last time."

"Heard that before too."

"Give me a break Dan. What else am I supposed to do?"

"Let him sort his own shit out for once. You don't owe him anything."

Jack's stands behind the chair, knuckles paling as his grip tightens. "Trouble with that Dan, is I do."

He walks to the door and when he turns back to Dan, his smile has returned. "Catch you tomorrow. Take care of those war wounds. It's good to see you."

"Yeah, yeah. Good to see you too." Dan's voice follows Jack through the door. "You and all that joy…you're killing me." He sighs, watching Jack hop into his truck and reverse out of the drive. "And get rid of that beard!" He shouts from the window pointing to his own chin.

Jack waves, beeps the horn and disappears around the corner.

Its midnight when Dan wakes with a start on the sofa, dry mouthed, hands and knees throbbing. The room is black aside from the flicker of his laptop screen saver in the far corner. God, why did he finish that bottle of red?

He'd felt belligerent, sitting on his own, pouring the third glass, telling himself he needed a few drinks, just to relax. It's a funny thing having no-one to observe your actions, no-one to question your intentions or justify your behaviour to. Liberating yet lonely.

He loves living alone. He's tried twice to live with partners, but both attempts at domesticity were a disaster. He'd hated having someone in his precious space, and both good relationships quickly turned sour. Living alone, Dan can keep to his routine, can micro manage the aspects of his life that give him peace. Yet tonight, he feels different. Dan feels the quiet, the lack of empathy from his sparse furnishings and designer kitchen appliances.

He wants someone to talk to, someone to listen, someone that gets him. Because this feeling is a new one, this sourness with life and his place in it, it's strange and unwelcome. He's never questioned his profession or his vocation. It's what he was born to do, it's what he's good at. He's familiar with tragedy, illness, disease and depression. So why now, does he feel shaken by the futility of it all, and his inability to make a difference?

Reaching above he flips on a lamp, drinks some water and heads to his laptop where the email icon celebrates the arrival of 7 new items in his inbox.

Roitner has replied already: a short business-like note, updating Dan on his latest projects and the health of his wife and children. Attached are two recently produced papers on cystic fibrosis, describing trialling of new treatments and drugs, new statistics and information on progress with existing studies.

Dan taps the paperclip icon and the first 37-page document opens readily. His eyes reflect the white, blue glare of the screen in the semi-dark room, blinking and refocusing from sleep to study.

Scrolling down, he reads carefully. Gradually the quiet despair is replaced, page by page with calm resolve. He is a professional, a scientist, grounded by research and medicine. An internal tug of war is underway as Dan tucks away the personal. Fact by precious medical fact, illness and cures, patients and ailments become separate, unrelated to anyone he knows or loves. Disease: a collection of diagnosed problems to be researched and treated appropriately.

His head begins to pulse with the beginnings of a hangover and he winces, removing his attention from the bright screen to rub his temples gently. Medicine has never felt so claustrophobically close. Never in all his years of studying, never in his time in practice has it seemed so closely aligned with his own emotions. Tonight Dan's resilience is depleted, but he knows in the morning things will be different. With this thought, he carefully closes the laptop and hobbles down the hall to bed.

Tomorrow is always the best place to start.

Chapter Eight

Jack

Driving in the dark, around the narrow, twisting roads of St. Cloud is something Jack can do with his eyes closed. He knows the island like a lover. Each bend is familiar. The rise and fall of the asphalt trails that traverse and caress it, etched to memory, beloved. This island is home and he has travelled these roads most days of his life.

There are memories embedded in these roads; some he likes to recall and others he tries to forget. But the familiarity is comforting; on these roads Jack knows where he's going.

Driving in the dark with Raife beside him Jack can only remember where he's been.

Tonight there is no comfort in the familiar roads. Familiarity rests in the tension that crackles between them - tension felt most strongly here on these roads. Where the last time they drove side by side was the moment one life ended and another began.

Raife looks relaxed, leaning back in the passenger seat, one arm resting against the closed window smeared with rain. Jack hadn't expected this; the sudden rush of fear, the tightness in his chest and throb in his temples. They say the body remembers.

Instinctual knowledge of the road and its predictable route is gone. Jack frowns, concentrating on each bend, anticipating disaster around each corner. The rain falls steadily and he's sweating, palms slippery on the steering wheel. As he flips the wipers on high their rhythm becomes frantic, a wild squeal of wet rubber on glass as they push streams of water across the windscreen. The sound does nothing to calm his racing heart.

He needs to settle down. He feels trapped under an incoming tidal wave. Sweating heavily his breath comes short, his chest tight. Panic, fear borne from shadows made physical through denial. If he doesn't push it away it will stop. Self-talk meant to reassure, is quickly overwhelmed by frustration and anger. He's a fool - a desperate fool - scared of the past and tortured by his inability to change it. In this car, at this moment, Jack is seventeen and scared, and no-one can help him.

Raife leans his head back, closes his eyes and begins to whistle quietly. The memory is complete; the radio playing the same song, the rhythm of the rain and bleak darkness of night. A drive that's endless in his memory with Raife - and Lil.

"Stop it."

Raife stops but doesn't look at Jack, he stares out through the rain streaked window. "Don't you like that one? Funny, used to be my favourite, but not anymore." He traces a line across the foggy glass of the passenger seat window. "Not anymore."

Jacks hands tighten on the wheel. He'd like to shout, maybe lash out, hit the self-pitying asshole in the face. But he doesn't. Instead he breathes and drives, focusing on the road and the safe passage of the truck home. What's between them can't be solved or healed. They won't talk about it or try to make it better - they can't. Jack will wear it. Like he's always done. He'll wear it and live it because he deserves to.

As the truck weaves its careful route home, Raife begins to whistle again. Jack doesn't protest or look around. Beside him the relaxed expression on Raife's face masks an unforgiving tension in his rigid body.

Pulling into the drive at Frontiere Point Jack breathes, air floods his lungs with welcome relief. The panic has subsided. The vivid images are gone. He turns off the ignition, and flips off the high beams. Heavy rain on the roof is a whisper amidst the thundering silence between them. A series of excited barks break the taut air as Louie and Bets bound through the darkness, coats gleaming wet, tails wagging furiously. Jack opens the door to the rain and wet-dog-welcome as Raife reaches for his arm.

"Do you ever wonder what would have happened if things had been different?"

Raife's voice is sincere, his question disarmingly honest. For a moment Raife's guard is down and as Jack turns to him, he is sure the pained expression is real.

Frozen by the half open truck door, Jack watches Raife, trying to gauge if this is just another game. "I think about it all the time."

By the time the words are spoken, Raife's expression has changed and the air crackles once again. The glimpse of vulnerability gone. He's out of the car and jogging through the rain to the house with Louie and Bets on his heels.

Jack sinks back in his seat and lets the half open door swing closed. Ahead the light clicks on in the house above the workshop, a watery glow smeared and unfocused though the rain-soaked windscreen. He closes his eyes and sees her, Lil smiling and beckoning him forward. The past is all around, soaking the present red.

Like a conduit to the past, Raife's presence plunges him back into a sea of regret. Eyes on the light flowing in pale wet rivulets, he wonders if he ever really left that sea. If maybe he's survived the past few years on an insubstantial life boat. He feels heavy. Maybe it's the rain and the distant sound of the ocean, but the feeling of sinking is everywhere. His lifeboat is no longer seaworthy.

Jack presses his hands heavily over his face till the darkness behind his eyelids flashes with pinpricks of jagged light. If he's to have a future, he must reconcile the past. Lowering his hands to his beard he rests his fingers on the course hair, rubbing his cheeks and chin methodically until he knows how to begin.

Billie

Such a lot of rain this month, St. Cloud streets puddle and pool and the skies loom moodily, always threatening downpour. I miss the light. When it remains low and the day stays grey, my mood seems to follow.

For days now, the light has barely lifted from black to inky grey. Sullen skies remain till sunset, when the grey turns gradually darker and dissolves into night. Storms are regular. If you watch closely enough you can see the cycle: the gradual darkening of clouds above, until so heavy with moisture they hang desperate for release, then the first drop, followed by the inevitable downpour.

The bush drips and vibrates with rain. I imagine I can hear the celebration of all those vines and palms as they drink and bathe, lavishing their leaves and roots in the joy of monsoon. Aside from the grey, weighty feel of the skies and the damp air, there's something else, something quite beautiful. Life becomes a fluid watercolour image of itself. Details are blurred and the edges of form uncontained. From a distance things seem to merge and flow in a way that makes the world seem less formal, less deliberate. And I find myself thinking about just that; the form and outline of life.

Are the edges of our life paths blurry like the watercolour rainy garden? Is the future shaped with the pull of self will or simple fate? Does it merge and flow more freeform than planned path? This lack of rigidity in what I see transmutes to what I feel. I find myself more open to a future that I cannot plan nor predict. So far, trying to control and sway my destiny and that of those I love has been spectacularly unsuccessful.

The air is warm and moisture laden. It's 11pm and I can't sleep. Rain is loud on the roof, but that's not what's keeping me awake. I'm unsettled for reasons I can't explain. I can't sleep. I can't write. I don't want to read.

I'm not sure why.

The twins sleep peacefully in two twin beds, not cots. Another change I am getting used to. I lie on the cool floor between their beds and their quiet breath brings me comfort. After the lying, and the listening, and the reassuring myself I'm an okay mother, and contemplating how much I love my children (especially when they're asleep), I still can't sleep.

Heading to the deck outside I lower myself into the swing seat. This part of the deck is covered and so I recline back to look out on the damp darkness, and listen to the rain. I hear the sound of a car approaching, headlights shine down Jack's driveway illuminating his house. The dogs are barking and running. I hear voices, a door slamming and shortly after Jack's lights flick on.

It's nice to know he's there. I imagine what he might be doing, and now I really can't sleep. Watching his window, I see Raife, not Jack, moving back and forward and I'm momentarily angry. It's irrational, I know, but he's spoiled my fantasy.

I extend a toe to push down on the ridges of warm wood below and the swing seat rocks back and forward, creaking on rusty fastenings. Raife stands by the kitchen window where Jack should be, nursing a glass in his hand, and he's looks over like he can see me. I know that I'm invisible, bathed in darkness, all the lights behind me are out and there's no moonlight through the low cloud, so I watch him too.

He stares, lifts the glass to his lips then brings a hand to his face, he runs the hand through his hair and seems to be nodding. That's when I realise that of course he isn't looking at me, he's looking at himself, appraising his reflection. The blonde head turns and disappears from the window. Moments later I hear music, turned loud, the sound softened by heavy rain.

"Hey."

The shock of the voice in the darkness makes me slap my hands to my mouth in fright, pushing back the scream that was about to rush forth. Luckily the scream heads south, but my deft motion sends the swing seat flying and I'm propelled face forward, down on to the deck.

"Are you okay?" Jack steps into my line of vision.

"Jesus Jack! I just lost a life."

I'm on all fours on the deck, the swing seat rocking behind me, making contact with my butt and nudging me forward. "God, you scared me." The swing seat comes forward again, "Ouch." I struggle to stand and he extends a hand to help me up.

"Sorry."

He guides me to my feet by my elbow. I'm sure I can see the corners of his mouth upturn with the hint of a smile.

"You don't sound sorry." I rub my butt and frown up at him. "What are you doing here?" He doesn't answer. "Scaring the crap out of a lady trying to relax of an evening."

"That was the funniest thing I've seen all day." He's still holding on to my elbow.

"Well, good for you. Glad I could help." I pretend to be annoyed but, of course I'm thrilled to see him.

"I was getting out of the car and saw the swing moving. I figured you might have another touch of insomnia. So I thought I'd…"

"You thought you'd come help the insomnia by giving me a heart attack?"

Now he does smile, releasing my arm and rubbing his beard with a hand. "Something like that."

"Are you okay?" He looks exhausted. "Want to come inside? I'll make some tea."

"I don't want tea." Despite the smile there's something serious in his eyes.

"Okay." I nod.

He holds the swing seat steady and motions me to sit down. I do and he sits heavily beside me. We swing in silence for a while, but it isn't awkward. Silence has never been awkward with Jack. It's another blurry line; the fade between talk and silence, one seamlessly drifts into the other and both always feel natural. The rain batters above. My toes are wet so I lift my feet and hug my knees as we sit side by side, swinging gently in silence.

"Will you do something for me?" He looks ahead into the darkness and the rain, past the light in his window, beyond the place where the music emanates.

"Of course." I answer without hesitation, and I mean it, although I have no idea what I'm agreeing to.

The air crackles with the possibilities in his question. What would I do for him?

"Will you shave my beard?"

I bite my lip in a bid not to laugh because his eyes are wretched. He watches me carefully; the air between us suddenly charged and expectant. I wonder if he's joking, but his eyes are dark and he isn't smiling. The moment is so unexpectedly intimate I look away.

"Will you?"

"You want me to shave your beard?" I smile, my expression incredulous. "Right now?"

He nods without a trace of humour and I realise that this is of course, not about the beard. There's an entire lifetime of Jack I don't know, a past I haven't been part of and might never understand. Consumed by my own struggles, I always assumed Jack was okay, never swayed or unhinged. I'm the one that does the wobbling. Yet here he is unsteady and unsure. For the first time I see him clearly, looking beyond what I've always needed from him, to wonder what he might need from me.

Smiling, I lean forward and lay my hand flat on the side of his face, his beard is damp and rough beneath my fingertips. "Let's do this."

I can't say what has propelled him through the rain with this request that makes no sense, but I clap my hands together seriously and assume the expression of someone planning major surgery.

I tiptoe back through the dark house with Jack behind me. In the bathroom I fill the sink with hot steamy water and rummage around for the appropriate hardware necessary for the task ahead. When I return from the kitchen armed with scissors and a fresh towel Jack stands awkwardly in the centre of the bathroom, the low ceiling making him appear much taller then he actually is.

"All systems go." I brandish my scissors. He doesn't move. "Come on, you'll have to sit down. I can't reach you up there." His expression is far away and I doubt he's heard a word I've said. "Jack." I touch his arm, he blinks and smiles quickly. "Are you okay?"

"Sure."

"I mean, I'm okay with weird, you know me, but this is - well - really weird."

"I know."

He begins to unbutton his shirt and I stand before him scissors in hand, pulse quickening. He removes his shirt then pulls his tee-shirt over his head. I'm staring but can't look away.

Stillness. Jack before me, watching me watching him. A force inside wills me forward. It would be the most natural thing in the world to take a step toward him, place a hand on his chest, reach up and kiss him. But I will my feet to stay where they are as my eyes travel up over his chest to meet his stare. Flushed and unsteady I look at him as long as I dare, waiting for him to look away first. But he doesn't.

The Jack I know would smile right now and make a joke. I'd laugh too, punch him on the arm and the moment would diffuse - but things have changed. We have changed. Life has changed around us. Jack doesn't smile, he watches me and I'm the one forced to look away.

"You'd best sit down."

He does, and sitting on a stool like this his head is level with mine. I take a breath and pray not to sever an artery with the razor. This suddenly seems like such a bad idea.

I'm channelling my grandma again, trying to keep steady. I mustn't let myself think too much. *Okay shearing sheep, that's the way forward, sheep shearing.* Every time that calming, fluffy sheep is fixed in my mind, Jack's bare chest gets in my line of vision and I have to look away.

"Are you okay with this?" Jack asks as I comb the beard and begin cutting shakily with my scissors.

"Of course." I smile. "You know there I was, lounging on the deck in the dark, wondering when another hairy guy would come and ask me for a shave. You've no idea how busy business is. I hardly get any sleep these days."

He smiles and I relax a little. "What's going on?"

"Nothing." He pauses. "I just want to start tomorrow fresh."

"And shaving the beard will help you do that?" I giggle a little. "You could try showering, that always works for me. Although I have to be honest, I'm glad the beard's getting the heave ho. It gets in my way."

"It does?"

God, I feel a blush rise quickly and remind myself every thought does not need a voice.

"Be quiet, you'll make me spear you." Feigning concentration, I push ahead and dark hair falls in soft clumps on the tiles below. When the scissors have done their work Jack soaps his face and I ready the razor. He sits before me all serious eyes and Santa-Claus-soapy-beard.

I take a moment to capture the image in my head: *Jack half naked in my bathroom with white soapy beard.* I let the razor warm in the hot water.

"You could have done this yourself."

"I know."

I take a step forward and begin the slow smooth glide of blade over skin. "And why didn't you?"

"Because I wanted you to."

I don't pursue this because I like his answer, and I like the deep timbre of his voice as he says it.

Stroke by careful stroke Jack appears. I can't help but smile. The disguise falls away and soon he sits before me as I remember him: the strong lines of his face and jaw, the curve of lips and square set of his chin. His skin gleams. When I'm sure every hair of the beard is good and gone, I wipe a warm towel across his face gently, drying and stroking, letting my fingers brush the softness of his skin.

Jack's eyes are closed and his breathing even. There's no trace that he feels anything other than sleepy, but as I dab the towel around his ear he reaches up and grabs my hand. The hold is tight and I freeze. His eyes flash open and the look takes my breath away. I stand before him unable to move, locked by the hand that holds me. He reaches for my waist and pulls me in. The towel drops to the floor and I let myself fall into him.

The kiss is slow and tender. Jack lifts me gently and I wrap my legs around his waist. He tastes of sadness and soap. And there in the bathroom, amidst the remnants of his beard, we kiss.

As his hands tighten behind me and I feel the press of his chest and thump of his heart, I pull away. He lets me, and we sit like that for a while, foreheads together, lips inches apart. He strokes my back gently, my legs knotted tightly around him. We don't have to say it, we both know. Not now. Not yet. We must tread carefully; our pasts gather heavily around our ankles.

Much later, after he's gone, after I've swept the bathroom floor and showered in cool water, I return to bed. But sleep is far away. Rain is relentless on the roof and my mind is full of Jack.

Do I deserve two great loves in one short lifetime? Is there room in my packed heart for the love Jack deserves when Evan will always rest there? I think of Cam having lost Mom, content to be alone, with his one great love gone he had no need for another. Then I think of Mom, if she hadn't made room in her heart for Cam after Dad, then a lifetime of happiness would be lost.

What feels so right and true seems wrong. Is it too soon? Am I fooling myself and Jack? Is it really possible to love fully after Evan, after everything that happened? It doesn't seem so long ago I'd embraced a stronger, independent self. Alone without Evan I could see how my life had been shaped and controlled by him. I'd become lost in him. I can't afford to let that happen again.

But is love something we can control? I might fight it forever and live a lesser life; what for? Evan can't be betrayed now, he is gone. I am the one left here alone. My thoughts leave me exhausted. There are no simple solutions. My heart tells me one thing and my head another. There is so little I seem to be able to control, why would love be any different?

When finally I fall to sleep, my dreams are littered with birds and rain. I dream I am flying but keep returning to the same spot. No matter how many graceful flights I take, my wings deliver me to the same place I started. When morning rushes in I wake unprepared for the day. The rain has stopped. The birds sing, and the morning sun glows pale and promising, rising slowly over the edge of the ocean.

Dog's breath isn't the ideal welcome to his day but it's what he's used to. Raising himself slowly on to an elbow, Jack yawns and squints through the sharp fingers of sunlight that cross the dusty workshop floor. Louie shifts his position and stretches his body, letting the sun caress his back. Sensing movement, Bets trots from her spot in the corner to lie beside Louie. She flops in the sun behind him letting her head rest on his back and both dogs close their eyes once more.

In the house above Jack hears the thump of feet, walking back and forward. A radio plays and the pipes creak as water flows to an open faucet in the kitchen.

He has overslept; first peaceful sleep in months and his body feels good. A little stiff maybe, but good. Returning from Billie's last night he wanted to be alone with his thoughts, didn't feel like dealing with Raife. He'd come straight to the boatshed where he'd lain down on the old sofa with Louie and Bets beside him. He'd fallen asleep amidst the wood shavings with the taste of Billie still on his lips.

He didn't dream, thank God. The dreams of late have been more frequent; each time another memory in random order, the details different but always Raife, always Lil.

Last night his sleep was black and dreamless, silence in his head for a time. The phone rings but he doesn't jump to answer it. He sits for a while, stroking the dogs, looking across the workshop at the sunlight. Golden beams slice across the unfinished hull of his latest boat, another labour of love. She's a real rescue, an old sailboat he found in St. Eloise. Left to age ungracefully on a private mooring, he'd enquired about her and found she'd belonged to an elderly local who passed on two years before. The man's family had inherited his farm and the unseaworthy boat had been left to the elements. Untended the weathered craft had deteriorated further and the family had been happy to sell it. Jack had arranged for her to be towed to St. Cloud where he'd picked her up at the docks.

She'll take a lot of work but that's exactly what he needs. Given time he'll bring her back to life and be able to sell her for a sweet price. She has good bones. Sometimes it's hard to see beyond the rot and neglect to what's underneath. To see what a boat once was and what she can become again. That's the part he loves the most, seeing beyond the imperfections and work, the vision of possibility. He's is a patient guy. He knows what's worth waiting for and working for. It's what he's best at.

Listening to the muffled tone of Raife's voice upstairs on the phone he rises. The dogs stir then relax as he moves slowly around the dilapidated boat. He lets a hand trail the rough surface of weathered wood stopping where a sunbeam falls on barely visible script. Once brightly painted the letters are faded; sun and sea have robbed her of her name. Jack traces a finger around the washed out script: *Galileo.*

Ten minutes later he heads upstairs to grab some coffee before a day in the workshop. Raife's voice can be heard from the top of the steps; deep, silky tones that drift out on to the deck from the open door.

"I will, soon, I promise…No, not right now. I need to straighten some things out first."

Raife lies on the sofa his back to Jack, feet up; one hand supports his head, the other holding the phone to his ear. He doesn't hear Jack behind him.

"Yeah, Jack mentioned it… tell Saul to stop fretting like an old woman." Raife laughs. "They wonder why I've been away so long. Between Jack and Saul you'd think…" Jack coughs interrupting the conversation. He walks in through the open doors toward the kitchen.

"Aha, here he is now Jess. Yep, he's been out all night. No, he's fine, Jack's always fine, right Jack?"

Jack smiles, Jess will be checking in, checking up on Raife. She knows him well enough. She'll want to know when he's going to go see Joseph and Amandine.

"I'm gonna play some music. I got a gig at Santos. Bastion's a funny old bastard, had to twist his arm but Josefina persuaded him to let me play next week…Yeah… Hey listen I gotta go. Jack's making me coffee."

Jack rolls his eyes and pulls another cup from the cupboard.

"Take care of yourself now. I'm real happy Saul wasn't firing blanks after all." Raife laughs, obviously being scolded on the other end from Jess who won't find the joke at all funny. But then, maybe she will - everyone has a soft spot for Raife. "You want to speak to Jack? No…Don't get her… I'll speak to her next…"

There's a long pause, when Jack turns around Raife's face has dropped. When he speaks the confidence of before has gone. Jack hears Raife's voice slow and soften, a tone reserved solely for their mother. He doesn't want to eavesdrop. Picking up the coffee cups he walks toward Raife. He'll pass him the coffee then give him some privacy. Raife needs to speak to Amandine alone.

Jack has tried to talk to him about her, but Raife doesn't want to hear. He shrugs off the topic, telling Jack to *quit being the family drama queen'*. A conversation with their mother is the only thing that will make Raife take it seriously. Until now it's a conversation he's expertly avoided. But now as he hears Raife speak, he can't help but hope Amandine is lucid, if only to delay the inevitable moment of realisation. The conversation will crush him.

Raife has stayed away for a long time not only to escape from the past, but to put distance between himself and Amandine. Their mother was the only one Raife never tried to wise ass or lie to. She always knew him better than anyone. He couldn't bear to hurt her and staying away made that easier.

"I'm good Mama…Soon, I promise."

Raife glances up at Jack as he places the steaming cup on the table before heading to the door and the quiet of the workshop. But Raife raises a hand to stop him, the action a plea. Jack stops coffee in hand, waiting awkwardly by the sofa. He shakes his head but Raife motions again for him to wait. Childish fear flashes across Raife's face and Jack is transported back in time.

Jack was younger but somehow he'd always been the one to cover for Raife, stand up for him and clean up the mess he usually left behind. He'd grown up knowing that's what you did for your brother, Raife said so, and he'd always done it. Always.

The look is the same but this is different. He doesn't want to see Raife crumple, it's not fair.

"It's okay Mama. Stop…It's okay…" Raife looks away and runs a hand over his face. "No… it's Raife… Mama, it's Raife."

There's a long pause as Raife listens, eyes open, expression closed. When Jack reaches the deck he hears Raife repeat himself; his tone less soft, less sure.

At the bottom of the stairs he hears only the murmur of conversation above. He can't hear the words or the tone. He waits. Jack stands back to the wall, hands clenched around his cup, eyes on *Galileo*; no stars.

Moments later Raife's footsteps beat down through the boards; a few swift strides and a slamming door. Something flies overhead, a sweeping arc of silver and black as the phone soars and spins over the yard before descending gracelessly into the bush. The footsteps retreat and the door bangs a noisy conclusion before silence.

Jack exhales slowly and sets his coffee down on the workbench. He is bound to Raife. He knows what he's feeling and there's nothing to be done. Their gatekeeper is slipping into another world?

They were all gone, avoiding life the best they could. They neglected her, wasted time hoping for some kind of repentance, each living out their guilt in different ways. Those years had been hard on Amandine and they hadn't known, wrapped up in getting through.

They'd neglected their foundation, the mother that built her world on her boys. Amandine had slipped away and they hadn't been there. Only Saul stayed, his proximity blinding him to gradual change. Facing a confused and upset Amandine, it was easier to blame it on something else, tell himself she was just tired. Now, only when the truth is unavoidable he is forced to face it.

Thank God for Jess, brave and practical. But what now? Now that they can all see it. Now that they can't pretend or deny, what now? The options are unclear and he's afraid. He'll call Saul tonight and talk it through. He'll give Raife time, maybe then he'll want to talk. Maybe it's time they went home together.

All is quiet in the work shed, not a sound now from upstairs. Jack examines *Galileo* critically, reigning in untidy emotions to store them safely in the confines of the work shed where his tools will make good of them. His attachment to the past and need to recreate it will find its channel here.

Jed

The phone rings out. Where is she? Jed sets the handset on the counter and smiles reassuringly at the line of customers extending out of the door.

"Hell Jed, what's the deal today? "Felix's blond head towers over the line of increasingly impatient locals. "Do friends get to line jump?"

Jed doesn't normally do 'stressed' but his cheeks are red and there's a hum in his ears. "You can get your ass behind this counter and give me a hand."

"But I can't make coffee."

"Get back here anyway." Customers' heads turn from Jed to Felix, listening with faint amusement to the exasperation in Jed's tone. "Come on man. Sadie's late and I'm on my own! I'll make you free coffee for the week."

Felix considers the offer, then weaves his way through Beaujangles to reach the counter littered with orders scribbled on paper, coins, take away cups and paper trays. "You owe me." He smiles widely at the waiting customer who looks apprehensive.

"Two takeaway lattes and a long black with soy…but I don't want you making them."

Felix places a hand on his heart. "I'm crushed." He rings the order into the till. "Jed did you hear them? They don't want me."

Jed slides four coffees along the counter to Felix signalling lids and a paper tray. "Don't let them get to you. I want you. These are for Marianne waiting over by the window, then take these over to table seven."

Felix shrugs, smiles at the waiting line and gets to work.

Half an hour later the early rush has passed and Jed leans on Monica, wiping his forehead with the back of his forearm. Felix reaches the cluttered counter with another tray of dirty cups, a tea towel draped over his shoulder and an apron around his waist.

"Thanks man. You saved my life."

"Who would have known waitressing was my thing."

"Yeah," Jed smiles, Felix looks so out of place. "Anytime you need a career change, I'm your man."

"What time is it?" Felix's smile evaporates. "Shit I was supposed to get coffee then go pick up Zoe from her doctor's appointment." He throws the tea towel at Jed and pulls at his apron strings.

"Sorry man. Tell her it's my fault. I don't know where the hell Sadie is. She was supposed to be here at eight."

"Quick, whip me up a couple of coffees before I run. If I turn up late and without coffee, I'm done for."

Jed gets to work. "She doing okay?"

"Three weeks to go. She's grumpy as hell." He sinks into a chair while Jed finishes the coffee.

The door dings as Sadie enters, she smiles quickly at Felix avoiding Jed's eyes.

"Hey guys."

She glances around at the mess of dirty cups and uncleared tables. "What are you sitting down for? Look at this place." She tries to scurry past Jed, grabbing a few cups from a table on the way past.

"Where have you been? I called home four times and you didn't pick up." Jed's usually easy-going expression is tight.

Sadie shrugs. "Sorry, I overslept."

"Overslept? Are you kidding me? Its ten o'clock. Jesus Sadie, I was swamped and if it hadn't been for Felix, I'd have been screwed."

Her pale face flushes red. "I said I'm sorry." Turning on her heel she strides to the kitchen.

Felix stands awkwardly, picking up the coffees he heads to the door. "I'll let you know when I need that career change."

Jed's eyes turn from Sadie's retreating back to Felix, he opens his palms mouthing *'What the fuck?'*

Felix shrugs. "Have fun with those dishes Sadie. Don't let him work you too hard."

Sadie's voice answers from inside the kitchen. "You bet Felix. Say hi to Zoe."

With Felix gone and Beaujangles empty of custom, the sound of angry dishes clattering in the kitchen rises above the music. Jed stands listening, his arms folded across his chest. As he rounds the corner, he's greeted by a chorus of breaking porcelain as a tray of cups slips from Sadie's hands and smashes on the tiled floor splattering his Converse with coffee dregs.

"For God's sake Sadie! Take it easy."

She's already on her knees scooping broken porcelain on to a tray. She doesn't look up. Shaking his head Jed bends down beside her, lifting shiny white cup pieces, handles, brims and broken motifs; the Beaujangles logo adorning the front of each white cup cracked in two.

"I can do it. I'm fine."

"Yeah, you sure seem fine." Her cheeks flush over the pale canvas of her face. "What's going on?" Jed asks the question before he has time to think about the repercussions of her answer. He feels closer to Sadie than anyone but it's a closeness he knows she controls. She lets him in, but not all the way. There's a part of Sadie he doesn't understand, because she won't let him. At this moment he has no idea what her answer might be: *'I'm leaving you', 'I'm pregnant', 'I have a secret life as a high class call girl'.* There are days when he's pretty sure nothing would surprise him.

Today is one of those days and today he's over it. He doesn't do well with high maintenance and lately she's been testy over a whole bunch of things. He waits for her answer, watching the top of her head bent over the mess on the floor, clearing the debris and salvaging remnants with shaking fingers.

"I'm sorry. I won't say it again. I didn't feel great this morning and I slept too long. I didn't mean to let you down."

"You can't just sleep in Sadie. This is my business. If I can't make coffee for people they'll start going someplace else. It might not seem like a big deal to you but this café is pretty much all I've got. I've worked my ass off to make it good and if you were anyone else, I'd probably fire you."

He feels better getting it all off his chest. Beaujangles means the world to him. He's built the place up from scratch. He's proud and it irks him when she acts like it's not a big deal. She still hasn't looked up from clearing the mess. "I need to know I can count on you."

She stops, frozen on her knees, hands full of broken pieces. "You know Jed…" Her eyes close and she takes a long slow breath while he waits for the words she's struggling with. "I really wish I could give you the answer you need."

Jed stands, hands on hips, head shaking in confusion. "What the hell is that supposed to mean?"

Her face snaps closed and she turns away. "Just forget it."

"You're acting crazy. I just want you to turn up when you say you will. It's important to me."

"Will you shut up? I know what's important to you. I really do. And you want to know what? I think about it all the time, and actually

I'm tired. I'm so fucking tired of always thinking about what's important to you."

She's still on her knees, sweeping shards of broken cups along the floor into an open hand.

"Hey, can you stop for a minute? Slow down, what is all this?" Anger makes way for concern. "Here, let me get that." He guides her up by her elbow but she pulls away.

"I'll get a brush."

"Stop, come here."

Sadie still won't look up. "It's fine. I'm on it. Just give me a minute and I'll get all this cleared up for you."

Jed reaches out for her retreating back. "Wait up." He pulls her around to face him. There's blood on her hands and hot tears course down her cheeks. "Hell Sadie, what is it?" The tension is gone and now he's worried.

She stands in front of him, eyes pressed tightly closed as he reaches for her hands, cut and bleeding from the broken porcelain.

"Are you okay?" She nods but doesn't open her eyes and he wraps her hands in a clean tea towel. "Do you want to talk to me?"

"There's nothing to talk about. God Jed! I was late. I broke some cups. Big deal."

"Would it kill you to be honest with me, and stop acting like a bitch?"

She pulls her hands away and brings them to her face, covering her eyes completely.

Jed's anger and hurt are overwhelmed by confusion. He doesn't get any of this and doesn't know what to do. Instinctively, his arms reach out and pull her into his chest. They stand there, beside the storeroom, folded around one another till Sadie's body quietens and the sobs that make her shoulders shake, slow and stop.

He kisses her head and she looks up, really looks at him for the first time that morning. The look is defeated, sorry and sad. Bringing a hand to his face, she smiles and runs her thumb over his eyebrow. Stroking her thumb back and forward, she watches him carefully, his expression relieved and tender. He's not sure what they've just come through, but it was something. The barrier is slowly fading and he just caught a glimpse of the other side.

There's a shift in energy, from tenderness to something quietly charged. It starts from the rhythm in her fingers, hushed tension that spreads in a careful breath.

"I love you." She speaks quietly, eyes locked on his, careful and steady.

He blinks, the spell breaks and her hands move to his belt. Jed's eyes close, his fingers slowly trail her body, finding her breasts loose under a button down shirt.

She pushes him back against the store room door. The light is low. They're alone.

He knows she's distracting him. He was too close to the boundary and now he can think of nothing but her hands easing down his Levis, and her mouth - God, that mouth. He whispers her name as his breathing comes fast and ragged.

Hands in her hair, Jed let's go as Sadie takes him, the act a small substitute for all the things she can't say. He comes quietly, hands twisted in her hair, body gradually uncoiling, softening and quietening. When he opens his eyes she's on her knees, a hand on his waist another brushing gently across her mouth. Her eyes watch him but her focus is far away.

Their breathing has barely returned to normal when a voice hollers from the café.

"What is this? Make your own day? Are you even open?" Dan's voice is irritated. "What kind of a business is this?"

Jed adjusts his jeans, heading through the kitchen and around to the café front, his face flushed and smiling. "Dan, who else would come disturbing my peace? The usual?"

Dan frowns. "Disturbing your peace? Sorry, I thought you were a bustling coffee shop. I must have made a mistake and come into the St. Cloud Centre for Meditation." He tosses his hair and looks around the empty café still cluttered with dirty cups and plates. "What happened here and where are the customers? Has there been an earthquake I missed?" He turns back to face Jed who is already at Monica loading Dan's double espresso. "And yes, I'll have my usual."

"Hey Dan." Sadie breezes around the corner from the kitchen, tying an apron around her waist, her cheeks flushed.

Dan looks carefully from one to the other and raises his eyebrows, turning back to Jed. "Really?"

Jed laughs, throwing his hand out toward the mess in the café. "We've been packed out, last customers only just left. We haven't had a chance to clear up the carnage."

"Uh huh." Dan nods sagely, hands on hips turning to watch Sadie as she busies herself, loading trays and carrying them to the kitchen. "Why do my busy mornings only consist of snotty noses, viruses and boils? You're in the right trade kid."

The opening door disturbs Dan's stream of sarcasm. In minutes several tables have filled and a new queue has formed. Dan sits at his usual table, opens out the newspaper and waits for his order. When Sadie arrives with his coffee and pastry, Beaujangles is filled with sounds of life.

"Time for a quick sit down?" Dan pats the chair beside him.

"Jed will kill me. I was so late this morning." She glances furtively over to Jed who is busy making coffees. "Just for a minute."

"How you feeling?"

"Okay, a little rough this morning. Just tired, first time in a while it's been that bad. Had to spend an extra hour on exercises. You know, those nice ones where I bash myself good and hard to get my lungs working."

Dan nods. "Maybe you're overdoing things."

"Any good news for me?" She is quick to change the subject.

"Have you spoken to the marshmallow yet?"

She flushes again and examines her hands. "Not yet."

"Sadie you need to do that. Real soon."

"I don't want to force him into a corner."

"What are you talking about?" Dan watches Sadie's serious face. Her eyes move from her hands, across the café to the coffee counter and Jed who is singing whilst frothing milk.

"I'm just afraid he'll start to feel sorry for me and it'll change the way we are together. That I won't ever really know how he feels because suddenly he's trying to take care of me." She blows out a long heavy breath. "Worse, that he'll feel trapped into staying with me."

"Jesus Sadie, how about you give the guy a little credit and let him decide for himself. Don't you think he deserves that? If the tables were turned how would you feel? Would you want him to lie to you, to try and be the tough guy?"

"I'm not trying to be tough Dan."

"Really? It sure looks that way. You don't want to accept help and you won't tell the guy who's your ticket to love and happiness what's really going on. You won't give him the chance to support you."

Sadie drops her head. "It's just that…"

"Listen, don't say anything else, I don't want to upset you." Dan squeezes her hand. "I just emailed you over a bunch of new research papers." He lowers his voice. "It's really interesting stuff: latest findings and therapies, clinical trials, new stats and facts on fertility and pregnancy. Things have come a long way in a few years. Have a read and see what you think."

She dabs at her damp eyes and throws her arms around Dan's neck. "You're such a great guy."

"I know." Dan shrugs.

"I don't mean to be a bitch."

"Who said you're a bitch?"

"Jed did." She sniffles again, "I deserved it."

Dan considers this, eyes fixed across the café at Jed behind the counter. "You know, I think you're going to find your marshmallow over there is a lot tougher than you think."

I was going to tell him just before, I really thought I would."

"And?"

"Well, then we both got mad and then…well…"

"You decided to have a quickie instead?"

Sadie blushes, fanning her face with her hands." Something like that."

"Uh oh, you've been busted. Here comes the stallion."

Sadie gets to her feet as Jed motions across the room, heading toward her.

"I'm coming!" She smiles and turns back to Dan. "Thank you. I promise I'll read your stuff tonight."

Dan nods "…and then tell lover boy."

Sadie sighs, "and then *maybe* tell lover boy." She winks and weaves her way back through the tables toward an exasperated Jed who rolls his eyes as she approaches, gesturing toward two trays filled with steaming cups.

Dan sips his coffee slowly, carefully folds his newspaper and salutes a goodbye before heading back to the surgery and the snotty noses, viruses and boils that now seem so uncomplicated and easy to treat.

Chapter Nine

Jack

From: *jessandsaulkelly@santenet.co.el*
Subject: *News*
Sent: *24/7/2008 9:42pm*

Hi Jack

Thought I'd write a note - it's easier sometimes than the phone. I never know when you'll be home, or if you'll be banging away in the work shed and not hear it ringing anyway.

I've been thinking about you and Raife and wondering how it's all going. I know what you're like. Try and be patient with him. Give it time. Saul thinks the stability of being home will be good for him. Funny, after all these years we're still trying to sort Raife's shit out. Just remember, under that tough exterior there's a good heart.

I've been worrying that I shouldn't have let Amandine speak to him on the phone. I thought it would be good for her to hear his voice, maybe jog some memories, that way she'd stop thinking Saul was Raife. I think I made things worse Jack.

She's unwell and I really want to take her to a doctor but I can't if Joseph won't let me. Saul finally realises she needs more help than we can give her. He tried to talk to Joseph about it but that went pretty badly. Joseph was drunk for two days and didn't speak to either of us for a week. I know how you feel about him right now but maybe if you'd call him it might help. Will you?

Everything else is fine, try not to worry. I think with some help from the doctor things might improve.

Work is keeping Saul busy, he's out fishing most hours, then in the orchard when I can get him on dry land. We had to get a little help from some local boys in town to harvest this year. I'm useless, you should see the size of my belly. It's incredible!

Still a while to go, I can't imagine the size I will stretch to. Saul is so excited I think he might combust by the time this baby pops out. It tires me watching him.

Nursery is all finished and looks perfect thanks to the furniture from Uncle Jack. Finishing on a happy note after pouring my worries on you…we were wondering if you'd be Godfather. What do you say? We think maybe this way, you'll have to come visit more often.

Waiting to hear from you…

Jess :)

❧

It's early when he reads Jess's email. He can hear Raife snoring next door, the damn noise is driving him crazy. Raife is driving him crazy. Something needs to happen; he just wishes he knew what it was.

He feels the weight of expectation, Jess, Saul and Joseph. They all believe he can somehow help Raife and get him back on track. What does that even mean? *Back on track*. Jack has an idea that the track Raife was headed even before the accident was never a good one.

That one night has become the reason nothing turned out as it should for Raife. It's become his excuse for everything: his *'if only'*. No-one regrets that night more than Jack, but he's pretty sure Raife would have been in trouble with or without a reason. What makes it tough is that now and forever more, the reason is Jack.

His reply is brief. He loves Jess and wants to reassure her everything's fine. He writes that he's honoured to be asked and that of course, he'll have to come home more often being that he'll be a *'kick-ass'* Godfather. He tells Jess that Raife is doing well, settling down and that soon they'll both come home.

The truth is, he's not sure when that will be. Right now Raife won't talk about going to see Amandine. Since the call where he launched the phone into the bush, he won't talk about home at all.

Jack gives Jess all the answers he hopes she needs: telling her to rest up and take care of his Godson/Goddaughter, that he'll talk to Joseph and will make sure Amandine gets the help she needs.

Happy with the letter, he feels is only partly true he presses 'send'. The thought of Jess and Saul and their baby pulls him away from the worries which will wait till later. Pulling on some old running shoes and whistling quietly for the dogs, he exits the house and the snoring and the drama.

Night makes way for day as he runs to the beach. Here he stands ankle deep as the tide pulls and rushes around his feet. Louie and Bets race back and forward for each stick he throws. Swimming and searching; all eyes and sleek black noses above the water, back and forth searching for the stick they know will be tossed once again back into the waves. The fruitlessness of their mission unimportant, lost in the thrill of the swim and chase and the white frothy caps of sea foam that follow.

Billie

"Hello? Anyone home?"

I knock again, hoping Jack will put down whatever he's doing inside and come open his front door. The twins bang with little fists and shout for Louie and Bets but no-one's around.

I'm carrying a dish of lasagne and a cheesecake on a large wooden tray. It's shameless I know, but bribery via food has worked well for me so far. I have been trading home cooking for DIY help. Jack's cooking repertoire is limited. So when I offer dinner for DIY, he seems happy to oblige.

Setting the tray down on the doorstep I motion for the twins to follow me down to the work shed. Jack's truck is in the driveway. I deduce if he isn't upstairs then he's probably down there. Evie runs ahead, pushing her way into the dusty work shed. No signs of life here.

In the middle of the room reaching almost to the roof is Galileo, Jacks current project. We stand, the three of us, in a small line, entranced. The boat glows in the afternoon sun, a shabby chic relic destined for greatness. She stands naked. Jack has stripped away everything that couldn't be salvaged. All the bad wood and rot gone. She waits proudly, quite bare but self-assured, as if she knows she will be beautiful again.

Sunny wanders forward, extending a small hand to touch the curve of the hull. He pats it like a dog then runs the flat of his palm along the side, walking as he goes till he has completed a full circuit. When he comes back around to meet us, Evie joins copying his movements exactly. The lap of the boat soon turns into a game of chase and they race round and around Galileo squealing with laughter, until finally I intervene, grab them both around the tummy and head for the door.

With both hands occupied, I push the heavy door with my back but it doesn't budge. Damn, it's always getting stuck. I bend and flex then thump the door with my bottom. Nothing. Again, a little harder. Still nothing. Evie and Sunny giggle and yell as I try for one last powerful butt thump to the stubborn door. This time it flies open, and I fly backward at speed with a small child under each arm, directly into the arms of Raife.

"Easy there." He catches me deftly, arms locked around my waist as I lower the twins shakily to the ground. "You okay?"

"Sorry, I was looking for Jack and the door got jammed."

"Right." Raife's arms remain firm on the sides of my waist.

"Thanks, I'm fine." The moment is awkward. "You can let me go."

"If you say so."

Raife is barefoot, wearing old jeans and no shirt, and my back presses into the sinewy muscle of his chest. I can smell him; an oddly erotic odour of cologne and sweat.

Blushing, I look quickly away, flustered and embarrassed by my internal reaction to 'man smell.' God, what has become of me? I'm a sex-starved, beard-shaving, man-smelling, widowed, mother to small people who are, incidentally, running around my ankles as I contemplate the eroticism of the male smell and sex.

I can't help it! I'm thinking about sex. Not with Raife, but sex, in general. And, to be honest, Jack parades around in some small shorts in this quickly formed fantasy.

Oh my God! Lock me up!

"Are you okay?" Raife's eyes twinkle in amusement.

I shake my head, clearing the fantasy which was quickly turning into a soft porn movie without the seventies moustaches. What's wrong with me?

Raife is waiting for an answer and I bluster, "Sorry for bothering you, I just came round to…"

He interrupts me. "Bring Jack food? I saw the tray. Sweet."

I don't like his tone. It makes me feel like some needy, pathetic female. "He's doing some jobs for me."

"Uh huh."

I'm hot and flustered, and a little cross. Raife is looking at me like he was privy to my private fantasy and I hate that I'm blushing.

"Look, can you just tell him I came by when he gets back?"

Raife's arms are folded across his chest, the smile on his face looks too much like a smirk for me to feel comfortable.

"You can wait for him if you like."

"No that's okay. I have plenty to do."

"Can I help you with anything?"

I smile confidently. "Thanks, but I'll wait for Jack."

I shout to the twins, who have ducked under the fence and are already in our back garden playing in the sandpit.

"Hey you two, wait up!" I notice Louie and Bets are in my garden jumping around near Evie and Sunny. I look around wondering where they sprang from.

Jack comes jogging down the path bare-chested, in shorts and runners (not *little* shorts, but shorts nevertheless) looking like he's just run a marathon. Another sweaty, man too close to my raging hormones for comfort.

"Hey." He smiles as he reaches us, and the light from his smile makes everything else fade, just for a moment.

Just for a moment, I forget that the twins are wrestling with the dogs in the sandpit. I forget that Jack's gorgeous but strange brother is hovering over me. Just for a moment, I forget that I chose another man; one that I loved deeply who's no longer here. I forget that I ought to feel sad and full of regret, because I betrayed that other man with this one. The smiling one, walking towards me like I'm the best thing he's seen all day.

"Jack." Raife sighs and his eyes narrow as Jack approaches. "Billie and I have just been hanging out."

Jack slows to a walk. His hands rest on his waist as he catches his breath, eyes moving quickly from Raife back to me.

Raife waits for a moment, watching me and watching Jack. He mirrors Jacks pose; hands on hips and nods. "Billie was just filling me in. Things were just getting interesting." He grins, reaches a hand out to squeeze my shoulder and turns back to the house where he takes the stairs two at a time. In moments the sound of his guitar strums beautifully though the thick air. Plaintive chords, followed by the hum of his voice in rehearsal; much more is to come.

I turn my gaze from the stairs and the beautiful music, back to Jack who is closer, hands still on his waist, breathing heavy and eyes pained.

I blow a breath of air out forcefully, the hair around my face lifting and settling limply in the heat. "Your brother is…" I frown, trying to think of the perfect word to do his uneasy presence justice without offending Jack. "He's…" Didn't I recently resurrect my clever writer self, where is my bank of perfect adjectives? "He's weird."

Jack's eyes are on Louie and Bets and the twins running in circles in my garden. He nods but I don't think he's listening.

"You okay?" I ask, because there's something in his expression I can't fathom.

His eyes snap back to me quickly, "Yeah." His smile looks forced.

"I wasn't filling Raife in on anything, just so you know." Sunny notices Jack and ducks back under the fence giggling. Louie follows closely. "We left dinner on the front porch."

"Hey buddy." Jack squats down level with Sunny. "What you got there?" Sunny looks at me carefully, worried that he's about to get whatever is in his grubby little mitt confiscated. He leans in theatrically toward Jack.

"It's a bug."

Jack looks serious, he glances up at me just as Sunny did and says in a low voice. "Can I take a look?" Eagerly Sunny opens his hand and I yelp. I was expecting a squished worm at worse, but in Sunny's open hand is a large cicada, or more accurately what used to be a large cicada before Sunny held it in an affectionate embrace and its guts spilled out.

Sunny seems unaware that the cicada is as good as gone. He looks up at me, little palm open, bug guts on show, then back to Jack. "Mommy doesn't like bugs." Jack's eyes are warm, the troubled look gone. They twinkle as he examines Sunny's palm. "His name is Jojo."

"That's a good name."

Sunny grins at Jack like he just knew Jack would get it. Every bug deserves a name right? I'm wondering how to explain to Sunny that his bug friend is dead when Evie comes running up, her hands full of sand.

"Mommy, look it's raining, it's raining!" She throws fistfuls of sand in the air and it showers down on Sunny's head. The open hand displaying Jojo the dead bug is now a small desert, Jojos' remains buried.

"Mommy Evie sanded me!" He wails as Evie turns to run.

Sunny, quick off the mark forgets Jojo the bug and everything else. In his moment of sibling revenge, he drops the bug and races after her. I watch open-mouthed as a tussle ensues. There's some scrabbling in the grass, some hair pulling and just when I move to go separate them, the squealing turns to giggling and all is well again.

When I turn Jack is close behind me, almost touching, the humid air charged with his proximity. He doesn't speak and we stand there watching Sunny and Evie. I let my body lean back till there's barely a breath of air between us. Close enough to hear his heart, I reach a hand carefully behind me, and let my fingers touch his leg and rest there.

"I need you."

His words are barely audible above the beating of my heart, his breath close to my ear as he whispers. I shudder and hold still, feet firm on the earth below. I want to hold the moment; have it wait here like this till I'm done. Till I'm done rolling those words around in my head and letting their warmth sink deep into my bones.

I close my eyes holding the moment next to my heart, storing it away - a stash of quiet joy. This memory will sustain me, because winter is always coming. Life has taught me this much.

I lean in to him and breathe the musky air heavy, fragrant in the hot afternoon sun, amidst children's laughter and dogs barking, the strum of Raife's guitar and call of distant seabirds by the cliff. Amidst all this life, I lean in toward Jack, I let him hold me and I hold my fragile heart as it swells and aches with grief and hope in equal measures.

He needs me and there is beauty in this need. That despite my heavy baggage and healing heart, I fulfil a need in him. *Not a want but a need.* That somehow the person I have become has been moulded by fate and circumstance to fill the space that waits in his heart.

He moves my hair to the side and gently kisses the back of my neck, then turns and walks toward the work shed; to his life of boats and brothers, family drama and sick mothers. And I return to my side of the fence; to the twins and the dogs, sand fights and laundry, bedtime stories, snotty noses and pet bugs. Two lives once separate now tangled and bound.

"Hello? Anyone home?"

I recognise Virginia's voice and know I won't have to race to answer the door, she will let herself in.

"In here!" I dry my hands and pop my head round the corner from the laundry to see Virginia making her way across the kitchen to unburden herself of a large cardboard box and a few other plastic containers.

"There we go," she arranges the collection of cartons on the counter and stands back to survey them proudly.

"What's all this?" I look from her satisfied expression to the crowded counter.

"Well, after seeing Zoe yesterday, I thought maybe we should take her some dinners, you know, stock up the freezer. She's looking a little tired."

"Ginny, you are a sweetheart. God I'm a terrible friend, I haven't spoken to her in a few days. Is she okay?"

"Oh she's great, blossoming beautifully, although I think she might have just hit the *over it* stage. It's hard having two busy boys at home when you can barely walk up the stairs." She looks around. "Now where are my little darlings?"

"Evie! Sunny! Aunty Ginny's here." I call down the corridor to the bedroom where the twins are holed up, playing in a fort made with blankets draped over beds and dressers. Evie comes running first wearing a bumble bee costume, Sunny in hot pursuit poking her with a foam sword.

"My favourite bumble bee." She scoops up Evie and tickles her, producing a yellow lollypop from her pocket. Sunny watches closely his bottom lip trembling, sure he's been forgotten. Virginia puts down Evie who runs to me to unwrap the lolly.

"Excuse me." Virginia turns to Sunny, bending down to kneel in front of him. "Mr Pirate Man. I'm looking for my friend, Sunny Skylark. Have you seen him around?"

The trembling lip breaks into a disbelieving smile. "It's me Ginny, it's me."

"No, you can't be Sunny, you look too much like a fierce pirate. Tell me where he is!"

Sunny is laughing hard now, jumping up and down, waving his foam sword at her. "It's me, it's me!"

She grabs him by the waist and tickles him before presenting him with a green lollypop. "You are the cutest, I mean scariest pirate in St. Cloud." She unwraps the lolly, "Truly Sunny - and I've seen a few."

Soon we are bundled in the car and all the food Virginia has carefully prepared is stacked in the trunk to deliver to the overtired, and almost over ripe, Zoe. I drive and Ginny takes care of the boxed chocolate cake she has brought to share around for afternoon tea. We're hoping this will help Zoe's mood. Chocolate cake usually works in Zoe currency.

The heat of the day is slowly waning as we drive up Zoe and Felix's curved tree-lined drive. Their house, settled just up the hill is surrounded, by bush and native forest, but the upper lever of the house rises just out of the tree line and the deck has a view to die for.

We meet Felix in the driveway. "Ladies," he smiles warmly. "Have you come to save me?"

"Move aside." Virginia says forcefully. "We've come to save your wife."

Felix grins and steps aside, noticing the boxes and containers his smile widens. "You shouldn't have."

I roll my eyes. "If you did more than barbecue a few sausages, we wouldn't have to."

Felix looks wounded, "Zoe loves my sausages."

I punch him affectionately on the way past. As we reach the front door, I hear him shouting for Mattie and Nate who must be playing in the bush. The house smells like an odd combination of lavender and burnt toast.

"Zoe?" Virginia calls as we kick off our shoes and head to the kitchen with our offerings, the twins follow behind, looking in each room for Mattie and Nate or at least their toys.

"In here," calls a voice feigning cheer. Plopping the containers on the table, we enter the living room to find Zoe sitting on an upturned bucket in the middle of the floor. Lavender scented candles burn on all the window sills and a pile of burnt toast sits on a plate on the floor beside her.

"Hey." Her eyes are tightly closed and her hands rest on her bent knees.

"What, are you doing down there pray tell?" Virginia's maternal tone is scolding.

Zoe opens an eye, "It's the only way I can sit comfortably. I couldn't find a stool so Felix found me this bucket."

"And did Felix make you this appetising snack?" Virginia asks unimpressed, pointing at the plate of overdone toast.

Zoe actually smiles. "I asked for something plain, you know, nothing that would give me indigestion being that my actual stomach is the size of a peanut. This is what he brought me. I had been thinking maybe soup or macaroni cheese." She gestures to the toast. "He's a literal thinker." She reaches out an arm and makes to stand. "So nice to see you gals. Feel free to help yourself to my toast, I'll put the kettle on."

I step forward and steady her with a hand. She really is quite a size, poor Zoe. "Your guardian angel Ginny here has been busy in the kitchen. We come armed with food for the week and chocolate cake for now."

Zoe wobbles and grips my hand tightly. "You didn't." Steadying herself she beams brightly and waddles over to Virginia to throw her arms around her in gratitude. Only her hands actually reach Ginny as the huge belly gets in the way, and we're laughing as Felix arrives back in the house with Mattie and Nate in tow.

Soon we're all ensconced round the big kitchen table drinking tea, eating cake, chatting, teasing Felix and doing our best to take Zoe's mind off her stretched belly and aching body. Mattie and Nate have exhausted the twins on the trampoline and Felix settles them all on the sofa for a movie.

Zoe has been transformed from the blotchy faced picture of abject despair seated on an upturned bucket back to the glowing, smiley fun-loving self we all know and adore. Felix looks relieved.

"Listen, I have a great idea." Zoe claps her hands together. "Let's call around and get everyone over and have dinner here. I know Jed has Thursdays off, I bet Jack will be free, and Dan can bloody well miss yoga. Let's have a celebratory dinner before this baby pops and I'm out of commission."

Soon, Zoe is on the phone rekindling her role as social organiser, persuading everyone to drop what they're doing and head round for an impromptu dinner. Virginia busies herself in the kitchen, making a salad, heating up a few of the dishes she has made, I set the table and in thirty minutes the house is full. No-one can say no to a heavily pregnant woman, so here we all are. It's a gorgeous excuse to get together and soon conversation and laughter fill the house.

Dan arrives in lycra pants with a scowl on his face and a yoga matt rolled under his arm. The pretence of annoyance is only for our benefit, and he's soon enjoying centre stage, telling funny stories with his usual sarcasm and making everyone laugh. Jed and Sadie sit side by side. Jed drinks beer and talks football with Felix but I notice Sadie sips on water looking pale and a little distracted. I can't help but wonder if things aren't going well.

At 7pm Bastian pops by with a crate of beer and a tray of Josefina's Chilli Rellenos. Zoe had begged them to come but Santos is open and they couldn't get away. Bastian drops off his offering and has a quick drink before heading back to the bar.

Jack is the last to arrive, Raife comes too. I'm happy to see him but the sight of Raife makes me uneasy. There's a strange distance between the two. I haven't yet seen them smile or laugh together. It's odd; brothers so close in age yet seemingly not close at all. Maybe sibling love is always complicated, not that I would know personally. Jack smiles at me across the room and everything feels right. All around me is my other family; all of us quirky and imperfect, but together we work and with them I feel loved.

By nine thirty the twins, Mattie and Nate are all asleep on the sofa. Despite the noise they snooze peacefully, little bodies wrapped around each other in slumber. I cover them in a blanket, pour myself another glass of wine and wander to the kitchen to begin clearing up.

Zoe, with only 2 weeks till her due date, has allowed herself a glass of wine, the first all pregnancy and I think she's a little buzzed. She's sitting on Felix's knee. His arms wrap around her and rest gently on her tummy and he looks happy, more relaxed than I've seen him in a while. Dan sits across the table from Jed and Raife, they're all in some discussion about bands and live music. Sadie and Virginia chat at the other end of the table and it's all just so easy.

I clear plates and watch my friends from the kitchen, even Raife seems relaxed. The edge around him that unsettles me has faded. He looks more like Jack as he sits, elbows on the table, beer in hand, absorbed in the discussion about music.

"Need a little help in here?"

Jack enters laden with plates. I nod and smile. Together we scrape, rinse and stack the dishwasher. Van Morrison plays in the background and when the surfaces are clear and the kitchen quiet we lean side by side against the counter looking out to where our friends chat, laugh and sip drinks. It's a beautiful scene and it needs nothing, one of those rare moments when life is perfect just as it is.

I'm watching Felix and Zoe thinking what a lovely couple they are when suddenly, Felix's eyes widen and he sits bolt upright. Zoe who is still on his lap has an odd expression on her face - shock maybe.

"Oh my God."

I see her mouth the words. Deep in conversation, no-one else has noticed.

Felix takes his hands from their resting place on Zoe's belly and holds them, palms out in disbelief. "Zoe did you just…?"

"Oh my God!"

She yells now and everyone jumps and turns. Together Jack and I run through from the kitchen.

"Oh my freaking God."

Water drips through the cane chair on which Felix sits, his expression mortified. We look down at the small pool of water on the floor, then back up, wide eyed to their shocked expressions.

"My waters just broke!" Zoe yelps.

"On me!" Felix is looking down at his lap as Zoe stands up shakily.

She turns to Felix and claps a hand over her mouth. "Oh my God sweetie, I'm so sorry. That's a little gross." She clutches her tummy. "But so exciting! Oh my God this baby's on the way!" She claps her hands together in joy and kisses him full on the mouth. Felix hasn't moved, trapped in the cane chair, crotch soaked in his wife's amniotic fluid.

Here follows much fussing and clean up. Zoe is terribly excited and begins bossing Felix around. It takes him a few moments to recover from the shock, but soon it's all action stations. Raife, looking awkward leaves and the rest of us finish clearing whilst Virginia takes Zoe through to the bedroom to check things out. I run around packing a hospital bag with all the things I think she might need, and more, just in case.

Felix is changed and waiting in the kitchen for news from the bedroom where Zoe and Virginia are.

"Don't worry man, it could take a while yet. Don't get all worked up." Dan pats Felix on the arm and Felix nods trying to look calm.

"Save your energy, could be a long haul." Dan speaks so assuredly we all breath out, relaxing a little. No hot towels needed, the baby mightn't be here for days. A scream from the bedroom makes us jump and we turn to Dan, he shrugs. "A guy can't always be right."

Virginia strides calmly from the room. "Right Felix, get the car going, we should leave for the hospital now. She's 5cm dilated."

"Holy crap!" I'm amazed, "She was in labour through dinner and didn't even know?"

Felix doesn't move. His mouth is slightly open. His feet stuck to the spot. Virginia claps her hands together and he jumps.

"What about the boys?" Felix is pale, his deep voice an octave higher than usual.

"Don't worry, I've got it" I say patting him reassuringly on the arm. "Go!"

Sadie grabs the packed hospital bag and passes it to Virginia whilst Jack gets their car running. Felix emerges from the bedroom carrying Zoe who smiles weakly at us and moans again as they help her into the backseat.

"Don't worry about a thing. We'll be here with the boys." I shout after them. The car whooshes off down the driveway, red tail lights disappearing quickly around the dark bends. We stand in shock, watching the dark space where the car had been.

Jed is the first to speak. "That was wild."

Dan shakes his head, "That, was labour… Zoe style."

Sadie's hands are over her mouth, "My God, it was so quick. Please let them get to the hospital in time."

Jed slings an arm round her shoulder, "She's in good hands with Ginny."

"She is." I concur thinking back to my own experience when once again Virginia had been there to take control.

Sadie shivers and starts to cough, taking herself inside for some water.

"I think she's getting sick." Jed's arms are folded as he stares out into the darkness. "I'm going to tell her to come see you." He sighs, turning to Dan. "If she wasn't such a hippy she'd just take some antibiotics like the rest of us."

Dan looks away and doesn't answer. And I'm only half listening, distracted thinking of Zoe, babies, labour, and the messy, scary business it is, wondering if I'll ever go through it again.

Jed and Sadie head home shortly after and Dan follows. We promise to keep in touch if there's any news. Despite the warmth, I shiver too and head inside to check on the kids. Jack has carried Mattie and Nate up to bed and has put Evie and Sunny to sleep in the spare room. All is quiet and still. Zoe's lavender candles still burn and the room flickers and glows.

I collapse into the sofa and bring my hands up to cover my face breathing carefully, examining my thoughts quietly behind the darkness of my hands. Jack lowers himself beside me and we sit there for a while. I know that something isn't right, something is eating at him, I feel it. His easy presence is cluttered, his attention distracted.

"What is it Jack?"

He looks down at his hands and grins. "Other than Zoe's waters breaking on Felix's lap and her almost having the baby in the bedroom?"

"Yep." I nod. "Other than that."

He shakes his head, taking my fingers one by one, rubbing his thumb down their length. "Nothing."

"That's not true."

"I know, but it's nothing that I want to think about right now."

"Okay."

I watch the candlelight for a long minute. "When you want to think about it and you need to talk, will you come to me?"

"I'll come to you."

He brings my hand to his mouth and kisses my fingers and I turn to him bringing the other hand to his face and letting it rest there till gently he pushes me back on to the sofa. We kiss, and he runs a finger slowly down over my closed eyes, my lips and neck, around the curve of my shoulder down to my breasts. In one careful motion he slides his hand gently under my top to touch bare skin. His hand strokes my breasts, the sensation so exquisite my thoughts are quiet, silenced under his touch.

"Just this." His voice is low, barely audible; his lips pressed to my neck.

When I open my eyes he is watching me, I nod slowly answering in a whisper. "Just this."

We lay side by side facing each other, the quiet privacy an unexpected treasure.

I fall asleep holding his hand and wake startled in the blackest part of the night, the candles burned out, the screen of my phone flashes brightly with an incoming text.

Baby Freya here, all well.

I laugh and Jack wakes. I throw the phone toward him, my eyes clouding with tears. His face lights as he reads the words and we talk for a while, and hold each other, and together share in the joy of new life.

"We have flown the air like birds and swum the sea like fishes, but have yet to learn the simple act of walking the earth like brothers."

Martin Luther King. Jr

Raife

The darkest part of the night sees Raife walk alone. Alone, along the side of the curving, tree lined roads of St. Cloud, another road that inevitably leads to the ocean. Past houses, tucked safely amongst the trees, lights on here and there but no noise. It's too late. Even the cry of a baby awake is swallowed by the forest. Endless windows into the *'happy ever after'* of others brings bitterness to fill the space where sadness sat briefly. He lowers his head, sinks his hands deeper into his pockets and walks on.

At the beach Raife walks to the water, kicking off his shoes and heading along the tide line. There's a small bonfire on the far edge of the shore. The light in the darkness draws him closer.

A party, a group around the fire, bottles scattered, guitars, couples draped around each other. They're young. It's a scene he would have been in the middle of ten years ago. He wanders closer. It's almost 1 am. and the expected chaos of too much booze and pot around the

campfire is evident in raised voices and tangled limbs. A few couples
are making out, shabby guitar chords strum from lazy fingers and up
ahead he can hear voices in the water; the obligatory late night skinny
dip.

"Hey man, what's up?"

A male voice calls him over and he strolls toward the scene. It's
the guitarist, a kid of maybe twenty with scraggy hair and a nose ring.
"Good night for it, eh?"

"Is it?" Raife answers with a smile.

"Sure, always is." *Nose ring* strums a chord then pauses as a girl in
a bikini passes him a bottle.

"Want a drink?" She looks up to Raife, smiles slowly and gestures
for him to sit. Raife shrugs and eases down on the sand beside them,
the girl passes him a bottle of beer. "How come you're all alone?"

"Because I like it that way."

She shrugs, undeterred. "You sure?"

He smiles, sips his beer and watches the crowd, taking his turn
with the guitar as it passes round the circle. When he plays there's
silence all around, conversation stops and glazed eyes try and find
focus looking for the source. His music is beautiful and hard to ignore;
attention is all on Raife.

When he stops the hush lasts, no-one speaks for a moment, unwilling to break the spell. The girl moves closer and passes Raife a
joint. He smiles taking it in exchange for the guitar which continues its
round of the circle, although no-one is keen to follow his act.

"Wait a minute…" The girl in the bikini is staring at him. "I know
you."

"I doubt it sweetheart." Raife sucks on the joint, holding his
breath then slowly, slowly, exhaling. "I'm a little old for you."

Her eyes widen and she looks suddenly clear headed. "You're
Raife Kelly."

Surprised he turns to her. "Yes, I am." His eyes narrow in a frown
as he looks at her more closely. "And you'd know that because?"

"Because I'm Niki." She stares at him like he should recognise her
too.

"Good to meet you Niki," the marijuana is kicking in and he
blinks to clear the glaze in his vision.

"Niki Freeman…Lil's cousin."

Raife shakes his head as though readjusting the frame, erasing what he thought he just heard, trying to replay the scene correctly. "What did you just say?"

"Lil's cousin."

Raife breathes out slowly and takes her in. She's watching him, waiting for a reaction but his face remains blank.

"I was ten."

He catches his breath. "I remember you."

"Where did you go?"

Raife shakes his head, "I've been away."

"You've been away since? It's been more than ten years?" Her voice is incredulous. "You must have really loved her." The air has become thin and he's pale and clammy. She moves closer. "Do you still hurt when you think about her?" She's touching him, her hand carefully stroking his forearm. "She loved you, you know."

He shakes his head as the scene spins. "I've got to go, the pot…I don't feel good."

Nearer, "I'm all grown up Raife." Her breath is close, sweet from wine as she presses herself against him. "Stay a while…we'll make it all okay."

Raife pushes her gently to the side where she collapses on to the sand and starts to laugh. He stands too quickly and staggers but she's not watching him anymore.

Her eyes are closed. "Guess I'm no match, huh hot shot?" Her laugh is grating, it scrapes and tears at his thick skin. He needs to get away. Raife turns, trying to run despite a sudden weakness in his legs. He runs till he reaches Jack's place where he lies in the moonlight on the deck with his hands over his face waiting for the world to stop spinning.

Jack isn't home and the house is quiet. Calm comes slowly, and when he finally sits up his face is no longer afraid but cold and closed. Anger, cold and familiar descends. Raife Kelly knows anger; he relies on it. Descending the stairs to the garden, he crosses to Billie's yard where he walks quickly to the back door. He knows she won't be there. She's with Jack.

He tries the glass sliders - locked, then makes his way around to the laundry door. As predicted, there's a key under a plant pot. He lets himself in.

Taking his time, he walks from room to room. A purposeless intrusion. But his anger clouds reason, bitterness spreads with each quiet footstep as he surveys her house. Quiet but clear words in the still air of the empty house. "Fucking Jack." He looks around at the chaos of toys, and mess of clothes and kitchen clutter. "Happy fucking families… fuck them all."

There's a door at the end of the corridor, a room he hadn't noticed before. He tries the handle then enters. Boxes and canvases are stacked and labelled against the far wall and the faint smell of oil and paint hangs in the air. There's a photo, just one on the window sill. He picks it up surveying the dark haired man, his arm around Billie. He stares for a time, feeling a strange connection with the face he'll never know.

"Poor bastard." He mutters, flipping off the light and walking silently back through the house to where he knows her bedroom is.

Without caution he flips the light and moves around her room running his fingers over surfaces, pictures and through clothes. He sits heavily at the end of the bed, head in his hands, eyes closed tightly. A sheer curtain ripples in a rare breath of air and the room is calm despite the tension that tightens his nerves like strings on a fret. Slowly he lies back on the bed face raised to the roof, hands braced behind his head. He watches the moonlight on the ceiling until his eyes close and he drifts to sleep.

At 3 am he rises, drinks water from her glass then opens a bedside drawer. He sees a ring, a plain golden wedding band and slips it into his pocket. Letting himself out, he replaces the key then returns to Jack's place where he enters the workshop.

A spotlight illuminates *Galileo*. Raife stands a moment taking her in, sulkily admiring his brother's work. Pulling the gold band from his pocket he presses it into the smooth wood of the hull and runs it carefully around, cutting a shallow but distinct groove of suppressed anger. A clear line from this side to that, just like the one they live by; then to now.

Raife steps back, surveys the damage and lets out a long slow breath. Falling back against the wall he slides to the floor, head on his knees. "What the fuck?" The empty question falls on the dusty floor and Evan's ring glints as it falls from his hand, rolling and settling under the work bench.

Chapter Ten

Jed

"Damn!" Jed tries to boot up his ancient computer again. He should have bought a new one a while back but he hasn't been able to afford it. He doesn't use it much but this morning he has two bills he really needs to pay before the start of business. Shit, he meant to do all of this last night, but with the dinner party and the baby, it completely slipped his mind. If he doesn't get these bills paid he'll be slapped with a late payment fine.

"Perfect timing." He flips the power switch again and gives it one more shot; nothing.

It's 5.30 am and this needs to be paid before he leaves for Beaujangles. He jumps to his feet and paces the apartment. God, he could do with a coffee. He drank a few beers last night and he's a little sluggish.

He hears Sadie cough. She's still asleep. Man he'd love to crawl back into bed but that won't be happening. He clicks his tongue in frustration and walks to the desk where Sadie's laptop lies open. He'll borrow it for a minute, just to do the banking, she won't mind.

Jed pulls up a chair and flips open the laptop. The screen snaps to attention opening directly on to Sadie's email. He moves the cursor over to close the mail but his eyes are caught by Dan's name at the top. He shouldn't read it. It's none of his business but a few keys words flash from the text, demanding his attention: medication, drug trials, side effects, and his own name; Jed. What the fuck? Before he knows it he's halfway through, banking forgotten.

It's still dark but the light from the screen reflects on Jed's face, features frozen and expressionless. Elbows on the table, hands shaking slightly he rubs a hand over his eyes and reads again. He opens the attachments and reads them too. In the bedroom he hears Sadie cough and call for him. He closes the laptop carefully and heads to the bedroom door, searching the darkness for her voice.

"You okay?" His voice is flat; shock has sucked the marrow from his words, the sounds thin and hollow.

Sadie's voice is raspy from sleep, muffled in part from the duvet, "I forgot to set the alarm Will you call to wake me at seven?"

Jed smiles weakly, glad she can't see his face. "Sure."

"I won't be late babe." She yawns. "See you there."

"See you." He closes the bedroom door quietly and stands still, resting his head against the door frame.

When the shaking stops, a seed of anger takes its place, flooding his senses. Grabbing his skateboard, he leaves the apartment and takes off running down the sidewalk, board under his arm, laces undone. He throws the board on the road and jumps on at speed weaving his way too quickly down the empty road. His lace catches under the wheel and the board stops abruptly throwing him up in the air to land on his knees on the asphalt.

"Fuck!" The word echoes in the early morning quiet. Knees bloody and jeans ripped he stands, grabs his board and swings it hard against the sidewalk. "Fuck, fuck, fuck." With each word he smashes the board against the kerb until it's splintered and broken.

He sinks to his knees beside the shattered board waiting for the 'wake up' part. The moment when he hears the alarm and realises with relief, it was a stupid dream. A dream where he reads his girlfriend's email and find's out she's sick, really sick.

When the waking up doesn't happen and the light begins to lift, Jed stands slowly. He picks up the broken pieces of his beloved skateboard and throws them one by one in a nearby trash can. His knees throb and his elbows sting, but he doesn't walk to Beaujangles. Screw the café. Screw it all. What the hell does any of it matter anyway? He starts running and doesn't stop till he reaches Dan's house.

Dan has been awake since 5.00 am. - too much on his mind to sleep. Thank God Zoe made it to hospital in time. Poor Felix, the look on his face when her waters broke. He smiles a little then frowns again, remembering Raife looking awkward amidst the drama.

He's been a real prick to Raife. They need to talk, try and put the past behind them. But it's hard, so many lies. He heads to the kitchen and pours himself another coffee. Sipping slowly, he enjoys the quiet, a welcome ease into another busy day ahead.

The bang on the door is so loud and unexpected Dan jumps, throwing his coffee in the air and down his robe. "Who the hell…at this time?" He glances up at the clock, heading to the door which quivers under the force of another heavy bang.

Jed stands outside, sweating and panting, face pale but cheeks flushed.

Dan is immediately afraid for Sadie, "What the hell's wrong?"

Jed steps in and swings a fierce punch that strikes Dan just underneath the chin, knocking him out cold. The action releases the last of his anger. With the fire gone, Jed deflates. Rubbing his knuckles, he surveys the crumpled heap on the floor; a mess of coffee stained white towelling. Jed steps inside and kneels down beside Dan who is slowly coming round.

"You okay?"

"What the fuck?" Dan voice is woozy and he brings an unsteady hand to his chin.

"You deserved that." Jed helps him to his feet.

"I should kick your ass." Dan growls as Jed guides him to the kitchen. "Ice packs in there dip shit," he points to the freezer. Jed pulls out some frozen peas and throws them at Dan.

"Do I need to tell you what this about?" Jed sits on a bar stool, arms folded, head down.

"No, I don't think you do, but maybe you can tell me why you hit me."

"Why didn't you tell me?"

"I couldn't."

"You should have fucking told me Dan." Jed turns to look out the window, the sun pokes over the tree line unsure of its reception. "Why didn't she tell me?"

"She hasn't told you? Then…?"

"I saw your e-mail."

"You read her email?"

Jed flushes, "I didn't mean to…oh fuck off, don't look at me like that, it's lucky I did. Was anyone going to fill me in anytime soon? Or did I have to wait for her to collapse as I over-fucking-work her in the café? Jesus Christ. I gave her such a hard time yesterday."

Dan closes his eyes and rubs his chin, "How can you *not mean* to read someone else's e-mail?" He opens his eyes to Jed's glare. "Okay, I get it. You didn't know because she was afraid you'd treat her differently."

"What? That's crazy."

"Is it? Look at you now."

Jed rubs a hand over his face. "Christ Dan, how bad is it? I don't know anything about this."

"Take it easy. It's okay. You need to go home and talk to her, it's nothing you can't deal with."

"I know I can deal with it. Why the hell did she think I couldn't?" He looks up. "Listen to me? I don't even know what I'm saying I can deal with."

"Hey." Dan stands and moves across the kitchen but Jed looks up quickly.

"Don't fucking hug me! I'm not good with that."

Dan suppresses a smile. "Right, reining that man-hug right back in." Jed nods, but his eyes are wet and Dan pretends not to notice. "Listen, how about I don't hug you, you don't punch me and we'll take it from there."

Jed nods, "Right. Sorry man, about the punch. I didn't plan that."

Dan points a finger. "If you'd chipped a tooth there would be hell to pay. Now pour yourself a coffee and wait till I get changed. I'll print you off some stuff to read. Once you know what you're dealing with, you two can talk it through."

"Thanks."

While Dan's in the bedroom, Jed's phone vibrates and he pulls it from his jeans pocket. A text, from Sadie: *'Come home. Now.'*

It's an hour later when he arrives. He's read every paper Dan had on cystic fibrosis. His head is spinning, but like Dan said, now he knows what he's dealing with.

It's the first day in eight years he hasn't opened Beaujangles. Truth is, he hasn't even thought about it. He climbs the stairs slowly, opens the door quietly and kicks off his shoes.

She's on the couch waiting for him, staring at the door. Her knees are pulled up under her chin, arms hugging her legs. Waiting.

"Hey." She speaks first and he's relieved.

"Hey."

She looks down at his torn jeans and bloodied knees. "No Beaujangles today?"

Jed shrugs. "Fancied a change."

Sadie nods and Jed sits down opposite her. The laptop is open on the desk and the email glows. He glances over, sighs and rests his scraped elbows on his thighs.

"Been reading my email again?"

"Gets better every time."

"I'm sorry I didn't tell you."

"I didn't mean to snoop. I was going to use your computer for the banking and…"

"It's okay."

"Right."

The silence is heavy and the distance between them large. They both go to speak at once. Jed gestures for Sadie to go first.

"I didn't tell you at first because I didn't want 'it' to be who I was to you. We weren't serious so there was no reason to say anything."

He looks up. "And then?"

"And then…hell, then I just didn't want to. I liked who we were together without all that shit. I liked that you thought I was tough and fiery and strong and independent. I didn't want you to know that really, I'm the opposite of all those things."

Long, delicate arms hug her knees tightly, hands knotted together, knuckles white. He notices how pale her arms are and wonders why he hadn't noticed before.

"Then the pretending had just gone on too long. I know how to take care of myself, and it was easy to pretend, soon I got to where I didn't even know how to talk to you about it. I'd let it become this big secret when really, it's just how it is." Her hands move to cover her face. "And then you went and asked me to marry you and that really screwed things up." She pauses but he doesn't interrupt. "The past couple of weeks I haven't been feeling so good. I had to talk to Dan, and once I'd actually told someone here in St. Cloud, someone that wasn't you, it felt deceitful, like a lie and…" Her voice fades out.

"I just don't get it." Jed shakes his head. "Did you think I wouldn't want to be with you?"

"No, are even listening? You don't deserve to choose a girl who will compromise your life. Do you hear me?" She flushes with anger.

"Then who gets to choose what I deserve?"

"Do you know my life expectancy Jed? Do you know that I probably can't have children? Listen to me, I'm telling you what you deserve and it's not this."

Hot tears flow down her cheeks and she jabs then away with the back of a hand.

Jed stands matching her anger with his own. "You don't get to make that choice for me. You don't have the right to say who I get to love and for how long."

"I can't give you what you want," she's given in to the crying, her words wet between sobs.

"You don't know what I want and you sure as fuck don't know what I need."

He won't let himself crumble seeing her cry like this, she has to know. He kneels down in front of her, wincing as his skinned knees hit the floor. "You don't know what I need Sadie, so look at me because I'm telling you right now."

The last rays of sunrise bathe the room in shades of yellow and for a moment he's silhouetted in light. "I need you."

A quiet follows the chaos. He holds her hands and looks steadily at her face. "I need you for however long you'll have me. That's all I need. Nothing else. And a day or a month, whatever the fuck you think you have, is worth more than a life without you."

The sobbing has stopped and she's still; eyes fixed on his. She squeezes his hands and blinks, letting another wave of tears free fall down her cheeks.

"Now will you quit with the crying and tell me you need me too?"

Sadie wipes her eyes and watches him, she takes a long careful breath before answering.

"I do."

"You do?"

"I do."

"Well, let's get married then."

She's laughing and crying at the same time and he watches the beauty of all that emotion flow, the boundary line finally fallen.

"Do you ever give up?"

"Never. Let's do it."

"Is that really your best proposal?"

He grabs her by the shoulders, pulling her down on to the floor where he wrestles her wriggling body into submission. He leans in and kisses her and it feels like the first time because it's honest.

"Sadie Brooks, will you fucking well finally say 'yes' and marry me?"

"Say it again without the fucking."

"Can we do that bit later?" She swats him with a free hand but he grabs it kissing it carefully.

"Marry me."

She takes her time, watching him watching her. "Okay."

"Okay?"

"Okay."

Morning light paints streaks of joy on his face. "I love you."

"I love you too."

He blinks and shakes his head like a wet dog. "You said 'yes'."

She smiles, nodding, "Technically I said *okay*."

"Say it again."

"Okay."

"*Okay* you're saying it again or *okay you'll marry me?*"

"Both."

"God, I love you."

With unsteady hands, he takes the edge of her shirt and pulls it slowly up and over her head. He touches her pale skin gently and she smiles up at him, never more beautiful than now. Taking his time, he traces her breasts with a finger watching her expression change. Suddenly he throws his head back, howls like a wolf and punches the air like a teenager at a ball game.

"Best. Day. Ever!"

Laughing, she tries to swipe him with a free hand but he's too strong and for now she doesn't mind. "You are such a kid." He answers with another howl and she only stops laughing when his fingers move inside her underwear, and he whispers it again.

"Best. Day. Ever."

While most of St. Cloud wind down by early evening, as cocktail hour approaches Bastian is busy preparing.

Happy Hour at Santos is a drawn out affair. It lasts for a few hours rather than just one. The routine is always the same. At 6.00 pm Bastian extends his outside seating area, pushing a few tables and chairs out on to the quiet sidewalk. He often has a musician or a band at night and sometimes they'll play in the covered area outside, the bar gets hot in summer.

It's been a spectacular day, another St. Cloud steamer, literally. At this time of year, the heat is usually broken by a heavy, warm rainfall late afternoon. The rain never lasts for long and when the sun breaks out again; steam rises from moisture-laden streets and sidewalks. The air is heavy and fragrant. A curious mix of hot city streets and perfumed foliage that rests on the skin in a soft misty layer.

Steam rises as Bastian readies his tables and chairs for the night, it's Friday and they should be busy. Back inside Santos the speakers hum and Josefina sings along to the Madonna track she has selected. Bastian grimaces and heads into the kitchen to negotiate.

"I'd do anything, for ma material girl. Cause I am a material girl…" Josefina is immersed in frying corn fritters. Bastian watches as she ladles the batter in time to the music, does a little dance until the bubbles rise and pop then flips each bite size fritter over deftly, not missing a beat. Beside her is a tray towering over with golden fried corn fritters.

He surveys the cycle once then steps in to sample the offerings.

"…living in a material world" Her voice rises as she sees his hand approach the platter," Materia… a… a… al… Hands off!" She snaps the spatula at his extended hand. "Okay, just one Bastian. You're getting fat."

Bastian laughs and pats his round belly affectionately, "I was a thin man till I met you." He grabs a fritter and bends down to kiss her on the cheek.

"Don't you blame me! It's the beer, not the cooking." She smiles at Bastian whose expression is far away as he savours the still warm morsel, the sweet flavour of corn balanced expertly with the zing of fresh chilli. She shoos him with her hands. "Now get out of my kitchen while I make some salsa."

Josefina's forearms are spectacular, quite out of proportion with her small, round frame. With her sleeves rolled up and a kitchen knife to hand, a tattoo or two wouldn't go a miss. They are strong, well-muscled forearms, tuned from kneading bread, rolling fajitas, chopping, slicing, mashing and beating. Food is her passion. It's her home. The kitchen her place of worship. It's the language she speaks and her offering of love. Bastian's belly had no chance.

Lifting a crate of ripe red tomatoes, she begins to chop rhythmically. In time, she lifts the chopping board deftly. A horror show of decimated tomatoes are tipped unceremoniously into a large metal bowl. The bowl is soon full, and she gets to work with red and green chillies, shiny purple onions, lemons, bulbs of garlic and coriander. The smells are heavenly and Bastian would stay and savour the sight of his wife at work but, he's had enough of Madonna, and he has other jobs to do.

Heading back out front he restocks the cooler and approaches the stereo apprehensively, waiting for the yell when he switches the playlist.

"Not again… Listen, I'd rather have Madonna than Boyzone. Seriously, it's too much for anyone, all that white-suited, shiny-faced, Irish heartthrob stuff. I can do without it. I mean, they didn't even look old enough to have pubic hair. Don't you agree?"

Bastian knows it's Dan before he has to turn around. "Rough day kid?"

"Same shit, different day and all that. Can I have a beer please?"

Bastian is still focused on the playlist, his large thumbs scrolling down the screen of the iPod. "I know I've said it before but I preferred it when we had CD's."

"Trust me." Dan grins, settling himself on a stool. "You've said it before."

Bastian turns to serve him, his lips shaped to sing along to the lyrics he knows will come soon. "A winter's day…in deep and dark December…"

"Simon and Garfunkel? Quick with the beer would you, I'm welling up."

Santos fills slowly, mostly regulars, a few tourists. Dan sips his beer thinking back for a moment to Evan, his airport and the changes that will inevitably come to St. Cloud. Since Evan's death, the controversy died down, no-one spoke about objections to the international airport anymore. No-one seemed to worry about the adverse effects of tourism. People's priorities were kicked back into place by his untimely death. Why stop the inevitable, change is always on its way.

"What happened?" Bastian points to the angry welt on Dan's chin.

Dan sighs, extends an arm to flex his well-toned bicep, then shakes his head with a frown. "Thought I had a future in boxing, but turns out it just isn't my sport." He rubs his chin tenderly. "Back to Tai Chi tomorrow."

Bastian is only half listening. He's serving. The bar is lined with custom; Happy hour begins. Soon Josefina walks around tables with small baskets of fritters, and ceramic bowls of salsa. Simon and Garfunkel have headed back to the seventies, and an island reggae band's latest tunes beat rhythmically from the speakers.

Dan is planning the set for his radio gig tomorrow. He meant to do it last night, he likes to be organised, but with the last minute dinner party he didn't have time. He likes to sit at the bar in Santos to plan his play list and topics for the show. He gets a feel for what mood the people are in, what they want or maybe need to hear, and usually he'll hear a few good bits of island gossip that he can joke about.

Sipping his beer, he scribbles notes on to a wire bound note pad, chews on his pencil for a time and watches the crowd. It's nice; he likes this part of his routine. Usually, because mostly everyone knows who he is, when they see him with the pencil and the notepad at the bar they give him peace. He likes a bit of quiet and refuses to talk *doctor shop*. The pencil and pad are the sign: *don't disturb…or else I might bitch about you on air.*

"Dan."

Surprised at the break of protocol, Dan looks up from the page. Raife slides on to the spare stool beside him.

"Raife." He tries a little warmth in his voice, remembering he'd decided only this morning to be nicer.

"Busy?"

"Planning tomorrow night's show." Raife looks bemused. "I DJ a couple of nights a week."

"You do?" He shakes his head like the suggestion is ridiculous.

"A lot changes in ten years Raife."

"Yeah." Raife looks around and breathes out slowly. "I hardly know anyone anymore."

"Maybe that's a good thing, fresh start."

"Right." Raife takes a long sip of beer from his bottle. "I don't even know if that's possible here."

"Why not?"

"Don't talk like a fool Dan. You know why." Raife looks away and Dan stiffens.

"Well maybe you need to take a look at all the reasons you ran away and deal with them. Try starting from there."

Dan places the pencil down carefully on the note pad watching Raife, waiting for the inevitable backlash. Raife was never one to let anyone tell him what to do.

"How do I do that? You tell me. I see Lil everywhere. I want to punch Jack's lights out. I've got no home, no fucking job." He pauses, closing his eyes. When he opens them he turns directly to Dan. "You know the rest." For a moment he's vulnerable, but the moment passes quickly and the cool, closed expression returns.

"You'll always see Lil, of course you will. That won't go away. Jack does too, he doesn't talk about it anymore but I know he does."

"Good old Jack, cruising on with his life like none of it ever happened. *Mr Fucking Perfect,* always was. He screwed up and I paid for it."

"Are you for real? Don't you think Jack's paid enough? Get off your self-pitying ass and be a brother. He's paid his dues. You weren't around. I saw it all."

Raife shakes his head. "I don't want to talk about it anymore."

"Really? Well I do, because you know what the problem is? You can't be honest. You can't tell anyone how it really is because you're a fake. Be a man Raife and step up."

The bar is busy and no-one but Bastian has sensed the tension between the two. Before Raife can answer Bastian is in front of them offering drinks, attempting to diffuse whatever has started.

"Raife Kelly, you causing trouble in my bar again? It's been a long time since I kicked you out on your ass but I can do it again." Bastian is smiling. The tension is broken and soon Raife and Bastian are making plans about the gig Raife will play with a few local musicians the following weekend.

Dan takes a while to settle. He knew eventually he'd have this conversation with Raife; it was never going to go well. He doesn't know whether to be angry with the guy or feel sorry for him. All the lies and self-pity are why Raife is a fuck up. He can't help him. He was stupid to think he could.

God, the conversation brings it all back. A memory faded from neglect and tainted with chaos, buried deep for so long. But the anger and proximity to Raife are such clear triggers. It's all there, hazy but fully formed; that night and how it had felt like waking up. It was the first time the pieces of his life seemed to fit and the understanding had felt like freedom.

Then, so quickly, the chaos.

When Raife stands to leave he lays a hand on Dan's arm. "Thanks. You're one of the good guys."

Dan rolls his eyes. "And who the hell are you - Roy Rogers?"

Raife grins. "I'll see you."

"No doubt."

"Maybe I can play on that radio show of yours?" He calls back to Dan as he weaves his way through the crowd.

Dan sighs, "Why the hell not?"

He watches Raife disappear into the night, his hand resting where Raife's arm lay.

Billie

I haven't gotten to the end of *The Grapes of Wrath*. I can't bear to. I stall as I near the last hundred pages because I can't take it; the sadness of what I'm sure is coming will be too much. Bloody Bruce Springsteen and his 'Ghost of Tom Joad' song. I mean really? Of course now I know there's no happy ending for Tom Joad because Brucie bloody well wrote a whole album about it.

Thing is, I love Tom Joad. I love that guy with his crooked teeth and his big heart and all his imperfections and quiet observations of the world. I love his devotion to his family, and I just know what's coming and I can't read on…you see, I need a happy ending.

I need a happy ending because they don't ever happen in real life. You might think you've got yourself a happy ending, but give it long enough and you'll find out like the rest of us, that the shitty part is on the way. It always is.

It's part of being alive. Happiness comes with no guarantees. Maybe that's what makes it so special, the fact that it's fleeting. Sadness follows happiness like a sullen shadow; where there's one, the other is never far behind.

So far life has taught me that the pursuit of happiness is just another distraction. If we could be settled in each moment we're given maybe we'd quit looking for happiness. Maybe then our smarter, less self-seeking side would know that happiness isn't a destination but a way of living. The thing is I get all of that, and much as I'd really like to, I don't live it. I seek out happiness and run from sadness, and that's a lot of running over the past few years.

So you can see why I'm struggling with Steinbeck, all that sadness. But the more I think about it; about Steinbeck and the way he wrote, about the Joad's and their journey to the Promised Land, I realise the happiness, the real joy, is in love.

That amongst the despair of almost every character in *The Grapes of Wrath*, the absolute desolation around them and that bright future that is never, ever within reach, the beauty that shines is the love from character to character. Tom Joad and his mother, Uncle Al, Rose of Sharon, the preacher, all of those keen characters brought to life with words. It's the raw love that sustains despite crippling circumstance.

And so I stay here on page 390 and worry about Tom Joad, and what is to come.

Evie and Sunny are asleep. It's been a big day and really I should sleep too, but instead I decided to read. Unable to proceed with my book I sit down to write, head cloudy with life all around and the terrible tangle it inevitably is.

I save and close my manuscript and write a long overdue email to Iris:

To: Bumlikeapeach-iris@yahoo.com
Subject Heading: Help
Sent: 27/9/2008; 10.32pm

Dear Iris

What should I do? I'm a sex crazed, melodramatic, hormonal wreck.

- *I can't stop thinking about men's armpits - is this normal grieving or would you say I've moved on to a new level of mourning?*

- *I check the twins fourteen times a night to be sure they're still alive.*

• *I keep wanting to write sex scenes, and to be honest, my work is heading for the 'Private Shop' in the High street. Should I give up literary ambition and settle for a career in soft porn?*

• *It's so hot here I'm considering shaving my head. New approach to life, revealed in baldy, earthy beauty and all that. Is it too much? (Please say yes. I like my hair…maybe a nice bob would remedy the situation.)*

• *I keep crying; like all the time. What to do? I'm dehydrated…seriously. It won't stop. The scent of the wrong laundry detergent sends me into spasms of 'remember when I washed this dirty t-shirt of Evan's' patheticness. It makes no sense. I don't cry when the twins ask me where he is, but cry instead over the smell of his shirt.*

• *I feel like I'm on the verge of moving forward but I'm afraid. I feel like the world will think I love Evan less because I want to start again with Jack. Would Evan hate me for it? Does that even matter now?*

• *Sorry for the decent into nonsense, I stopped for a glass of wine; now the world is beautiful, but my writing less so.*

Write to me soon. I love you.
Ignore my depressed every silver lining has a cloud shit - I want to hear your good stuff, your happy stuff: luscious Marcus, the wedding plans, the lot.
Write me soon.
Yours… a little pissed but feeling quite wise.

Billie xxx

Chapter Eleven

"Some people walk through the rain, others just get wet."

Roger Miller

Jack

Briny smells of salt, seaweed and dead fish hang in the still air. Broody low clouds gather; a weighty angst of inky grey. Jack likes the stillness before the storm; acceptance and inevitability. The earth's wait for coming chaos.

There's been a storm every day now for weeks, frequent downpours that deluge the island. It's the rainy season, a time of year where sunshine must be grasped and held whenever it appears. It won't stay for long and no-one expects it to. Here in St. Cloud, islanders quickly come to respect the weather and accept it can't be controlled. Weather in St. Cloud is not personified; hated or gossiped about like an unfaithful neighbour. The weather just is. Jack is used to working in the rain. He likes it.

Here at the dock the stillness brings a subtle change in gear. People work quickly; gathering in the day's catch, fixing boat moorings and readying vessels for the potential buffeting of the coming storm. Dusk is approaching, and with the dark another downpour.

Raife sighs, struggling to keep pace with Jack's stride. "What's the hurry?"

Jack glances over, "I want to get the wood loaded into the truck before the rain."

"What did you do before your man-slave Raife arrived?"

He smiles at the irony. "I managed."

"Never used to manage without me."

"Maybe - when I was fifteen."

Raife's eyes are on the water. "Hell of a long time ago."

Silent agreement passes in a nod, acknowledgement of how things were and how different they are now. But it's not just time. Time doesn't make decisions and wear the repercussions; people do. Jack does, and so does Raife, but for now they walk side by side over the rough boards of the dock, happy to blame the present on time and its disrespectful passing.

The wood has been shipped and waits dockside, delivered by boat yesterday. The only downside of St. Cloud's isolation, as far as Jack can see, is the inaccessibility of certain supplies and the cost of shipment. There are materials, wood types and tools he can't get here. The trip to pick up shipped goods at the docks is a regular one when he has a boat undergoing reclamation.

He doesn't skimp. He could do it differently, substitute wood and fixtures, but Jack has always had vision; knowledge of what each boat will become and he won't compromise. It's why his work is sought after and commissions regular. It's the reason he's able to make his living this way. He is an artist and a craftsman. Vision and construction give him equal pleasure.

As the first fat raindrop descends the brothers have only just begun lifting and loading planks on to Jacks truck. There's no real rush, the wood won't spoil, it's ready for the ocean; the rain a tepid rehearsal for life ahead. People instigate rush. They hurry to avoid another downpour, hustling as though this rain brings more than sodden clothes and damp hair. As though the downpour is irreversible and they've forgotten that eventually everything dries.

Dark skies exhale in collective relief as rain falls. Light fades, the sun lost behind watery clouds. Planks on the dock hiss and creak with steam as warm rain soaks aged wooden walkways.

Jack works methodically, lifting, carrying and resting each plank on the truck bed to be bound and transported back to the work shed. Raife's actions are urgent, anxious in the heavy rain. Jack stops momentarily, eyes closed, face raised to the damp heavens, revelling in the pleasure of warm rain on hot, tired skin. Raife dodges the drops like each movement this way or that might somehow despite the odds, keep him dry.

Soon the truck is loaded with mahogany planks, colouring deeper and darker with the rain. This will be their permanent colour once sealed and finished as the keel and hull, a rich, ruddy brown, hard and dense, naturally resistant to decay and marine borer. Jack loves to work with mahogany. The work is tough and refined skill is required but the results are always worth it. It will give his boat a timeless quality both aesthetically and practically.

Quiet and sullen, Raife bangs the last plank into place and circles the truck, slamming the passenger door as he gets in. Jack ties the tarp, covering the planks and securing them to the truck bed. With a hand he bangs the side of the truck to signal the job complete and hops into the cab beside Raife, whose arms are folded, his gaze fixed out past the dock and beyond the line of ocean.

As Jack turns the ignition the sound of the engine is barely audible amidst the drumbeat of rain on the roof. In the ferocity of the downpour people have disappeared. Streets and sidewalks are empty. Signs of life gone, vanishing in perfect synchronicity, gone to ground until the rain eases.

Inside the steamy windows of bars and cafes, proprietors will be serving quickly, making the most of the influx of business before the sun returns. This weather imparts recklessness: people make impetuous purchases and linger over late lunches that extend into cocktail hour. Quick stops for shelter turn into boozy afternoons and impulsive retail therapy.

Jack drives on slowly through the deserted streets, bright coloured signage now blurred watercolours of words and images. St. Cloud will always be home. This place and these people have always brought him comfort.

For a time, it might have been easier to run away, to start again like Raife, but he stayed. He stayed while others left. Some travellers returned home later, their understanding of the paradise they'd grown up in freshly formed. Others stayed away, happy to sacrifice the tropics for anonymity in big cities in busier parts of the world.

Jack had meant to travel, he'd planned to. But after the trouble, after Raife left, then Joseph and Amandine, he'd felt himself begin to slide. He knew then that to leave would be the end. He'd really screw up and never come back. Here in St. Cloud he'd let himself slide alright, but never off the edge. Here he had friends and they'd always been there; through the drunken years, the toxic marriage and the rest. If he'd left home to escape he'd have been a drifter forever.

He turns to Raife, glancing at his brother's profile; composed and rigid. The cool edge of distance overpowers the intimacy of the cab. Jack remembers the night in LA; the fight, Raife's vulnerability and how, after Jack had fought for him that distance had gone. They were brothers, a flashback to childhood, them against us, doing what it took for your brother, your blood. That same blood is the only thing that unites them now.

Back in St. Cloud, Raife's hard edge had resurfaced, a protective layer to keep out people and the past. And it works. No-one gets in and he lets nothing out. But it keeps him drifting and, as far as Jack can see, Raife has no anchor.

"I can't go back."

Raife's words are spoken quietly, his eyes fixed on the rain smeared window. Jack doesn't answer and Raife turns to face him, "I can't go back and see her like that."

Jack nods, eyes focused on the road ahead.

"I just don't know." Raife lowers his head, hands twisting in his lap. "I don't know how I'll be, what I'll do seeing her like that." His voice fades and the rain beats harder.

"We have to."

"Why didn't you tell me how bad she was?"

"I didn't realise myself until I went home." Jack exhales heavily, "I hadn't been back in a while." His knuckles tighten on the wheel. "It had been too long, I should have gone home before. Jess told me she was worried about her but I didn't realise how bad it was."

"Why the hell has everyone let it go?"

"No-one let it go Raife. Don't start judging, where the hell have you been?"

Raife lowers his eyes. "I had no idea. If I'd known, I…"

"You'd have what? You'd have pulled your head out of your ass, sobered up and come to the rescue with a cure for fucking dementia?"

Raife bangs the dashboard with the flat of his palm. Silence follows the impact.

"I'm sorry." Jack shakes his head.

Raife nods but the edge has returned. Jack takes a long slow breath before speaking again. "She's deteriorated quickly. I used to call her maybe every month - a least that - and she'd sounded pretty much the same until recently. Even then she'd just sound tired, maybe a little forgetful but, not like this."

"I won't go."

"I think we should, both of us, we can talk to Papa, see if he'll agree to get her some help. There must be something. He'll listen to you."

"I said I won't go."

The rain has eased, the sky lightens and all around St. Cloud shimmers. Jack rolls down the window, the cab is suddenly claustrophobic and he needs air. They're on the bush road that winds around the islands bends and curves leading home. It's the same road, the same fucking road, and driving it with Raife is the trigger. He feels it descending; a dark, heavy mist and there's nothing he can do. Suddenly the need to run is everywhere and foreboding gives way fully to panic.

The sensation is a physical blow, an impact hard on his chest as his body remembers what his mind has locked away. Sweat prickles his skin and his muscles spasm in nervous tension. His scalp tingles, nerve ends on standby as his heart begins to race and the panic settles. This time he can't control it, side-swiped when his resistance is low, wave upon wave of nausea rise and fall. He tries to focus on his breath but it's ragged and short. With a jerk of the wheel, he pulls over to the side of the road, jumps from the truck and pushes through the tree line where he doubles over and vomits as Raife looks on.

The scene that greets us when we arrive at Zoe's is blissful. It's a snapshot moment of perfection that should be taken and gifted to every new mother later, when her baby is a mischievous toddler, emptying kitchen cupboards and pulling cats' tails.

Zoe is asleep on the sofa and Freya, baby of newborn deliciousness, has fallen asleep on her chest, skin to skin. Zoe is flushed and beautiful and Freya is perfect in every tiny, delicate detail of newborn, wrinkled newness. Her little head is turned to face us and her mouth is open. A shock of dark hair caps her head and tiny hands lay in fists on Zoe's chest.

Ginny and I stand transfixed at the door, unwilling to go in and break the moment. We all know how precious a baby's sleep is, better still the miracle of mother and baby asleep at the same time. Ginny grasps my hand and squeezes it as we stand side by side in the open door frame. The afternoon is warm and the distant sounds of Mattie and Nate playing in the garden drift through the fragrant air. When I glance around Ginny's eyes are wet but she doesn't move to wipe them or turn away.

The tranquil bubble bursts as Evie and Sunny, who I'd momentarily forgotten about come racing up behind us, tussling to get through the door first. I haven't time to quieten them. Zoe's eyes snap open and little Freya reflexively jumps.

"Hey guys," Zoe says softly, her voice slow with sleep.

"So sorry, we didn't mean to wake you." I apologise as she smiles and waves my words away with a free hand.

"It's fine. She's due for a feed." Zoe sits up slowly lifting little Freya, who doesn't cry exactly but makes a sound like a small cat mewing. Evie and Sunny are struck dumb having never seen such a small person before.

Eyes like saucers, Evie points a finger toward Freya. "Baby."

I kneel down beside her. "This is baby Freya darling."

Her eyes don't move from the tiny bundle. "Who brought her?" She walks slowly forward to Zoe who is positioning Freya to feed. I'm about to give some fabulously creative, *sort of true,* pre-schooler answer to the innocent *where-did-the-baby-come-from* question but Sunny has moved in and squeals loudly, making us all jump.

"Look Mommy! Look!" He has muscled his way past open-mouthed Evie to the edge of the sofa. One hand rests on Zoe's leg, the other points to the baby whose small mouth is open, searching for a nipple. Without a trace of inhibition Zoe has whipped out an engorged breast and is trying to get Freya to latch on. "Mommy, look at Zoe's boobies!" He starts to giggle and Evie quickly recovering from her open-mouthed stance joins in. The phenomenon of milky boobies and feeding babies cause much hilarity between the twins for maybe thirty seconds. Mattie hollers from the yard and sensing fun, babies and boobies are forgotten as they race outside.

"She's so beautiful." I lower myself gently on to the sofa beside them.

"I know." Zoe can't take her eyes off the tiny face.

My attention is swayed a little by her breast which still hasn't made full contact with Freya's grasping mouth and has begun to spray small jets of warm breast milk. "Zoe…" She is smiling at me, full of the joys of motherhood. I gesture toward the breast.

"Oh." She shifts quickly and the breast squirts in my direction. A little stunned I glance down at my t-shirt which sports a small dark wet patch mid chest. She whistles in surprised appreciation. "Woops, don't know my own strength."

I can't take my eyes off the squirting milk and the little mouth that has now dextrously found its target and sucks thirstily. "That was…"

"Awkward?" Zoe finishes, giggling. "Sorry, I have a lot of milk."

"No, amazing," I'm in awe. "It's amazing, your boobs are…well, amazing."

I shake my head in wonder, remembering how I struggled with breast feeding and how my own milk had come in like a lactose heavy tidal wave that had trickled out shortly after. I'd put it down to stress and had subsequently beaten myself with the mother's *guilty stick* over my inadequacy.

"Are you sure you're a writer? Three *amazing's* in a row? I was hoping for a *spectacular* or maybe a *super sexy*."

"Super sexy wouldn't be my first choice right now."

We all laugh, despite the glow in her cheeks and the content aura that surrounds her, Zoe hasn't brushed her wild hair in a few days and its curly mass frizzes around her face in a voluptuous afro. She wears stripey pyjama bottoms and an industrial sized, beige feeding bra.

"Someone call me?" Felix enters on cue.

"No, but we should have." Virginia answers from the kitchen where she is filling a teapot with boiling water. "Poor Billie here was just given a dose of breast milk."

"I'm here now, happy to help." He grins and bends to kiss Zoe on the top of her head. "Just yell when it's my turn."

Zoe throws a cushion at him as he heads to the kitchen returning a second later with a big bag of potato chips. "Just distracting the hordes with some junk food, shout if you need me." As he reaches the door we hear his voice greet Sadie who enters the room moments later laden with a cake box and a tray of take away cups.

Zoe claps her hands together making poor Freya jump. "Sadie! Come in, meet Freya and feed me cake and coffee!"

Sadie's smile lights the room. She places the box and cups on the table and moves to hug Zoe and coo over Freya who is still sucking ferociously. "Oh she's perfect Zoe, and you look incredible. How are you feeling? Was it awful?"

Zoe waves her hand dismissively, "Gory details later. Pass me that coffee cup and let's talk more about how great I look."

"Hey, I just made you a nice pot of milk thistle tea." Virginia's head pops round the corner from the kitchen, "It's good for breast milk." We all turn with expressions of disdain, free hands reaching for Beaujangles take-away coffee cups.

"I don't think Zoe needs any help with her breast milk." I reassure a miffed Virginia. "Come taste this." I take a sip of my latte and hold a paper cup out to her. "Trust me, let's give the milk thistle to the plants."

Soon Ginny is seated cross-legged on the floor beside Zoe, coffee in one hand, pastry in the other, all thoughts of healthy consumables gone. United in self-indulgent sweet treats and caffeine, we are one. We pass the gorgeous Freya gently from one set of arms to the next, oohing and aahing over her tiny, sweet-smelling perfection. We share news and laugh a lot, and a great deal of mileage is gained in the retelling of the *dinner-party-water-breaking-incident*. Ginny does a hilariously accurate impression of Felix's face when he thinks Zoe has just wee-ed in his lap. Little Freya sleeps and feeds, and Sunny and Evie run in and out, happy in their playtime with their big-boy friends.

It isn't long before someone brings out a bottle of bubbles. We clink sparkly crystal glasses to toast the newest member to our small family of fabulous women.

Another hour later and we are still there, camped out in Zoe's living room. On the floor and sofa, glasses in hand, faces flushed and cheeks sore from laughing: Zoe, Freya, Virginia, Sadie and me. We have somehow through the passing of time and life's ups and downs, become a misfit sort of a unit. The company is comfortable and easy, I don't have to pre-empt words, hide feelings or disguise emotions. Here it's all okay. These women know and love me, they'd do anything for me, they already have and I'd do the same right back.

Entirely outnumbered, Felix has taken the boys and Evie down to the den to eat pizza and watch Star Wars. The twins, far too young to understand the intricacies of space combat were just glad to be part of the action. At last check both were asleep on either side of Felix. Unphased by Darth Vader's creepy deep breathing, they did that beautiful thing that little people do. No matter where they are and in spite of noise, vibration, music, chatter, and intergalactic battles to save the earth; they sleep. They feel comfortable and safe. They're warm and their tummies are full of cheese pizza, so despite the mayhem around them they sleep tucked under Felix's arms.

Freya has fed, burped, vomited, pooped and been changed copious times since our arrival and I'm secretly high-fiving myself. Only a few years ago I survived this, times two.

"It's a miracle we've made it this far." I announce taking another long full sip from my glass. "I mean look at us? Look at how needy our babies are? Wouldn't you think that another species, one whose young were up and running and getting their own dinner by three weeks old would be dominant?"

The others turn to look at me, with James Bond-esque raised eyebrows. "I thought we were talking about Spanish men and their sex drive." Ginny queries. If she had half-moon spectacles, she'd look over top of them right now and give me *the frown*.

"We were, we are, but it got me thinking about sex, and then that led to babies and then, well you can see the connection. Don't you agree? How did we make it this far? It's not like we're terribly well designed either, so complicated, no wings and no fur, too many dangly bits. I mean, so many things to go wrong."

"Speak for yourself on the no fur!" says Zoe rubbing a hairy leg.

Sadie nods sagely, "I agree, it doesn't make any sense." She takes a deep drink from her own glass, "but then what does?"

"Exactly!" Ginny concurs, slamming her glass down on the table too hard. Everyone jumps and Zoe throws a peanut at Ginny's head. "Sorry. But you're right it doesn't, it doesn't make sense, and that ladies is the difference. Humans try to make sense of it. It's what sets us apart, our intelligence. We think and we question."

"And we like sex," hoots Zoe from the sofa.

We all laugh, Ginny stops mid science lecture flow then slaps her thigh with her hand. "My God we do, where do I get me some?"

This causes another wave of hilarity, but Virginia who has loosened up considerably with the bubbles carries on. "I'm here to tell you girls…" she pauses dramatically, her eyes flutter a little and she raises a hand. We wait expectantly, all eyes on Ginny whose lipstick has smudged a little. "You can be happy in marriage…" she raises her head proudly, "…after twenty-one years with sex once a month." Another small frown, "Okay, maybe once every six weeks give or take work schedules etc."

There's a slightly awkward silence then a snort, a throat clearing 'bullshit' and an explosion of belly laughter. Ginny starts to laugh, "I'm serious!" She waves a hand and sips her drink. "Trust me sisters."

Zoe sits stock straight, thankfully Freya ensconced on her chest doesn't stir. "Are you freaking kidding me?"

"No."

There a sudden seriousness to the moment none of us had expected, least of all Virginia. She looks suddenly deflated; girlish and unsure. Zoe who is completely sober, thank God, rescues the moment quite perfectly. "Okay…well, do you have a vibrator?"

Virginias mouth drops open in genuine shock. "My God, no." She looks carefully around the room, we are all laughing hysterically. "Why do you?"

"Hell yes!"

Virginia surveys us all as though for the first time. "Hang on a minute, why have we never had this discussion before? I feel like I've missed something vital."

"Zoe, you're terrible." I laugh patting bemused Virginia on the arm. "Don't worry Ginny, she's being silly."

"No. I'm not. Honestly why would you be without one? Instant gratification for the busy mother."

"Does Felix know?" Ginny asks, desperately curious.

"Of course, he bought it for me. I think it's a bit of a relief - less pressure on him."

At this moment the laughter is interrupted by Felix who strolls into the room looking sleepy, fresh from a doze on the sofa with the kids watching Star Wars. The abrupt break in laughter stops him in his tracks and he looks around sheepishly.

"Should I come back later?"

We all start to laugh again. "No Felix stay. Zoe was just filling us in on some new hardware you've been purchasing." Sadie grins innocently as Felix rubs his head looking confused, no doubt wondering why we're talking power tools. Zoe throws a peanut at Sadie this time but Sadie is too quick and catches it in her mouth, crunching it with a cheeky wink.

Freya rustles, saving Zoe the hardware/power tool explanation. She heads off to the bedroom with the baby for another round of nappy and onesie changing. Felix, heads to the kitchen and hurries back through the room moments later with a beer, cheeks a little flushed. Keen to be away from the cackling lady folk.

Ginny sighs, extending her legs out in front of her, wriggling her toes, watching the glint of her shiny pink toe nail polish. "I'm not sure what to do."

Sadie has grabbed the bowl of peanuts and is honing her 'throw-and-mouth-catch' trick. She answers between mouthfuls. "I'd wait till they come up with a solar-powered one."

Ginny and I exchange confused glances then turn our gaze back to Sadie and her adept peanut-eating technique. She continues, "Otherwise you'll just end up spending a fortune on batteries." A nut bounces off her nose then rolls across the floor. "So un-environmental."

"I'm not talking about vibrators you lemon." Virginia rolls her eyes, "Mike, I'm talking about Mike."

"Oh." Sadie stops mid-throw and the last flying peanut bounces on the hardwood floor.

"I don't know what to do about Mike."

"I thought you were here to tell us how great it was after twenty-one years." I touch her hand gently.

"I lied."

Sadie and I glance at one another, unsure what comes next. Virginia brings her knees up to her chest and hugs them tightly as she continues. "Oh I sound terrible. I don't mean that its bad, really things are fine. But that's just it, they're fine. I think I just always thought we'd, well…"

"You'd what?" I ask.

"We'd be more." Her flushed face droops and her eyes fill again.

I can see these are barely processed thoughts. Things she's been pushing away, filing in the *too hard basket.*

"He's a good man." She turns to us reassuringly, keen to pledge allegiance to the husband she feels she's bagging on. "You know that. Gosh listen to me, he's a wonderful man."

"We know that." I squeeze her hand again.

"It's just that together, for a few years now, we haven't been wonderful." She bites her lip. "We used to be, at least I thought we were. But now we're sort of just another average couple, just partners stuck in the same routines." She looks at me like I should nod and agree and so I do. "It's not that I want to be with anyone else. I just want more. It won't go away, this feeling that what we have is only a tiny taste of how we could be." She pauses, eyes fixed on her feet, the pale pink toes now quite still. "I always thought we'd grow together you know? You do don't you? You think together you'll grow out of all your problems, that you're just at the beginning of this long journey and that somewhere along the way you'll sort it all out."

I keep nodding. Sadie has joined suit and Zoe has tiptoed back into the room and is curled on the sofa quietly listening and nodding too.

"But we're here, we're at that place and things are the same. I'm 47 and Mike will be 50 this year. He's still more passionate about work than me. We do the same things week in week out, and here I am joking about it, pretending like it's okay to have sex once a month."

It must be the bubbles. I've never heard her like this but I'm pretty sure she means every word. Usually Ginny is the one who clears up the mess for everyone else. She is the fixer, the stable-headed, *got it together* Agony Aunt. When you create that role for yourself there's no room to be needy or confused, you don't often share because it's just not what you do.

"And you know what? It's not enough. And it's not the lack of sex, it's so much more."

There's a long pause and we are silent, waiting for her to continue. She takes a long, deep breath then exhales. "So, in summary darlings, I don't think a vibrator is going to cut it." She sniffs and Sadie passes her a hankie. "God, if only it were that easy. It's more, it's being interested in each other. I don't even know if Mike wants more. Maybe he's quite happy with what we have." A little sob escapes. "That's even worse, don't you think?"

I sling an arm around her while she has her moment. Sadie fills Ginny's glass till bubbles froth happily over the top and down the side. She smiles and sips and we don't say anything for a while. There's nothing to say. None of us can make it better, or offer anything that might help. Not right now. It's Ginny and Mike's business to figure out, to work out together, to realise that together they can be more; if together they want to be.

We sip our glasses in synchronised thoughtful reflection. I pat her shoulder and hope that she feels the support that surrounds her and remembers tomorrow, that although her glass might seem a little dusty and tired, it's almost always full.

Zoe frowns then pads out of the room and returns a moment later carrying a brown paper bag. She has a quick look right and left, then throws the package across the room at Ginny who manages to catch it spilling some bubbles in her lap.

"No." she shrieks breaking into a toothy smile.

Zoe shrugs, "I had a spare." She grins. "Don't worry! It's still in the box, unused. What sort of a friend do you think I am?"

Sadie grabs the package from a wide-eyed Ginny and rips it open extracting a large white, diamante-studded vibrator. She holds it gingerly, then throws it with a whoop of laughter to Ginny who seems to have regained her sense of humour. Despite her assurances that it would take more than a vibrator to fix her troubles Ginny soon has the 'Rabbit Deluxe' tucked away in the depths of her handbag.

It's almost seven and my cheeks are sore from laughing. I make a move to leave but as Evie and Sunny are asleep on the sofa Zoe persuades us to stay for one more drink, promising that Felix will drive us all home.

Sadie is all smiles, she sits cross-legged on the floor, takes a little sip of bubbles and hiccups. I decide I prefer her without the dreadlocks. She has such a pretty face; heart-shaped, with a nose like a Disney princess; small with a perfect upturn at the end. Her beauty is very natural: the short blonde hair, pale skin, freckles around her nose and sparkly hazel-coloured eyes.

The hiccup turns into a cough, one of those coughs that starts small then grows like a thunderclap. A small splutter that she struggles to suppress but the deep rumble has begun and soon she's coughing persistently and loudly. It's a deep wet cough that makes her eyes stream and her face red. Virginia rushes to the kitchen for some water whilst I give her a good bash on the back.

"I'm fine." She splutters between coughs. "It'll stop in a minute."

"Bubbles must have gone down the wrong way" Zoe offers. "You just need more practice drinking champers Sadie. That's the problem."

Sadie tries to smile but the wet cough carries on despite the water, and she excuses herself to the bathroom.

"That girl is too pale for my liking." Virginia has returned to her mothering role. "Really, she needs a tonic. I'll bet she's anaemic. I'm going to tell Dan to have a word with her, get her some iron supplements."

"I think she just drank too quickly Ginny, you can relax." I say.

Moments later Sadie is back, eyes watery and cheeks flushed. "Sorry about that girls, all good."

Ginny can't help herself, she stands with a little wobble and places an arm on Sadie's. "Darling, I've been saying it to you for ages and I just wish you'd listen. I may specialise in vaginas and ovaries but I know a thing or two about general health, and I'd say you really need a check-up. Get Dan to do some bloods and check your iron." She sits down again pulling Sadie down with her, passing her back the offending glass of bubbles. "Trust me on this, I know what I'm talking about."

"Thanks Ginny." Sadie pats Virginia on the arm affectionately. "I don't need a blood test."

"Oh but really, I honestly think you should."

Sadie waves her hand to swat away Ginny's words, clearing the air. "Ladies, being that we're celebrating, I may as well share a little secret I've been keeping."

This pronouncement is met with much *oohing* and clapping of hands. Sadie stands, does a little twirl and a courtesy. "I, Sadie, who swore she'd never, ever, well, not least till…"

"Get on with it," Ginny heckles.

"Okay, okay." She laughs, "I am…" dramatic pause, "…getting married."

There's a collective hush, then a unified collection of *wow, no way, oh my God, do we know him?* and other such exclamations of surprise. It's not that we didn't know Jed and Sadie were serious but after the hooha over Jed's radio proposal we were all pretty sure that marriage wasn't an option.

Zoe jumps off the sofa and throws her arms around Sadie. "Just tell us it's Jed."

Sadie is laughing loudly as Zoe practically squeezes the air from her lungs. "It's Jed!" she yelps. "It's Jed."

After we've all hugged her and toasted some more, we get down to the business of what sparked this change of heart. Zoe as usual, is the first with the questions.

"Tell us, please, how did he ask you this time? I mean, how did he manage to top the radio show stunt?"

"Oh my God! Yes. "Virginia claps her hands together remembering the evening in Santos. "That was perfect. I loved it, poor Jed. Remember the reception he got when he came back?"

"That was so not perfect." Sadie shakes her head. "It was awful. But you're right, poor Jed. I did make him pay."

"So what did he do this time? Or is it X-rated?" Zoe is on the edge of the sofa.

"No, it is not X-rated. Zoe, you're an animal."

"It's just the hormones."

"So? Tell us? You have our undivided attention, we need the scoop." I fold my arms and give Sadie my best no-nonsense look.

She laughs. "Okay, okay. But there's really nothing to tell. I just changed my mind. I needed to think a few things through."

"And?" Ginny smiles, looking much more like her maternal self.

"And we talked, and I realised that life's short and sometimes we don't get too many chances." She stops abruptly and glances over at me. "Sorry Billie, I hope that didn't…"

"Stop it, don't be silly."

I focus carefully on my smile, telling it sternly to stay there. I never know when the smallest throw away comment will start me off. So, I look at Sadie and think about smiling, and the fact that I'm happy. I am happy, and life right now is good. Sometimes sad yes, tragic yes, unpredictable always, but right now, good. "Carry on will you?" I pinch her affectionately.

"So, I thought, well why the hell not?"

"Amen!" says Zoe.

"Sadie that's great, really great, I'm so happy for you both." I really am. I am so happy for Jed and for Sadie, they are perfect for each other and she's right, life is short. "Jed is a great guy."

"I know." Sadie smiles widely. "And I figured if I didn't get around to saying yes he might go off and ask someone else."

We become spectacularly, stereotypical females for the following ten minutes. With great excitement we discuss weddings, rings, dresses and such like. We compare experiences and imaginatively plan the perfect ceremony, dress, cake and party for Jed and Sadie.

Sadie humours us and lets us get carried away on her behalf even though she's probably rolling her eyes inside, knowing that really, they're planning to pledge their love over a few beers on the beach. She listens, relaxing into the imagined future we are creating. Soon we've planned a Chanel dress, a seven-layer cake, crates of Moet and a reception for one hundred where Radiohead make a guest appearance.

"Too depressing," Sadie shakes her head solemnly.

"Are you kidding me? What's wrong with that plan? That is so the perfect wedding." Zoe exclaims, offended.

"No, just Radiohead. Too depressing."

"Really? "Zoe frowns for a moment, "I do love them though, and of course it's all about me." She smiles and we eye roll. "How about Dan throws together some happy tunes and DJ's for a bit, then Radiohead make a guest appearance and do a few numbers near the end?"

Sadie nods but her eyes are far away. Bringing her knees up to her chest she wraps her arms around herself and looks out the window where the sun is beginning to set.

"God, what time is it?" I sit up, if the sun is setting then we must have outstayed our welcome. "We should go. I need to get the twins to bed, poor things."

"Oh my gosh, you're right." Ginny follows my gaze out the window. "How did it get this late?"

"It got this late because you sat here all afternoon drinking bubbles and keeping me company while I sit here like a big cow, being milked on the hour. But don't go yet, Felix can babysit a bit longer."

"No," Sadie turns to us looking so serious I wonder if I missed something, "there's something else."

There are occasional moments in life when understanding passes in a glance. It's a language beyond words, subtle and powerful. The flicker of an eye might speak in a voice you recognise. A fleeting expression from another can be so familiar, that for a moment, you might believe their feelings are your own.

As Sadie looks at us I see loss and I recognise it. I see sadness in loss, and the feeling expressed in a glance is like an old friend. She watches us warily, composing her words. And although I know the loss is not mine I'm suddenly afraid, afraid of what I see in her eyes and afraid of what she is about to say.

Maybe I'm the only one that feels the moment so intensely, maybe when that feeling of loss still weighs on your heart, only then can you sense it in others. Everyone looks expectantly at Sadie but no-one shows any apprehension. She takes a breath then speaks quickly - too quickly.

"I have this thing…"

All eyes are on Sadie, unsure of what *thing* she's about to divulge: a birthmark shaped like a two finger salute on her left butt cheek, a hairy mole on her boob, an addiction to re-runs of Dallas. But I know, I know before she has to tell us something is wrong, very wrong.

"So don't get all weird on me. It's just one of those things. I'm used to it and Jed knows and…"

Virginia can't take any more, she raises a hand palm-up like a traffic warden. "Stop, I've had a little more to drink than the rest of you but you're making my head spin. Will you spit it out! What thing?

"Cystic fibrosis."

She throws the words, then having delivered them, looks around at our wide eyes, assessing our expressions carefully. "I have cystic fibrosis."

There's a stunned pause, a sobering moment before anyone responds.

"Oh sweetie," Virginia is the first to speak, laying a hand on Sadie's leg. "Why didn't you say anything before?" By our silence it's pretty obvious Zoe and I aren't actually sure what cystic fibrosis is.

Sadie shrugs, "It doesn't have to be that big of a deal. That's why I don't talk about it unless I have to."

"Sorry, I'm a ditz Sadie. What does that mean for you?" I ask.

Sadie quietly explains her condition and how she lives with the genetic disease. She tells us of how she manages it with daily routines and medications, and she tells us of the risks. We ask questions and she answers. Sadie talks of the disease like an experienced doctor, unemotionally, just the facts.

We are suddenly all quite sober, we talk with careful tones; afraid to overreact and cause upset, or the opposite and appear heartless. After the science, the facts and treatments she drops the clanger.

"You see, I can accept it, it's all I know, but it was Jed. I was afraid of telling him, then I was afraid of not telling him, then he went and asked me to marry him. That really threw me." She takes a sip from her glass, more relaxed now. "I mean how could I say yes when he didn't know my big ugly secret?"

"It's not ugly." Zoe says firmly.

Sadie continues "Then I got to thinking that I'd missed the boat, I'd really screwed things up because if I told him after he'd proposed then he'd feel obligated to go ahead because you don't dump the *sick girl.*"

"Why would it stop him from wanting to marry you?" I ask, confused. I must admit, the revelation of her illness is almost a relief to me. I had imagined far worse was about to come.

Sadie looks imploringly at me and that look of loss is right back in her eyes, they ache as she reaches a hand out to mine. "That's just it Billie, he wouldn't. It wouldn't stop him and I can't give him the time he deserves."

And I understand now the loss is hers. It's the loss of the life she might never see and a love that can't last.

"What does that mean?" asks Zoe, very still, eyes fixed on Sadie's sombre face.

"These days' people with CF are lucky if they live till forty."

We're all very quiet. I realise that of course Virginia must have known this, her face is unchanged, open and understanding. Zoe and I are shocked and we show it.

"That's ridiculous," Zoe announces. This makes Sadie smile.

"I know. I think so too but there we go, life's a bitch."

"No, I mean, surely with new research and all that stuff…I mean forty's so…"

"Young. I know. There are some people that live happily for longer, others don't make it that far. But hey, let's not talk about that part."

"Of course," I say. "God Sadie, what a thing to carry around and not tell."

"Believe me, it's just easier sometimes. Dan knows. He's been great."

"So what changed, why did you tell Jed? I mean it's all okay because we just planned your wedding right?" Zoe is perplexed.

"Yes." Her face lights up. "It all sort of took care of itself in the end."

She's quiet for a moment. "It was stupid thinking that I could keep it from him for long. I've had a lifetime of trying to be normal, whatever the hell that is." She rolls her eyes. "Pretending to be normal, managing myself so I wouldn't have to tell people. The 'sick-girl sympathy' kills me." She pauses and frowns. "Bad word choice." We're all quiet, awkward in the dark humour we're not quite ready to share.

"In the end, Jed found out anyway, and it wasn't like I'd expected at all. He wasn't like I'd expected." She smiles and her eyes sparkle. "He talked me round, and finally I got to thinking that he's right. It doesn't matter, we're happy now and I can't plan his happiness for him. I can't make choices for him and you know what?" Sadie pauses for dramatic effect. "I've never been so God damn happy!"

Moments later we're in a group hug, Felix times his entrance badly once again. "Should I come back later?" He smiles awkwardly from the edge of the room.

Zoe extracts herself from the tangle of girlfriends in bonding, her eyes streaming. "Get over here and give us some man-love." Felix looks a little stunned as we turn to face him, we're all sniffling. Zoe reaches an arm for him and Felix approaches, his expression bemused but soft. He knows something has passed between us, he's unsure what, but he knows better than to ask.

The scene would be funny if there weren't so much crying. Felix towers over the standing circle of entwined, teary females. He wraps his arms around us and we lean into him. And although he has no idea of what's going on, he knows what to do. His warm, solid presence forms a wall of comfort and steadiness. He knows the room is a wobbly fusion of hormones and champagne but he simply smiles and joins the shaky hug until we're all hugged out.

I'm not sure how long it takes, maybe just a few minutes, maybe more, but after a time Sadie starts to giggle and we follow suit. All except Felix, who shakes his head, kisses Zoe on the head then asks who needs a ride home.

It's 9 pm by the time we're putting Evie and Sunny to bed. Jed, having had a tip off from Felix, arrived to take Sadie home and Felix delivered Ginny and I here with the twins to Frontiere Point.

Ginny had insisted she should help me put the twins to bed. Together we tuck them in, a little slower than if we were sober, and retreat back to the kitchen where I find some more wine and we sit at the kitchen table to talk some more.

My head thrums and I've reached a point where usual reservations and inhibitions are pushed aside. The slow stream of alcohol trickles steadily through my veins, numbing my senses and delivering me to an unfamiliar, but quite wonderful place where I feel fit to burst with emotion.

I feel brave and angry, and plain pissed off at life's continuous kick in the ass; the kick which seems harshest and hardest to only the best and most beautiful people. I'm angry that at every turn someone I love gets served a kick up the pants from life.

I open the bottle and pour two large glasses and a flash of guilt illuminates my boozy fog. *Didn't you blame it all on the booze? Didn't you tell him this was where it started?* I wobble uncertainly, balancing for a second between guilt and oblivion.

"Fuck it." The wine sloshes over the edge of the glass and I jump, steadying myself and the bottle.

"Excuse me?" Virginia peers out from the kitchen cupboard where she is rooting around for potato chips.

"Fuck it!"

"Fuck what exactly?"

I sit down heavily at the kitchen table, pick up my glass watching the golden glow of wine circling as I swirl. Unceremoniously I gulp half of the contents down in one go. "All of it."

Ginny's head tips slightly to the side, like she's thinking carefully about something terribly insightful I've just said. She nods, throws a bag of salted chips on the table and lowers herself into the seat opposite nodding sagely. "All of it and the rest!" She raises her glass, clinks it with mine and takes a large gulp.

The house is quiet, the twins are asleep, the sun has set and outside the sky fades, reddish gold fading to indigo blue. I watch it, the light on the ocean and the deep forever of the night sky.

"It's not fair Ginny," I shake my head wisely, a woman of the world. "It's not fair." In my drunken haze I am un-contradictable. You see I have suffered; I have been on the *unfair* side of life. I sink with the wine to the bottom of my glass.

Ginny is at the same stage of drama as I, having drunk too much wine and heard the same sad news. She's in no position to kick me up my melodramatic ass.

"Poor, poor Sadie." She shakes her head and sips from her glass again. "I'll never understand why things work out the way they do. Why the worst people get all the luck and the best never do. I mean really Billie, I've been lucky and I can be one serious bitch!"

I start to giggle. "Get out, everyone loves you."

Ginny ignores me entirely. "I mean really, there's no sense in the workings of the world. Good, young, beautiful people get sick and suffer and old miserable bastards just go on and on." She frowns at me, then grins. "Oh Billie, there's nothing to be done. Nothing at all. Sadie and Jed will be fine and with the way things go in this funny old life, Sadie will outlive us all. It's just…"

"It's just…?" I prompt when her focus begins to wander. "It's just what?" I'm hoping for the perfect wise summary, the one liner that will put my angst to rest. But she looks up at me like she's forgotten what we were talking about.

"Call Mike for me will you darling? I need to go to bed."

I do, and ten minutes later Mike arrives to pick up his sozzled wife. I wave them goodbye, Ginny blows me kisses from the passenger seat as Mike frowns, heading for home.

Alone inside the house I walk slowly from room to room. I check Evie and Sunny again, laying a hand on their chests and pressing my lips to their foreheads. The night is hot, airless and still and I open the windows and remove my sandals and dress. I move through the dimly lit house trailing a hand over wall and window, trying to feel at peace but unable to lose the seed of anger and despair.

Outside everything is black, there is no moon. The sky is heavy with weighty clouds, more rain on the way. There is no reflection of moon or starlight on the ocean, no glimmer of light in the sky. Jack's house is in darkness and I feel alone.

I know the timing is wrong but I don't listen to my more rational self, bitten by something I can't explain, an unfamiliar, self-destructive force drives me forward.

I enter Evan's studio. The one room I have left untouched. Its walls remain unpainted, windows shut tight, the smell of linseed oil and wood shavings stop me in the doorway. The pain is momentary. Driven forward by anger and wine I push the door wide and flip on the lights.

Nothing is as it was, yet everything still is.

There are no models hanging, no half built sculptures on the worktable, no music playing, no warmth, yet something of him remains. It is the only place left I can still feel him, despite the passing of time. In the naked yellow light, the studio is barren. Maybe it's my mood, the booze, the news of Sadie's illness, or simply a general disillusionment with life and the hands we're dealt. But I don't cry or speak softly to him as I have in the past. I feel a rush of anger flood my chest and soar through me like a trapped bird and I let my wine glass fly. I throw it as hard as I can against the wall where it explodes in a thousand sparkling pieces of fractured glass.

Nothing is as it was, yet everything still is.

I wallow in fate's shitty dealing of my cards this far. I allow myself to be the victim, waiting for the time when it all turns around, when poor old Billie gets a good deal.

Well hell, is it okay to finally be done waiting? God dammit, what good will waiting on life's perfect course get Sadie? What good did it do Mom? What good did it do Evan? Life doesn't do waiting, it doesn't do fair, it doesn't wait around for *should have's* and *what if's*. Life doesn't give a shit, because really, no-one's watching. It's a fucking lottery, a gamblers game, who gets what, and when, and how long. No-one knows and dammit no-one cares?

Master plan my ass. It's all a bloody mess and you can only do the best you can, and hope for a lucky deal.

Standing still in the corner of the room I survey the broken glass in pieces on the floor. No moonlight to reflect my ignorance in the broken shards that lie scattered. The yellow overhead bulb casts a jaundiced glow on the scene and I feel no shame in my drunken drama. I leave the mess, and the smell of linseed oil, and Evan. I flip out the light and retreat back to the den where comforting darkness allows me to wallow in self-inflicted pain.

Sinking on to the sofa I watch the darkness, steady and reliable and I rally my heart to find its equilibrium. Anger slowly subsides but that seed of unrest persists and I watch the night, waiting for a star.

Instead there is rain, a signal of the sky's discontent; a rumble, gentle pattering, then the drumbeat, heavy and unrelenting. The sound is everywhere and its persistence blocks out everything for a time.

Maybe it's right then, or later, an hour, maybe more, but head-lights shining on the side of Jack's house startle me. His truck moving steadily into the drive, a flash of brightness then nothing, a slamming door then another. I watch as lights appear in his house, but even the thought of Jack gives me no comfort.

My thoughts spin recklessly. I am a stranger in my own head.

Chapter Twelve

Jack

The drive home seemed endless. It takes time to shake the desperate fear. The descent of relentless panic and its complete hold leave him weak.

Inside Raife heads to the fridge and pulls out a beer. They don't speak. Jack is shaken and ashamed. He thought he had it under control, to lose himself in front of Raife leaves him exposed. Raife hasn't spoken about it. He sips his beer, grabs his guitar and heads outside to the deck to play music in the dark.

The quiet of the house is good. Jack's colour begins to return and he strips and showers under heavy jets of cool water. Slowly the anxiousness and fear wash away with sweat and grime from the boatyard. When it's gone and the tension recedes from his chest, he closes the shower faucet, towels off and changes. A heavy throb in his temples reminds him of what he must do.

In the bedroom he places the laptop on the bed and opens the window. Rain falls steadily and from here he can just make out the strums of the guitar. Sheltering under the covered deck Raife plays and sings, competing with the rain for attention.

Resting on the edge of the bed he powers up the computer and connects to Skype where he clicks on Jess's photo and the automated ringing sound begins. The first time the connection goes dead; call failed. He waits a moment, gathering his words, and tries again. This time within a few rings the screen flickers to life and Saul's weathered features look down at the screen through a tangle of untidy hair.

"Jack?" Saul's brow is furrowed in frustration.

"Hey, yeah it's me. Didn't know you knew how to turn that thing on."

"I don't. That's why it took me so long." The frown turns to a half grin as he relaxes, sitting himself down to face the screen. "Can't you just use the phone?"

"You don't answer that either."

"Right."

Jack shakes his head, smiling warmly at his dependable, older brother. "Why the hell are you answering anyway? I thought Jess was your PA."

Saul hates technology in all forms. "I'm flying solo man."

"Jess run off with Isa from the fish market?" Jack laughs and Saul grins in response.

"Not yet, but he keeps trying. Nah, she's down at the clinic."

"It's 10.30, what's up?"

"They tell me there's nothing to worry about, but her blood pressure's up and they wanted to keep her in for the night."

"You gotta stop working that girl so hard."

"You try and stop her! I'm damned if she'll listen to me." Saul rubs a hand over his forehead. "You should see the size of her, God. I really didn't know women could stretch like that."

"Well that baby will be a good size if you're actually the father, although if Isa got a look in she'll be okay."

Saul throws his head back and laughs heartily. "Don't, you're killing me."

"So, she's okay then?"

"Think so, just got back from there. She's still bossing me around so that's a good sign." Saul's face becomes sombre when he speaks again. "She's more worried about Mama, so I'm gonna head over there now and check on her and Papa."

"How they doing?"

Saul shrugs, collecting his words. "Not so great." His gaze refocuses on something below the screen. "How's crazy? You beat him up yet?"

Jack's turn to shrug, aware of the quick shift in topic. "Same, same. You know Raife."

"I do. He needs a job, some kind of a focus. Maybe he could do some work with you?" Jack shakes his head but Saul continues on. "He needs a girl, that would sort him out. Forget the job and find him a woman."

Jack doesn't feel like talking about what Raife does or doesn't need. "Listen, I'm gonna come over soon, see Mama. Maybe we can talk to Papa together. Jess said he won't get any help. Thought I'd try and get Raife to come too."

"Papa won't listen, I've tried. I don't know what you can do, he doesn't listen much to you anyway." Jack winces. "Sorry bro but you know it's true. As Mama gets worse he gets more stubborn. He's fixed on having no-one else look after her, says he can manage fine on his own."

"But she needs looking after, right?"

Saul's eyes shift off to the left. He won't look at Jack as he answers. Jack knows he's lying. "She'll be okay," he pauses then turns back to face the screen, "I got it under control kid. Now I'd better go and check on them or Jess won't sleep tonight."

"Listen, I've been doing some reading…"

Saul interrupts. "I'll put an ad in the papers."

"Shut up and listen, I've been reading about what she's got."

Saul pauses and takes a deep breath. "She's gotten old Jack, that's all."

"Come on Saul, you know it's more than that. Don't tell me you don't believe it's more serious."

Saul brings two hands to his face and rubs them carefully over his eyes. The silence is drawn out by the flickering screen and the grainy image of his despair, in and out of focus. When he answers the screen has cleared but his expression clouded. "I don't know what the hell it is Jack. Some days she's fine, just fine, she's back to her usual self and it's the strangest thing. Then we're all too afraid to talk to her about the days before, the days when she forgets, or talks like it's twenty years ago."

"Saul, she has dementia." Jack waits a moment for the words to settle. "There's no cure, it only gets worse." His voice is soft but firm. He wants Saul to understand.

Saul looks up, then turns away again before responding. "Yesterday when I went by she's making dinner and says to me, *Now Joseph, set the table will you. Set it for three, there's an old fella out there on the porch that I might ask to stay for dinner.* It throws me for a minute then I realise she thinks I'm Papa, and Papa is the old guy outside."

He pauses, running a hand through his hair. "Hell, Jess is so good with her but she wasn't there. I didn't know what to say. Do I tell her I'm her son Saul and the old guy is her husband? What would she do?" Shaking his head in despair he continues. "Know what I did Jack? I gave her a hug and I said thank you and I set the God damn table and went to tell Papa dinner was ready. What was he going to say when he hears her calling me his name? What would that do to him? I know why he's pretending it's not happening Jack, how the hell else would he cope? When I came back to the kitchen the pots were burning, she'd just walked away and left it all. I went to look for her and she was in bed, asleep, peaceful as anything."

Saul lowers his head, Jack waits a time before speaking. "It will get worse, we need to do something."

"What?"

"I'm not sure yet, but we have to take her to see someone."

"We'll never get Papa to agree."

"I don't think he has a choice."

"Right, of course." Saul rolls his eyes," I'll just head over and tell him now. Say nice things about me at my funeral."

"Listen we'll sort it out together when I come over."

"Sure." Saul is quiet, then jumps suddenly noticing the time on the bottom right corner of the screen. "I got to go."

"Call if you need me, right?"

"I will."

"Take care of Jess."

"Take care of Raife."

The screen flickers. Saul's image is gone, and despite the comfort found in talking to his older brother, Jack's unsettled. Sadness and anger in equal measures; frustration, guilt and regret. Can sorrow and stress trigger the onset of dementia? They're to blame; him and Raife. Another fucking tragedy as a result of one senseless mistake.

He paces the room, replaying Saul's words, trying to figure out a way forward. Fuck Raife. Saul's last request leaves a bitter taste. Always the focus on Raife, even now when Amandine needs them. Why is it that Raife continues to suck the air from the room when he's not even there? Will he ever be able to shift the bitterness and guilt that overwhelm him at the mention of Raife's name?

He exits the house taking the steps two at a time. Dull chords of Raife's guitar drown tunelessly in the darkness and rain. Jack jogs down the drive and out on to the slick road. He runs to the end of Frontiere Point where the land meets the sea then turns back and runs to Billie.

❧

Billie

I might have dozed for a short time, I'm not sure, but when I wake there's a steady knocking on the back glass door. The door that faces the ocean, the yard and Jack's house. In seconds I'm up, awake and alert as though I'd been waiting for his arrival. I open the door and usher him in to the dimly lit room, only half sure I'm not dreaming.

"I'm sorry. It's late." He runs a hand over his face, wiping the rain, clearing his features; serious and unsure.

"It's fine." I blink and steady myself but it's no use, I'm not sober. "I was still awake."

"Billie, I…" His head is down, wet hair dripping on to his chin and shirt. "I just wanted to see you." He raises his chin and blinks away the rain that drips into his eyes.

He is beautiful. I watch him through the haze in my head, looking down at me, eyes dark and troubled. I ache to be held, to be touched by someone who wants me, to feel the complete release of sex.

"You should…" he gestures a hand toward me and I remember I discarded my clothes in the heat and stand in my underwear. Sober, I'd have cringed. My underwear is not of the *let me seduce you* variety - cotton sports bra and jockey high waists. But my undies are the last thing on my mind. The only thing on my mind is sex…

Sex with Jack.

The Jack I'm used to would smile at me right now. He'd realise I wasn't behaving like myself, he'd tease me and not buy into my drama. But this isn't the Jack I'm used to. This Jack is edgy and unsure and I know he needs something from me but misinterpret what that is.

The sliding door is still open behind him, warm rain falls hard but the real storm is yet to come. "Is it okay?" He asks quietly and I nod as he reaches behind and pulls the door closed.

"Let me get you a towel."

"It's fine."

"Will you let me get you a fucking towel?" I hear myself and stop, shocked by the sound of my voice. Jack nods gently, staring at me warily.

I try to walk nimbly to the bathroom but stumble a little on the three steps leading up to the corridor. When I return he's kicked off his shoes and stands barefoot, arms folded, back to me, eyes on the rain outside.

I throw the towel toward him and it lands in a heap on the floor. He bends slowly to pick it up watching me, aware that something has shifted. "Are you okay?"

I collapse back on to the sofa. "I'm great, just great."

He lifts the towel to his face, then drags it back over his hair. His eyes remain on me as I lean back sulkily on the sofa. "Billie, I…"

I give him no time. It's all about me and my skewed perception on what must happen now. "God Jack, I can't do it anymore."

"Can't do what?"

"This. I'm sick of waiting. I'm sick of being the good girl that waits for life to give her what she needs. That's all I've ever done. Waited for life to give me what I think I need. Then when it turns to shit, I wonder what I did wrong. I blame myself for not being good enough." I stop, breathe in deeply then blow that breath back out angrily. "I've been wrong all along."

Jack shakes his head. He knows he has to hear me out before he interjects with sober wisdom.

"Life doesn't actually give a shit. I just figured it out Jack and I'm pissed." I blow out another hot breath of angry air. I am on a righteous roll. "None of it bloody well matters. How good we are or how good we've been? What we want or deserve, what we God damn well ought to have? It doesn't matter. Life deals you a card and that's it."

"Billie…"

"Let me finish."

I feel sure for the first time in forever and the certainty is powerful. I'm done waiting around for divine deliverance. Why not go out and get what I want? And right now I want Jack. I want him to stride over here, all damp and troubled, and rip my bad underwear right off. I want him to make love to me right here on the floor and I want it to feel so good I forget everything. I want to forget it all and start again.

"Nothing makes sense Jack." I pull myself up to stand, squaring off to face him, "nothing except you."

His eyes are closed and he's very still, but I can't wait. The surge of confidence will soon dissolve so I press on. "I need you now." He folds his arms across his body, head down, eyes still closed. "There's no reason to wait, tomorrows a cheat and I want this now."

I'm a little woozy, but I manage quite quickly to pull my bra up and over my head. God damn him, he will look up.

Jack does look up and he doesn't flinch or look away. He also doesn't race over and have his wicked way with me. His eyes are dark and heavy, his mouth set in a hard line. I walk over and stand before him, close but not touching. I want him to want me. I want him to reach for me, but he doesn't and I feel myself wilting. I keep my head held high and stare him down, but with every passing second my self-assurance fades.

"You don't want me."

"You know I do."

But he's wrapping me in the towel, covering me up and everything starts to spin.

"Get away from me! All this time I thought this was what you wanted. I thought you loved me." I free myself from the towel and flail unsteadily, fists flying, desire transmuted to jilted rage.

"I've always loved you."

These words only reach my ears as my fist makes contact with his mouth, and I smack him harder than I knew possible.

"What the fuck Billie?"

He grabs me firmly by the wrists and I struggle, half naked, flailing and lashing out like Jack is responsible for everything bad that's ever happened to anyone.

"Stop it."

"God damn you!"

"Stop screaming, you'll wake the twins."

The word *twins* breaks through my hysteria and stops me mid-pummel.

"Take it easy, calm down." He scoops me up like a child, holding me tightly to his chest. And just the feel of him straining below me, his arms that grip tightly around my shoulders and legs brings me back. I slump in his arms and begin to sob.

"Stop it Billie. Just stop."

Jack sinks back on to the sofa with me in his arms and catches his breath. His heart beats loudly where my head lies.

"There's more to love." He waits letting his breathing slow. "Yes, I want you. I've spent years thinking about making love to you, but not like this. Me all messed up, you drunk and angry. You don't want this for us either, the way you're feeling tonight I could be anyone. I want you to remember how we are together. I don't want you to mistake me for Evan, and I want to be ready to give you everything you deserve." He lets his head lean back and his eyes close.

I lift my chin and rest it on his collarbone, "But I love you now, the way you are. You don't have to fix anything for me."

"I have to fix it for me." He nods as though talking has given the thoughts clarity. "I've made mistakes, bad ones in the past, and I have to be sure for your sake, and for Sunny and Evie that if you let me into your lives I'm good enough."

"I don't understand." I sniff.

"You still need time, time to be sure."

"I'm already sure God dammit." I wipe my eyes with the heel of my hand and pull the towel around me.

"You're not going to hit me again are you?" He tips my chin toward him and kisses me gently, a soft careful kiss then something deeper, longer and less contained. And I know he is right, the time isn't now and if I weren't stupidly drunk I'd have known before. My experience with love so far has taught me that sex comes before everything. It's what I know, but I am learning, slowly, there are so many ways to love.

"I'm sorry Jack."

He kisses me again, cupping a hand around a towel clad breast. "Don't be." He pulls back and grins. "I just came for a chat - these babies were an unexpected bonus."

He's laughing and I'm laughing too and it feels nice. As anger seeps out, hope returns and with it a level helping of joy. Beautiful but unfortunately short-lived; the laughter sends my tummy in spasms and in seconds I'm racing to the loo to vomit out the excessive bubbles. The hangover I deserve begins slowly, and with aching limbs and a pounding head I shower then return to the sofa where Jack waits for me. We sleep, fully clothed, his arms around me, my back to his chest, his hand stroking my damp hair.

Just like the first night so long ago.

In that quiet place just before sleep, I wonder about those mistakes, the ones that keep Jack from ever being really happy. When he speaks of the past, the spaces between the words are louder than his stories. The words he won't say weigh heavier now than ever. I fall asleep feeling sure it's my turn. I must step up and be the rock he can lean on.

Dan

Dan can't sleep.

He's had trouble sleeping this past week, too much on his mind. All the usual sure-fire fixes he uses to switch off his mind after a long day don't seem to be working. He's done an hour of yoga, stopped in to Santos for a cold beer, had a long bath at home with scented candles listening to some Bach, then, still feeling twitchy, poured a red wine and watched an old Audrey Hepburn movie. And still, no sleep. There's something he needs to do, something to help resolve the turmoil. He just wishes he knew what it was.

After a few fitful hours of dream laden sleep, he rises at 5.00 am. It's not his thing but this morning he needs more than a few sun salutations. He needs to run, get sweaty and work off this nervous energy.

Designer running gear on, Dan could be mistaken for an elite athlete. Lean and well defined, hairless, tanned legs, broad shoulders and muscular arms he looks the part; until he starts to run. Running really isn't his thing. His stride is uncoordinated and his arms don't seem to know what to do. He hopes he doesn't bump into anyone - he likes to be good at everything - but this morning needs must.

He runs down the side of the road toward the beach in the dim light; two kilometres of tarmac before the sand and a hopeful breeze. Despite his total lack of co-ordination, he moves quite quickly and the heaving of his lungs and burn in his thighs begin to make him feel better.

Maybe he needs to talk to Jack. Maybe not telling Jack what he knows hasn't been the noble act he once thought. Maybe keeping quiet all these years has simply been cowardly. The thought makes him stride out faster, one clumsy footstep falling flat on the road after another. But would it change anything? He turns as the road curves, thinking his way carefully once again through the same question. Would it change anything?

By the time he reaches the beach the sky is grey, no hint of sunlight yet, but the pale ocean reflects the transition from night. No-one around, his stride shortens and slows to a walk as his feet meet the sand. He stops, chest heaving and bends over to catch his breath, thighs supporting his hands. He thought he'd put all this behind him but Raife's return was always going to rock his boat. Jack wasn't the only one disturbed by his presence.

When his breathing returns to normal, the light is brighter and a pale shimmer of orange and gold lines the far edge of the ocean. There's nothing to be done that won't somehow cause damage. He's a doctor; he's supposed to heal and cure, to alleviate suffering, not re-open old wounds.

Hands on hips, he watches the morning arrive on the horizon. His troubles dilute a little with the light and he sighs. Bending over he stretches out his aching muscles then decides to jog to the surgery. Another three kilometres will do him good, make sure he's sweated those worries right out. He'll shower and change at work, at this hour he should make it without being spotted.

❧

"What the hell happened to you?" Jed's forehead creases, the resultant expression a mixture of concern and disgust.

Dan raises a hand then collapses forward, hands on his knees again, breathing like a fish.

"That must have been some damn yoga class." Jed grins and goes about grinding the beans to make Dan's coffee.

The noise of the grinder gives Dan a moment to catch his breath and recover his sarcasm. "You have no idea." He staggers to the counter and pours himself a glass of water.

"Hey, stand back, you're sweating over stuff." Jed throws him a clean towel from the kitchen and Dan gratefully mops his forehead, drinks some more water, then drapes the towel around his neck. "So what is this? You training for something or running from someone?"

"Neither."

"Okay." Jed pushes a double espresso across the counter. "I'm suspicious though, I don't think I've ever seen you sweat. Look at you, dripping all over my floor, looking like you've just circumnavigated the island in your Nikes."

Dan smiles weakly and sips the coffee closing his eyes reverentially. Jed watches the transformation. A subtle change is underway. Dan takes a long slow breath and when he opens his eyes the sparkle has returned. "I couldn't wait."

"For me?" Jed places a hand on his heart. "But Dan, I'm spoken for."

"God, that's better." Dan continues, ignoring him. "I just ran further than I've run in my entire life." He waits expectantly but Jed just raises his eyebrows. "I feel like death, but I'm coming right."

"Oh good, the local Doc feeling like death isn't good for business in the surgery." Jed smirks but Dan's gaze is far away, looking out through the café's glass front and beyond. "Just think if you'd stopped at the surgery first Muriel might have had to give you mouth-to-mouth."

Dan stretches a long leg out in front of him and leans his head side to side. "You know, I actually feel quite good now. I may have missed a great career in endurance sport."

Jed stifles a laugh, "Dude, you ran five kilometres. I don't think Lance Armstrong needs to worry yet."

Dan sighs, "Lance…cute, but definitely a cheater. And he dumped Sheryl! Who does that?" Shaking his head, he finishes the last of his coffee then bangs the cup over enthusiastically onto the counter. "Now before you start getting the impression I'm here for small talk, and coffee - which incidentally, is partly true - I need to discuss a few hot topics and I only have a few minutes."

Jed stands squarely behind the counter and folds his arms firmly across his chest, assuming a serious stance. "Hit me."

Dan glares and rubs his chin briefly where Jed's fist left its mark only a few days ago. "I should, but I'm waiting till you least expect it." Jed grins. "Okay, now that you and Sadie are tying the knot I think the three of us should sit down together. I don't know what she's told you or hasn't, but I think it'd be good to talk things through, the three of us. She's a master of downplay, and this way you can have her back."

Jed's face softens and he smiles at Dan. "Thanks man, I'd like that."

"She probably won't."

"I know."

"But we'll bully her into submission."

"I'm all for submission."

"No more of this *do it by myself* shit. Life will be easier now she can ask for help."

Jed's smile is warm. "Thanks Dan."

"You already said that."

"I know, but I really mean it. Thanks."

"Your welcome."

The phone rings and Jed answers, writing the days' specials on the chalkboard as he talks, obviously placing an order. In minutes he's back. "Right, next?"

"Next what?"

"You said you had a few hot topics. What's the next one?"

"Oh right? "Dan nods. "Are you going on Friday?"

"What's Friday?" Jed frowns, lines on his forehead clearing as he remembers. "For sure, Raife's gig at Santos? Said I'd give Bastian a hand behind the bar, Sadie's going to help Josefina in the kitchen. Should be a great night, heard he's really good."

"He is."

"Have you heard him?"

"Long time ago. Listen I was thinking, the guy needs a job, a chance to meet people, make some friends. You got any work going here?"

Jed looks surprised. "Thought you didn't like him."

"I never said that."

"Didn't have to, you get all moody when he's around, I just figured…"

"Well, you and your *figuring* don't always get it right junior. I grew up with him. Raife's okay, a cocky pain in the ass, but he's okay."

Jed checks his watch and starts stacking cups as he speaks. "Can't see him fitting in here."

Dan raises his eyebrows. "Why not? Another misfit to your crew, what's not to fit in?"

"Fuck off."

"You could do with the help."

"Let me think on it." Dan waits expectantly as Jed toys with the idea. "What's in it for you? Since when did you care about Raife Kelly?"

Dan shrugs, "I think the guy just needs a break." Jed's turn to raises his eyebrows. "It's just my Buddha nature coming through." Dan sighs bending to re-lace a shoe. "Good hearted compassion, seeing ourselves in everyone, everyone in ourselves, all that jazz."

"Okaay," Jed drags the word out, the sound drips with sarcasm. "Could you ever just come in for coffee like a normal person?"

Dan straightens stretching his hands high above his head. "Normal people don't do coffee here."

"Fair point." Jed glances out the window, the sun is fully risen and he has a lot to do before the crowds arrive. "Okay, what's the next thing? I need your sweaty ass out of here."

Dan grins, "Keep talking dirty." Jed throws a wet cloth across the counter which makes a direct hit with the left side of Dan's face. "Okay, okay! Have you seen Jack? I need to talk to him."

Jed's busy sliding a tray of warm pastries out of the oven, "Nope, not for a few days."

Dan rubs his chin, eyes fixed out of the window, "Has he spoken to you about anything?"

"Anything in particular you're fishing for here?"

"Why am I asking you?" Dan sighs heading for the door.

"What are you asking me?" Jed is confused.

"Never mind, if you see him today tell him to come by the surgery. It's important."

"Okay, are you done?"

"I'm done."

"Now get to work."

Dan salutes as he leaves. "Keep it tight junior."

Jed turns the music up smiling. The smell of warm pastry wafts through the air and Ella Fitzgerald begins to sing about black coffee. He hops over the counter and flips the *closed* sign to *open*, humming to himself.

Across the road Dan opens up the surgery feeling better than before. He heads for the staff shower hoping that the warm water will wash away the last threads of tension that remain.

Jack

Teak, totara, cedar, oak, mahogany. He runs a hand carefully along the line of sanded planks, the workshop walls are lined with the woods he loves best. Okoume, iroko, greenheart, ironwood. Each distinct in colour and grain, touch and smell. He knows them by sight and appreciates their qualities.

Like people each wood has its own special quality, something that makes it unique and precious. He knows which to use and when. He knows what attention each needs to become perfect for his purpose; to be reshaped and formed into a boat of beauty.

It started early, this fascination with boats. Growing up on an island like St. Cloud, boats are a part of life. Saul taught him to sail, not Joseph. It would never have been Joseph. Patience was not a quality Joseph possessed. Teaching his boys anything had never been an option. Saul taught Jack most things, how to fish, play soccer, ride a bike, sail a dinghy.

The free feeling of being out on the water, steering a boat, being in control, learning the waves and respecting the ocean. The independence and freedom. These were the things he'd loved. Working with wood came naturally and he'd started helping out at a local boat builder's after school. He worked and they let him sail for an hour after work.

It had been a natural progression. Over the years he'd refined his skills and carved out a reputation for himself. It was lucky really, who else would have employed him? Especially back in his twenties. It's the thing that has held him together; a constant that's always been there to distract and consume him.

He might sometimes build from scratch, working toward a craft of classic design with a modern edge, but his passion has always been restoring. Saving those old boats others have given up on. Bringing back what once was, second chances, new life after old. It's a beautiful thing and it's what makes him tick.

Fingers of sunlight shine through the workshop windows, resting on the wall, giving warmth to the wood. True colours radiate under the sunlight's touch. Each is unique, each scent enhanced by the warmth. Jack's finger stops on a cedar plank, the pads of his fingers pressing flat on the smooth surface, imprinting the grain and scent on his hands. He brings his fingers to his face and inhales.

Methodically, Jack organises his tools and supplies for the day. He lays out hand tools and resins, oils, rags and brushes, sand paper, brass fasteners and bronze screws. He dusts off the bench saw, sander and planer then stands back to examine *Galileo* in the light. Bright morning rays travel to the keel and bow. She shines, basking in her new beauty, a loveliness Jack has reclaimed day by patient day since bringing her home.

He's glad he chose mahogany. He will prepare and begin working with the wood they brought in last night, although not much is needed now. She is beginning to resemble the boat she once was. Jack pats her with a rough hand. He hopes she'll be more beautiful than before.

He watches the light play on the wood, watches the golden red hues and perfect seams from panel to panel. He is happy with his work so far. But as his hand moves a roughness catches his finger. Moving closer he sees the small but definite ridge that runs along the portside. He follows it with his finger and the rough groove guides him around *Galileo* in an almost complete circle.

"What the hell?" He bends close and examines the gouge, an indentation forced with something solid. Standing back, he brings his hands to rest on his head, eyes fixed on the angry mark. Sun gleams on the now obvious imperfection and it's all he can see. How did he miss it before?

But it wasn't there before. He sanded and sealed these planks only days ago. They were perfect. Leaning back against the wall of wood, he folds his arms across his chest, eyes stuck on the imperfection. There is nothing now but this, this mark which tarnishes everything. Frustration mounts as he walks lap after slow lap of *Galileo*, index finger running the length of the groove from bow to stern. Frustration blossoms into blame, and resentment follows like a guilty shadow.

Upstairs Raife plays his guitar and sings, his voice, dulled by the dense floorboards is still beautiful. There's a sense of impending doom, inevitability to the moment that fuels the anger which swells in his chest. There is satisfaction in the bitterness, quiet resentment turned loud. He strides from the workshop taking the stairs two at a time.

"What the fuck did you do?" Jack stands on the top step facing the deck where Raife practices his set.

Raife doesn't jump or startle, his reaction is slow and measured. He raises his head slowly, "Can you be more specific? Are we talking right now, or way back when? I did a lot of stuff Jack. Which do you want to talk about?"

"You know exactly what I'm talking about." Jack strides across the deck to where Raife sits, guitar balanced on knees, eyes fixed lazily on Jack's advancing form. He grabs Raife by the shoulders pulling him gruffly to his feet. The guitar clatters to the ground as Raife struggles to steady himself.

"Easy man. Watch the guitar."

"Why are you even here? Why the fuck are you here, leaving your mark everywhere? Are you afraid I'll forget? Is that it?"

"Easy with the drama, you're not that important Jack. You think I'd waste my time hanging around here just to piss you off? Get your fucking hands off me."

Jack pushes Raife hard and he staggers backward before righting himself against the wall. Jack's anger is beyond words. He doesn't want to listen to Raife. It's all he's ever done. In three strides he's one pace away, lunging forward he throws a punch that knocks Raife to the ground.

Raife's reaction is careful. He takes the blow and is still for a moment. His hand cups his cheekbone where Jack's fist struck but he doesn't retaliate, instead he smiles slowly. "Nice, better than I remember. Got another one hotshot?"

Jack fist makes contact with Raife's mouth before the last word is spoken.

The release is exquisite; the first blow soothing, the second stunning. As his fist makes contact with Raife's jaw something toxic exits Jack's body: primal communication, pure and uncomplicated, feudal resolution of fraternal complexities. Then the quiet, the echoing stillness following violence. He knows the peace will be short-lived. But for now the shaking anger is gone, tension dissolves to stillness and his head is silent.

Raife slumps against the wall sliding to sit, elbows on his knees, hands to his face. Louie whines from the edge of the deck pacing anxiously from side to side, head darting from Jack to Raife uncertainly. The sound brings Jack back from the red line and his breath escapes jaggedly as his fist begins to throb in time to the thump in his temples.

Raife looks up warily, bringing a hand to his lip which bleeds freely down his chin and over his shirt. "You done?"

Jack leans back against the house and slides slowly down to crouch on the deck beside Raife, eyes closed, forehead creased in impending regret. He nods. "Why did you do it?"

Raife's eyes focus on the ocean and the birds that swoop and soar above the breaking waves. He shrugs but doesn't answer.

When Jack speaks his voice is quiet. "I thought eventually you'd stop blaming me, but it's never going to happen. You can't move on. Sometimes I don't think you even want to." Raife's expression is still, his focus fixed far out to sea. "I get it Raife. I wear it every day." He nods slowly as he speaks. "You have to leave. I can't be around you. Life's moved on. I'm trying to start again. You need to get away from me and try and do the same."

"I don't know where to go." Raife raises a hand to his bloodied lip, turning his head away, eyes squinting in the midday sun. Jack stalls, anger turned to sympathy in a heartbeat, but Raife smiles slowly, glancing over to Billie's just visible house. "Time to get on with your own little *happy ever after*, eh?"

Jack tries to ignore the sneer in Raife's voice. "You can't stay here anymore, we're no good around each other. It's like no time has passed. I need you to leave."

They're interrupted by the low thrum of an old engine as Dan's Chevy pulls into the drive. Raife grasps Jack's arm before he can stand. "You should wear it every day."

Dan's voice calls from below and Jack shakes his arm free, the sound of feet taking the stairs two at a time accompany Dan's offended tone. "Where the hell are you Jack? I'm not used to being stood up, we were supposed to…" Dan stops abruptly on the top stair, seeing the two slumped bodies, side by side, bloodied and bruised. "Is this a bad time?"

Raife manages a half grin through his swollen lip. "You're just in time. Jack's giving me some advice for the future."

Dan turns to Jack who shrugs. "Your timing's perfect." He struggles to stand, rubbing his knuckles as he gets to his feet. "Raife needs a hug." Jack pats Dan on the shoulder as he walks past, and into the house.

"Fuck you." Raife calls after him.

"Glad I came by." Dan's hands are on his hips, eyes flitting between the brothers. "You okay?" he gestures to Raife's bloodied lip and nose.

"Never been fucking better."

"What happened?"

"Jack giving me a bit of what I deserve." Raife doesn't look up. Down below in the work shed Jack's sander roars to life, the grinding impact on wood grates the air around them.

"What do you deserve?"

Raife raises his head, heavy eyes on Dan. Dan holds the stare but his composure is momentarily lost. The grind of the sander stops abruptly, Louie and Bets bark from the yard and the tension dissolves. "Do you want me to look at that?" He gestures again to Raife's face. Raife shakes his head, and turns away.

In the work shed Jack is barely visible under a cloud of wood dust, the sander is so loud he doesn't notice Dan standing by the door. Sweat glistens on his forehead and forms a dark stain down the back of his shirt as he works; face set, jaw clenched tightly. When finally he notices Dan he doesn't stop. Dan waits patiently, leaning against the wall, arms folded.

When he's ready he turns off the sander, the grating sound seeps from the room as the dust slowly settles. "Don't ask."

"I'm not going to."

"Good." Jack wipes his brow and runs a hand around the edge of *Galileo*. "I don't want to talk about him. I'm done."

"Okay, well you be sure and tell me when you're ready, because when you are, I'll be telling you that this isn't like you. That you're going to regret this, and that you need to suck it up and sort this out without your fists."

Jack's eyes remain on *Galileo*. "And I'll be sure to tell you to fuck off and mind your own business."

Dan sighs, "I get the picture, I'm leaving." He sneezes, and brushes his shirt, wood dust lifts and settles in a small cloud.

"Sorry I didn't stop by yesterday, I got caught up. Shouldn't you be at the surgery?'

"Yeah, I had a cancellation, I wanted to have a talk."

"About what?'

Dan looks away, out of the window where the mid-morning sun bears down, the light too bright. He shakes his head briefly, eyes focused on the glare. "Nothing really, better get back. Take it easy man," he frowns at Jack, "maybe I'll catch you later." Turning for the door he stops, holding up a paper folder he's been clutching. "I've got a little reading for you, I'll leave it upstairs.'

"What is it?"

"Some stuff to read and maybe give to Joseph and Saul. It's about Amandine." He pauses. "It's about dementia."

Jack puts down the sander and nods as Dan opens the door. "Thanks."

Dan gives a strained smile as door closes. "You're welcome."

Upstairs Raife is in the kitchen, running water on to a cloth, attempting to clean the blood from his face. "You still here?"

Dan puts the folder on the kitchen bench. "Let me look at your face."

"You should see the other guy."

"Shut up and let me help you." Raife shrugs and turns to face Dan who takes the cloth and cleans efficiently around his nose and face. Raife sinks into a chair wincing as Dan touches the gash on his lip. This is where Dan would normally be sarcastic and witty, where he'd joke about Raife usually being the tough guy. But instead, as his hands touch Raife's lips, words stick in his throat and his long fingers tremble unsteadily.

Billie

"God… oh my God."

Bringing my hands to my face I cover my eyes and take a deep breath. The memory of last night is so horribly cringe-worthy, every time I think about it the same thing happens; *Oh God…oh God - hand wringing head in hands moment.* Over and over.

I'm currently hanging out the laundry, Evie is trying to help, which translates to tipping the peg basket upside down and making several peg families. Sunny is pulling a red plastic cart around, filling it slowly with dirt and the odd lucky pet bug.

As I peg a bra on to the line I'm once again faced with the God-awful hazy memory of me propositioning Jack. My cheeks flush and a hot tingle spreads, making my legs feel weak. I sink to a sitting position on the grass where Evie flings herself on to my lap and introduces me to *Boobee* the blue peg. The irony of her peg name turns my blush to a smile and I take *Boobee* the blue peg and join in a short game of peg families. Evie has a yellow peg who is *Boobee's* sister so peg play begins and the washing is forgotten for a bit.

It doesn't take long before Evie's attention wanders from peg friends and she's off to check out Sunny's cart to be sure he hasn't got any cool stuff in there she should fight him for. I stand to resume my laundry hanging when I hear the low growl of a familiar car exiting Jack's driveway in a hurry. I'd recognise Dan's Chevy anywhere.

Running to the fence I see him in a blur as he revs past, accelerating along the road. I'm waving wildly because I'd love to see him and, well, angry driving isn't like him and I hope he's okay.

At first I think he hasn't seen me and my hand drops limply to my side, damn. Then there's the sound of brakes screeching as the Chevy halts abruptly one hundred meters along the road, reversing quickly back to where I stand. The car pulls level and Dan raises his arm in a feeble salute.

"Where are you heading in such a hurry?" I lean in to kiss him on the cheek.

"Away darling, away from this hell-hole." He smiles and blows a kiss at Evie who is charging toward the car grinning.

"Hell-hole? That's a bit much." I try to examine him a little more closely, but he's shielding his eyes from the sun. "Please have coffee with me, I need you. Stay with me in this hell-hole for another half hour."

"No can do sister. Just stopped so you can smooch me, I'm a busy guy."

"I have Tim Tams."

"Damn you," he smiles weakly. "Double dip?"

"You bet."

"I'm coming in." He revs the engine and pulls into the parking bay as I clap my hands together.

Evie and Sunny run to greet him and soon we're inside where the twins climb on him like an indoor Jungle Jim and I brew some fresh coffee.

"So what's up fella? I miss you."

"I miss me too." He grins, flashing those shiny, straight white teeth. "No, no, no, I don't. I take it back." He yelps as Evie pulls on his ears and Sunny tickles him. "I miss you guys terribly. I've been so busy, mercy. Save me Billie, and get me a Tim Tam."

Half an hour later and half a packet of Tim Tams down, Dan is fully reclined on the sofa. Evie snuggles under his arm and Sunny has a pretend stethoscope around his neck and is studiously taking Dan's vitals.

"So Muriel is driving me crazy, she keeps rearranging the furniture, and get this, yesterday I came in to a big vase of plastic carnations on the front desk and The Carpenters on the sound system." I nod sympathetically. "I mean, who can work in those conditions?"

His phone buzzes, his eyes snap open and he fishes around in his pocket whilst Sunny continues prodding him with his toy doctor set. Dan's face pales at the number on the screen.

"Muriel, hi! Yes, sorry. Won't be long darling got caught up on a home visit." He winks at me. "I'll be there soon." He snaps the phone closed and shrugs. "She's a scary old dragon. I'm going to have to keep the plastic blooms but maybe I can sabotage the stereo."

Sunny and Evie take off, realising they are no longer the centre of Dan's attention. He sits up, brushes down his shirt and trousers and smiles at me. "You look good."

"Thank you. I'm not sure I'm deserving of such a compliment, but I'll take it anyway."

"You do, best I've seen in a long time. Sort of shiny happy…wait I feel a song coming on… hang on, R.E.M. already covered it."

"Stop it." I laugh.

"So, do I take it that things are getting better?"

"Much better." I nod, "Then some days they're not, quite spectacularly not in fact. But for the most part I have more good days than bad."

Dan smiles warmly. "I'm proud of you girl."

I want to say thank you and accept this compliment too, be gracious and mature, but I don't. "I'm not sure if you should be."

"Oh God, here we go again." Dan rolls his eyes. "What is it now? Did the play dough turn out the wrong shade of blue? You can tell me? Dr Dan is here to absolve you of all parenting guilt."

I laugh, embarrassed. "I hit on Jack."

"Excuse me?" Dan's face is a picture, his mouth forms an exaggerated *Oh* but his eyes are twinkling.

I can't even look at him, but I have to tell someone. "God, I did Dan, it's terrible. I really threw myself at him last night."

"And what happened?"

"What happened?" I repeat in disbelief. "Well, he turned me down but that's not the point."

"He did?" Dan looks surprised. "Well, I didn't expect that, the guy's full of surprises."

"Dan are you even listening to me?"

"So you're looking for a little comfort. It's what we're all looking for, a little love, a little joy and some good sex. So what? Go easy on the guilt. A little jiggy jiggy would do you the world of good." His mouth is set but his eyes are definitely laughing. "Besides, Jack would be a great lay."

"Dan!" This is not the reaction I expected.

"What?" He shrugs like none of this is a big deal.

"Aren't you going to tell me I'm terrible person, and that it's too early, and it's wrong, and I'm rebounding and all of that other friendly advice?" He sits quietly, an odd expression on his face. "Well?"

"Well, what would you like me to say Billie?"

The twinkle has gone, and I'm unprepared for his question. "I'm not sure." I search his face for a clue. Is he disappointed in me? "Just tell me what you think."

"Okay." His face has lost all humour. "I think Jack loves you and I don't want you to hurt him. I think it might be too soon and I worry you might not be ready. But more than anything I think that you're lucky Billie, you're damn lucky you have that kind of love - and you know what else? I think I'm a little jealous." The serious expression quickly transforms into a gentle smile. "Jealous of all those great loves." He shakes his head again and looks at me carefully. "There are no rules to who we love and when we love them. I know how much you loved Evan, but I also know how hard things were." He turns away to look out of the window. "Your feelings for Jack have always been clear Billie." Turning back, his blue eyes meet mine. "I knew this would happen sometime, I've always known, and I wonder maybe if Evan knew too.

"Dan…" I bring a hand to my mouth and extend the other one to him palm up, to urge him to stop. This is not what I wanted to hear, not at all.

"I'm not giving you the sugar-coated version sweetie, you're too smart for that. Love's complicated, hell is that ever the truth." He runs a hand through his hair.

"Is it wrong?"

He looks surprised. "How can it be? Love's never wrong," he pauses to rub his temples, "although it can sure feel that way sometimes."

I'm trying not to cry. God I'm sick of crying and it's the only thing I seem to be able to do without mammoth effort these days. Dan folds me into his arms and hugs me while I dampen his shirt - not for the first time-with warm tears. "It's not wrong darling, just take your time and let Jack take his."

"And Evan?"

"Feeling something real for someone else doesn't change any-thing. Evan understood you better than anyone and he'd understand now."

Dan hugs me until Sunny and Evie come running back into the room and look at us with bewildered expressions. "What did you do to Mommy?' Evie asks suspiciously, noticing my wet cheeks.

Dan laughs and raises his hands like he's surrendering, "Nothing, are you kidding me? She's been tickling me and teasing me and I only just stopped crying myself."

Evie frowns, her little arms folded across her chest.

"Listen, I'd better go before Muriel begins redecorating." He squeezes my arm. "You okay?"

"Sure." I shrug, "No Tim Tams for you next time, I was hoping for a few laughs."

Dan winks and kisses me on both cheeks. "Love you girl, go easy on the big guy." He gestures toward Jacks house and I punch him playfully in reply.

We walk to the car arms linked. "I didn't even ask how you are." I sniff apologetically.

Dan waves my words away with a free hand as he opens the Chevy and hops inside. "We wouldn't have time darling. The things I could tell you. I've already reduced you to tears once." He grins playfully and pulls out of the drive, Lyle Lovett crooning from the stereo.

I watch the red Chevy disappear and think about Dan, and wonder who listens to his worries. Who makes it better when Dr Dan is the one who needs fixing?

I wander back inside feeling humbled. In the kitchen my shopping list dangles on the fridge, secured by a magnet that says *Carpe Diem*. "Whatever." I grumble, grabbing a pen and scribbling *Tim Tams* in bold shouty capitals.

Chapter Thirteen

Billie

Cam sends a monthly letter. It arrives like clockwork on the last few days of the month. It's written in black ink on thick white paper, folded and stuffed into a stripey-edged airmail envelope. Quite often there are a few Scottish bank notes folded into the paper and it's a given that this be spent on a *wee something* for the twins.

I have created quite a ceremony around the letters. I look forward to them and savour the opening and reading, imagining him writing and the people and places he writes about. The letters have become a little lifeline to my other home, to my other family; Cam and Mom. And although the words are Cam's, I always feel Mom in the sentiments. Funny how love can blur the edges from one heart to another. When I think of him, I think of her, and when I read his words I hear her voice.

Silly really, but sometimes I find I can't open the letters straight away. I don't want to. Sometimes I sit them on the hallway table. I examine the envelope propped up and waiting to be opened: the stamps, postmark and the hand written address. I imagine the journey it's taken, from Cam's old kitchen table and the red post box in Arrasaigh's main street, over oceans and through the air, all the way here to me. I wait until the moment is perfect to read his words.

Today there are two letters, right on time: my expected envelope of treasures from Cam and another, a thick cream envelope, long and elegant with a red seal and a London postmark. Evie and Sunny are in the garden with Louie and Bets playing fetch and squirting water guns.

It's a gifted moment of peace to read my mail, so I grab my coffee and head to the swing seat outside.

Down on the grass Sunny is digging with a plastic spade for treasure while Louie watches, barking loudly. It's an odd sound, not his usual playful bark but something different, he sounds almost grumpy. Poor old thing, I best check Sunny hasn't been trying to ride him like a horse again.

"Louie, here boy!" I try to coax him away, making a mental note to tell Jack Louie seems a little out of sorts. But in seconds he seems back to his playful, affectionate self and is wrestling Sunny's spade from his little hands.

"Louie, it's not a stick. Mommy tell him it's not a stick." Sunny is yelling and chasing him, but Louie is off at top speed. Evie meanwhile has abandoned her water gun and lounges on her tummy on the grass transfixed with a small red pickup truck she is loading carefully with leaves.

I take a sip of coffee and weigh the letters in my hands. Cam's, a little crumpled, the envelope stained on the corner, the letters spidery, practiced script in blotchy blue biro. The other letter seems very formal in comparison. God, it must be another bill. Since Evan's death I've had a few surprises. Evan's student debts, the ones he'd told me were all paid off were evidently not.

Once again I say a silent prayer of thanks for our insurance policy. Without it, things would be very different. After the birth of the twins Evan organised life cover, a safeguard I'd believed wasn't necessary. I'd told him we didn't need it, that we should put the money into the house and fix things up. Thankfully Evan went ahead, and I wonder now if back then he sensed trouble ahead.

I wish I could say all his financial decisions were as well considered, but the bills that arrive periodically tell a different story. I sigh and place the formal letter underneath Cam's, study the old fashioned hand writing for a bit longer then prise it open.

The careful writing and heartfelt words give me great comfort. As I read news of the island and farm, Nell and the locals, I can hear Evie and Sunny's giggles and yells from the garden, lost in play. Closing my eyes, I take a moment to savour the letter. I'm picturing Spring in

Arrasaigh, birthing of the lambs, Cam's frazzled expression and wild hair as he returns from another long day out in the fields. Although he complains about how busy he is, I know he loves it. Lambing is his favourite time of year on the farm, the anticipation of new life, spring and an end in sight to the long grey of winter.

I imagine Nell in the kitchen, fussing over Cam. He becomes a shaggier more dishevelled form of his usual self this time of year. Unkempt and exhausted, he often doesn't return to the farmhouse until evening. Nell will leave a fire in the grate and a warm meal on the table. He'll sit at the old kitchen table with Samson at his feet, toes poking out of old woollen socks, whisky to hand.

Taking a long slow sip of coffee, I read on, ready to hear the rest of his news, which really is always the same as last month's news; but that's why I love it. The swing rocks gently below me, toes and heels pushing alternately encouraging the tiniest breeze amongst the heat.

"And so, it seems right that I should tell you love, I've been seeing a wee bit of Janey McGowne. I never thought I'd say it, but it's nice to have someone to share an evening with. She's a lovely woman, widowed ten years back, two kids at the university in Glasgow. She's a teacher here at the primary school. I think you'd like her…"

My heels sink to the deck with a thump and the swing stops abruptly. I look up to check the view ahead. Evie and Sunny are still in the yard with Louie and Bets and the sun still beats down overhead. Everything is the same. I'm not dreaming, I didn't just imagine that paragraph…

I read it again, this time aloud. Cam's letter falls on my lap and I rest my hands there, palms down, on top of the words that mark change.

Cam has found someone new.

I can't say why this shocks me to the core but it does. And it's not that I'm upset, I'm not. I'm stunned. Cam and Mom are my forever, my image of eternal love, mated for life, my evidence that there is only ever one perfect love. And because Mom won't ever have another love, I imagined Cam wouldn't either. It's been such a long time since her death, I suppose I expected things would always be the same; that Cam would be alone and I would be his first girl.

"Mommy!"

I paste on a smile and wave enthusiastically at Evie who is trying to show me something she's unearthed in the garden.

Cam has found someone new.

"Mommy!" Sunny this time, pointing at whatever it is Evie has, trying to get my attention.

Cam has found another love.

"Mommy!"

Evie and Sunny in unison, Louie and Bets have disappeared. I see a sheepish face appear from behind the hedge, then a fuzzy rear end, tail tucked safely between legs, heading round the corner of Jack's workshop.

It's a good thing. I breathe deeply and stand, the letter falling to the deck. No, I take another careful breath, composing my inner child and telling her to back off. It's a great thing. Cam is all alone, he has been all alone for too long. Is that what I want for him? To be old and alone in the farmhouse, his only happiness memories of another life? Mum has been gone a while and come to think of it so have I. What about Cam? Doesn't he deserve another chance at love?

I'm getting ahead of myself, Janie McGowne might just be a friend, another dowdy village widow who brings him the odd apple pie. But then Cam wouldn't have written about her. I know him well enough. She would have to already mean a lot for him to have felt the need to tell me. Janie McGowne is no dowdy widower bearing apple pie, although let's hope for Cam's sake she does bake apple pie. No, Janey McGowne is… I take a deep breath and clasp my hands to my chest; Cam's new love.

The breath out is a long one, very controlled and together. *I am an adult, I am an adult, I am an adult.*

Evie yells, having stuck a finger in her mouth she screams wildly, waving her hands. Honestly what now? Gathering myself I take a few steps toward the edge of the deck, smiling, beckoning her to come over for a cuddle. Now that I'm closer, I see quite clearly the source of hysteria.

Evie has dog shit in her hands. Evie has also got dog shit in her mouth.

Screaming like a grossed out teenager I'm off the deck and beside her in four loping strides. She holds the offending smelly hands out to me, wailing, her mouth open, teeth smeared brown. Mustn't vomit, mustn't vomit…the garden hose isn't far away but the smell is overpoweringly awful. Sunny is on my heels whooping and clapping, "Evie's eating poop! Evie's eating poop!"

Hose on full blast, Evie has a shocking power shower, silencing her yells for a second or two. When the shock subsides she opens her mouth to wail again. Without thinking I aim the hose for her once white teeth. Eyes wide she splutters and gasps for breath. Oh God, is anyone watching? Even Sunny is quiet and wide eyed, he looks warily from Evie to me, afraid the hose is coming his way.

"I'm sorry darling," I scoop her up and run for the shower, this could be a national disaster, my reaction quite disproportionate to the event. But really, dog shit in her mouth? It's beyond bad mothering! It's down in the too-preoccupied-to-care category. Shitty parenting at its best! The thought doesn't make me smile. All humour has been blasted with the garden hose and as I strip her clothes and rinse her little mouth I dry gag again.

Bloody Jack, bloody dogs, bloody Cam. I cuss under my breath, brushing her teeth, gums and tongue with a *My Little Pony* toothbrush and liberal dollops of Spiderman toothpaste.

Naked but still smelly, I put her small confused body under the hot shower, then realise the remaining smell is actually coming from me. My t-shirt is stained brown where I lifted her, and the ends of my hair are matted and pongy. As I begin to strip off Sunny joins in, pulling off his clothes, thrilled with his dog poop cupcake prank.

Soon we three are all in the shower, the yelling and crying have turned to giggles and the stench transformed to fragrant soapy bubbles. Evie stamps her feet in puddles of water that gather by the plug, asking why the mud tasted so bad. Sunny draws stick men on the steamy glass and I let the hot water run over my head; perspective beautifully restored.

✑

It's almost 6.00 pm when I remember the other letter.

I'm leaning in toward the bathroom mirror applying a fine coat of mascara to tired eyes. Maybe it's the tired eyes that remind me. The concealer applied to dark shadows camping out beneath my lower lids might fool others but not me. My eyes have aged. There's a lifetime of melancholy bagging underneath these eyes, and let me tell you, no amount of concealer and no ignoring of bills can remedy the situation.

Yes, that bloody bill awaits me, probably still upside down on the deck, waiting to be opened, surrounded by the faint odour of dog shit. What an afternoon. I check my reflection again, choosing to delay bill opening a bit longer.

It isn't often I take the time to *beautify* myself. In fact, looking back, the last night out I had in St. Cloud was the mid-winter carnival, almost two years passed. The night Evan had his pre-death experience. The warm up that should have warned me of what was to come, of what I should have pre-empted and prevented.

Shaking my hair out with such force I feel dizzy, I push the negative memories away. I haven't the strength to deal with them now. Tonight is another first, a night out with friends and I am determined to enjoy myself. Raife's gig is tonight at Santos and I am *making the effort*. I am going out. I have a babysitter and God dammit I will have a good time.

As I brush my hair I remember Cam's letter and instinctively smell dog poo, there's an alternate sad/happy/disgusted reaction to the thoughts and I smile, leaning in to the mirror to apply some lip gloss. God, if Iris were here she'd rugby tackle me with a damp flannel, rub off the sallow gloss and slap some sassy red on my pout. But she's not, so I purse my pale lips together, try to ignore the baggy eyes and smile at my reflection; which half smiles back looking just the littlest bit unsure.

By 7.00 pm I'm standing in quiet disbelief in the middle of the toy scattered living room. All around is quiet, really quiet, as in, *just me and the birds, no children* quiet. It's very strange and I'm not sure I like it. I stand for a minute more, taking in the chaos of the floor: Lego, stuffed animals, books, crayons, unidentifiable game pieces scattered, play dough remnants pressed into the rug. Nodding slowly, I decide the quiet is in fact good. Better than good. It's exactly what I need.

My neighbour on the opposite side to Jack, Marlene, has always been very generous with her time when it comes to Evie and Sunny. Her children have long flown the nest and she loves to see the twins, always offering to babysit. Tonight the twins will stay at her house meaning I have a whole night off and a possible sleep-in tomorrow.

Turning on the radio I hear Dan's silky voice and relax. Tonight is his early show, the reggae is nice and I pour myself a wine, slip into my dress and wait for Zoe and Felix to pick me up. They're late as usual. I imagine Felix, arms folded, waiting in the car while Zoe fusses. Felix's mother has arrived from Germany, hence their first venture out since baby Freya.

Such a nice time of night, the sun is low and the evening light soft. Relaxing into the swing seat with my wine I rock gently, watching the glimmer of ocean and the changing green of the bush ahead. The light casts pale shadows on the grass, low sun behind tea trees and pungas, spiky long leaves and elegant pale bark in vague hazy shapes that move and change as the wind breathes and the bush sways. The gust lifts and deposits something white on the lawn. I watch as the rectangle of paper rises, tumbles and falls with the same timed perfection as the leaves. The letter.

Crap. Tempting as it is to leave the neglected bill to the fate of the wind, I chase the letter down the lawn until after a few near misses I catch it firmly. My neatly brushed hair has frizzed in the wind and I sigh, feeling my calm joy in nature ebb slightly. Back on the deck I slug my wine and rip the envelope open. Outside a car beeps and I hear Felix's baritone calling my name.

Distractedly I read the first line once, then again. The horn beeps a second time and I read it a third. The envelope drops to the floor and I let my breath go, exhaling for the first time since I began to read. Carefully I fold the letter and place it in my bag.

"Come on, we're already late!" yells Zoe.

Slamming the front door behind me, I jog to the waiting car and slide into the back seat smiling. Zoe is staring at me, her small nose screwed up in minor disgust. "Are you going to wear any shoes?"

Looking down I blush, "Woops."

Sandals on, hair re-brushed I'm back in the car moments later, flushed and excited. Zoe shakes her head in despair. "Let's go Felix, this one's forgotten how to function without two babies in tow. Put your foot down before she changes her mind."

Felix smiles and winks at me in the mirror. "You good to go Billie?"

I beam. "Get us out of here." He salutes and revs the engine, the sound isn't terribly impressive as we're in a Toyota family wagon. Zoe claps a hand to her forehead as the tires do a mini screech out of the driveway into the night. I settle back to enjoy the drive, fingers clasped tightly around my bag.

The family van hugs the tight corners of the winding roads heading to the city. Felix sings along to Bon Jovi, and Zoe leans back trying to be heard over the noise. Her hands gesticulate, she nods, her mouth opens and closes almost in time to the music. I mirror the nod occasionally and smile. I can't hear a word she's saying but I'm not really trying to listen. I'm taking in the familiar sights and smells, the music, the friends and the happiness, shiny and bright and real as the night air and the musky smell on the breeze.

Amidst it all I hear my own voice, small but proud, echoing over the music, Felix's singing and Zoe's chatter, repeating the words in type that lie folded in my bag; "…publication of your debut novel…negotiation of terms and contract…three book deal." I blink a few times readjusting focus, pinch myself discreetly on the soft inside of my wrist, but so far I'm still awake.

It must be true. In my bag lies folded an offer of publication for *St. Germaine*, the novel I'd almost forgotten I'd submitted in the clouded month before Evan's death.

Joy and despair in equal measures.

"Music was my refuge. I could crawl into the space between the notes and curl my back to loneliness."

Maya Angelou

The city at night: a potent blend of sensual pleasures. Lights sparkle and blink from cafes and bars, neon signs find life in the darkness after a day of faded identity under the suns' bright rays. Smells of street food waft on heavy air and music is everywhere.

Bars open their doors to the streets and tables and chairs spill on to sidewalks. Jazz and reggae mingle disrespectfully, somehow creating an offbeat rhythm that works. Sweet and salty opposites attract, sounds, smells, flavours and people.

As we walk down Main Street, the vintage piano that lives under a sheltered awning by a tall hibiscus tree plays Mozart. A small crowd gather and an upturned straw fedora catches money from generous listeners. An old man, stooped and unshaven wearing a faded hawaiian shirt plays expertly. Gnarled fingers caressing the keys and calloused bare feet on the pedals. The clear melody rises above the chaos of music and conversation all around, his rhythm and timing exquisite.

We stop on the edge of the crowd, it's impossible not to. Felix's set expression softens and Zoe links arms. We are a small chain of togetherness in the midst of unexpected beauty. The old man's eyes have yet to open, his face shuttered, fingers speaking through the keys. Felix fishes around in his pocket for a note and I follow suit. Bending to place the paper bills in the upturned hat I notice the torn refuse bag by the man's feet. As he presses the peddles of the old piano his belongings rustle in the plastic bag that contains his world.

Santos hums. A steady stream of people flow in and out of the wide doors, open to the warm evening. Small clusters of friends sit around tables sipping drinks, others stand talking and laughing, bottles of island beer in hand. Strings of lights shaped like red chilli peppers hang from the overhead veranda and tables glow with votive candles.

Inside the crowd is thicker and the light low. The scene slow and syrupy, filtered through the low reggae beat. Despite the crush of bodies, the atmosphere is relaxed. At the bar is a three deep line of patiently waiting locals. Behind the bar Bastian pours, mixes, uncorks and serves drinks twice as fast as anyone else. The Santos staff are at full capacity. There are six bodies serving including Josefina and Jed. As we weave our way through the crowd I see Sadie balancing a tray of glasses heading back toward the bar.

"God, I hope it doesn't get any busier." Zoe leans in. "Bastian will put us to work."

I'm thinking that actually that might be a nice option. I'd like a reason to be busy, to forget that the last time I was here at night was St. Cloud Fiesta, a lifetime ago. And although the world has turned since then, all around these smells and sounds are the same.

Felix, a head above the line at the bar is noticed by Bastian who grins broadly; one night like this and he can take a month off. "Nice crowd." Felix reaches a hand out to high five Bastian.

"Who'd have thought young Raife had so many fans?" Bastian is passing drinks over the bar to Felix, quickly moving on to next in line, no time for small talk.

I take my bottle of cold beer from Felix's outstretched arm thinking that Raife's looks may have a lot to do with the turn out. But then Raife is a local, a boy born and bred in St. Cloud. He must still be a familiar face to many. People will be curious to see what he's been doing since he left, to see if he's made good. And if he has they'll say he's a good St. Cloud boy; it's all down to his roots. If he bombs they'll say he should never have left.

We clink bottles and try to chat above the noise but I'm only half listening. Santos is a sensory overload and my existence for a while has been closeted. I want to watch and smell and listen and feel my way around this forgotten world, and so as Zoe chats in my ear I listen distractedly. Bound with threads of anticipation and anxiety I wriggle my toes, feel my feet firm on the dusty bar floor and breathe. It's all okay. I'm okay. I'm holding on and moving on, and today someone wants to publish my book.

"What are you smiling about?" Dan nudges my shoulder. He looks around the bar with a disapproving eye. "God, who are all these people?"

"Nice to see you too." I smile as he frowns, a perfect picture of gloomy couture. "Who's ruffled your feathers?"

"Nobody."

"Is that the problem?"

He breaks into a small smile but doesn't answer as Felix moves in offering drinks and man banter. Zoe is talking about Freya and the boys and to my shame I'm half listening again; on the small stage area I see Jack.

In a pale grey t-shirt and old jeans, he moves in and out of the light, carrying an amp, arranging some wiring, then connecting what seems like too many instruments and speakers on such a small stage. His expression is composed and careful.

Dan and I are pressed closely side by side; dreamy and grumpy, two gnomes left behind by Snow-White. "Ginny told me to tell you she won't be coming." He slugs his beer, eyes straight ahead, fixed on the stage set up.

"Why not? She promised she'd be here."

"Well, she's not." His arms are folded tightly across his chest.

"Okay." Eyebrows raised I give a sideways glance toward Zoe, who grins looking relaxed and radiant. *What's up with him?* I mouth silently, signalling my eyes toward old gloomy couture.

She shrugs and throws a peanut at Dan's head. "What's going on Dan? Had a rough day?" The peanut bounces off his forehead and plops into his drink. Zoe gives him no time to react, which I suspect from the look on his face is a good move. "Did you see that?" She nudges Felix, shaking her head in awe of her aim.

I try not to giggle, and when I turn back to Dan he's gone. As the lights dim and the crowd begin to clap, I see the back of his golden head at the edge of the bar.

One perfect halo of light shines down on a stool set centre stage, the crowd are shadows as noise falls away replaced by expectant hush. Then there's Raife, all alone, head down, taking his time, tuning his guitar. Suddenly he flashes a smile and starts to play. It's a long, acoustic solo, fingers picking a melody, the sound so simple yet complete that when he starts to sing I'm taken by surprise. His voice contrasts the clarity of chords so perfectly the sounds seem made for each other. It's that sweet and salty contrast, perfection in polar extremes; the broken scratchy voice amidst the clear, melodic tune.

With each chord his voice catches and pulls across the melody. Where the guitar guides the song his voice blurs the edges of the notes and there's magic in the sound.

It takes the entire first song, start to finish before I can look away. In music Raife is transformed, all the edges have fallen away and I realise for the first time since I met him, he sounds sincere. Now those eyes match the words, there's no hiding and what's even lovelier is his apparent lack of self-consciousness. Maybe it's another act, so well-practiced he's got me truly fooled, but I can't help feel that what I see and hear are real, that there are no games or pretence, that this expression through music is true.

All around me are wide, dreamy eyes, every face angled toward Raife. Zoe takes a long, deep breath and Felix catches my eye, shrugging his shoulders and smiling. From Felix this is praise in the lesser known language of *grunty male*. He can't get too enthusiastic over anything that doesn't involve a drum set and a bass guitar. Felix doesn't have long to wait, after a few solo acoustic numbers leaving lady folks with their tongues lolling Raife brings a few local musicians on to the stage to join him.

In no time the energy has changed completely as two more guitars, a banjo and a full drum set ramp up the sound. Soon people are dancing, the bar gets busier and the air thicker. Raife stands, his guitar strapped across his body, strumming, foot keeping time and singing along with the band. They play like they've been together for years and I can't help but wonder what the hell Raife has been doing. Why isn't he signed up by a label and making a living from this. I'd put money on his success and if his reception in Santos is any reflection so would most.

Zoe has dragged Felix up to dance. Jed who has been bopping around behind the bar has made a dash for the dancefloor with Sadie. Poor Felix looks a little lost, trying not to stand out too much even though he's a head and shoulders above most. I can't bring myself to dance, tonight it just feels good to watch. I look for Dan and see him at the far side of the bar, leaning against the wall, eyes on the stage, sipping beer from a long necked bottle looking sulky and drunk.

A hand settles on my shoulder and I turn to meet Jack standing close behind me.

"Hey." I reach for his hand and give it a small squeeze and he pulls me gently back toward him, his hand moving slowly to my waist.

"You okay?" He leans his head carefully toward my ear so I can hear him over the music. I nod and smile, grateful he's here. Jack doesn't dance, this I know for sure. Jack Kelly doesn't dance and I don't think I could bear to watch if he ever did.

"He's pretty good." Jack gestures toward the stage where Raife shines.

"He's incredible."

Jack nods, his fingers moving gently along my waist.

There's a buzz of electricity that spreads from his fingertips and I focus on the sweaty dancers, feeling a blush rise to my cheeks. My heart is suddenly beating in my knickers. Oh God, I'm sure he must know. I am a lusty desperate woman. Blushing, I quickly cover my face with my hands.

"What's wrong?"

"Nothing," I speak through a small gap in my fingers. "I'm hot."

"Do you want me to take you home?"

My hands drop quickly from my face. Am I that transparent?

"Yes." I turn around crimson-faced. "I mean no." Placing a palm on my forehead I take a slow deliberate breath and ask my heart to return from my knickers to my chest cavity. "Maybe I'll just have a drink."

Jack smiles and my wayward heart flutters happily. That's the smile I love, not the composed expression of before but this. This smile, reserved for me, a smile that never seems rehearsed or planned. His eyes sparkle in the dim light, he's teasing.

"What?" I frown, thoughts manifest in a glitzy sign above my head. *Horny*, in flashing capitals with an arrow pointing my way.

"You."

I'm about to answer when there's a small commotion to our right. Someone has stumbled, and as they struggle to right themselves they pull over a few more chairs and spill a few drinks. Through the heads, I can just about see a crumpled version of Dan. He raises a hand in greeting and stumbles again. Jack reaches to steady him and Dan grabs hold, pulling himself toward us, hand by hand up the length of Jack's arm. Trying to right his tall body he slings an arm around Jack's shoulders and sets his face. It's the overly serious face of one who's really believes no-one has noticed they're drunk.

"You okay champ?" Jack asks.

"Never been better."

Dan's expression is flabby and un-composed. I've never seen him like this. "Want to sit down?" I offer.

"Nope."

"Let's go outside and get some air." Jack begins to steer Dan toward the doors.

Raife has just announced he and the band are taking a break and sweaty bodies move from the dance floor to the bar or outside to the veranda.

"Think I need another drink." Dan gestures toward the bar.

"Come on buddy, let's have a breather first." Jack doesn't wait for Dan's reply but steers him around toward the door. I lock arms on his opposite side and together we guide him through the crowd and out into the night air.

There are as many people outside as in, and no seats to be had. Jack leads our wobbling threesome out toward the sidewalk where together we lower Dan to sit on the kerb. The road is wide and few cars pass. Beyond the tarmac, the line of palms and long stretch of beach is endless ocean. We sit side by side, elbows on knees, the sounds of Santos behind us and the dark glint of waves under moonlight ahead.

"Did I just fall over?" Dan murmurs.

"You did." Jack answers.

"Hell."

I giggle and turn to look at poor Dan. This out of control behaviour is very unlike him. "Do you want us to take you home?" I squeeze his leg. "You're not yourself, I…"

"And who the hell am I?" I flinch at his tone, he's angry. "Tell me sweetheart? Because…" he pauses and his face clouds. He turns to me concerned, "Did I just yell? God, I'm an ass! And you know what else?" We listen, stunned by his outburst. "I hate this place, I'm sick of it. We never move on." He gestures to Jack. "None of us. No-one ever moves on."

"Come on Dan, lighten up." says Jack ignoring the jibe.

"What's to move on from? I love it here! I'm going nowhere," I sling an arm around him. "Anyway, you love this place more than anyone, you can't go anywhere. How would we all survive?" I lean in and kiss him on the cheek.

"I hate my life."

"Oh my God, now you're being melodramatic." I give him a good nudge in the ribs. "Come on now desperado, you're killing my night out."

"I need to move on."

"Have you been on the whisky?" I lean past Dan whose head rests in his hands and stage whisper to Jack. "My step-Dad, Cam gets really depressing after too much whisky." I'm about to offer some more sage advice to Dan when we're interrupted.

"Hey kids, what's all this? Are you coming back inside?" It's Zoe, all smiles.

"No, I'm depressed." Dan mutters into his hands as Jack claps him heartily on the back.

Felix and Jed are close behind armed with more drinks. We stand up and take the cold bottles, drinking thirstily, happy for the distraction. Everyone is buzzing from the music and the atmosphere.

Raife approaches, just managing to avoid the table of ladies vying for his attention. "Thanks for the beer," he claps Felix's shoulder. There's a flurry of compliments and more back slapping as everyone tells Raife how great he is. Everyone I notice, apart from Jack. He has turned back to the kerbside seat and is side by side with Dan.

Minutes later there's a call over the sound system, Raife starts, intermission over. "Best get back up there." Running a hand through his golden hair he dazzles us with a smile and turns to leave. And as I watch I see something flicker in his eyes as he catches sight of Jack and Dan sitting behind us facing the street, his smile is gone.

Everyone is talking and beginning to head back inside, but Raife ducks around and bends down behind Dan and Jack. Jack nods and stands as Raife leans in to Dan. Jack is heading toward me, he smiles gently and gestures toward Santos but I'm distracted as behind him I see Dan shake his head and give Raife the finger.

Undeterred Raife jogs past, winks at me and weaves through the remaining crowd to reach the stage where he hops up, nods to the band and begins to play. In the doorway I look back but Dan's gone and I'm swallowed by the crowd, the music and mayhem before I can worry much more. Raife plays on. Santos is at capacity and all around people dance, sing and laugh fuelled by the magic that accompanies great music.

I lean into Jack and feel the night around me.

It's 1.00 am when I stumble through the door, and not because I'm sozzled but because I'm bone achingly tired, my feet throb and ears buzz. The taxi beeps its horn as it reverses out of the drive and I hear Zoe shouting something unintelligible. Poor thing, she'll be up and down with a baby whilst I get to sleep late, no kids for me in the morning. The thought is wild, and the brief feeling of freedom has me whoop out loud. But there's no whoop in response, no-one to party with, and that's probably a good thing. I'm too tired for shenanigans.

Humming, I kick off my shoes and do a little twirl. Throwing my bag on the sofa I whoop again remembering the letter folded neatly inside. I take a run and jump on to the sofa belly first, rugby tackle the bag and fish out the letter to read again, then again, then once more this time out loud. Sighing happily, I'm asleep on the sofa with the letter clutched to my chest in approximately three and a half minutes.

My hazy half-formed dream features Billie Skylark the critically acclaimed, hugely successful writer. I have dark-framed, uber-cool glasses, hair in a messy bun secured with a pencil and I'm wearing some smart, but casual, clever outfit, featuring a matching pashmina draped casually around relaxed but terribly assured shoulders. I'm being interviewed for Mindfood magazine and I'm trying not to intimidate the interviewer with my wit and intellect. Just as the photographer arrives on the scene I get a bad feeling, the foreboding gloom that descends when part of your brain figures out you're actually dreaming. Damn, something is not right, the pashmina is gone and looking down I can see my elegant pumps have been replaced by very bad HI Tec trainers; *so* not the look I'm going for. I smile anyway but the photographer who has been a little blurry till now swims into focus. It's Evan and he smiles conspiratorially, his hair has grown, now he's the one with the messy bun, a pencil behind his ear saying loudly. *I hate my life, I've got to move on, no-one ever fucking moves on.*

I wake abruptly, gasping, the precious letter crumpled and damp in my hand. *Dan.* Sleepily I fish around for my phone and text him: *Hope ur ok, call me tomorrow after Advil. Bx.*

I wait for a moment just in case he might miraculously be awake and text me right back, but he doesn't and I pad through the dark house to bed, wishing I'd gone to sleep there in the first place.

When I feel his hand on my leg I know it's time.

He has come to me, he's ready. I stretch lazily, welcoming him like I'd always known he'd be here. He lies behind me, a hand stroking my leg, up and down, slow and steady. He is my future and I'm ready. His hand travels up, grazing a breast, moving to my throat where a single finger traces lines back and forward, shoulder, collarbone, neck, pausing on my lips. He whispers something I can't make out, my mind still heavy with sleep, words float and rise to the ceiling where the overhead fan spins and sends them back, rearranged and indistinct.

Again the hands and their gentle caress, I reach to touch them and here time stops. Reality crashes through the imagined dream and my head swims desperately for the surface. These hands are not Jack's and I am not dreaming.

The gasp before the scream sucks the air from the dark bedroom and powers my lungs with a force borne of instinct. The sound is terrifying, fear driven and desperate. As the scream fades my body is transformed; from rigid to feral and I lunge and kick, scrabbling my way off the bed. But nothing happens, there is no counter reaction, the intruder doesn't move or speak, doesn't try to run or wrestle me to the ground. Terrified I grab the book on the nightstand and hurl it toward the still figure, there's a muffled moan as I lunge for the light switch.

Lying on his side, propped comfortably on an elbow is Raife. He watches me carefully, one hand rubbing his jaw, a slow smile creeping across his face.

"I thought you were enjoying it. You could have said, that hurt." He rubs his head, *The Grapes of Wrath* lies spread-eagled on the floor, the spine broken and pages scattered.

"What the hell are you doing here?" I'm leaning against the window, trying to cover myself with a sheet as he continues to smile and stare. "How dare you let yourself in. Get out! Get out before I call the cops."

"Billie." He says my name with such familiarity, like we're lovers having a small tiff. "Don't be like that. Come back in here, shut the light off and we'll carry on. Jack won't ever have to know."

"Are you insane? Get out!" I'm shaking, my voice breaks. "Get out."

"Come on baby, I know what you need. I see the way you look at Jack, I know you leave the door open for him every night. I've been watching. But he's not interested, never was."

"Shut up and get out."

Raife sits up slowly, raising both hands in a gesture of surrender. "Okay, I'm going. It might have been nice for both of us you know." He shrugs looking vaguely bored. "You're not really my type anyway."

I'm so angry I want to hurt him. How dare he? I dive toward him and swing as hard as I can, but he's too quick and is up off the bed, leaving me to fall sideways, my fist making contact with the wall. Pain radiates through my hand as I scramble to my feet, swinging for him again.

It's then that I hear the banging; loud, angry banging coming from the deck. I open my mouth to scream his name but find my voice is gone. Another bang and a dull thud as a shoulder makes contact with the door. Raife doesn't move and I wait, terrified of what will happen next and what this must look like.

Raife stands by the side of the bed, arms folded, waiting patiently. Huddled on the floor, wrapped in a sheet I sob. I know now that this was Raife's intention, to create the scene and wait for Jack. I hear him call my name loudly, his footsteps racing through the house. As he bursts through the door, the world is still for one interminably long second. In a glance he sees me half naked on the floor sobbing and Raife standing by the bed, eyes dark, face impassive.

"Don't you ever knock Jack?"

Raife is about to grin, about to try and spin his story and make Jack hurt, but the words never make it to his lips. The punch is so hard Raife's feet leave the ground. Jack barely looks at him before bending toward me, lifting me up. "Are you okay?" I can't talk through my tears and bury my head into his shoulder as he holds me. "Tell me you're okay, please…are you okay?"

I nod and he lays me on the bed before turning to Raife who is getting slowly to his feet. Jack doesn't wait, he pulls him up roughly but Raife is ready and takes a hard punch at Jack's gut. He doubles over and Raife slaps him across the back of the head. The action so disrespectful it is more shocking than the punches that follow.

I scream at them to stop, but my voice drowns in the swirling fury of the room. Time stretches and contracts, and all around is the dull thud of blood in my ears and the impact of fist on bone.

Raife seems to deflate, the will to fight gone with the last hard punch. Jack's fist makes contact with his stomach and he doubles over. Before he can fall Jack grabs his shoulders and pins him to the wall, a glass framed photo of me and Evan shatters and hits the floor.

"Get out."

Raife blinks dazed, he nods slowly, tongue licking a small trail of blood that trickles from the corner of his mouth. I don't look up till he's gone.

It's a while before I'm calm. Raife has taken off in Jack's truck, the doors are locked and curtains pulled. Jack has bathed my hand and strapped it. I'm clothed in warm sweats, with a hot cup of tea and we sit side by side on the sofa.

"I thought he was you."

Jack closes his eyes and leans forward, elbows on knees, letting his hands run through his hair. "I heard you scream, I couldn't get in, I…" his hands are shaking, "You should press charges, we need to call the cops."

"No."

"I'm so sorry Billie."

"It wasn't you."

"But he was trying to get at me, it's my fault."

"I don't understand, what do you owe him?" He shakes his head but doesn't answer.

"He didn't…?"

"No, he didn't."

"What a fucking mess." He lowers his head again, hands rubbing the top of his scalp, he takes a long slow breath. "I want to kill him."

"What happened between you two?"

Jack turns away and I reach for his shoulder to pull him around, his eyes are closed. Without thinking I crawl into his lap and he buries his face in my hair whispering he's sorry over and over. I find his mouth and kiss him slowly and he returns the kiss with such tenderness I almost forget the drama that brought us this. He kisses me again and there's desperation in the act; words he won't say, the act a step toward their delivery.

Later, we fall asleep entwined on the sofa once again, and when I wake the light is new. We are face to face, my head rests on his arm, chests almost touching, legs twisted. Jacks eyes are open and despite the nights events his eyes clear.

"I love you." He pushes my hair back from my face and a tear escapes, sliding carefully toward his fingers.

"I love you too." I touch his cheek and wince, my bandaged hand tender and aching.

"Want to hear a story?"

I nod and close my eyes. "It's my favourite thing."

I know the decision to talk has lightened the load he carries. Whatever he tells me will be okay, I have prepared in my head for this story many times.

"When I was seventeen I killed Raife's girlfriend."

Chapter Fourteen

Billie

The words echo around the room, unsaid till now they bounce from walls and deflect on shiny surfaces, returning again before resting in the air between us.

I don't answer because there's no response that will do.

I want to say,…*Excuse me? Come again? My mistake but I thought you just said killed, did you mean kissed?"* As my internal narration quietens, the moment extends in contemplative silence. I take my time, tuck judgement away as best I can to leave my mind open and free to listen. He waits, watching me carefully, and the pressure of expectation is so high the air crackles with a thousand responses that would crush his honesty to shame.

"Tell me."

Two words, all I can manage. But I hold his hand as I say them, knowing that this story will change everything.

Jack breathes heavily, closes his eyes and is silent for a moment. I imagine him clawing back hidden memories, dusting them off, anticipating their jagged edges.

"We were in a car wreck, here in St. Cloud. I was driving. I'd been drinking." His tone is emotionless; these are the facts. "We were in Raife's truck, the three of us, high and drunk. Lil was in the middle without a belt."

"I'm so sorry." I don't know what else to say. There's nothing to say that can change anything, no comfort to be had, an accident with repercussions that ripple altering lives forever.

"She hit the windscreen and we rolled right off the road and into the bush. We were all knocked out, without her belt Lil was a mess. She was in hospital for a long time. She healed pretty well, but the scarring on her face was bad."

He stops for a minute and turns on his back, eyes to the ceiling. "She was beautiful." He takes a slow breath. "After, with her face scarred like it was…" he pauses, gathering himself then carries on, his words slow and careful. "She moved away. They didn't make it through the accident, her and Raife I mean. Afterwards things had changed, we all drifted. Lil moved to Australia, then after…Raife left for the States. I stayed and went down the tubes for a while. I'd fucked over everyone's lives, one stupid decision…" he tails off.

"But you said you…" I pause because the word is too weighty. "You said Lil was dead."

"She is."

"I don't understand."

"Lil was a mess. She felt like she'd lost everything. She came to see me before she left, told me it wasn't my fault. Said she had to get away from St. Cloud where everyone remembered how she used to be. She had to get away from Raife too. She'd loved him but Raife…he'd never really been serious about anyone. He'd strung Lil along for a while, he was a player. He liked her for sure but it had never been serious for him." He pauses watching the early light dance across the room.

"Something happened to Raife after the accident, like a light went out. He went to see Lil while she was in hospital but it didn't last. Mama thought he blamed himself but he didn't, he blamed me. He didn't say goodbye to Lil when she left. Two months later she was dead, an overdose. They found her body in a motel in Sydney. No note, all alone."

The story settles for a time and the light around us gets gradually brighter. I keep hold of Jack's hand and he lies still, eyes open, watching pictures of his past reflect in sunlight on the stark ceiling.

"When we heard, Raife went into a spin. You know St. Cloud, people were talking, saying Lil had killed herself, heartbroken, and it was the Kelly brothers' doing. One crashed the car, ruining her face and the other one dumps her because of it. Mama said Raife needed to get away. They paid for his ticket to the States. He left quickly and never came back. Not until now."

"But you never left."

"I had to stay, it was my fault. I deserved to live with it."

"But it was an accident."

"I was drunk Billie. It was my fault, there's no way around that. Lil died because of that night and Raife went off the rails. I've spent the last seventeen years feeling like I owe Raife. I screwed things up for more than just Lil."

"But you've no way of knowing how it would have turned out anyway. It's a terrible thing, I can't imagine what it's like to have to live with that. But you've become the scapegoat for everything that's ever gone wrong for Raife."

"Maybe you get what you deserve."

"Jack…" I reach out for him but he turns away.

"It's not as easy as that Billie."

I stroke his hair. "I know."

I wait, smoothing his hair back from his face, waiting till I hear him breathe. "Maybe if you were both able to talk about it, even just once, hear how he feels, say your piece, shout it out, whatever you guys do. Maybe it might be better." He shakes his head. "Have you ever asked how he feels about it? Who he blames? Maybe you'd be surprised by his answer."

"I know how he feels."

"Talk to him one more time Jack. Maybe not now, not when you've just punched his lights out." I lean in and gently kiss his cheek. "But before he takes off again. Maybe if you give him the chance to tell you properly how he feels he might stop being so angry, get it all out once and for all."

He turns back to face me. "Are you done?"

"Yes."

"How do you feel?" I can't gauge his tone. "I'm taking your advice and asking. How do you feel, knowing now what I've done?" His face is serious, eyes downcast.

I reach for his chin, shadowed and rough, tipping it up toward me so I can see his eyes. "You were seventeen. You made a mistake and you're still paying." His eyes are raised to meet mine, waiting, needing more.

I suddenly understand. Jack's life since then has centred on seeking the very thing no-one can give him. He wants to be forgiven, every act of reclamation, of second chances and charity are part of a subconscious bid for redemption, an attempt to barter guilt with good and make peace with God. And it's all so bloody tragic I'm crying again, just when he needs me not to.

"I'm sorry." Jabbing an eye with my hand I steady myself and carry on. "I'm sad Jack. It's been so hard for you. I'm sad for you all; sad that you've lived underneath that mistake since, sad that you've suffered because of it." I run a hand across my streaming eyes. "But you've got to stop sometime. It's become who you are. You can't wear it forever and neither can Raife. You're more than your past. We make mistakes and we make amends the best way we can but we have to live." He nods slowly. "We've seen enough life wasted."

We're both silent. All the words crowd out the light. I press my hand to closed eyelids, the red and purple psychedelic haze mirrors emotions raw and spent. Jack pulls me to him, prising my hands away, kissing each eyelid softly. Carefully he opens my clenched fists and rubs the palms where fingernails have left indentations.

Slowly, slowly an unravelling begins, and the need to give myself completely to him makes me dizzy. Moving to my mouth he kisses me with the same gentle intensity of before. An unspoken promise that leaves me breathless; my heart in my knickers once again.

A phone rings from somewhere in the depths of my bag and I pull myself up reluctantly, thinking it might be Marlene about the twins. Real life, my life calling, mayday; neglected and ignored. When finally, I find the phone it's Dan's number flashing impatiently on the screen. I ready myself to tease him.

"Hey, it's Dan. Is Jack with you?"

I hesitate, picturing him frowning, frustrated I've ignored his advice. "Uh huh," silent pause, "do you want to speak to him?"

"Yeah."

"Are you okay?"

"Been better. Sorry if I was an idiot last night."

"It's fine you were…"

"Let me speak to Jack will you?"

"Sure, hang on." I'm concerned, it's barely 7.00 am and he sounds upset."

Shrugging I pass the phone to Jack.

They talk and I head to the kitchen to make coffee in an attempt to give Jack some privacy. The coffee has barely started to brew when he enters the kitchen.

"Everything okay?"

"Can I take your car?"

"What's wrong?"

This is a funny question considering how long his answer might be if he were to answer honestly… *where to begin, well my brother's a mad stalker, I'm struggling with a few hang ups because I think I ruined a few lives drunk driving when I was seventeen, my Dad hates me and my Mom is losing her marbles…oh, and I fell for the girl next door whose husband killed himself because he was a little crazy too.*

Instead Jack simply shrugs. "Dan needs to talk to me. I'm not sure what the hell's wrong with him, but he asked if I could come over now."

"Now? It's just gone seven."

"He wouldn't call if it weren't a big deal."

"Right," I nod in agreement. "Here." I thrust the keys at him. "And tell him there's no room for any more drama right now." Jack turns by the door. "We have enough, ask him to put his on hold at least until Monday."

He smiles just a little before walking back to where I stand, two waiting coffee cups to hand. Cupping the back of my head with one hand he pulls me in, kisses me deeply then is gone.

As the tires of my old blue Honda skid out of the driveway I crumple just a little. Repercussions of last night and this morning make my head ache and my legs weary. The coffee bubbles in divine reply to my call and I pour the thick, black, aromatic brew into my favourite mug. Sip and breathe in that order, sip and breathe.

❧

Jack

The air is fresh and cool; heavy, humid night washed away by rain to leave a morning so clear Jack is dazzled.

Pulling his cap low to shield his eyes from the light he drives with ease around the tight bends of the bay. He will go and see Dan, find out what's going on, but first, he'll find Raife. He's pretty sure he knows where he's gone. He's broke and there's no other place else for his brother to go.

Raife will be licking his wounds and sulking. He'll be bedded down in Joseph's old boat; *Liberty*. The old vessel has been moored in the same secluded bay for years, not far from their childhood home, just another old fishing boat, weather worn and no longer sea worthy.

When they were boys Joseph used it to fish and escape. He'd take off all day, sometimes for days, fishing alone. When the chaos of his young family was too much he'd leave and Amandine was never sure when he'd return, or if he really ever fished.

The boat had a small cabin with a gas stove and single bunk, it was a refuge. Joseph had a place to go for solitude. The family were glad of the boat, not that they fished or sailed together, but because they too needed refuge from Joseph.

Driving slowly along the dirt road that leads to the water's edge, Jack parks, turns off the engine and waits. He watches the horizon, the edge of the ocean, the waves and the old boat. All is as it was. It's a private cove, no-one ever comes here. Access from the road is unsealed and potholed, the sailing route out past the sand banks difficult to negotiate. Years ago Joseph had paid a friend for a permanent mooring. The old man had since passed but no-one had ever asked them to move the boat, and so she floats lazily, moored to a wooden dock, at the far end of the sandy beach. The sight speaks silently of neglect, things that no longer matter, time passed and forgotten, age and decay.

There are no signs of life on the boat. Raife's probably still asleep, trying to avoid the hangover that waits. He clenches the steering wheel remembering last night; Raife with Billie, what Raife was trying to do.

God he's so tired, tired of it all. But maybe Billie is right. Maybe an honest talk, a chance for them both to say their piece might help. God knows he has nothing to lose.

He waits a while like this; uncertain, tossing emotional conflict and options for resolution back and forth. The tussle resolves in anger. Slamming the car door, Jack jogs across the sand to the old wooden walkway. Moorings long abandoned flank it's sides. At the far end is *Liberty*, the only vessel that remains. Obstinate and sullen like his father, she floats uneasily, aware of the gradual decomposing of her hull and the dampness that eats at her once solid boards.

Jack had asked Joseph if he could restore her then sail her to St. Eloise. He'd wanted to gift her back to his father, return her to the way she'd been when he was a boy. But Joseph had said no, shook the idea off like an ill-fitting shirt. His boat wouldn't be touched by anyone else.

Good intentions rejected turned inward mutate to bitterness. Jack can't help it, but he's found himself wishing the tables were turned and that Joseph was the one sick and losing his precious memories. Instead Amandine, whose capacity for joy and hope seemed infinite, watches her memories fade. Detailed recollections of people and places, time and events disappear one by one, day by day. A leaky tap with a slow inevitable drip, her memories disappear, leaving confusion and despair.

Still no signs of life. No-one on the deck and no movement from below. Jack jumps down on to the aged wooden planks and the boat creaks in weary protest.

"Raife?"

His voice seems unnaturally loud, the sound sharp and rough amidst the smooth lapping of waves on empty moorings. Again, "Raife?" He walks around the edge to the far side of the boat and stoops over a grimy porthole but the dirt prevents a view inside. *Liberty* had once been white and red but her paint has peeled and flaked, and the faded remains are dull and grey. The cabin door is bolted from the inside, he bangs twice then hits the door with his shoulder.

In one forceful push the rusty hinges give and the door swings limply. The light within is mottled, filtered grey through smeared windows. Pinpoints of golden sun push through the spaces alighting on Raife, curled on the single bunk. He lifts a hand to shade his eyes from the glare. A moment passes when they watch each other uncertainly.

Why is it that everything seems calculated, every word and action, every expression? Was Raife always this way or did Lil's death change him? His rehearsed responses paint a mask over the brother Jack used to know, the brother he's no longer sure exists.

Raife sighs, pulling himself slowly up to sit, his face is bruised, the remains of a nosebleed crusts on his cheek and chin. "What took you so long? Thought you'd be hot on my heels, ready to finish me off."

"Fuck you."

"Don't be a pussy Jack, just do it. You know I deserve it, get it over with."

"Don't go near her, don't come near me. I want you to leave or I swear I will fucking kill you." Jack's words are delivered slowly, he means them, and the reality is terrifying.

"That's more like it." Raife rubs a hand over his face then swings his legs over the edge of the bunk to stand stiffly. "I've spent years feeling that way about you. Makes me feel better knowing it's mutual." He shrugs and winces. "I'd go to sleep thinking about kicking the shit out of you for fucking everything up. Funny how far hate can take you."

Jack doesn't have time to answer, the impact knocks him backward, through the broken door and on to his back. Raife wastes no time, descending on Jack, reigning punches. Stunned, Jack is limp and unresponsive, the first punch close to a knock out. Raife pulls him roughly to his feet and hits him again, the pain brings him back and he responds in like, his head catching pace gradually with the instinctive reactions of his body.

The fight is ugly; every impact delivers a lifetime of wasted blame. There's torrid beauty in the scene, physical excellence in pugilistic combat. Primal expression in conflict, sleek shining muscle, bone impacting bone, the sound of breaking and smell of blood. There's tragic satisfaction in the hurt, the giving and receiving of pain, deserving and deserved, blow after blow.

The cabin is broken, boards smashed and glass shattered. Like an awkward, brutal dance the fight moves to the deck, a trail of blood marking their passage. Intensity slows with exhaustion, anger almost spent. Jack staggers to his feet to grab Raife by the shoulders, bloodied hands weeping over Raife's ripped t-shirt.

"Enough." He wrenches the words from his throat, but Raife hears nothing. Bringing a knee to Jack's belly he drives upward with all his remaining force. Jack stiffens and falls backward, over the side and into the water.

Raife isn't done. He follows and here the fight continues. Gasping for breath, shaking with exhaustion they brawl in the shallow water. But Jack is struggling now, the punch to the head and the cold water leave him disorientated, his strength zapped. His response is too slow as Raife grabs his shoulders and pushes him roughly underwater. He struggles, legs kicking, arms flailing, fingers grabbing and pulling, but he's held firm. Raife's hands are around his neck and time slows, sounds quieten and the world stills. Jack forgets the pain and the air he needed so desperately, something cold and soothing flows through his veins and calm understanding comes with the stillness.

Time passes in a vacuum.

"Jack." Again, his name, louder, urgent and afraid. "Jack!"

Pain comes first, sharp and insistent, then the voice again. "Jack! Come on man!"

Sand packed beneath him, rough against the side of his face, his eyes flicker uncertainly and open to the bright light around the silhouette of Raife's head.

"Thank God…" Raife doesn't finish the sentence, he collapses back on to the sand beside Jack breathing hard. Jack's head is slowly finding focus, remembering where he is and what happened. He searches for his voice, but what comes is a hacking cough, wet and salty. He tries to stand but his legs are weak, on his knees he doubles over and vomits the sea water that nearly drowned him. Collapsing back on the sand, they lie side by side: silent, bloodied and broken.

Jack has lost track of time, how long have they lain here? He's cold and disoriented.

"I'm sorry." Raife's forearms cover his eyes, his body shaking. "I lost control," the unfamiliar honesty drags uncertainly. "I wanted to kill you."

Jack's voice returns broken and hoarse. "Why didn't you?"

"What a fucking mess." Raife's sobs silently and Jack can't watch, doesn't want to hear. He pulls his aching body up to sit, his head pounding, he has to get away.

"Are we done?"

Raife nods. "Are you okay?"

"Fucking fantastic." He tries to stand but his legs aren't ready and he sinks reluctantly back on to the sand.

"Hear me out…"

"I don't want to talk to you, or see you or fucking think about you anymore Raife. I'm done. We're done. Do you get it?" He lowers his head, elbows on raised knees, waiting for steadiness to return.

"I never really blamed you. I blamed myself, but I was too much of a coward to wear it. I convinced myself it was your fault. It was easier that way."

"I crashed the car."

"I made you drive."

"We fucked up Raife…both of us."

"I'm still so fucking angry." Raife laces his hands behind his neck, head down he rocks gently. "I didn't want you to be happy. I'd screwed my life up, why should you move on? When I saw you with her, I was so fucking bitter. I'm sorry, I don't expect anything from you." He pauses to breathe, eyes pressed closed. "When I was holding you like that under the water, and you were kicking and fighting for your life, I saw it all, for the first time. Saw it clearly, I'd spent all that anger on you and suddenly I could see past it. All this time, I've been hiding behind you."

Jack breathes carefully, eyes ahead, letting Raife speak. He's carried it too; the blame, the guilt and the shame. The unexpected confession churns up a decade of distraction and despair, he fights for composure.

"It was a bad time for me back then Jack. I just…" He shakes his head and runs a hand through his hair. "I was fucking mixed up. Messing around, smoking weed and drinking seemed to be the only way to feel okay."

"Not much has changed then."

Raife exhales, nodding ruefully. "Do you want me to go?"

Jack waits, letting his thoughts slow and find clarity. He shakes his head and nods toward Joseph's boat. "Fix her up for Papa. I'll give you what you need. He'll be happy for you to do it. Do something useful with those hands, live on her for a while and sort your shit out."

"Tell Billie I'm sorry."

"Don't fucking talk about her. I'm not ready to hear you say her name."

Raife raises his hands in surrender. "Okay."

"We should go see Dan, get cleaned up, we probably both need some stitches." Jack gestures to Raife's face.

"I'm okay, you go."

Jack shrugs. "I'll be back with tools later."

Raife nods and Jack turns to leave, walking slowly back to the car. His body aches; weary and sore but his heart is a little lighter. It's when he reaches the car that he hears Raife's voice again.

"Jack." Turning he sees Raife trying to run across the sand "Wait up…there's something else."

Billie

When Ginny calls the twins have just arrived home with Marlene. It's true what they say about absence and hearts growing fonder. Although it's hard to imagine you can become *fonder* of your own children, *fondness* already runs at maximum. What's different this morning is that I appreciate them so much more than yesterday. My love is renewed and so it seems, is there's. They scream excitedly to see me like they've been gone for weeks and I respond in like.

So when I scramble to the phone I have a giggling child on each hip, of course they are far too big for me to manage this manoeuvre with any degree of comfort. "Hello?" I'm breathless as I answer.

"Billie, its Ginny…are you alright?"

"Ginny," I exclaim loudly, my inside voice has gone outside. It's loud and rambunctious over here since the twin's return. "How are you? What happened to you last night?"

"What's all the noise?"

"Evie and Sunny are a little hyper. They stayed at Marlene's last night. I thought they'd hate it but apparently not. I'm not quite as indispensable as I thought." Ginny is unusually quiet. "Are you okay?"

"I am."

"You're what? You're okay?"

"No, not okay, but it seems I am dispensable."

"Excuse me?"

"I'm dispensable."

"I heard that bit, what are you talking about?"

"Mike's having an affair."

I suck in my breath, shocked and unsure of what to say. "Oh Ginny, how do you know? I mean, are you sure?" I can't believe that Mike, the quiet, retiring, work-obsessed geek that he is would be the type. Is there a type?

"He told me last night. He told me, when I was getting ready to come to Santos. He told me quiet plainly, as I was applying my lipstick, like it was nothing really, just a small detail."

"I'm so sorry." In the background the twins are yelling and it's hard to hear. It sounds like maybe she's laughing, or crying, I'm not sure, something hysterical. "Come over."

"I'm coming."

There's a click as she hangs up and I stand holding the receiver stunned. The last man I would have believed was capable of cheating on his wife, old *Harry high pants* Mike. Poor Ginny. Poor, poor Ginny. I'm imagining her face, hearing his words, dropping her lipstick on the floor. Her recent confessions regarding their relationship, how she'd wanted to bring the spark back. God it makes sense now, all of it. His emotional distance, the long hours, the lack of intimacy. I want to kill him, but first cut his nuts off.

Instead I race after Sunny, scoop him up, tickle him mercilessly and vow to make him the kind of man who'd never, ever treat a woman like that. As he laughs and squirms, his eyes twinkle like Evans and I catch myself.

Is the cheating gene inevitable? Is it present in all males, activated in most by presentation of a particular sort of women at a particular time in their lives? But hang on, a small internal voice becomes louder till it's a shout. A shouty voice that's angry and hurt. It sounds a little like Evan, a little like me, it's saying; *don't forget, you cheated too, you cheated too…YOU CHEATED TOO!*

There's a knock at the door. Sunny is wriggling in my arms. I'm hugging him too tightly and my eyes are wet. Another knock and Ginny lets herself in, looking quite unlike the Ginny I'm used to.

"What's wrong?" she asks me, when plainly I should be asking her.

"Hay fever." I set Sunny down and he runs for cover. I move to Ginny and wrap her in the biggest, most comforting hug I have.

"Okay, I can't breathe Billie," she muffles after a few minutes. "You can let me go."

"Sorry." I release her and take a step back. "You look… amazing. I mean, you always look lovely but I'd expected you to look a little…"

"Heartbroken and dowdy? Well yes, that's all there, but I thought I'd go for the vampish *here's what you're missing* look."

"Of course." I nod and take her hands, she's straightened her usually frizzy hair, has on a full face of makeup, a dress and heels. As I squeeze her hands she crumples a little, one tear then a small tsunami. While the twins play in the yard we sit together on the swing seat with a view of the ocean.

"It's been going on for over a year." She pauses and sniffs, I pass her a hankie. "Her name is Helen and she's a nurse in ER."

"I can't believe it." Shaking my head, I squeeze her hand again. "I mean, he never gave you any reason to believe that…"

"Actually, now that it's all come out I can see that the signs were there. I just wasn't looking."

"Oh Ginny, what did you do?"

"I told him to leave, and I was calm. In fact, I don't know how I did it. Pride maybe, I told him I would never forgive him and not to come back. Didn't shed a tear. I waited till he was gone of course. He looked wretched."

"He bloody well should look wretched. God what a bastard."

Ginny shakes her head, eyes on the twins running around with Jack's dogs in the yard, she smiles sadly. "You know Billie, I actually felt sorry for him. I know that makes no sense, but I did. I found myself thinking *you stupid old man, look what you've gone and done, it can't be fixed, and you won't ever be truly happy.* I know him and he'll always be plagued with guilt."

I pass her another hankie and she wipes her eyes. "Stupid old fool. God I wonder what she's like. What if she's young and gorgeous? What if they end up having a family together?" Ginny now looks wretched herself.

I shake my head. "I'll bet she's in her fifties with a flat bottom. I'll bet she wears tan tights and those awful white nursing Crocs. She's probably even got a hairy mole on her chin." Ginny bursts out laughing but it doesn't last long, the laugh fades to a sniffle that turns into a sob. She's processing the thought that Mike might start a family with someone else. "Oh Ginny, I'm so sorry."

She shakes her head but continues to cry quietly and we sit for a while like that, watching the afternoon sun reach its peak in the sky then begin its slow slide downward.

Sunny and Evie are in the sandpit and Louie and Bets loll in the sun. The twins run them ragged, they're forever fetching and chasing. I've noticed that lately Louie seems slower, maybe a little sore and I realise I don't know how old the dogs are, or how long Jack's had them. Rising from the seat I head inside to get the twins some snacks and the dogs some water. Ginny has closed her eyes and I wonder if she might have fallen asleep, her head is tipped back on the cushion and her red lipped mouth is relaxed and slightly open.

What a day. It's four pm and I feel I've come through a year's worth of emotional drama. There's a bottle of white wine in the cupboard, I pop it into the refrigerator and head outside to the kids and dogs, snacks and drinks on a tray.

Evie and Sunny are beginning to get a little grouchy, they are tired too. They gave up on the afternoon nap a month ago and the *witching hour* quite often begins right about now. Being that bedtime is seven, technically the witching hour has become 'hours', three to be exact. Evie squeals as Sunny takes an apple slice that apparently she had earmarked for herself. A bop on the head follows the squeal and soon Sunny is squealing too. Bets pads over and licks Evie on the ear whilst Louie makes a groaning sound and curls himself under the shade of the gum tree.

Evie begins throwing the snacks around and squealing, soon Sunny has joined in. It's noisy but everyone seems happy. Ginny sleeps on, only Louie looks twitchy under the tree, he stands turns around in a circle then settles again, trying to get comfortable. I watch as he repeats this funny little cycle, a few times before whining, settling and finally closing his eyes.

I remember the wine cooling nicely in the fridge, and as Ginny sighs and rouses gently from her doze I decide a nice chilled glass is just what we both need. The day's dramas might fade a little and some alcohol fuelled philosophy will be nice.

It's when I'm pouring the second glass that I hear it, a sound so violent and terrible that I drop the bottle on the floor. It smashes instantly, but I barely notice the glass that slices my feet as I run to the garden.

The sight is one that will stay forever etched in fearful memory, one that will form the basis of nightmares to come.

Evie is under the tree with Louie and he holds her to the ground, jaws clamped around her small face. The screaming that began as Evie's becomes mine as I run to the nightmare scene, lunging at Louie who releases Evie as I strike him across the head. I grab Evie who has gone quiet and limp. Louie cowers, bearing his teeth, blood on his mouth. Sunny screams from the sandpit and Ginny runs from behind striking Louie with a child's plastic spade. I'm afraid to look at Evie, I don't know what I'll see. I'm in shock and so is she.

"Tie him up! Tie him up Ginny, quick!" I scream whilst running to the kitchen with Evie bundled in my arms, her face so covered in blood I can't see how bad anything is.

Events blur from here, an ambulance, hospital, emergency surgery, me, Ginny and Sunny in the waiting room. Sunny sleeps on my lap and Ginny and I hold hands, all other events of the day pale now beside this new and unexpected disaster.

I try again to call Jack, but his phone goes straight to message.

Where is Jack? Where the hell is Jack?

Chapter Fifteen

Jack

Dan's head is in his hands when Jack arrives. Jack doesn't knock, he lets himself in, walks through the house and finds Dan sitting on the edge of the sofa.

"I should have told you." Dan speaks without looking up.

Jack, bone-achingly tired, lowers himself slowly into a chair opposite Dan, every muscle protesting, his battered body trying to find a position that doesn't ache.

Dan speaks, head still angled to the floor. "There's something you don't know, something I should have told you a long time ago."

"Dan…"

"It's just that I pretended to myself it wasn't my business to tell you. That it was up to Raife."

"Dan." Jack's voice is louder now and Dan looks up, eyes bleary and red. "I know."

Dan takes a deep breath, bringing his hands to his head, slowly running his fingers backward through messy hair. "How?"

"Raife just told me."

"I'm sorry."

"You don't have to be. You've done nothing wrong."

"But I didn't tell you. I stayed quiet, knowing." Clenching a fist, he bangs the table and the sound echoes around the sparsely furnished room. "I knew that Raife was messed up. I knew he'd go out that night and drink to forget. When I heard about the crash I wasn't surprised. Desperately fucking sad, but not surprised. The only shock was that you were driving and not him."

Jack turns to the window; it's all too much, all of it. And this new and unexpected angle was not, has never been, part of the story. The story that mapped out his life for seventeen years. Seventeen fucking years of believing the world looked one way, only to find he'd been looking at the wrong picture.

"Well, say something." Dan looks up for the first time since he's arrived. "Jesus Christ, what happened to you?"

He doesn't have the energy to explain. "Got any beer?"

Beers to hand they sip as Dan works, cleaning and mending Jack's face and hands. The silence is good and by the time the slice across Jacks eye is sutured and the crusts of old blood washed and cleared, a quiet healing has taken place.

Jack hadn't been angry at Raife's confession, just shocked. He's still shocked, the news that Raife is gay circles around his head, settling only to be shaken off in disbelief.

Raife is gay. Raife has always known, and most of his life he's hidden it away. Ashamed of who he is and how he feels, then later of what he did. Raife and Dan together, just once. The night before the crash - the night life changed for everyone.

For Raife, the repercussions were evidence of everything that was wrong about who he really was and how he felt. For Dan, his night with Raife had brought an understanding of who he was and why he'd always felt different, a joy of connection and a reason not to feel alone.

Two teenage boys in a small community where differences are bigger and gossip louder. They'd agreed not to talk about it again, to tell no-one and to carry on like normal. Dan felt happiness believing he'd found something he hadn't known he'd been looking for. The experience changed his world. Raife felt terror. The experience changed his world too.

The next day, he'd gone on like nothing had changed, although everything was different. He'd kissed his girlfriend Lil like he meant it, he'd gotten them drunk, found some good weed and got everyone high. He was afraid. He knew now why nothing fit and why he was different, and later why he was always angry. He would never be truly happy because back then he could never, ever admit how he really felt.

That was the night of the crash, and here they are years later hashing it all up. Years later, when everyone's life should have moved on and grown roots, blossomed and settled. Instead they remain moored there, unable to move on from the tragic accident and the heavy load of blame.

"It was the first time for me. I mean, the first time I realised fully." Dan speaks quietly as he dabs Jack's face with a cotton ball doused in antiseptic. "I knew the kind of guy Raife was; I knew he'd pretend like nothing had happened. Then, the next night…" Dan stops and Jack pushes his hand away from his face.

"It's okay, that's enough, it's all good," he feels his cheekbone where the new sutures sting.

"But it's not, is it?" Dan sits down beside him.

"Dan, I've spent a lot of time blaming myself for Lil's death, for Raife taking off and screwing up. Now don't get me started on feeling bad because you've been nursing guilt all these years." He reaches out squeezing Dan's forearm. "You're a great friend, I know you, I know how you are. None of this, you hear me? None of this was ever your fault. If I've learned anything today, it's that it was all fucking tragic accident." He sighs heavily and sips his beer. "If Lil was here she'd be kicking all three of us up the ass and telling us to move the fuck on."

Dan turns away to hide the tears that fall silently.

Jack pulls him in, Dan's head tucked tightly into his chest. No words, but comfort, forgiveness and acceptance of differences and mistakes.

Outside in the car, Jack's phone lies face up on the passenger seat. Missed calls: seven. It rings again but he won't hear it, not yet.

Billie

Sadie and Jed came to take Sunny. I was a mess and he was scared and confused. I couldn't get hold of Jack, his phone rang and rang, I'd left messages. Ginny had called Sadie and they'd come straight away.

Jed promised to find Jack and Sadie swooped up Sunny and plied him with smiles and the promise of treats at Beaujangles. He was a little dazed and unsure about leaving, but I'd lied and promised Evie would be just fine and so would Louie, and we'd all be at home together tonight.

Sunny kept talking about Louie and how Ginny was hitting him with the blue spade. He'd somehow blocked out the sight of his sister's mangled face and for that I'm glad.

Scratch that, I'm not glad or sad, or angry. I'm terrified. Shaken to the bone, waiting to hear if my baby will still be able to see. If her face can be mended and if her life will be marked by this terrible moment; before and after.

Ginny waited with me, no word from the doctors yet, nothing. The nothing is too much to bear. I can deal with something, anything, but the nothing is killing me.

When Jack strides through the double doors I crumple. His face looks like he's wrestled a crazed dog too but I don't care. Sobbing I rush to him; his eyes are dark his expression barely composed. He becomes the focus of everything that's gone wrong and for a short hysterical time I lose complete control. As his arms open to me, I bat them away with my fists and launch myself at his chest, punching and pummelling and yelling. If there's a scene and people are staring, I don't notice or care. Jack takes the blows then after a time pulls me in, crushing my flailing arms against his chest, burying his face in my hair.

"I'm so sorry, I'm so sorry."

"Don't tell me your sorry Jack, don't tell me you're sorry." I drop to my knees and sob.

He picks me up, and asks the nurse if we can go somewhere quiet, she ushers us into a small empty room where Jack lies me down on the bed. I'm shaking but so is he, it's not his fault, but I don't know what to do.

He holds my shoulders firmly. "You have to hold it together Billie." I nod desperately trying to. I can't let Evie down, I must hold it together.

Shakily I tell him what happened. He nods, hands tight around my shoulders, eyes closed, feeling his way through what comes next. I pull the hand that holds my shoulder around to my lips then bring it to my heart as fat, heavy tears roll silently down his rough and bloodied cheeks.

When the surgeon knocks a few minutes later, he looks kindly at us both. His eyes are warm and caring but they widen a little at the sight of Jacks battered face.

"Mr and Mrs Skylark?"

We're on our feet. "No, I mean I am, he's not, sorry. How is she?"

"She's asleep now, the surgery went well. She's a very lucky little girl."

I breathe, but it's a careful unsure breath. "What does that mean?"

He smiles, ushering us to sit but I don't want to. "The puncture wounds missed her tear ducts and the lacerations on either side of her eyes have been stitched and should heal with minimal scarring."

"She'll be able to see?" I don't wait for his answer? "Her eyes are okay? I mean, it just looked so bad, the bleeding was terrible and…"

"Mrs Skylark, facial lacerations are messy and the bleeding is always heavy, luckily the wounds were not deep and her eyesight will be unaffected. You can go in and see her now, she's asleep."

In a haze of relief, we thank the surgeon profusely and are led into the recovery room where Evie lies heavily bandaged, her eyes swollen and bruised. She looks peaceful despite everything. It will be okay, we have dodged another bullet, but we will be okay.

I sleep at the hospital in an armchair beside her bed. Jack waits till we are settled then leaves. We haven't talked about what happens next, for now I know Evie will be okay and that's about all I can deal with after this day of days. I kiss him goodbye, pretending I don't know what he has to do. But I know.

Jack

He hears the howls from the road. Tied up beneath the gum tree, Louie cries and Bets answers, cowering under the deck, alone and afraid.

He'd known Louie was old, but he hadn't known he was sick. He must be in pain; he must have been hurting to do this. Wrapped up in himself he hadn't noticed the change in his faithful dog. Louie howls again, and Jack waits in the car, head in his hands.

He has to be strong and do what's right; he must fold his heart away till it's done.

It's raining again, and there's no beauty in this rain. It's cruel and colourless, but when it's over everything will be washed away. Unlocking the box in the work shed he pulls the gun free. Bets whimpers beside him, he stoops and ruffles her smooth fur, motions her to lay down then locks her inside.

As he crosses the fence to Billie's yard Louie's howls soften to a whine. He can sense Jack is coming, he'll soon be free. Jack keeps his eyes to the ground, tries not to look as Louie wags his tail, ears back, flooded with happiness that he is no longer alone. It has to be quick, he mustn't stall, but he has to say goodbye.

He lays the gun on the ground and kneels to Louie who folds himself into Jacks arms, licking and wagging, all eyes and tail. "Good boy, good boy." Jack strokes his back and lets his face rest against the wet nose, "I'll take care of you boy, it's okay." He brushes his lips on the silky wet head, steps back, picks up the gun and fires.

The gunshot is muffled by the heavy rain. He unties Louie and holds the limp body for a time before carefully wrapping him in his jacket. Walking slowly to the end of his garden, he lays the bundle down and begins to dig.

Billie

It's our first night home from hospital, the twins are asleep and the house is dark. It's good to be home. Moving out into the still darkness I walk to the edge of the deck and down the steps to the grass. There is no breeze, tree frogs and mosquitoes drone and chirp as wafts of heady perfume rise up from the earth as it cools.

I'm drawn to the gum tree. On the grass below lies the rope that tied Louie, and alongside, lying awkwardly is the blue plastic spade, its handle broken. Kneeling down on the soil I say a little prayer to Louie, hands flat to the spot he took his last breath.

As I untie the rope and pick up the spade a light comes on in Jack's workshop. I hear him opening the door, he moves slowly and without meaning to I say his name aloud. He turns, and the door to the work shed gapes open, light spilling across the yard to where I stand, on the other side of the fence beneath the gum tree.

Jack comes to me slowly, his steps careful and quiet. We have not been alone since the accident. I want to hold him and comfort him and have him hold and comfort me in return, but I feel a barrier between us. Both too sore, too sad, guilty, and needy to be of any use to the other. I hold my hands out to him wondering if there will ever be a time for us, the fences that separate us grow higher. He takes my hands but doesn't pull me in and doesn't speak. We stand there in the sliced, electric light, arms length, holding hands, together but apart.

Nothing is the same after Louie and Evie. We're all dejected, a little broken and desperately sad. I keep my distance from everyone for a time, not wanting to spread the despair that has settled in my heart. It will pass I know. I've been here before but for now, I can manage only my own feelings. Take care of the twins, be a good mother, small steps every day. It's all any of us can do.

Is it possible we are at the mercy of the stars, the pull of the moon and tides? Or are pawns in a chess game of life controlled by the heavens? Sometimes it's easier to believe that we have no control and we deal with what we're dealt. And that what we're dealt is not necessarily a reflection of what we deserve but what we can manage. In the inevitable stew that is life and living we are each given our portion.

Evie is happy at home, battle-scarred but smiling. She doesn't seem to remember much of what happened so we don't talk about it. Her bandages are off, her eyesight is fine, her tear ducts weep, but the doctor says it's a reaction to trauma and soon it will pass.

Mike moved out permanently and Ginny has their house up for sale. She's put in a bid on an apartment downtown, a new beginning and I think it's good.

Sadie and Jed are due to be married next month, here in St. Cloud at La Misère, our most beautiful beach. Sadie has good and bad days but as she tells me regularly, her head is always good; it's her body that lags a little behind. Jed is generally the happiest guy around and the coffee is so damn good I think profits are soaring in Beaujangles.

Dan comes by every day to check Evie and dress her wounds. We drink coffee and eat Tim Tams. We talk about something and nothing, and it's exactly what we both need.

Zoe and Felix are underground with their little family, absorbed in the intense first few months of a new baby with a big personality.

Raife has been at Sentinels Bay, repairing their father's old boat, keeping out of Jack's way for now. He came to me not long ago and apologised, I accepted, Jack had told me everything; and I have to believe that everyone deserves a second chance.

Jack and I circle around one another, so much has happened and we both need time. I see him at night, down at the end of the yard where he buried Louie, Bets at his heels. The words I rely on are empty, there's nothing to say to change or make it better. Today, he leaves for St. Eloise and Raife has agreed to go too. Together they will return home, spend some time with Amandine and Joseph and help Saul and Jess with the farm. Their baby is close and there is much work to be done. We said goodbye this morning, and the departure has left me with a heavy heart.

The phone rings and reluctantly I put down my pen. I'm journaling, before I get down to the real work of editing. The *being signed by a publisher* malarkey isn't quite the quick road to success I'd first thought. God damn they want me to change things! And much as it galls me, I know they're right. So we communicate by email, they send me their *comments* and I go about editing. At this rate my book might be for sale by the twins' eighteenth birthday.

I grab the phone impatiently but it's Cam, and I'm so thrilled I forget about my journal, and my book, and my heavy heart. And I listen happily to his news before telling him mine.

When I hang up I feel lighter, less sombre and self-indulged. I pick up the phone and call Ginny, she answers first ring. "Ginny, it's me, Billie. I think Sadie needs a hen party."

✑

They travel in silence, he thinks this is what they need. To learn to be around one another again; removing the resentment leaves their relationship saggy and wavering. They need time to let it find its shape.

It's a beautiful road and Jack enjoys this drive, Bets lies in the bed of the truck, mouth open to the breeze. She's happy to be with them but looks at Raife like he should know he's no replacement for Louie.

The drive has been peaceful, the weather good. They'd stopped and camped on route. Soon they'll take the boat to St. Eloise. It feels right, like the last piece in the jigsaw, to go home and try and make peace with Joseph and see if together they can support their mother.

Jack's not sure how things will go. Raife hasn't spoken to Amandine since the last call when she didn't know who he was. Saul has gone quiet, snowed under with the orchard and the fishing business. With Jess unable to work and a handful of unreliable island staff he's just getting by. It will good to be there for a while and help, even if the help is only physical.

The radio plays and Raife dozes in the passenger seat. They haven't spoken again about the past; about the accident, about Billie or Dan. Jack doesn't want to and he assumes neither does Raife. He has no expectations of what might happen with Raife, where he will go and what he'll do but he's willing to give him a chance.

Together they are all starting over.

It's dark when they arrive. Saul hasn't come to meet them and they hitch a lift the last few kilometres. The driver drops them at the intersection beside the dirt road leading to Saul's place and together they walk through the night with Bets at their heels.

"Do they know we're coming?" Raife sounds anxious.

"I called, they know."

"No welcoming party huh?"

"That what you were expecting?"

Raife shrugs. "I'm still getting used to the fact the world doesn't revolve around me."

Jack hears the smile in his voice. "Good, you'd better. Saul will have you working for your keep starting 5.00 am."

"Jesus."

They can see lights now, two houses, set well apart. As they reach the gates a voice breaks the dark.

"Is that you boys?" A flashlight flicks on, dazzling Raife who raises an arm to shield his eyes. "Holy shit, it's the prodigal sons." Saul laughs, vaulting the gate and jogging toward them.

It's nearly midnight and Jess is asleep on the sofa. Saul's voice is so loud she jumps as they enter, smiling and struggling to her feet. "You're here." She's up and across the room before they can stop her.

"Are you sure there's only one in there?" Jack embraces her, although her tummy makes the manoeuvre a challenge.

"So they tell me," Jess smiles indulgently at Raife and moves toward him as he waits awkwardly in the corner of the kitchen. "Look at you."

Raife nods, grinning. "I should say the same to you." She pulls him into a warm embrace, manoeuvring her belly sideways to get close.

They spend the next hour around the kitchen table. Raife entertains, telling stories of his time away, leaving out the bad stuff and exaggerating the good. It's what he does and Jack doesn't mind. Saul talks about the orchard, the crop and the coming season, the fishing boats, the days' catch and finally, the locals. The brother's talk boats a while longer - its safe territory and a shared passion.

Jess excuses herself after a while shuffling uncomfortably across the room, kissing them all goodnight, saying how happy she is they're all home. The stairs creak as she ascends to bed.

"So, she's been okay since that last stay in hospital?" Jack asks.

"Yeah." Saul sighs. "They're keeping a check on her blood pressure, seems okay for now. She's been worried though. I think that's the problem, not the size of the baby."

"You sure?" Raife pipes up. "That's one big baby."

Saul ignores him. "We're falling behind here, it's just timing. We've had a few guys quit at the same time and we lost a fishing boat. It needs a new engine we can't afford to buy and it's almost harvest. I'm trying not to let her hear too much, she's worried enough. But if we take a hit on the harvest this year, it'll be tough to recover."

"Why didn't you say things were bad? I could have come before." Jack eyes Saul reproachfully. "I'd have been happy to pitch in. We'll muck in now, get you through."

"You've got a business of your own to run Jack, things will be fine here. It's just a bad phase, you know how it is. I've been over at Mama's a whole lot too, just those few hours a day has got me behind. Now you guys are here, you can spend some time with her and I can put in some extra hours."

"How's she doing?" Raife asks uncertainly.

Saul shrugs. "Ask Jess you'll get a better answer. I don't know what to think right now, you'll see what I mean tomorrow. He shakes his head. "You'll see. Anyway, I'm beat. See you guys in the morning." Saul rises and passing behind Raife's chair ruffles his hair. "Good to see you kid." Raife doesn't look up.

Jack wakes early. It's still dark, barely 5.00 am, but he wants to walk to the beach and swim. Sunrise will be beautiful.

The house is quiet aside from the sound of Saul's snores as Jack lets himself out into the pre-dawn air; soft and still with a hint of promise. He walks barefoot along the dirt road between the two properties. A light burns brightly from this parents' house and as he approaches music drifts from an open window. Puzzled he follows the sound, stopping abruptly on the porch with a view into the small living room.

Inside lights burn brightly and Elvis Presley croons from an old record player in the corner. In the middle of the floor stands his father - his sullen, quarrelsome father - wearing pyjamas, dancing barefoot on the rug. Across from him, twirling and snapping her fingers, smiling like she's the happiest woman in the world is Amandine in a white nightdress.

Transfixed he stops, then steps quickly into the shadows, unwilling to intrude on the strangely beautiful scene. He watches his mother and father together in a way he's never witnessed before; comfortable, happy, relaxed and unselfconscious. God damn it, he's quite sure Joseph is smiling.

The record stops abruptly and Amandine stops with it, like a puppet the music has propelled, the dancing stops and her face regains the years. Joseph changes the record quickly and the sounds of The Drifters croon through the bright room and out into the early dawn.

"Come on now, one more." Joseph entreats.

"I'm so tired darling."

"It's important, one more and then we rest."

"Of course."

Joseph claps his hands and the dance begins.

Jack slips away, feeling he has intruded on something private, but he can't help feeling glad he saw them. That for a moment he could imagine their youth, how it once was and what they once had; perhaps still do. Despite how he may feel about his father and what he's always believed his mother deserves, somehow together they work and there is love, deep and lasting.

Reaching the beach, he swims as the light lifts, and later back at Jess and Saul's he sees the magazine open on the bench. Some journals Jess had borrowed from Joseph - an article circled in pen, the page edges well thumbed: *Dancing Away Dementia.*

After a few hours in the orchard they had gone to Joseph and Amandine's house. Jess had prepared Amandine for the visit, worrying the surprise would be too much. But when they'd arrived she was waiting, smiling, delighted to see them, looking older and frailer but sharp. The light in her eyes was bright, brighter maybe then than ever.

Raife's relief was evident. He'd smiled at Jack and shrugged his shoulders as if to ask what all the fuss had been about. Jack had to admit he was relieved too, maybe the dancing was helping, who knew? Only Saul seemed unexcited by her manner, he stayed a short while then headed back to the orchard. Amandine had fussed over Jess, and Joseph complained about everything. Things felt very normal.

Later, Raife and Joseph had gone for a walk together. Their father's manner toward Raife had always been different, even before the accident. They'd all known who the favourite child was, and Jack had always been fine with it. What hurt was the blame; Joseph's anger directed solely at Jack. When they had returned from the walk something had changed; a subtle shift in energy, both Raife and Joseph seemed somehow lighter.

Later after lunch, Joseph thanks Jack for bringing Raife home. The words of gratitude are bittersweet, too little too late, but none of it matters now. He tries to be gracious and accept the thanks. He must focus on a new start with his family and leave old baggage behind.

By evening Jack has almost relaxed. He'd spent the afternoon on one of the fishing boats with Saul, the catch had been good and Saul's easy company was a tonic of sorts. Being out on the water, absorbed in the ocean, the boat and business of fishing; it was calming. He'd remembered how much he loves his work and was happy at the thought of *Galileo* in the work shed, close to complete. It had been a good day, one to remember. Heading to dinner with his family he feels a seed of something good settle and take root. A seed of happiness that might have room to grow.

"God, that was good Jess." Raife pushes his plate forward and rocks his chair back from the table. "Thank you. You are an amazing woman and if Saul hadn't married you, I know I'd have talked you round."

Jess laughs piling dishes up at the sink. "You Raife Kelly, were never my type, too much trouble."

"I'll say." Jack pipes up, finishing the last mouthful of pie and standing to help Jess. Joseph as usual had read the newspaper throughout dinner despite it being the first time they've all been together in years. Some things just don't change.

"When the hell will they stop opening damn tourist bars around here? The island's full of damn tourists. There'll be no place for community soon."

"Because you're so involved in the community Papa." Raife teases. Joseph glares over the top of his glasses but doesn't respond; only Raife could get away with back chatting him.

Amandine sighs and claps her hands together. She's been quiet throughout dinner, seeming restless and uneasy. "When can we go home Saul?" She's looking directly at Joseph. "I want to go home now.

I don't much like it here. The food's no good and there's a man I don't know, he keeps looking at me." She gestures toward Raife.

There's a terrible silence, hope falls from the table and spills messily on the kitchen floor.

Raife speaks first, his face pale. "Mama, this is your home, this is your kitchen, you cooked dinner with Jess, remember?"

She looks at him, eyebrows raised and turns back to Joseph. "Who is this man? Why is he here? Take me home."

Joseph lowers his head then reaches slowly for her hand but she pulls it away and begins to look frantically around. No-one speaks for a moment then Jess steps forward "Amandine," she speaks gently, "shall I help you upstairs to bed? Come now."

"Whose baby are you carrying? Are you his other woman? I always knew." Her voice becomes louder, on the edge of hysteria. "He thought I didn't, but I knew about you. Don't talk to me you whore, go back to Joseph."

Joseph slams a hand on the table and Amandine jumps, frightened again. Saul steps forward, his face dark and angry. "Let's go." He ushers a shocked Jess out of the kitchen as Amandine starts to weep. Jack helps her to her feet, she doesn't say a word, doesn't ask him who he is or why he's here. She wobbles weakly and Joseph turns away. Jack lifts her like a small bird and carries her upstairs where he lays her down and sits at the end of her bed till she closes her eyes.

When did they lose her?

Jack's feet crunch the gravel road, the question repeating with every inhale, every exhale. Was it after the accident when Lil died and Raife left? Was it when she left St. Cloud forever, isolating herself with Joseph?

He picks up his pace and the movement feels good. When did they lose her and why didn't they see it? Was it here in the quiet of St. Eloise with no friends and two of her boys gone? The truth is it was all of these things, not one of them. It was life. And the change was so gradual they'd barely noticed.

Lost in thought he doesn't notice her on the porch watching him as he runs, past the house and down toward the ocean. A slight figure in a nightdress, white hair cascading over thin shoulders. She raises a hand, palm open, fingers reaching to touch him. He is gone. Her frail hand, translucent in the pale morning light flutters farewell.

On the sand Jack watches the sunrise, basking in the sensation of salt water drying on warm skin. Birdsong works in harmony with the tide, and as waves lap gently, sun-warmed, dewy leaves diffuse a musky, earthy fragrance in the still air. All around is a sense of calm, for now he is at peace. He waits, enjoying the solitude, sounds and smells of St. Eloise. He'll take his time and think things through, for now no-one needs him.

The sun is bright over the farm as he jogs the trail home to Saul's farm. Pale sunlight has turned bright and warm. He'll have breakfast with his parents, then take the boat out with Saul. Maybe today he'll have that chat with Joseph, convince him to get some support for Amandine.

When he reaches the orchard he hears the shout. He stops dead, hoping he imagined the sound, a call loaded with panic. Hands on hips, catching his breath his eyes search for the source, he sees her running, stumbling ungainly in his direction. She shouts his name again, fear in her voice.

"Jess! What the hell? Stop running! What is it?" Determined to reach him she keeps moving, waving with one hand, the other supporting her belly. "Stop! What the hell's wrong?" She bends over, hands on her knees, breathing heavily, bump hanging like a pendulum about to overbalance her small body.

"What is it? Are you okay?'"

"I was…" she gasps for breath, "trying to find you. Amandine's gone."

"What? What do you mean gone?"

"She's gone Jack, disappeared. She wasn't there when Joseph woke up."

"Shit." Jack's hands move to his head, palms pressing down on his hot scalp. "Where could she have gone?"

Jess is pale but her cheeks flushed. "Oh God, I need to sit down." Before he can answer she plops herself on to the path, breathing heavily. "You need to go looking with the others."

"Okay, calm down. Let's get you indoors and I'll go. Let me help you up." He levers Jess to her feet and she winces, breathing heavily. "Jesus Jess, what were you thinking trying to run?"

"I'm fine, just out of breath, take my arm."

At the house he lowers her into a shady porch chair and brings her some water.

"They've all spread out. They've been gone about an hour. Joseph went up through the orchard, Raife's headed down as far as the neighbours' farm and Saul was heading down toward the beach. Trouble is, we don't know what time she left or how far she could have gone." She winces again. "Oh God Jack, what a mess, get out there and find her please?"

"Don't worry, we'll find her. She can't have gone far. I'll head to the other end of the beach and work my way back."

Jess nods, her eyes closed. "Good, go…" She ushers him off with a hand.

He nods then turns, taking the steps from the porch two at a time. At the gate he glances back, her eyes are closed, hands gripping the corners of the cane chair. "Jess…?"

"I'm fine Jack, just tired, go please." She shoos him away, waving a hand but he's torn, an ominous dread sinks over him as he runs through the bush calling Amandine's name.

He reaches the beach ten minutes later. He's seen no-one, heard nothing. The sand stretches out ahead; there is nowhere here to hide. He jogs along the tide line, at the far end of beach he sees Saul, they exchange notes quickly on the places they've covered and set off again. Dread settles, a heavy weight pushing down on his chest. When he closes his eyes he sees Jess on the deck, knuckles white, face pale.

Shit. He turns, racing back through the bush, toward the house, trusting instinct. Jess is no longer on the cane chair but the glass of water has fallen and shattered on the deck. Running inside he calls her name and finds her on all fours in the kitchen.

"Shit Jess, I knew you shouldn't have been running. Let me…" He steps in to lift her on to her feet.

"Don't touch me! I can't move." She tenses and her face contorts as her body stiffens and she whimpers. He kneels beside her watching helplessly. It seems like an hour before she opens her eyes. "I'm so glad you're here. I thought I was going to have to do it on my own."

"Just breathe, it's okay. You've overdone things, it's too early for this baby. I'm going to run and get Saul and we'll get you to hospital."

"Did you find her?" Jess cries as another wave of contractions descend.

"Christ. I'm going to get Saul, hang on Jess."

"Jack Kelly!" She screams his name with such violence he freezes. "Don't you fucking leave me, do you hear? Stay right there! Don't. Go. Anywhere."

"But…"

"It's coming Jack. Don't tell me it's not, and you're going to have to help me." She takes a long steady breath gaining composure. "Saul isn't here and until he gets here you have to help me."

"It's okay, I'm staying. I'm with you, but I don't know how to do this."

She manages a small smile at the terror on his face. "Me neither so we're going to have to wing it. Get some towels."

Jack runs from the room and returns moments later armed with clean towels to find her once again mute with pain. Grabbing his cell from his pocket he speed-dials praying for a real person and not an answer machine.

"Jack! What's up? Thought you were in St. Eloise."

"I am. Dan, I have a big fucking emergency and I need you to help me."

Jess looks up between contractions. "Jesus Jack, tell me you're not on your cell phone. If you dare to video this, I will have your balls!"

"Who the hell is that and what are you doing?

"I don't have time to explain. I'm putting you on speakerphone. Jess is about to have her baby on the kitchen floor and I'm the only one here."

"Christ almighty! Jack, this is serious."

"I know it's fucking serious. You have to help me." In the background Jess cries out. "Tell me you've done this before?"

"No, I haven't!" Dan snaps, sounding terrified. "I'm a GP not a midwife, hang on…" Jack hears muffled shouting and a clatter as the phone falls.

"Jess are you okay?"

"Do I sound like I'm okay? I'm dying over here."

"Right."

"Lay out the towels and help me turn over." Giving up on Dan he puts the phone on the counter and does exactly as she asks. "Okay, can you take off my underwear, I'm sorry." She apologises seeing his face.

"Don't you dare say sorry Jess. I'm on this, just relax. It's going to be fine."

He doesn't really believe his words but saying them somehow reassures them both. He slides off her blood stained underwear and eases the towels beneath her.

Just then a high pitched female voice speaks from the kitchen counter. "Jack?" There's a surreal moment when he forgets he left the phone on speaker. Ginny has manifested just when he needs her. "Jack, it's Ginny. How's she doing?"

"Hi." Jess answers weakly, not caring where the voice is coming from, it sounds comforting and authoritative. "I'm getting close I think."

"Okay Jess, I'm Ginny, Jacks friend, you're going to be fine. How far apart are your contractions?"

From here Ginny takes over like she's in the room with them. Jack becomes her hands; he does as he's told. He holds Jess under the arms as she bears down. Then, when she's ready he props her up, and as instructed prepares for the baby. As Jess screams he sees a crown of black hair appear between her legs.

"Almost there Jess, you're so close. Almost there, just a few more pushes."

Dan and Ginny speak words of encouragement via speakerphone and Jess braces her back on the cupboard and pushes her feet into Jack's shoulders. *Once more, and breathe, and again,* he hears the words and Jess's screams and feels his fear ebb away as he reaches forward to grasp the tiny body that slides its way into the world.

His face is wet, his hands hold the tiny baby steady. A girl, a baby girl. He wraps her carefully in a towel and places her in Jess's arms, and they're all crying and laughing at the same time.

"We did it." Jess squeezes his hand.

"We did."

Dan and Ginny whoop with delight from the counter, but Ginny is soon all business. She explains the checks Jack must do, how to cut the cord and what to do with the placenta.

It's around this time that the door swings open and the others enter the kitchen. There's a shocked silence, lingering disbelief as the men process what they see; silence broken only by the soft crying of a new-born. Jess smiles up from the floor. There's a baby and there's blood and there's Jack looking like a trained medic. Saul tries to speak but can't. He drops to his knees by her feet.

"It's a girl Saul, a beautiful little girl."

Chapter Sixteen

News travels fast, and by lunchtime everyone has heard how Ginny and Dan helped Jack deliver Jess's baby from the store room in Beaujangles. It's a source of great excitement in the café all day.

My first reaction is not to laugh as it seems most others are doing. Although picturing Ginny and Dan in the store room talking Jack through labour via cell phone does make me smile. The story made me cry. Of course, this is no local newsflash; I am the woman whose default setting is *the quiet sob*.

Just imagining Jack, and Jess, his adored sister-in-law. Imagining the scene, the beauty of new life and that Jack helped bring his little niece into the world. It's just so beautiful, I was sobbing for most of the telling. Of course Ginny who was terribly proud of herself rolled her eyes and moved on to tell Zoe the details, hoping for a reaction more in keeping with her magnificence as an on-call midwife.

Dan had been having his usual morning coffee in Beaujangles when he got the call from Jack. As luck would have it Ginny was walking past, heading to work. Dan yelled out of the window, pulled her inside and together they fielded the call. Beaujangles had been busy and Jed was a little nervous with the loud talk of vaginas, contractions and placentas and had ushered them into the storeroom. The story goes that as the baby was born Dan came running from the storeroom hands in the air shouting joyfully for all to hear, *It's a girl, we did it, it's a girl!*

I haven't spoken to Jack since and neither has anyone else, no doubt his family are celebrating the birth together. The first of a new generation, maybe the baby might give Jack's mother a lift.

Tonight I've invited the gang over for takeaways and drinks to celebrate the fabulous threesome; Jack, Dan and Ginny. Even though Jack's not here we'll celebrate on his behalf. I scoot around the chaos of the living room, chucking toys in boxes or under the sofa. I have no time to vacuum crumbs and so, to my shame, lift the edge of the rug and sweep the mess underneath.

I'm done. Kids are in bed, wine is chilling, takeaway menus are to hand and all that's missing is Jack. I pour myself a wine and sink into the sofa. God, I miss him. What if he doesn't come back? What if he decides to stay away from the drama and hurt and complications I bring? Maybe too much lies between us. I must face the reality; I love him but may never have him.

There's a gentle knock at the door, a welcome interruption to my thoughts.

"Hey," Dan's handsome face appears around the corner. "Tell me I'm not the first, it's so not my style."

"You're the first." I smile and pat the space on the sofa beside me.

"Glasses on the counter."

"That's my girl." He grabs a glass and brings the wine. "Well, it's been a quite a day." He opens the red and pours himself a generous glass. Catching me smiling he frowns. "I deserve it."

"You so do." I squeeze his thigh as he rests back beside me, glass to hand.

"Would you look at us, like an old married couple." He slings his free arm around my shoulder. "…but not really."

"Sometimes, I think it would all be easier just to…not." I look at him like he should get it.

"Not what?"

"Too not have to *want* people. To be content on our own." I nudge him affectionately. "Like you and me, remove the whole attraction/love/soul mate thing and it's easy."

He's looking at me like I have a large pimple on my nose, a little interested but mostly disgusted. "No darling, it would be dull. To love, one must live and to live one must truly love…or something like that."

"Did you just make that up?"

"I think so. Anyway, that's what you need to remember, in amongst all that 'Billie angst'…"

"I don't have 'Billie angst'!" I slap him on the arm, offended. But I'm frowning. "Do I?"

"Come on, it's the writer in you, don't fret. Life never goes your way, and I don't just mean you, I mean all of us. It doesn't go our way only because we've been silly enough to make a way. Do you see what I mean?" I shrug, sort of with him, sort of not. "I mean, when you stop thinking you can decide the best way, it takes a load off. If you tell yourself that every happy moment, every problem, challenge, bump on the road was always meant to be there. It's a hell of a lot easier."

The door knocks again, Dan's philosophical speech interrupted. He sighs and settles back on the sofa as I go to greet our friends.

Ginny arrives, closely followed by Jed and Sadie. Then Felix and Zoe, who to my delight have managed to sort out a sitter. Soon my dearest friends are spread around the living room floor, drinking wine or beer, eating take-aways from plastic cartons, taking loudly and laughing.

We toast Jack and his new found capabilities in baby delivery. We toast Dan and Ginny and their role in the drama. We toast Sadie and Jed whose big day looms only a few weeks away. I'm sure we toast pretty much everyone and everything we can.

It's the first time we've all been together like this since the night Zoe gave birth. It's a night only for happiness. No-one talks of Evie and Louie, of illness and life expectancy. We don't mention absent husbands; cheating or dead. It's a night to be thankful, and we are, and I realise that I'm not trying to be happy, this is not an act. It's no longer the *act as if until*. I am in the *until*. I am happy, genuinely and truly happy.

It's midnight when everyone leaves, everyone except my darling Dan. Together we wash the plates and glasses, both a little tiddly and talkative.

"Jack told you right?"

"He did."

Dan turns to me, dishtowel in hand, eyes terribly serious. "Raife was my first." I watch him recalling a distant memory. "It was like the world changed, I'd finally figured it out."

I nod, yellow rubber gloves submerged in soapy water. "What did you figure out?"

"That I wasn't really different. I wasn't a misfit. I did fit, just not where most people expected. It was a relief." He sighs, mopping his hot forehead with the dishtowel. "I can't tell you what a relief."

"And did you…" I pause, unsure of how to word my question. "Did you…?"

"I didn't love him, if that's what you're asking. I thought I did, for a long time. Funny how your first time stays with you. I used to dream about him, even though I suspected he probably hated me. I'd screwed it all up for him, he couldn't pretend anymore, not really."

"Oh Dan."

"No, it's not an *Oh Dan*, he did me a favour Billie. For a long time I was angry with him for being a coward. Now I suppose I'm just sad it all turned out so badly for him."

"And afterward?"

"We didn't speak, the accident was the next night and then everything went crazy. When he took off to the States I thought it was for the best. I didn't really think about Jack and what might happen."

My hands are white with soap suds, holding them aloft I examine those sparkling bubbles. "Poor Jack."

Dan claps his hands together and I jump. He grabs me by the shoulders, my yellow rubber gloves pressed together as though in prayer. "You, my girl, are beautiful." He curtsies before me. "And trust me when I say, you will get everything you deserve." I roll my eyes. He releases me and snaps his fingers at the stereo. "Just one dance then I must go fair maiden."

I curtsey in reply. The stereo kicks off and we're soon dancing to the Dixie Chicks like an old couple. We waltz, holding each other up until the wild chorus when the banjo and harmonicas kick in. Then, with no-one watching we dance like a pair of crazy teenagers.

When he leaves at 1.30 am, I kiss him on both cheeks and tell him he's the best boyfriend I ever had. He bows and leaves with an extravagant wave. And I think it must be true that we make our families where we go, we choose them and they choose us, and together we forge familial bonds that hold us together. This way, home is never far away.

∽

That night I dream like I used to, those vivid dreams of before when Evan was here.

There are birds, there are always birds; skylarks above, circling and flying in great flocks that create patterns in the air. Shapes and letters, like a message I can't read. I'm standing in a white nightdress, in the middle of the yard watching the flocks above me swoop and dive in the evening sky.

"I can't read it!" I yell impatiently to the heavens. "Make them stop." But the skylarks don't stop and I'm getting upset. I want to figure out what he's trying to tell me. "Evan!" I call his name and the dream changes. Just like that, like the Magic Faraway Tree and the world above its topmost branch, everything is different in an instant.

The light is bright all around, like the dawn of a new day, and my heart feels happy and light. I look up for the skylarks but they're gone. I search the skies but they're empty; all is quiet and still and the light grows brighter by the second. Turning slowly to face the old gum tree I see a single bird fly from its branches, something pale and indistinct caught in its beak. I raise my hand to the bird, following its flight with the tips of my fingers as it leaves a paper trail in its wake.

Like Hansel and Gretel, I'm in a forest chasing the bird and the paper trail. Each piece has one letter, the letter forms a message. I run and I run, picking them up, holding them in order, desperate to read the message that's been left for me.

Something's happening, the forest is falling around me and the sky above looks strangely like my bedroom ceiling. Sunny stands by the bed, pulling my hand. "Mommy, I had an accident."

I sit bolt upright exhaling one long, shaky breath. I am awake and Sunny has peed, metaphorically on the cryptic message his dead Daddy was trying to deliver. I smile sleepily and I scoop him up. Heading dozily to the bathroom I decide to go easy on wine before bed.

༄

"For life and death are one, even as the river and sea are one."

Khalil Gibran

Amandine's body is found at dawn the next day, washed up on the beach, dressed in her dancing clothes.

The discovery is made by a local fisherman on a small beach to the east of the island. Jack and Raife identify her body and arrange the small ceremony in Saul's orchard where they will say their goodbyes.

For those few days between, the days before they really let her go, Amandine is everywhere.

Jack can smell her fragrance, hear her voice calling, and her soft hum, always the same song in French; *'Quand le soleil dit bonjours au montagnes. When the sun says hello to the mountains.'* You'd know she was happy when she hummed that song. He hears it now in the trees, in the waves and on the breeze.

Every place, every corner, every object is a jagged memory. Suddenly everything is associated with her. He knows it's his inability to let her go. He wants to feel her everywhere because it can't last. She's gone and soon her image will fade and he'll struggle to see her face and hear her voice. The thought is heart-breaking.

Losing her removes an anchor from his world, a vital root that held him, gone forever. Now comes the crushing grief, the helpless despair and irretrievable loss before the slow acceptance that he must live on in a world without her. The wrench leaves Jack and his brothers lost and broken. They must find a new way, readjust their footing on the earth and move on slowly. Each day a careful step in a new and different world.

There are moments when he believes he might wake, that none of it is real, but as the days pass the feeling fades. This morning they must say goodbye. He's come to the beach to see the sunrise, maybe that's what she'd done. Maybe this was the last thing she saw.

At the far end of the beach walks a familiar figure, strolling along the water's edge, eyes on the sunrise. Noticing Jack, Raife raises a hand in greeting and walks to meet him. Together they walk in comfortable silence. Bets races back along the sand and drops a piece of drift wood at Raife's feet. Smiling, he stoops, picks up the wood and tosses it out into the breaking waves. She barks and chases it into the surf and they watch as she disappears under each wave, only to reappear as the surf crashes over. Her small wet head emerging between surges, her legs paddling furiously under the water to catch up with the drifting stick. Finally, she reaches it, and with the treasure lodged firmly between her teeth she turns and swims for shore.

"I'm sorry about Louie." Raife's eyes on Bets as she fights the rip.

"Thanks."

Bets surfaces dripping, and proudly drops the drift wood at Raife's feet. As he bends to pick it up she shakes violently, showering them both in sea water and dog hair.

"Jesus Bets!" Raife wipes his face. "Damn crazy dog." He hurls the drift wood with force and watches it spin then plummet down into the foamy surf. Bets barks ecstatically and races after it once more.

"What are you going to do?" Jack's arms fold across his chest and his gaze follows Bets as she swims.

"Have a shower."

"After the shower?"

"Help scatter Mama's ashes."

Jack sighs. "And after that?"

"Hell Jack, I don't know." Raife rubs his face wearily and sinks to sit on the sand. "So far none of my plans have turned out too well." Jack raises his eyebrows and Raife shrugs. "Okay so far I haven't worked to much of a plan. I don't do plans."

"How's that working out for you?"

"Yeah well." Raife takes a long, slow breath. "Might be time I made a few changes."

"You sticking around?"

"For a while. Maybe I'll give Saul a hand here, keep Papa company." He nods as though the idea has only just occurred to him and he likes it.

"That's a good plan." Jack frowns as he turns to Raife. "But you'll need to work. If you're staying Saul will expect you to pull your weight."

"Thanks for the advice *Mr Got it all figured out*. I can manage." Jack stiffens. "Sorry, I'm trying Jack. Give me some time, being an asshole comes so easily." Raife forces a smile. "Listen, I want to make a fresh start and I know you do. I don't want to keep hashing over the same shit forever, but…"

"But?" Jack shrugs.

"But thanks."

"What for?"

"For beating the shit out of me, for letting me stay." Raife stoops to throw the drift wood back into the waves. "For giving me another chance even though I sure as hell didn't deserve one, not from you." Jack raises his hands to fend off the apology he can't manage, but Raife ignores him. "I know how hard I made things for you. I wanted to hurt you. I know how wrong that was."

"It's over."

"I know." Raife's eyes are wet. "But she didn't." He looks away, wiping his eyes with the back of his hand. "Mama didn't know. You know how happy it would have made her, knowing we'd made peace, knowing we'd moved on. She never fucking knew and it's because I've been a selfish asshole, hell bent on blaming the world for everything. I fucked up and she'll never know I'm sorry."

He stands slowly reaching out to clap Jack on the shoulder. Jack steadies his arm, holding it firm before pulling him into an awkward embrace. There is more intimacy in the exchange than they've shared in a decade. When Jack loosens his grip Raife holds on, head lowered, shoulders shaking. The tide creeps in around their ankles and Bets barks, pushing her wet nose against Jack's bare legs.

"Look at me." Jack holds Raife's shoulders, easing him back. Reluctantly Raife looks up. "We'll be alright." Jack raises a hand and holds it against the side of his brothers' tear stained face. Raife nods and they stand together on the beach till fingers of sunlight prise open the day bringing light, warmth and peace.

It's barely 6 am when Jack enters the kitchen. Now the light outside is bright, the sun a hopeful pink laced orange as it breaks the horizon line. As he pours coffee Saul tiptoes into the kitchen with a tiny bundle cradled in his arms.

"Get any sleep?"

Saul shrugs, eyes on the baby. "A little, Jess is sleeping now." He shakes his head and looks up at Jack with a sad smile. Jack nods, knowing that Saul, for now is not thinking of his brave wife, who sleeps upstairs. The sadness suggests the thoughts are of their mother.

"We failed her." Saul's dark eyes rest on their parents' home across the orchard.

"We did our best."

"Did we?"

"You were here for her Saul. You've nothing to feel sorry about."

"Yeah, I was in charge right? And I let it slide thinking it would all be okay, she'd come right." His jaw is clenched, his features tight as he speaks. "You want to know the truth Jack? I knew she wouldn't come right, I knew what was going on, but I stuck my head in the sand." His eyes cloud with shame. "It was all too fucking much. I was under pressure with the business, Jess was sick, and Dad was a pain in the ass, so I put it in the too hard basket. I thought we'd have time. Jess would have the baby and things would calm down. Then we'd get Mama sorted." He stops and takes a long, slow breath, drawing his eyes away from their parents' house. He looks up at Jack and his shoulders begin to shake. "I wasn't watching."

"None of us were, no-one was to know. At least you were here for her, you've always been around. Me and Raife, we were too busy feeling sorry for ourselves."

Saul rubs a hand across his eyes and shakes his head but doesn't answer.

"No-ones to blame Saul. It's not that simple, and anyway it doesn't help a damn." Saul nods slowly and runs a finger down the baby's smooth cheek. "Come on, let's get some air. It's a beautiful sunrise." Jack pours Saul a steaming mug of coffee then opens the screen door leading to the porch. Saul follows, carrying the baby with the careful steps of the first time father. He lowers himself on to a porch chair facing the sunrise. "You going to get used to all this?" Jack smiles watching Saul, oversized and unshaven with the tiny sleeping baby. It's a nice sight.

Saul grins. "Hope so, I'm screwed if I don't?"

Jack sits on the rail, looking out over the orchard. "I'll say."

Together they watch the sun rise higher, colours changing and spreading. Joseph and Amandine's house awakens as shade peels away to warm light. The baby stirs, Saul kisses her head and she settles back to sleep.

There's movement over on the other porch, and as they watch they can see Joseph lifting something bulky, like a large box. He descends the front steps slowly with the box in his arms, and walks across the lawn to the place they have prepared for Amandine's memorial. Just a grassy patch they'd tided and flattened and a hole ready to plant the Hibiscus tree. It would be simple: a blessing, they would plant the tree and scatter her ashes beneath.

Joseph has set the box down, but now he's putting something together. After a minute he disappears back into the house, then reappears dragging a long chord behind him.

"What the hell is he doing?" Saul asks, Jack shrugs in reply. Joseph hasn't spoken since they found Amandine. It's hard to know how he's doing.

The sound of Elvis Presley croons out over the orchard; "Love Me Tender," and Jack realises the box is the old record player. It stands on four wooden legs, playing Elvis out into the early morning light.

Jack closes his eyes as a wave of grief takes his breath away. Saul stands and together with the baby they walk across the orchard, to Joseph who stands alone, head down, eyes closed.

"Papa." Saul touches his shoulder and Joseph clasps a hand over Saul's. Elvis sings and the three men and the baby stand in an awkward line, facing the old record player and the hole in the ground.

When the record finishes Joseph looks up, his eyes spilling over, he turns to Jack then back to Saul, "You're good boys." Reaching out he opens his arms for the baby, tenderly Saul hands her to him. He sinks slowly to his knees, eyes fixed on her tiny face and begins to cry.

Jack reflects later on the day, and how Amandine would have thought it perfect. A few friends and locals paying their respects, offering food and sympathy, flowers and kind words. They had planted the tree together, the three brothers and Joseph, there was quiet singing and then of course, there was Elvis.

And as the sun began its descent and the long day drew to a close he'd felt the change. Something powerful and whole, a feeling in his chest, a simple understanding that finally it was done. He had made his peace the best way he could, and it might not be enough, and it might have been too late, but he can do no more. It's done, and now he might live.

❧

After Evie and Sunny are asleep I gather a few boxes and bin bags and approach Evan's studio, expression set but hands shaky.

It's time to finally sort and clear out the room. It's time to stop holding on, using the space as a quick fix, my phone line to the afterlife. The studio has become a presence, a solemn purveyor of sadness taking up more room in this house than it should. The decision to finally clear it was one I should have made a long time ago.

The truth is, I couldn't until now; I needed some part of Evan with me. Despite the passage of time, my need for him kept hold. I needed him in death as much as I'd needed him in life, my life still somewhere in the subtext of his.

I can't say what changed. There was no single event where an internal light bulb sprang to life. I didn't step out into the world of the living and announce, *I'm ready!* There was no lip synching to *I will survive*, wearing a spangled leotard.

None of that. Instead life simply went on.

I am a walking cliché of *shit happens, life goes on.* Life goes on around me, and in that full and beautiful life there is more sadness, more joy, more death and more birth. And it's impossible to remain in one place indefinitely. We adapt and learn, it's in our nature, we become more resilient, less dependent and a little more grounded in the terrifying fact that life will ultimately go just the way it was always meant to.

And so, if I choose to take Dan's advice and embrace life as it flows, then I must let Evan go and know it's okay. This is also the way our story was meant to go. He can't remain immortalised here in his studio any longer. I'm reminded of the skylark in the dream, scattering the message, letters on ripped paper. And I know in my heart Evan would want this; this new life for me and the twins.

Pushing open the door to the studio I inhale the gradually fading smells of linseed and wood shavings for the last time. I open the windows wide and begin to sort through everything that remains. Ruthlessly I bag all the things that must go, and box the few things that must stay. I will make a box each for Evie and Sunny, things to remember their Daddy by and with this in mind I tuck away sketches, brushes and a few small sculptures.

Fortified with the things I need to make the next step forward I drag furniture outside; his worktable and chair, the old metal storage shelves and a chest full of paints, charcoals, oil pastels, books and canvases. Dragging them as far as the garage I leave them to be dealt with later. With the studio clear I clip my iPod to my belt, plug in my earphones and turn up The Pogues; a suitable choice for the occasion. I sweep, dust, clean, mop and polish until eventually the room looks and feels new. Finally, with a cold beer to hand I sink to the floor in the middle of the empty room.

I sip the beer and look around at the transformation. A fresh start for an old room that deserves a change. The same could be said for me, and maybe that's the point. Smiling I raise the bottle and toast Evan. Everything feels lighter.

Thank you. I say the words before consciously thinking them. I say them in response to a conversation I might be having with him on another plane. It would have gone a bit like this.

Me: I can't' keep up anymore.

Evan: I know.

Me: These wings I borrowed, they don't fly. I'm giving them back.

Evan: I'm sorry baby.

Me: Me too, I'm just so tired.

Evan: Go on now.

Me: I love you.

Evan: It's time.

It is time. I hear his voice teasing, his slow smile shining from each word, and one fat tear slides carefully down my cheek; just one. It's time.

With a last burst of energy, I'm up, hurrying through to the toy cluttered living room. I drag the toy box, a throw rug, the doll's house and lightsabres. I sort and arrange, organise and art direct and by 1.00 am the studio has become a playroom.

The Incredibles, Buzz Light-year and Dora the Explorer smile down from posters hastily pinned on plain walls. A small table and two little chairs await play dough artists, soft toys gather brightly in a corner on a polka dot beanbag, beside a bookshelf stacked with favourite stories. Admiring the transformation, I ask Evan what he thinks, but this time he doesn't answer.

My heart is spectacularly light and until now I hadn't realised what a dead weight it had become. Quietly, me and my fluttery, light, little heart head to bed.

No more tears.

I take a quick jab at an eye to be sure a rogue wet one hasn't slipped out. Dry-eyed and weary I climb into bed. When I lean over to flip off the bedside light I notice in the corner of the room my copy of *The Grapes of Wrath*. An involuntary pang of anxiety reminds me why it's there; face down, a few pages loose in its bindings. I had thrown it at Raife.

Funny, I was mad at John Steinbeck that night anyway. Before Raife turned up I'd only just finished the last few pages and I was mad. I'd stalled on reading the last chapter because it had all been so unbearably heart-breaking and I knew there was no happy ending.

But that night I'd been in such a good mood, after the night out in Santos with friends. I came home and believed that maybe I'd missed the deeper meaning, maybe somehow there was hope in Tom Joad's story. Tucked up in bed I'd read that last chapter, and later slammed the book closed, feeling sad, and mad, and entirely unsatisfied.

I pick it up now and replace the torn pages back in their rightful spot. I flip back to Tom Joad's speech to his Mama when he knows he'll be dead soon, when he's reassuring her in his simple way that she needn't mourn him. When he's gone she need only look around, because he'll be everywhere, in everyone and everything; a little piece of a big soul.

I think of Evan and am comforted. Tonight I am saying goodbye but not really, because like Tom, Evan is everywhere; in our children, our home, in the ocean, and the sky.

"…a little piece of a big soul, the one big soul that belongs to everybody."

John Steinbeck

I read the last few pages again and understand them differently.

There is hope in the conclusion. The last scene: the offering of a mother's milk to a dying man, an act of kindness and compassion amidst sorrow and despair. Hope at the possibility of a tomorrow, despite the bleakness of today and the beautiful flow of life between us all.

It's not a happy ending but I don't feel sad, not anymore, because life goes on, and where there is life, there is hope.

Chapter Seventeen

There is a small wooden chapel surrounded by palms and native flowers, overgrown and a little neglected from the outside. White washed weatherboards now chipped and faded rise to a small bell tower, and a red corrugated steel roof. There are rusty patches on the roof and a few missing panes in the arched glass windows.

Holy Church of the Trinity is the oldest church on St. Cloud, and you can tell not a lot of care is put into its upkeep these days. Its congregation lie mostly in the cemetery nearby and Father Rene opens its doors only on special occasions: christenings, funerals and weddings.

Today the doors are open and the interior of the small church is a fiesta of colour; pews groan at capacity, seating a sea of smiling expectant faces dressed in their summer finest. Sundresses and hawaiian shirts, flowers adorn hair and hats perch on elderly ladies' heads. Oranges, yellows, purples and pinks; the vibrant congregation compliment the flowers. Island blossoms of hibiscus, frangipani and jasmine line the altar and drape in garlands from the edge of the aisles.

All around are people I know and care about. It's an occasion of joy, a coming together in celebration of love. Sun streams through the cracked church windows and a fan fixed high above turns listlessly, distributing the warm, muggy air. It's hot but no-one seems to mind. Shoulders press against shoulders and the heavy fragrance of summer blossoms blends with the musty odour of old hymn books and candle wax.

To my left is Dan, radiant in a pale linen suit, cool despite the heat. He catches my eye and winks. To my right is Jack. The low hum of quietened chatter stills as a guitar at the front strums a chord. All eyes turn to Raife as he plays the opening chords of Bob Marley's *One Love*, then begins to sing.

Everything about Raife seems softer, today he isn't performing but accompanying. He strums and sings softly as heads swivel to the rear entrance of the small church where Sadie stands framed by the arched double doorway. As she enters a collective sigh emits from the congregation. She walks slowly, head high, cheeks flushed, wearing a simple white sundress. A crown of fuchsia and hibiscus rests on her blonde hair as she smiles brightly and makes her way barefoot down the aisle to the Jed.

No-one gives Sadie away and Jed has no 'best man'. Somehow it feels like we are all one in those roles, in spirit we accompany Sadie down the aisle and stand together in support of Jed.

They'd tried to keep it all simple, just a small wedding they'd said, but Jed is part of the fabric of St. Cloud and now, so is Sadie. Excited at the prospect of *newlywed bliss* Jed had given an open invitation to all. He'd pinned a sign on Monica the espresso machine telling everyone to come and help them celebrate. Of course, Jed may not have thought through the logistics of his generous invite. At the front of the church Father Rene looks hot and a little flustered, Church of the Holy Trinity is now at full capacity.

Raife and his guitar stop, he smiles at Jed who hasn't stopped smiling all day. Jed gives Raife the thumbs up, his eyes locked on Sadie. Father Rene welcomes us all and goes through the *dearly beloved* speech whilst Jed and Sadie stand facing each other, holding hands, locked in their own little bubble of bliss.

I take a mental picture. I want to remember their happiness: Jed with his slicked back hair and hawaiian shirt and Sadie with her crown of flowers. Today is the day she thought would never be hers. A love she didn't believe possible. Yet here they are, happy with however long they have together. It's their own version of perfect and it's beautiful.

Sunny squirms in my lap and Evie tries to stand on Jack's knee, waving as though the show should be about her. Jack whispers something in her ear, she giggles and sits back down on his lap. Sunny sighs and plops his thumb into his mouth. Jacks thigh presses against mine and it all feels right.

The *I do* and *I will* bit is followed closely by the kissing which makes Evie point and squeal loudly. There's more music, laughter, hugs all round and an exit down the aisle by the bride and groom who are showered with flower petals. The congregation rise to follow outside where bubbles and more music await. Here we will toast Jed and Sadie and some will later head to a small hotel in Plantation Cove for their reception party.

People file out; colours and wafts of heavy perfume, excited chat and laughter as rows of townsfolk pass where we sit. Dan rushes ahead to see the happy couple. Jack is off on the heels of Evie and Sunny who disappear mischievously between the passing herd of legs. For now, I'll let him play hide and seek. I need to sit just a moment longer.

Soon it's just me, a solo figure, seated mid-row in the petal-strewn church. I want to stretch out the moment: the people, the flowers, the music and the smells. So much of my faraway home condensed into this small place of worship. I say a silent prayer to the God I hope is listening, the God I seem to talk mostly too when things need fixing.

"Billie, will you join us outside? Even God couldn't bring us a breeze in here today."

I jump at the sound of Father Rene's voice. "Yes, of course, I was just coming."

He stands a little unsteadily by the arched doorway, outside voices and laughter rise from the heat haze. His balding head gleams, a few limp remaining strands of hair stick to his forehead. As I approach he reaches out and gently links arms with me as we make our way out through the shaded porch.

"And are you well?" He pats my hand as we walk slowly.

"I am, thank you." He smiles as I answer, his eyes warm in the cool shade of the porch.

We pause, not quite ready to face the glare. "These things take time." He nods as he speaks, his eyes looking out beyond me, out past the crowd to where Sadie and Jed stand, hugging and thanking people. "Love is a powerful healer."

My eyes follow his and together we watch all that happiness. "Sometimes."

"When you've lived as long as me you'll see that in the end, it always is." I look at his wizened face, held together by the creases, leather brown and careworn. He turns back to me, smiles and squeezes my arm. "Trust me."

"I do." He nods and descends the steps down on to the grass, moving gracefully through the crowd, smiling and shaking hands as he goes.

The last time I saw Father Rene was at Evans memorial. Although the occasion was one of loss and great sadness, his presence then had been the same now: gracious, gentle and knowing. An old spirit that understands how it all works. I watch as he disappears into the welcoming mass.

I hear my name and see Sunny hoisted onto Dan's shoulders, weaving through the crowd toward me. "Here she is." Dan grins and throws Sunny up into the air before depositing him at my feet. "One of your matching set, the other is terrorising Jack."

I kiss the giggling Sunny then tiptoe up to kiss Dan, who places a hand on his heart and drops on to a knee before me. "Should we have Father Rene marry us here while we have the rent-a-crowd?"

"Dan!" I laugh pushing him on the shoulder, he wobbles from his bended knee position and flops on to his bum on the grass.

"Oh come on, we'd be great together, it would be so easy. You could cook me chile rellenos and I'd share my music collection with you."

"Sounds like bliss." I roll my eyes and pull him to his feet as Jack and Raife approach, their heads weaving through the crowd from opposite directions.

"Damn and blast." Dan's hands move to his hips as he sees them. "I see how it is, you're hot for one of these Kelly brothers."

"Stop it." I nudge him as he slugs down some champagne.

"You're not alone sister." Before my smart retort finds voice he's gone, his golden mane swallowed by a sea of heads.

As Dan disappears, Jack and Raife arrive at my side and there is no tension, no weight of unsaid words between them. They smile at me, and at each other and together we turn to face the crowd centred by Sadie and Jed. Raife raises his glass and makes a toast to peace and happiness and we clink glasses and sip whilst Evie and Sunny make farty noises and run races round our legs.

It's close to midnight and the band is still in full swing. They play under a canopy at the edge of the beach facing the courtyard, which doubles as a perfect dancefloor. Tables, groaning under the weight of candles and half-filled glasses surround them. Guests resting from the rigours of the dance floor sit, deep in conversation, smoking expensive cigars, arms draped over loved one's shoulders, legs crossed at ankles, ties undone and high heels abandoned.

The night is black, no stars from where I sit eyes raised to the heavens. And I love that about stars, always there, only we can't always see them. Like Mom and Evan, like Amandine. All there somewhere.

Tonight those stars pale under the glow of paper lanterns strung from post to post. Small white domes that illuminate the darkness above. They hang from pillars connecting the veranda to the hotel and string in diagonals across the courtyard.

It's a magical scene. Dan dances with Ginny. Zoe who hasn't left the dance floor all night, cuddles up to Felix, who she has finally persuaded to dance. Felix holds on to Zoe and he looks a little afraid, he ought to be. Zoe with this much champagne on board is dynamite.

Jed dances with tiny Josefina, he's laughing hard, struggling to keep up with her bouncing moves. She dances like she cooks, fast and with passion. Over by the bar I see Bastian, all smiles. Tonight he gets to stand on the other side. He is sipping dark beer from a large glass with a handle; his hands gesticulate as he no doubt describes the intricacies of the flavour with the barman.

Sadie floats from table to table, a picture of flushed perfection. Still in her white sundress, her floral crown slightly askew, she chats and hugs, allowing herself to eventually be led off to dance by an elderly gent with a bow tie and white gloves.

Evie and Sunny were taken away after supper by Marlene, they will sleepover and I will stay here at Plantation Cove. I have a room, with a balcony and a view of the sea, crisp cotton sheets and a huge ceiling fan. What more could a girl want?

Jack skirts the edge of the dance floor carrying a tray of drinks. I watch him from afar as he heads carefully this way, smiling and stopping briefly to chat to friends, working his way slowly back to me.

He arrived home from St. Eloise only a few days ago, there hasn't been time for us to talk. He was swooped up by Jed and Dan, keen to have him help with plans for Jed's stag night. They were trying to keep him busy, give him focus after the tragic death of his mother. What a time.

I haven't had the chance to tell him how sorry I am. To help share his grief and let him talk it out. To tell me what happened and what it might mean for him, for Raife and their family.

The wedding has given everyone a joyful distraction from anything less than happy. Instead we celebrate with Sadie and Jed, friends who have found love and a future together despite the odds. We are grateful for this reminder that happiness is there to be taken even though life is short.

Raife arrived yesterday, to play at the wedding at Jed's request. Something has changed there, something big. Jack and Raife walk together, dragging nothing behind them. It doesn't matter why, but, that they can finally tuck their past away is a wonderful thing.

He's close now, just a few feet from where I sit. Tall, breathtaking in his suit. I realise I've rarely seen him in anything but shorts and a work shirt. Clean shaven and suited he might have walked out of the pages of a lady porn mag; one rip and the whole suit's gone leaving a muscly body in a gold thong.

Jack places the tray on the table and distributes drinks around, finishing with me. He sets down a tall stemmed glass whose bubbles rise frantically, bursting effervescently on the smooth surface. Smiling, I raise my glass toward him in a silent toast.

There's an unexpected thickness to the air that separates us. He lowers himself into a seat opposite, glass to hand, eyes locked on mine. Raising and tipping his glass he mirrors my action and I sip slowly, feeling the bubbles burst and dissipate on my lips. I watch him, afraid to break the moment. In this evening of sensory overload; people, music, conversation and dancing, quiet is far away. But right now that quiet is everywhere.

He nods slowly, eyes still on mine. The movement speaks a thousand unsaid words. Lowering my glass to the table I nod slowly in reply.

Jack stands at the same moment I find myself on my feet. He comes to me, around the edge of the table, past the people in conversation, past the laughter, past it all. He takes my hand and leads me out past the lights of the dance floor, under the soft glow of paper lanterns blinking in the darkness, around and out on to the sand and toward the water that laps gently to shore.

We stand in silence for a moment, facing out toward the darkness of water and night sky. Behind us is light and music, laughter and raised voices. Time moves slowly, seconds marked with the ebb and flow of the tide. Everything seems to lie here on this beach, grain by grain, layer upon layer; people, places, love, loss, hope and desire.

The past lies heavily at my feet, changing slowly wave by wave. Compacted yet malleable, the sand shapes and moulds anew with each wave. Life's constant ebb and flow in the force of the ocean around my ankles.

When I turn to him I'm steady, grounded in the moving floor of sand by the weight of my love. Love aged and gritty, layer upon layer, ground down, reduced, different in form from how it once began, but somehow more; certain, heavy and sure.

"I love you." For a moment I'm not sure whether the words are in my head or said aloud.

Jack doesn't answer, he leans in and kisses me slowly. And there's a yielding; a gentle tenderness that leaves me dizzy. We kiss on the beach with the slow understanding of old lovers, knowing and unhurried until suddenly we're hurried, and the tide is high and my dress is wet.

Jack scoops me up and carries me, striding quickly, back over the sand toward the hotel. And it's all a little *Gone with the Wind*, but I don't care. In fact I do, I care more than I knew possible. I love it. I love this. I love him.

In my room he sets me down and moves behind me, unzipping my dress, letting it fall around my feet. I lean back against his chest as carefully he undoes my bra. As it slides to the floor his face is in my hair, fingers running slowly down, over my breasts to rest on my waist. It's all I can manage not to turn to him, to lose control.

I wait, eyes closed, senses on fire.

"Jack." I breathe his name, the sound of my voice pulling me back to reality. This is not another fantasy.

His breath is jagged and he kneels behind me, hands carefully tracing my spine, kissing the small of my back before gently easing down my underwear. My heart no longer beats in my knickers which is good, as they're on the floor. My heartbeat is everywhere as I pulse to his touch.

"Billie." It's the first word he's spoken; the sound heavy with more emotion than I can bear to unpack. On his knees, his arms circle my waist, his face pressed into my back.

"Show me," I whisper.

And he does.

There's a blur of frenzied undressing, the suit loses a few buttons but the end result is worth it. I could look at him forever - well that's how it would go in a good romance novel. The truth is, I can barely look at him. I want him, all of him and the wanting is all consuming.

He lowers himself down and eases into me and I cry out, hands buried in his hair, body slipping into his rhythm. Slowly at first, gentle and tender we move carefully, finding our fit together. The feel of him is almost more than I can manage, something inside cries out, alight, more than a memory.

"Is it okay?" He whispers in my ear, pulling me up to sit astride him, hands on my breasts.

"It's okay." I smile down as I move to him, and he to me. I bend to kiss him.

"I don't want to hurt you." His eyes are dark as he looks up, hands circling my back pulling me deeper with every thrust.

I gasp feeling the tension build and pull me closer to the edge. "You couldn't, ever." And although my words are said in pre-orgasmic throes of passion, I know it to be true. I know he will never hurt me. I've never been surer of anything.

"I love you Billie." The words, deep and broken remove the past for now. For now, this is all there is.

We lose ourselves completely, no words or questions, no more declarations of love or plans for tomorrow. Jack pushes me back on to the bed and second by glorious second we lose all control.

When it's over, when we've cried out, and lain softly beside each other, hands stroking, eyes closed, we talk. We talk about the past and the future, about where we've been and where to now. We laugh, and cry, and then make love again, this time it's gentler, slower, less fraught. And when it's done we sleep knowing we have turned a page. Tomorrow a new life will begin. The deal is sealed, our new direction set, and it is our time for happiness and maybe a little peace.

The End

Epilogue

It seemed like the right thing to do.

The anniversary of her death day; she'd have thought it perfect.

They're together again, all of them, but how different life is from then till now.

Joseph carries Ana, it's her first birthday and the day is a celebration for all. He moves around the gathering of friends and family smiling warmly, shaking hands and embracing. Ana charms with a dimpled smile as Jess and Saul watch from the edge of the crowd smiling proudly.

Raife whistles, two fingers thrust into his mouth, the piercing sound too loud to ignore. Everyone stops and turns and he smiles weaving his way through the small gathering of people. In his hand is a small shrub, its roots bagged in brown sacking, its leaves young and tender.

Joseph lets the wriggling Ana down where she crawls at pace to Raife and the tiny tree. Everyone laughs as she shuffles toward him, smiling and grabbing on to the shrub as though she understands everything. Raife scoops her up beckoning for Jack and Saul to come forward. Saul takes a spade and digs a hole beside Amandine's hibiscus tree. Jack steps forward, takes the shrub from Raife's hands and places it gently into the hole.

One by one everyone approaches and carefully deposits a handful of earth into the hole, securing the small shrub, allowing its roots to feel the strength of solid earth around it.

One year since the death of Amandine and the birth of Ana. The perfect time to plant a new tree and give thanks for all that has come before and all that lies ahead.

One by one friends and family lay their handfuls of soil at the base of the small tree. Raife plays her song, *Quand le soleil dit bonjour au montagnes*. Jess begins to sing to Ana who snuggles close to her mother's chest. Saul joins, not so much in song but a hum, deep and baritone. The melody spreads like an ocean breeze and soon there is a quiet chorus.

When the sun says hello to the mountains. They sing and Raife plays, and the sound is togetherness. It is memories, time passed. It is a love story of sadness and hope and heartbreak and joy.

Beside him, Billie hums, she doesn't know the words. Evie pats dirt on to the base of the small tree and Sunny tries to strum the guitar with Raife.

For a moment Jack feels it all, the depths and giddy heights of love and loss, of living and being alive. He leans to her, inhaling the fragrance of her hair, gently kissing the top of her head. Naturally her body moves to his, her weight leaning gently against him. And he hums the words he won't sing, letting his hand rest on the swell of her belly. She smiles up at him and he's sure he feels the baby kick.

The shrub is planted and tributes are made, flowers are laid by the hibiscus tree. People drift gradually toward the light and music and cooking smells that emanate from Saul's house. A celebration of life, of family and friends, of living and dying, of loving and being loved.

The party is here, where the sun says hello to the mountain.

Acknowledgments

Thank you to the readers who make time to read when time is so precious.

Thank you to the fabulously eclectic group of readers who made Skylark, my well intentioned, imperfect, debut novel successful. Your reviews and recommendations made things happen. It is very humbling - thank you, thank you, thank you.

Thank you to all the readers who believed Billie's story wasn't finished. Your words encouraged Borrowed Wings to take flight.

Thank you to my tireless editorial team: Kate Hesson, Evelyn Armstrong and Jilly O'Brien – your time, passion and expertise is invaluable. Thank you for your patience with my never-ending commas, long sentences and hilarious timelines. Thank you to my dear friends who listen with great humour and tolerance to my latest story obsession, and always understand when I ditch them for a night with my laptop.

Last but never least – thank you to Richard and my tribe of littles, who become not so little every day: Oliver, Gracie, Emily-Rose and Leo. You are the foundation and inspiration to all the stories.